THE MOUNTAIN

LUCA D'ANDREA

THE MOUNTAIN

Translated from the Italian by
Howard Curtis

MACLEHOSE PRESS
QUERCUS · LONDON

First published in the Italian language as
La Sostanza del male
by Einaudi Editore, Turin, 2016
First published in Great Britain in 2017 by

MacLehose Press
an imprint of Quercus
Carmelite House
50 Victoria Embankment
London EC4Y 0DZ

An Hachette UK Company

A CIP catalogue record for this book is available
from the British Library

ISBN (HB) 978 0 85705 690 0
ISBN (TPB) 978 0 85705 691 7
ISBN (Ebook) 978 0 85705 693 1

10 9 8 7 6 5 4 3

Designed and typeset in Minion by Libanus Press Ltd
Printed and bound in Great Britain by Clays Ltd, St Ives plc

to Alessandra,
compass for my stormy sea

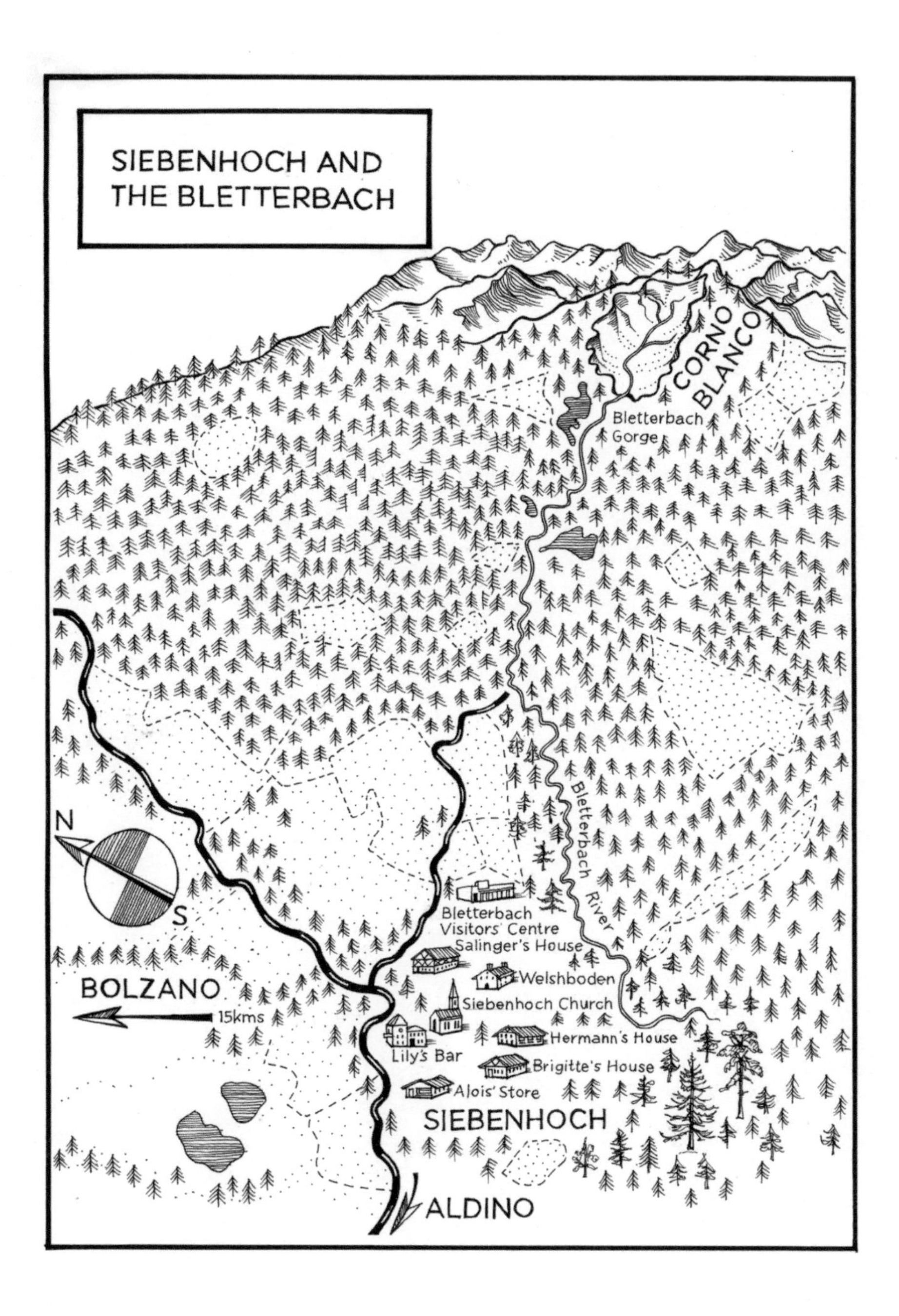
SIEBENHOCH AND
THE BLETTERBACH
CORNO
BLANCO
Bletterbach
Gorge
Bletterbach
River
N
S
Bletterbach
Visitors' Centre
Salinger's House
Welshboden
BOLZANO
15kms
Siebenhoch Church
Hermann's House
Lily's Bar
Brigitte's House
Alois' Store
SIEBENHOCH
ALDINO

That's how it always is. In the ice, first you hear the voice of the Beast, then you die.

There were seracs and chasms identical to those in which I now found myself, full of mountaineers and rock climbers who had lost their strength, their reason, and finally their lives, because of that voice.

Part of my mind, the animal part that knew what terror was because it had lived in terror for millions of years, understood what the Beast was hissing.

Two words: "Get out."

I wasn't prepared for the voice of the Beast.

I needed something familiar, something human, to tear me from the stark solitude of the ice. I raised my eyes beyond the edges of the crevasse, searching for the red outline of Dolomite Mountain Rescue's EC135. But the sky was empty, wide open, the blue of it blinding.

That's what made me fall apart.

I started rocking back and forth, my breathing rapid, my blood drained of any energy. Like Jonah in the belly of the whale, I was alone in the presence of God.

And God was roaring: "Get out."

At two nineteen p.m. on that damned September 15, a voice emerged from the ice, and it wasn't the voice of the Beast. It was Manny's voice. His red uniform stood out in all that white, and he was repeating my name, over and over, as the pulley slowly lowered him towards me.

Five metres.

Two.

His hands and eyes searched for injuries that would explain my behaviour. His questions: a hundred whats and a thousand whys I couldn't answer. The voice of the Beast was too loud. It was devouring me.

"Don't you hear it?" I murmured. "The Beast, the . . ."

The Beast, I'd have liked to tell him, that ancient thing of ice, couldn't stand the idea of a warm heart buried in its depths. My warm heart. And his.

And now it was two twenty-two.

The expression of surprise on Manny's face turning to pure terror. The pulley cable lifting him like a puppet. Manny being jerked upwards. The rumble of the helicopter's turbines becoming a strangled cry.

At last.

God's scream. The avalanche wiping out the sky.

Get out!

That was when I saw. When I was alone again, beyond time and space, I saw.

The darkness.

Total darkness. But I didn't die. Oh, no. The Beast mocked me. It let me live. The Beast that was now whispering, "You will stay with me forever, forever . . ."

It wasn't lying.

Part of me is still there.

But, as my daughter Clara would have said with a smile, that wasn't the *z* at the end of the rainbow. It wasn't the end of my story. On the contrary.

It was only the beginning.

One word, nine letters: "beginning". Five letters: "Beast".

Six letters: "horror".

(We Are) the Road Crew

In life, as in art, there's only one thing that matters: the facts. To know all the facts about Evi, Kurt, Markus and the night of April 28, 1985, you have to know everything there is to know about me. Because this isn't just about 1985 and the Bletterbach killings, it isn't just about Evi, Kurt and Markus, it's also about Salinger, Annelise and Clara.

Everything's connected.

* * *

Up until two twenty-two p.m. on September 15, 2013, in other words, up until the moment when the Beast almost killed me, I'd been defined as 50 per cent of a rising star in a field, documentary film-making, that tends to produce not so much stars as tiny meteors and a lot of hot air.

Mike McMellan, the other 50 per cent of the star in question, liked to say that if we'd been shooting stars on a collision course with the planet called Total Failure, we'd have had the privilege of disappearing in the kind of burst of heat reserved for heroes. After the third beer, I declared myself in agreement with him. If nothing else, it was a good excuse for a toast.

Mike wasn't just my partner. He was also the best friend you could possibly have the luck to meet. He was an irritating smartass, as egocentric as – or even more than – a black hole, obsessive to an unbearable degree, and gifted with the ability to focus on a single subject like a canary on amphetamines. But he was also the one true artist I had ever known.

It was Mike who realised, when we were still only the semi-talented, least cool pair in the whole of the New York Film Academy (the directors' course for Mike, the screenwriters' course for yours truly), that if we pursued our Hollywood ambitions, we'd get our asses kicked and end up as embittered and verbose as the dreaded Professor ("Call me Gerry") Calhoun, the ex-hippie who'd taken more pleasure than anyone else in pulling our first timid creations to pieces.

It was truly a magic moment – a flash of enlightenment that would modify the course of our lives, maybe a bit less epic than a Sam Peckinpah movie ("Let's go," William Holden says in "The Wild Bunch", to which Ernest Borgnine replies, "Why not?"), given that when it happened, we were nibbling on French fries in a McDonald's with our morale below our feet – but unrepeatable all the same. Believe me.

"Fuck Hollywood, Salinger," Mike had said. "People are hungry for reality, not C.G.I. The only way we can surf this fucking *Zeitgeist* is to forget fiction and devote ourselves to good old-fashioned reality. Satisfaction guaranteed."

I raised an eyebrow. "*Zeitgeist*?"

"You're the Kraut, partner."

My mother was of German descent, but don't worry, I really didn't feel picked on by Mike. After all, I'd grown up in Brooklyn, whereas he was from the fucking Midwest.

Genealogical considerations apart, what Mike was trying to say on that damp November day so many years ago was that I should throw away my (seriously bad) screenplays and join him in making documentaries. Taking moments and enlarging and transforming them into a narrative that goes smoothly from point *a* to point *z* according to the gospel of the late Vladimir Yakovlevich Propp (who was to stories what Jim Morrison was to paranoia).

What a mess.

"Mike," I snorted, "there's only one category of people worse than those who want to make it big in movies: documentary-makers. They own collections of *National Geographic* going back to 1800. Many of them have ancestors who died looking for the source of the Nile. They have cashmere scarves and tattoos. They're assholes, but liberal assholes, and that's why they feel absolved of every sin. Last, but by no means least, they have families rolling in money who subsidise their world safaris."

"Salinger, sometimes you're really . . ." Mike shook his head. "Just stop right there and listen to me. We need a subject. A strong subject for a documentary that'll break the bank. Something that people already know, something familiar, but that the two of us will show in a new way, different than how they've ever seen it. Rack your brains, think and . . ."

Believe it or not, it was at that moment that two losers discovered they could transform even the weirdest of pumpkins into a golden coach. Because yes. I had it.

I don't know how and I don't know why, while Mike was staring at me with that serial killer mug of his, while a million reasons to reject his suggestion were crowding in on me, I felt a gigantic explosion in my brain. An absurd idea. Mad. Incandescent. An idea so stupid, it might just work.

What was more electrifying, powerful and sexy than rock 'n' roll?

It was a religion for millions of people. A blast of energy that brought the generations together. Who hadn't heard of Elvis, Hendrix, the Rolling Stones, Nirvana, Metallica and the whole glittering caravan of the one true revolution of the twentieth century?

Easy, wasn't it?

No.

Because rock was also big, tall, black-clad bodybuilders who looked like double-door wardrobes, had the eyes of pitbull terriers, and were paid to get rid of cuties like us. Something they would gladly have done even for free.

The first time we tried to put our idea into practice (Bruce Springsteen in a pre-tour warm-up gig at a venue down in the Village) I got off lightly with a few shoves and a couple of bruises. Mike not so lightly. Half of his face resembled the Scottish flag. The cherry on the cake was that we almost got ourselves arrested. Springsteen was followed by concerts by the White Stripes, Michael Stipe, the Red Hot Chili Peppers, Neil Young and the Black Eyed Peas, who were at the height of their fame at the time.

We collected a fair number of bruises, but not much material. There was a strong temptation to drop the whole thing.

It was at this point that the God of Rock looked down on us, saw our pathetic efforts to pay tribute to him, and with a benevolent eye showed us the way to success.

* * *

In mid-April I managed to get us both hired setting up a stage in Battery Park. Not for just any band, but for the most controversial, diabolical and reviled band of all time. Ladies and gentlemen, I give you Kiss.

We worked like brave, conscientious little ants, and then, as the workforce was leaving, we hid in a heap of refuse. As silent as snipers. When the first dark sedan cars arrived, Mike pressed the *record* button. We were in seventh heaven. This was our big opportunity. And naturally, everything happened very fast.

Gene Simmons emerged from a limousine as long as an ocean liner, stretched and gave orders to his lackeys to drop the leash of his beloved four-legged friend. No sooner was it free than the demonic-looking snow-white poodle started to bark in our direction like one of Robert Johnson's hounds of hell ("And the day keeps on reminding me, there's a hellhound on my trail. / Hellhound on my trail, hellhound on my trail"). In two bounds, the dog was on me. It was aiming for the jugular, the bastard. That ball of fur wanted to kill me.

I screamed.

And something like twelve thousand brutes who wouldn't have

looked out of place in a Hall of Fame for cutthroats grabbed us, kicked us and dragged us towards the exit, threatening to throw us in the ocean. But they didn't do so. They left us black and blue, beaten and tired on a bench surrounded by trash, reflecting on how we'd been reduced to a Wile E. Coyote condition. We stayed there, unable to accept defeat, listening to the echo of the concert as it wound down. Once the encores had finished, we watched as the crowd dispersed and, just as we were about to go back to our mouse hole, while four big guys with Hell's Angels beards and faces like convicts started loading crates and amplifiers onto the band's Peterbilts, at that precise moment, the God of Rock winked down from Valhalla and showed me the way.

"Mike," I whispered. "We got it wrong. If we want to make a documentary about rock, the real rock, we have to aim our cameras on the other side of the stage. The other side, partner. Those guys are the real rock." And I added with a grin, "There's no copyright on them."

Those guys.

The roadies. The ones who do the dirty work. The ones who load the trucks, drive them from one side of the country to the other, unload them, set up the stage, prepare the equipment, wait for the end of the show with their arms folded and then once more, as the poem says, "Miles to go before I sleep."

Oh, yes.

Mike, I have to say, was *incredible.* With a lot of flattery, holding out prospects of money and free publicity, he persuaded a very bored tour manager to give us permission to do a bit of filming. The roadies, not at all used to so much attention, took us under their wing. Not only that: it was those bearded guys who persuaded the managers and lawyers to let us follow them around (them, not the band – that was the trump card that convinced them) for the rest of the tour.

That's how "Born to Sweat: Road Crew, the Hidden Side of Rock 'n' Roll" was born.

We worked our asses off, believe me. Six weeks of madness, migraines, terrible hangovers and sweat, at the end of which we had destroyed two cameras, developed various food addictions and a twisted calf (I had clambered onto the roof of a trailer that turned out to be as crumbly as a tea biscuit – and I was sober, I swear) and learned twelve different ways of saying "fuck you".

The editing lasted a summer of sweltering heat without air conditioning, spent endlessly arguing in front of a monitor that was melting, and by the beginning of September 2003 (a magical year if ever there was one), not only had we finished our documentary, we were actually pleased with it. We showed it to a producer named Smith who had reluctantly granted us five – and only five – minutes. Believe it or not, it only took three.

"A factual series," ruled Mr Smith, supreme emperor of the network. "Twelve episodes. Twenty-five minutes each. I want it for the beginning of November. Can you do it?"

Smiles and handshakes. Finally, a stinking bus took us back home. Stunned and a little dazed, we checked on Wikipedia what the hell a factual series was. The answer: a mixture of drama and documentary. In other words, we had less than two months to re-edit everything from scratch and create our factual series. Impossible?

No joke.

December 1 that year, "Road Crew" went on the air. It was a ratings smash.

Suddenly our names were on everyone's lips. Professor Calhoun had a photograph taken awarding us what looked like an abomination created by Dalí, but which was in fact a prize to honour deserving students. I emphasise: deserving. The blogs were talking about "Road Crew", the press was talking about "Road Crew".

It wasn't all roses, though.

Maddie Grady of the *New Yorker* cut us down to size with a blunt axe. A 5,000-word article that had me beating my brains out for months. According to *G.Q.*, we were misogynists. According to *Life*, we were misanthropists. According to *Vogue*, we embodied the redemption of Generation X. And that really got us down.

Some internet nerds started targeting us, with close readings of our work that in terms of prolixity and pedantry could have given the *Encyclopaedia Britannica* a run for its money.

Rumours started circulating, also on the internet, the cradle of fucking virtual democracy, rumours that were a mixture of the ridiculous and the disturbing. According to those in the know, Mike and I did heroin, speedball, cocaine, amphetamines. The roadies had taught us all of the hundred and one sins of Sodom. During the shooting one of us had died ("Mike, it says here you're dead." "No, it says one of us is dead, why should it be me?" "Have you taken a look at your face, partner?").

My favourite, though, was this one: we had gotten a groupie named Pam pregnant (have you noticed that groupies are always called Pam?) and had made her miscarry during a satanic ritual taught to us by Jimmy Page.

In March of the following year, 2004, Mr Smith got us to sign a contract for a second season of "Road Crew". We had the whole world in our hands. Then, just before leaving for the shoot, something happened that surprised everyone, me most of all.

I fell in love.

* * *

And, strange to say, it was all thanks to "Call me Gerry" Calhoun. He had arranged a special screening of the first episode of "Road Crew" followed by an unmissable debate for his students. "Debate" reeked of an ambush, but Mike (who may have hoped to get his revenge on our old teacher and the world at large) had insisted on accepting, and I'd meekly followed suit, as I always did when Mike got something into his head.

The girl who found her way into my heart was sitting in the third row, half hidden by a guy who looked like Mark Chapman and weighed around three hundred pounds (a fan from the blogosphere, I immediately assumed), in Calhoun's fearsome Lecture Room 13, the one that some students of the New York Film Academy called the Fight Club.

At the end of the screening, the fat guy was the first to have his say. What he said in a speech lasting thirty-five minutes can be summed up as: "What a crock of shit!" Then, satisfied, he wiped away a thread of foam, sat down and crossed his arms, with an expression of defiance on his pizza face.

I was about to retaliate with a long (very long) series of not very P.C. remarks about smartass fat guys, when the impossible happened. The blonde girl asked permission to speak and Calhoun, relieved, granted it to her. She stood up (she was really shapely) and said, in a very strong German accent, "I'd like to ask you. What's the exact word for *Neid*?"

I burst out laughing and mentally thanked my dear *Mutti* for her obstinacy in teaching me her mother tongue. Suddenly, I saw those hours spent flagellating my tongue against my teeth, aspirating vowels and rounding my *r*s as if I had a cracked fan in my mouth, in a completely different light.

"*Mein liebes Fräulein*", I began, bathing in the sound of eyes popping like champagne corks among that mass of horny students (including the fat guy). "*Sie sollten nicht fragen, wie wir 'Neid' sagen, sondern wie wir 'Idiot' sagen.*"

My dear young lady, you shouldn't ask how we say "envy", but how we say "idiot".

Her name was Annelise.

She was nineteen years old and she'd been in the United States for little more than a month, on a course. Annelise was neither German nor Austrian nor even Swiss. She came from a tiny province in the north of Italy where most of the population spoke German. The name of that strange place was Alto Adige, or Südtirol.

The night before I left for the tour, we made love to Bruce Springsteen's "Nebraska", which reconciled me at least a little with the Boss. The next morning was tough. I didn't think I would ever see her again.

I was wrong. My sweet Annelise, born amid the Alps eight thousand kilometres from the Big Apple, transformed her short course into a study permit. I know it seems crazy, but you have to believe me. She loved me, and I loved her. In 2007, in a little restaurant in Hell's Kitchen, as Mike and I were preparing to shoot the third (and, we had vowed, last) season of "Road Crew", I asked Annelise to marry me. She accepted with such joy that I did a not very manly thing and burst into tears.

What more could I have wanted?

2008.

Because in 2008, while Mike and I, exhausted, were taking a break after the broadcast of the third season of our *fuck-tual* series, on a mild May day, in a clinic in New Jersey immersed in greenery, my daughter Clara was born. And then: fragrant mountains of diapers, baby food decorating clothes and walls, but above all hours and hours spent watching Clara learning to get to know the world. And how to forget Mike's visits with his current girlfriend (they lasted from two to four weeks, the longest being a month and a half, but then she had been Miss July), during which he tried every which way to teach my daughter his name before Clara could even utter the word "Mamma"?

In the summer of 2009, I met Annelise's parents, Werner and Herta Mair. We didn't know then that the "tiredness" that Herta gave as an excuse for her dizziness and pallor was an advanced stage of cancer. She died a few months later, at the end of the year. Annelise didn't want me to go with her to the funeral.

2010 and 2011 were beautiful and frustrating years. Beautiful: Clara climbing everywhere, Clara asking "what's this?" in three different languages (the third, Italian, Annelise was teaching me, too, and I liked it a lot, I was a student motivated by a teacher I found very sexy), Clara simply growing. Frustrating? Of course. Because at the end of 2011, after presenting Mr Smith with something like a hundred thousand different projects (all rejected), we began shooting the fourth season of "Road Crew". The one we had sworn we would never make.

Nothing went right. The magic was gone and we knew it. The fourth season of "Road Crew" is a long, unhappy threnody to the end of an era. But the public, as generations of copywriters know, love feeling sad. Our ratings were better than for the three previous seasons. Even the *New Yorker* praised us, calling it "the story of a waking dream that crumbles".

So Mike and I once again found ourselves exhausted and apathetic. Depressed. The work we considered the worst in our career was being praised to the skies even by those who only a little while earlier had treated us like lepers. That was why, in December 2012, I accepted Annelise's suggestion to spend a few months in her native village, a little place called Siebenhoch in Alto Adige/Südtirol, Italy. Far from everything and everybody.

A good idea.

The Heroes of the Mountain

The photographs that Annelise had shown me of Siebenhoch didn't do justice to that little village clinging up there at an altitude of 1,400 metres. Yes, the windows with the geraniums were there, the streets narrow enough to keep warm in, the snow-capped mountains and the forests all around. Just like a picture postcard. But in the flesh it was . . . different.

Magnificent.

I loved the little church surrounded by a cemetery that didn't make you think about death but about the eternal rest spoken of in the prayers. I loved the pointed roofs of the houses, the well-tended flower beds, the streets free from cracks, I loved the frequently incomprehensible dialect that twisted the language of my mother (and, to all intents and purposes, of my childhood) into a dissonant, off-colour *dialokt.*

I even loved the Despar supermarket slumbering in a clearing torn by force from the vegetation, the interweaving of local and national roads, just as I loved the mule tracks half buried by the tracery of beeches, bracken and red firs.

I loved my wife's expression every time she showed me something new. A smile that made her seem like the little girl who had, I imagined, walked along these streets, run through these woods, played with snowballs, and then, once grown, had crossed the ocean to end up in my arms.

What else?

I loved *speck*, especially the matured kind that my father-in-law brought home without ever revealing where he'd procured such a delicacy – certainly not in what he called the tourist shops – and *canederli* cooked at least forty different ways. I devoured pies, strudels and lots of other things. I put on eight pounds and didn't feel even slightly guilty.

The house we occupied belonged to Annelise's father, Werner. It was on the western boundary of Siebenhoch (assuming that a village with a population of seven hundred could be said to have a boundary) at the point where the mountain rose to touch the sky. On the upper floor were two bedrooms, a study and a bathroom. On the ground floor, a kitchen, a cubbyhole and what Annelise called the living room, although "living room" was a bit of an understatement. It was huge, with a table in the middle and furniture of beech and Swiss pine that Werner had built with his own hands. The light came from two large windows that looked out onto a meadow, and from the first light of day I would put an armchair there for the pleasure of letting the space – the mountains and the greenery (which when we arrived were laden with a compact blanket of snow) – penetrate me.

It was while I was sitting in that armchair on February 25 that I saw a helicopter cut across the sky over Siebenhoch. It was painted a beautiful bright red. I thought about it all night. By February 26, the helicopter had turned into an idea.

An obsession.

By the 27th, I had realised that I needed to talk to somebody about it.

Somebody who knew. Somebody who would understand.

On the 28th, I did just that.

* * *

Werner Mair lived a few kilometres from us as the crow flies, in a place with very few comforts that local people called Welshboden.

He was a severe man who rarely smiled (a magical occurrence that only Clara could easily provoke), with white hair sparse over his temples, penetrating sky-blue eyes tending to grey, a thin nose and lines like scars.

He was pushing eighty, but in magnificent physical shape. I found him busy chopping wood in his shirtsleeves, even though the temperature was a degree or two below zero.

As soon as he saw me coming, he propped his axe against a rack and greeted me. I switched off the engine and got out of the car. The air was sparkling and pure. I breathed in deeply.

"More firewood, Werner?"

He held out his hand. "There's never enough. And the cold keeps you young. Would you like a coffee?"

We went inside and sat down by the fire. Through the smell of the smoke, there filtered a pleasant fragrance of resin.

Werner made the espresso (he made a mountain variant of Italian-style coffee: a tiny amount as black as tar that kept you awake for weeks), sat down, took an ashtray from a little cabinet and winked at me.

Werner told me he had quit smoking the day Herta gave birth to Annelise. But after the death of his wife, perhaps out of boredom or perhaps (I suspected) out of nostalgia, he had taken up the habit again. Surreptitiously, because if Annelise had seen him with a cigarette in his hand she would have flayed him alive. Even though I felt guilty about encouraging him with my company (and my discretion), at that moment, as Werner lit a match with his thumbnail, my father-in-law's tobacco dependence was convenient for me. There's nothing better for having a man-to-man chat than sharing a bit of tobacco.

I relaxed. We exchanged small talk. The weather, Clara. Annelise, New York. We smoked. We drank the coffee and a glass of Welshboden water to take away the bitterness.

At last I came out with it.

"I saw a helicopter," I began. "A red one."

Werner looked straight through me. "And you're wondering what it'd look like on T.V., right?"

Right.

That helicopter wouldn't make a hole on the screen. It would shatter it.

Werner shook the ash from his cigarette onto the floor. "Did you ever have one of those ideas that change your life?"

I thought of Mike.

I thought of Annelise. And Clara.

"I wouldn't be here otherwise," I said.

"I was younger when I had mine. It didn't happen by chance, it was born out of grief. It's never a good thing for ideas to come out of grief, Jeremiah. But it happens and you can't do anything about it. Ideas come to you, and that's it. Some go away and others take root. Like plants. And like plants they grow and grow. They have lives of their own." Werner broke off, examined the embers of his cigarette, and threw it in the fire. "How much time do you have?"

"Whatever we need," I replied.

"*Nix.* Wrong. You have the time your wife and daughter have granted you. A man must always think first of his family. Always."

"Right," I said, and I think I blushed a little.

"Anyway, if you want to hear this story, it won't take long. You see that photograph?"

He indicated a framed snapshot, hanging below the crucifix. Werner went over to it and brushed it with his fingertips. Like many mountain people, he was missing a few phalanges, in his case the first of the little finger and ring finger of his right hand.

The black-and-white photograph showed five young men. The one on the left, an unruly lock of hair falling over his forehead and a back-pack on his back, was Werner.

"We took that in 1950. I don't remember the month. But I remember them. And I also remember the laughter. That's one thing that doesn't fade as you get older. You forget birthdays and anniversaries. You forget faces. Luckily, you also forget the pain, the suffering. But the laughter of that time, when you're not yet a man but you're not a child anymore either . . . that stays inside you."

Even though I'd seen a good few springs less than he had, I understood what Werner was trying to tell me. I doubted, though, that his memory was failing. Werner belonged to a race of mountain people forged in steel. In spite of his white hair and the lines on his face, it was impossible for me to think of him as an old man.

"Life's hard down there in Siebenhoch. School in the morning, down in the valley, then afternoon till night breaking your back in the fields, in the pastures, in the woods or in the stables. I was lucky because my father, Annelise's grandfather, had survived the collapse of the mine, whereas many of my friends didn't have their fathers, and growing up without a father in Südtirol in those years was no picnic."

"I can imagine."

"Imagine, maybe," Werner replied without taking his eyes off the photograph. "But I doubt you can really understand it. Have you ever gone hungry?"

I'd once been robbed by a junkie who'd pointed a syringe at my throat, and a dear friend of mine had been stabbed on his way back from a concert in Madison Square Garden, but no, I'd never gone hungry.

So I didn't reply.

"We were young and carefree, in other words, we were happy. The thing we liked most was climbing mountains." An expression that was a mixture of sadness and irony crossed his face, then immediately disappeared. "In those days, mountaineering was something for foreigners and dreamers. Not a respectable sport like today. In some ways, we were pioneers, you know. With time, mountaineering has turned into tourism, and today tourism is the main source of income throughout Alto Adige."

It was true. Everywhere there were hotels and restaurants, and cable cars to ease the ascent to the mountain peaks. In winter, the tourists concentrated in the skiing areas, and in summer they devoted themselves to excursions in the woods. I couldn't blame them: as soon as the weather changed and the snow melted, I was planning to buy sturdy shoes and, on the pretext of taking Clara to get a little fresh air, to see if this boy from Brooklyn could compete with the local mountain men.

"Without tourism," Werner went on, "the Alto Adige would be a poor province, inhabited only by ageing peasants, and Siebenhoch would no longer exist, that's for sure."

"That would be sad."

"Very sad. But it didn't happen like that." He blinked. "Anyway, for people at that time, especially people around here, going into the mountains meant going to *work* in the mountains. Taking the cows to pasture, cutting firewood. Cultivating. That was the mountains. For us, on the other hand, it was fun. But we were careless. Too careless. We had competitions to see who could climb the steepest rock face, we timed each other, we defied the bad weather. And our equipment?" Werner gave himself a slap on the thigh. "Ropes made of hemp. You know what it's like to fall when you're tied to a rope made of hemp?"

"I haven't the slightest idea."

"Hemp isn't elastic. If you fall with modern ropes, the ones made of nylon and God knows what else, it's almost amusing. They stretch and absorb your weight. Hemp is another story. You risk being crippled for life. Or worse. And on top of that, the climbing spikes, the hammers and all the rest were handmade by the village blacksmith. Iron is fragile, extremely fragile, and expensive. But we didn't have cinemas, we didn't have cars. We'd been brought up to save every last cent. And we were really happy to use the money for our climbing expeditions." Werner cleared his throat. "We felt immortal."

"But you weren't, were you?"

"Nobody is. A few months after we took that photograph, there was an accident. Four of us went up Croda dei Toni – have you ever been there? In Belluno dialect, it means 'crown of thunder', because when it rains and lightning comes down it's a sight to give you goosebumps. It's a beautiful place. But that doesn't make death less bitter. Death is death, and nothing else matters."

I read it on his face. He was thinking about Herta, who had died with a monster in her brain, devouring her. I respected his silence until he felt ready to continue with his story.

"Three of them didn't make it. I survived only because I was lucky. Josef died in my arms, while I screamed and screamed, begging for help. But even if someone had heard me, you know how many kilometres there were between the place where the rope broke and the nearest hospital? Twenty. Impossible to save him. Impossible. I waited for death to take him, recited a prayer, and turned back. And then I had the idea. Or rather, the idea came to me. After the funeral, a few of us had a drink in memory of the dead. Around here, as you'll have noticed, drinking is quite common. And that night we drank like sponges. We sang, we laughed, we cried, we cursed. Then, when dawn came, I presented my idea. Even though nobody said it – some things you don't need to hear with your own ears – to the rest of the world we were lunatics who were asking for it. Nobody could have helped us, or even wanted to, if we'd got into trouble up there."

"To survive you could only count on your own strength."

"That's right, Jeremiah. So we founded Dolomite Mountain Rescue. We had no money, we had no political support, and we had to pay for the equipment out of our own pockets, but it worked." Werner granted me one of those smiles that only Clara managed to get from him. "One of us, Stefan, bought a first aid manual. He studied it and taught us the principles of resuscitation. Mouth-to-mouth respiration, heart massage. We learned how to splint a fracture, how to recognise a head trauma. Things like that. But it wasn't yet enough. The first holidaymakers, as we called them at the time, were starting to arrive, and with them, inexpert and badly equipped people. Our interventions increased. We were still on foot. We didn't buy our first van until '65, a rickety old crock that could take us only up to a certain point. After that, we had to manage in the old way. Transporting the wounded on our backs. And often the dead."

I tried to imagine the scene. It gave me the shudders. I hate to admit it, but they weren't just shudders of horror, because I, too, like Werner, had my own idea in my head.

"We'd arrive, we'd find the body, we'd say a prayer, then the oldest of the group would hand around a little bottle of cognac or grappa, one sip each, and the youngest would get the job of carrying the body. We'd go back to base. Which in those days was none other than the bar in Siebenhoch, the only place where there was a telephone."

"Shit," I murmured.

"To cut a long story short, here in Siebenhoch, real tourism arrived in the early '90s, when Hermann Kagol had the idea for the Visitors' Centre, but already by the '80s other valleys had their work cut out keeping up with the demands of the tourists. Tourists bring money. When money starts to change hands, as you yourself know, the politicians arrive, and if you have any kind of a brain, you can twist them round your little finger."

I wouldn't have liked to be in the shoes of the politician who tried to get the better of Werner Mair.

"So funds arrived. We made agreements with the Civil Defence people and with the Red Cross. At the end of the '70s, we used army helicopters for a special project. The results were incredible. If, before, three injured people out of seven survived an accident, with the helicopter it was six out of ten. Not bad, eh?"

"I'd say not."

"But we wanted more. First," Werner counted, showing me his thumb, "we wanted a helicopter that was at our disposal all the time without having to deal every time with the whims of some colonel or other." To the thumb was added the index finger. "We wanted to raise that statistic. We didn't want any more deaths. So . . ."

"You wanted a doctor on board."

"Precisely. The helicopter reduces the time, the doctor stabilises the patient. We managed to get our first helicopter in '83. An Alouette that was basically two pipes soldered together and a lawnmower engine. We moved our base from here to Pontives, near Ortisei, because there we had the possibility of building a hangar and a heliport. The doctor came only later, after Herta and I had left Siebenhoch."

"Why did you leave?"

A grimace on Werner's face. "The village was dying. There wasn't enough tourism. The Visitors' Centre was still just an idea in Hermann's head. You see how we keep talking about ideas? And I had a little girl to feed."

"You could have stayed and been a rescuer."

"Remember what I said before telling you all this?"

"No, I . . ." I stammered in embarrassment.

"A man should have just one priority. His family. When Annelise was born, I wasn't exactly old, but I wasn't a boy any more. It's true, Herta was twenty years younger than me and was used to spending her nights knowing that I was climbing some peak to rescue a climber in difficulty, but the arrival of the baby changed everything. I was a father now, you understand?"

Yes, I understood.

"A friend found me a job in a printing shop in Cles, near Trento, and we moved there when Annelise was just a few months old. It was only when she'd finished middle school that we decided to come back here. The fact is, she was the one who insisted. She loved this place. For Annelise, it was only the village where she spent her holidays, but she was tied to it somehow. The rest, as we say in such cases . . ."

"Is history."

Werner stared at me for a long time.

Werner didn't look. Werner examined. Have you ever seen a bird of prey? Werner had that look. They call it charisma.

"If you're convinced you want to do what you have it in your mind to do, I can make a phone call to a couple of people. Then it'll be up to you to earn their respect."

The idea.

I had it all in my head. The editing. The voice-over. Everything. A factual series like "Road Crew", but set here, in these mountains, with the men of Dolomite Mountain Rescue. I knew that Mike would be enthusiastic. I even had the title. It would be called "Mountain Angels" and it would be a hit. I knew it.

I *felt* it.

"But I have to warn you. It won't be the way you expect, Jeremiah."

The Voice of the Beast

A few days later, I talked about it to Annelise. Then I phoned Mike. No, it wasn't a joke. And yes, I was a fucking genius. I'd always known it, but thanks anyway.

On April 4, Mike showed up in Siebenhoch. He had a fur hat wedged on his head and a Harry Potter scarf around his neck. Clara intoned, "Uncle Mike! Uncle Mike!" and clapped her hands, as she had done when she was little more than a mite, something of which my partner was very proud.

On April 6, as excited as quarterbacks at the Super Bowl, we began filming "Mountain Angels" at Pontives in the Val Gardena, the headquarters of Dolomite Mountain Rescue.

* * *

The Pontives base was a two-storey building surrounded by greenery. Modern, with every comfort, and very clean and tidy.

It was Moses Ploner, the man who had taken over from Werner as the head of Dolomite Mountain Rescue, who let us make our first reconnaissance tour and introduced us to the rest of the team. People who had saved thousands of lives.

I won't hide the fact that we were intimidated.

We were on tenterhooks until ten in the morning, when the static over the radio gave way to a monotonous voice.

"Charlie Papa to Dolomite Mountain Rescue."

Charlie Papa stood for Command Post.

"Dolomite Rescue here, go ahead, Charlie Papa," Moses replied, bending towards the microphone.

"We have a tourist on the east side of the Seceda. Near the Margheri refuge. Over."

"Got it, Charlie Papa, over and out."

As the first day of shooting had approached, I had constructed a movie in my head involving strong-jawed Navy Seals types zooming from one place to another like balls in a pinball machine, sirens sounding, red lights flashing, and delivering brash lines like, "What are you, a bunch of girls, let's go kick some ass!"

Instead, there was no excitement.

I would soon understand why. The mountains are the last place in which the distinction between sounding authoritative and real authority still counts.

That April 6, anyway, I didn't have time to feel disappointed. Moses Ploner (with a slowness that struck me as truly exasperating) turned to Mike.

"Do you want to come?"

Slowly, Mike got up from his chair. Slowly, he hoisted the Sony on his shoulder. He threw me a terrified glance and climbed into the EC135 just as the noise of the turbines went up an octave. I approached the doors of the hangar, just in time to be flung backwards by the movement of air from the blades of the helicopter as it took off, and in the blinking of an eye the red outline of the EC135 had disappeared.

They returned about thirty minutes later. A routine mission for the team from Dolomite Mountain Rescue. The helicopter had reached the scene, the doctor had checked the injury (a sprain), the unfortunate climber had been taken on board and dropped at the hospital in Bolzano, then the EC135 had taken off again and on the way back Mike had received his baptism of air.

"We played at being the Luftwaffe, and Mike . . ." grinned Christoph, the doctor, displaying a small bag full of vomit, while my partner, as white as a sheet, ran to the bathroom.

Welcome to Dolomite Mountain Rescue.

* * *

In my memory, the next few months are like a speeded-up film.

The helicopter taking off in almost zero visibility and the exchange of quips between Mike and Ismaele, the pilot of the EC135 (Ismaele was the brother of Moses: Ma and Pa Ploner must have been great Bible fans): "Didn't you say we need two hundred metres' visibility to fly?" "But this *is* two hundred metres' visibility. Even three hundred if I shut my eyes, I think."

The faces of the injured, above all, blur into one. The terror in the eyes of a young man frozen by a panic attack. The pain of a shepherd with a leg broken by a landslide of rocks. The half-frozen tourist. The couple lost in the fog. An infinity of broken bones, dislocated pelvises, shattered joints, blood, sweat. Many tears, few thanks. Mike sleeping four hours a night, swept along by adrenalin. The radio calls that clench the stomach. Mike stung by thirteen different varieties of mosquito. My initiation: being mummified in a vacuum bag and left there to test the intoxication of claustrophobia. Mike shaking his head to tell me no, better not do interviews, there's no time. The request for "emergency spiritual aid" tormenting you day and night.

And of course, the Rules.

The men of Dolomite Mountain Rescue had one prophet (Moses Ploner), a chariot of fire to ascend to the Kingdom of Heaven (the EC135), and at least two hundred thousand rules transmitted from mouth to mouth. It was hard to keep up with them. Rules sprouted like mushrooms.

The Mealtime Rule may have been the strangest (and in some ways the most disturbing). Never mind if it was seven in the morning or four in the afternoon, at the exact moment when you sit down to eat, the alarm will sound and the team will have to leave for an intervention.

The first time, I told myself it was just a coincidence. The second time, I thought fate was playing a trick. By the tenth time, I had started to blame God and universal entropy. A few months into shooting, I just ignored it.

That was the way it was, period, so why worry about it?

For me, who as the writer didn't participate in the direct action (in Mike McMellan's immortal words: "You just have to figure out how the fuck to tell the story, the Sony will take care of the rest"), the Mealtime Rule had unexpected benefits. The alarm would sound, the team would go down into the hangar, the helicopter would take off and I'd finish the others' ice cream or dessert, sitting in the wireless operator's seat. The pen fattens quicker than the camera.

Until lunchtime on September 15.

* * *

Mike had been showing signs of fatigue for a few days now. He was pale and drawn.

The first operation of the day had gone smoothly. The weather was good, and the Milanese tourist involved had simply been scared and had the idea that the team's helicopter was a kind of taxi that could take him down to the valley. The second operation had been a photocopy of the first, but instead of the Corno Bianco they'd had to fly all the way to the Sasso Lungo.

When Mike came back, I noticed that he was dragging his feet. He changed the camera battery (*our* First Rule) and then collapsed onto a chair. Within a few minutes he was asleep, the Sony clutched to his chest.

Around one o'clock, since everyone's stomach was rumbling, Moses decided that the time had come to defy the Mealtime Rule. Stew. Potatoes. Strudel. We never got to eat the strudel. A pity, because it looked really appetising.

The alarm sounded just when we'd started filling our plates. Mike stood up, grabbed the camera and fell back on the chair, gasping.

Christoph soon announced his prescription: "Tachipirina, warm blankets, grandmother's broth and a good night's sleep."

Mike shook his head and stood up again. "I'm fine, no problem."

He didn't even have time to lift the camera before Moses took him by the arm and stopped him. "You're not coming. Send *him* if you like. You're not getting in the helicopter in that condition."

Him, of course, meant *me*.

Having said this, he turned and went down the stairs.

Mike and I looked at each other for a moment.

I tried to sound confident. "Give me the Sony, partner, I'll win you an Oscar."

"Oscars are for movies," Mike grunted. "We're making television, Salinger."

Reluctantly, he passed me the camera. It was heavy.

"Make sure to press *record*."

"Amen."

Christoph's voice from the stairs: "Are you coming?"

I went.

I had never been in the EC135. The seat reserved for Mike was tiny. The EC isn't one of those transport giants you see in movies, it's a small helicopter, agile and powerful. The best possible means of rescue in the peaks of the Dolomites, but damned uncomfortable if you have to do any filming.

As we left the ground, my stomach rose into my mouth. Not only because of the acceleration. Call it simple fear. Looking out of the window didn't help. I saw the Pontives base disappear and swallowed a couple of times in order not to throw up. Manny, the team member sitting next to me, squeezed my hand. His hand was as big as my forearm. A mountain man's gesture that meant: take it easy. Believe me, it worked.

No more fear: just the sky. Clear.

God, how beautiful it was.

Christoph gave me a wink and signalled to me to put on my headphones. "How's it going, Salinger?"

"Terrific."

I was about to add something else, but Moses' voice interrupted me. "Dolomite Mountain Rescue to Charlie Papa. Do you have any information for us?"

I started to film seriously, hoping that my lack of experience wouldn't give Mike hives when he saw the footage on my return.

He could be a real pain in the butt when he wanted.

"Charlie Papa here." The distorted voice of the 118 switchboard came over the radio. "German tourist, female, on the Ortles. Ended up in a crevasse at 3,200 metres. On the Schückrinne."

"Received, Charlie Papa. We'll be there in . . ."

". . . seven minutes," Ismaele said.

". . . seven minutes. Over and out."

Moses put down the radio and turned to me. I lifted the camera and gave him a beautiful close-up.

"Have you ever seen the Ortles?" he asked me straight out.

"Only in photographs."

Moses nodded to himself. "It'll be a beautiful operation, you'll see."

Then he turned, erasing me from his world.

"What's the Schückrinne?" I asked Christoph.

"There are various ways to reach the summit of the Ortles," the doctor replied, grim-faced. "The simplest is the Normal North, you need to be trained and it's no joke, but you don't go up onto a glacier unprepared, right?"

"We once pulled up a guy wearing flip-flops around there," Ismaele cut in cheerfully.

"Flip-flops?"

"At 3,000 metres," he said with a sneer. "People are strange, aren't they?"

I couldn't help but agree.

Christoph continued with his explanation. "The Schückrinne is the worst way. The rock is crumbly, some of the slopes are 55 degrees, and the ice . . . you never know when it'll do something strange. It's a bad place even for the most expert mountaineers. Charlie Papa says the tourist has ended up in a crevasse, and that's really bad."

"Why?"

"Because she might have broken her leg. Or both legs. And maybe also her pelvis. She might have hit her head. Plus the bottom of the crevasse in a glacier is terrible, there's water. You feel . . ." Christoph looked for the right image. "You feel as if you're inside a glass of *granita*."

"It's going to be fun," Ismaele said, giving the camera one of his unmistakable smiles, halfway between an abandoned cub and a mischievous little boy.

Another rule of the rescue team. Nothing is difficult. Ever. Because, as Moses Ploner said: "Difficult is only what you can't do." In other words: if it's difficult, stay at home.

The German woman would have done well to follow Moses' rule, I thought. It didn't occur to me that *I* should have followed it, too.

Seven minutes later, the EC135 was circling over the white slope of the Ortles. I had never seen a glacier before, and it was magnificent.

I would soon change my mind.

Moses flung open the door and an icy current swept over me.

"There she is."

I tried to film the spot he was pointing at.

"You see that crevasse? The woman is there."

I couldn't figure out how Moses could possibly be so sure it was the right crevasse. In that direction, there were at least three or four of them.

The EC135 was vibrating like a blender. It descended a few hundred metres, until the Sony framed the clue that Moses' eyes had caught before mine. A series of prints in the snow that suddenly broke off.

The EC135 paused.

"No way we can land there, boys," Ismaele said.

I stared open-mouthed.

Ismaele wasn't a pilot. He was the patron saint of all helicopter pilots. In Mike's footage I had seen him land ("park" was the word he himself used) on peaks not much bigger than an apple, surf on currents of air that would have brought the Red Baron down, and take the EC135 so close to a wall of rock, it seemed as if the blades would shatter at any moment. Without ever losing that Lampwick grin. But now this same Ismaele was worried.

Uh-oh.

"Manny? Go down with the pulley. Get her and bring her straight up. I'm not unloading anyone. It's too damned hot. And this wind . . ."

I didn't understand. We were on a glacier, weren't we? A glacier's cold, or am I wrong? So what the hell did "It's too damned hot" mean? And what did the wind have to do with it?

Now wasn't the time to ask questions. Manny was already securing himself to the pulley.

I looked at him and suddenly my heart started to pump gunpowder. So, as the EC135 hovered between two slabs of rock above the fissure in the glacier, words emerged from my mouth, words that would change the course of my life.

"Can I go down with you?"

Manny, already standing on the helicopter's runner, made a sign to Moses, the pulley taut in his leather-gloved right hand.

"What?"

"Can I go down with Manny? I'll film the whole thing."

"I can't pull three people up. Too much wind," Ismaele said. "And besides, the temperature's . . ."

Fuck the temperature.

Fuck everything. I wanted to *go down.*

"I can stay down there. Manny'll take the woman up and then come back for me."

Easy, right?

Moses hesitated.

Manny smiled. "I think we can do it."

Moses looked hard at me. "O.K.," he said reluctantly. "But hurry up about it."

I got up from my seat (it wasn't Mike's anymore, it was *my* seat),

Christoph passed me a harness, I put it on and tied myself to Manny. We leaned out of the door, our feet planted on the runner of the EC135. Christoph gave me the thumbs-up. Manny tapped on my helmet.

Three, two, one.

The void swallowed us.

I was scared. I wasn't scared. I was terrified. I *wasn't.*

I'd never felt more alive.

"Ten metres," I heard Manny say clearly.

I looked down.

It was too dark in the crevasse to see anything. I aimed the camera and continued filming.

"One metre."

Manny propped himself on the ridge of the crevasse.

"Stop."

The pulley stopped its descent.

Manny lit the lamp on his helmet. The beam of light plumbed the darkness. We immediately spotted the woman. She was wearing a fluorescent orange jacket. She was leaning against the wall of ice. She raised her hand.

"It's thirty metres," Manny said. "Down, slowly."

The pulley started humming again.

I saw the iridescent surface of the Ortles disappear and I went blind, while Manny controlled the descent. I opened and closed my eyes several times to accustom myself to the darkness.

"Five metres," Manny said. "Three."

There was a strange luminosity down there. The sunlight was refracted in a thousand flashes that blurred your vision, creating rainbow-coloured haloes and scintillas.

The bottom of the crevasse, two and a half metres wide, was covered in water. In the water, as Christoph had said, pieces of ice of various sizes floated. It was just like ending up inside a *granita.*

"Stop."

Manny unhooked his harness, then mine.

I was immersed in the icy water up to my knees.

"Are you alone, signora?"

The woman seemed not to understand the question.

"Leg," she stammered.

"She's in shock," Manny said. "Move as far away as you can. Let's see if we can do this."

I flattened my back against the wall of ice. My breath condensed in little clouds. I hoped they weren't going to end up in the frame.

The woman looked first at Manny then at her own leg. "It hurts."

"You see the helicopter? There's a doctor on it who'll give you a good dose of painkillers."

The woman groaned and shook her head.

Manny secured himself to the rope of the pulley, then, pulling on the cable, tied it to the woman's harness.

"Pulley, Moses."

The pulley lifted the two of them.

The woman screamed with all the breath she had in her. I held back the urge to raise my hands to my ears. If I had, I would have dropped the camera, and then Mike really would have killed me.

Slowly and painfully.

The ascent was textbook. The cable was like a straight line drawn in Indian ink.

I saw Manny and the woman go up and up and finally leave the crevasse.

I was alone.

* * *

What does the footage on the Sony show at this point?

The walls of the crevasse. Vague glimmers in the total darkness. The beam of light from the camera moving from one side to the other, sometimes in slow motion, sometimes hysterically. Iridescent little cubes floating in the pool of water around my legs. The reflection of my face against the ice. First smiling, then attentive, with the expression of someone trying to eavesdrop on a private conversation. Finally contorted, eyes like a trapped animal, cold-darkened lips pulled over my teeth in a sneer that didn't belong to me. A medieval death mask.

And over everything: the voice of the Ortles. The cracking of the ice. The hissing of the mass of the Ortles as it continued to move as if from two hundred thousand years ago to the present.

The voice of the Beast.

Manny descending, worried. My name repeated several times.

God's scream swallowing Manny.

The passing of seconds that stops making sense. The terrifying awareness that the time of the glacier isn't human time. It's an alien, hostile time.

And the darkness.

I sank into the gloom that devours worlds. I found myself drifting in deep space. A single, vast, endless eternal night of spectral whiteness.

Eight letters: "darkness". Three letters: "ice".

At last, salvation.

Too hot, Moses had said. Too hot meant avalanche. God's scream. And the avalanche had taken Manny. And along with Manny, through the pulley cable, the Beast had snatched the EC135 and dragged it to the ground, crushing it as you would a troublesome insect. Why hadn't Moses cut the cable? If he had, Manny would have been crushed but the avalanche wouldn't have touched the helicopter. The Carabinieri wondered that, and the reporters wondered that. Not the rescuers who pulled me to safety. They *knew*. It's all written in the Rules.

The pulley cable can't be cut because in the mountains you never leave anyone behind. For any reason. That's the way it is, and that's the way it has to be.

Nothing remained of Moses, Ismaele, Manny, Christoph or the German woman. The fury of the avalanche, which had been unleashed by the heat and the wind, had swept them away, leaving their bodies unrecognisable. The EC135 was a carcass further down the mountain.

But the accident on the Ortles didn't signal the end of Dolomite Mountain Rescue, just as it wasn't the end of my story.

As I said, nine letters.

"Beginning."

280 Million Years Ago

My body responded well to treatment. I spent less than a week in hospital. A few stitches, a drip twice to prevent the onset of hypothermia, and nothing more. The worst wounds were those I carried inside me. "P.T.S.D." was written on my medical record. Post-traumatic stress disorder.

Before bidding me farewell with a handshake and a "Take care of yourself", the doctor from San Maurizio in Bolzano prescribed some psychoactive drugs and sleeping pills, advising me to take them regularly. It was likely, he had added, looking me in the eyes, that for a while I would suffer nightmares and mild panic attacks, accompanied by flashbacks, just like war veterans in movies.

Mild panic attacks?

There were times when the voice of the Beast (mine were auditory flashbacks, I never suffered from hallucinations, thank God) filled my head with such intensity as to force me to the floor, sobbing like a child. Nevertheless, I'd sworn that I would do without the drugs and would use sleeping pills only as a last resort. Any two-bit psychologist could have sensed what I was really doing. I wanted to suffer. And I wanted to suffer because I had to. Had to? Of course, I had soiled my hands with the worst of sins.

I had survived.

I deserved punishment.

It wasn't until later that I realised I wasn't just punishing myself. I was also hurting Annelise, who had aged years in a few days and wept as

I wandered dazed around the house. Worse still, I was hurting Clara. She had become taciturn, spent hours in her room, immersed in picture books and God knows what thoughts. She ate little and had bags under her eyes that no child should have.

Annelise and Werner tried to help me in any way they could. Werner would take me to the back of the house for a smoke, or out in his jeep to give me a bit of fresh air. Annelise tried to rouse me with her best dishes, with the local gossip, with my favourite D.V.D.s and even with the most provocative lingerie available. Her attempts at using sex to revive me proved humiliating for us both.

I would sit apathetically in my favourite armchair, watching the leaves turn red and the sky take on the typical autumn colour of those parts, a glittering palette of blue and purple. When the sun went down, I would stand up and go to bed. I didn't eat, I didn't drink and I made an effort not to think. I jumped at the slightest movement. I could still hear that noise. That damned hissing. The voice of the Beast.

If the days were horrible, the nights were even worse. I would wake up screaming at the top of my voice. It was as if the world had split in two. One part, the wrong part, the one I called World A, had gone on as if nothing had happened, while the right part, World B, had come to an end on September 15 at two twenty-two p.m. with the obituary of Jeremiah Salinger.

I remember the day when Mike came to see me. Pale, eyes circled in red, he told me what he was planning to do and we talked about it. The network had cancelled "Mountain Angels", but we could use the footage we had shot for a documentary on Dolomite Mountain Rescue and what had happened in the crevasse on the Ortles. My partner had even thought of a title: "In the Belly of the Beast". In dubious taste, but appropriate. I gave him my blessing, then walked him to the door and told him this was goodbye.

Mike took it as a joke, but I meant it. This was the last time Batman and Robin would meet. I was trapped in an infernal loop, and as far as I could see, there were only two ways to get out of it. Explode or throw myself off some cliff or other. Exploding meant harming Annelise or Clara. I wouldn't even dream of that. As a brave idiot, withdrawn into my wounded egotism, the second possibility seemed to me less painful. I even began to imagine where, how and when.

So, goodbye, partner. Goodbye, everybody.

Then, midway through October, Clara came to me.

* * *

I was sunk in the armchair, gazing at the infinite, a glass of water now warm in my right hand, the left clutching an empty cigarette packet, when Clara came and sat down in my lap, a book clutched to her chest, as she did whenever she wanted me to read her a story.

With some difficulty, I brought her little face into focus. "Hey, kid."

"Hey, four letters."

That was Clara's favourite game, Numbers and Letters.

I forced myself to smile. "Stress on the second syllable?"

"Stress on the second syllable."

"P-a-p-à," I said, surprised how strange it still felt to hear myself called that. "What's this?"

"Five letters."

"Five? But it's a book. That's four."

Clara shook her head and her hair turned into a blonde cloud. The smell of her shampoo reached my nostrils and I felt something move in my chest.

A hint of warmth.

Like a fire in the distance during a snowstorm.

"Wrong," she replied resolutely.

"Are you sure it isn't a book?"

"It's a 'guide'."

I counted on my fingers. Five letters. She hadn't cheated.

Smiling came almost naturally.

Clara lifted her finger to her lips, a gesture she had inherited from her mother. "The thermometer says seventeen degrees. Seventeen degrees at this hour of the day isn't cold, is it?"

"No, it's not cold."

"Mamma says you hurt your head. The inside of your head," she corrected herself. "That's why you're always sad. But your legs are still working, aren't they?"

That was it. Papà had hurt the inside of his head and that was why he'd become sad.

I bounced her up and down on my knees. Soon that type of game would bore her, within a few years even embarrass her. Time was passing, my daughter was growing, and I was throwing away the days watching the leaves fall from the trees.

"I'd say so, eight letters."

Clara frowned and started counting on her fingers, concentrated. "'Sweetheart' has ten."

"'Honeybun' has eight. A point for me, honeybun."

Clara gave me a sidelong look (she hated losing) then opened the guide she had in her hands. I noticed she'd put some pretty bookmarks in it.

"We'll have Mamma make the sandwiches, we'll take some water, but not too much, because I don't like doing wee-wee in the woods." She sighed. "I'm scared of the spiders."

"Spiders," I said, almost choking with love for her. "Yuk."

"Yes, yuk. We'll start from here," she pointed at the map, "turn here, you see? Where the lake is. Maybe it's already ice."

"Maybe."

"Will we see frozen fish?"

"Maybe a few."

"And then we'll come home. That way, you can carry on looking at the meadow. Is the meadow so interesting, Papà?"

I hugged her. I hugged her hard.

Four letters: "fire".

* * *

That was how our walks started. Every evening Clara would sit on my lap, her guide in her hand, and we'd plan an excursion.

The autumn was a warm embrace, and those walks, but above all Clara's company and the mountain of chatter under which she buried me, worked better than any drug I could have taken.

There were also nightmares, and sometimes the hissing paralysed me, but these episodes were increasingly sporadic. I even managed to reply to Mike's questions by e-mail: he'd gone back to New York in the meantime to edit "In the Belly of the Beast". Even though I refused to look at even a single clip, giving him a few suggestions did me good. I felt alive again. I wanted to get better. World B, the one in which I was a corpse, no longer attracted me. Because that world wasn't the real world. Whether I liked it or not, I had survived.

It had taken a five-year-old girl to make me realise that.

* * *

It was towards the end of October when Clara, instead of showing me the guide as usual, sat on my lap and stared at me with very serious eyes.

"I want to go and see someone."

Theatrically, I turned to Annelise, who was huddled on the couch, absorbed in a book, her long, slender legs gathered under her, and asked her, "Is there something yours truly should know?"

"What kind of thing?"

"The kind that every self-respecting father should be aware of."

I heard Clara laughing at the ridiculous accent I was using: the one I called "Charlie the English butler". It was the mother's side of my daughter's family, the intelligent side.

"Let me make myself clear. Our first-born, Clara Salinger here present, five years old, and I underline five, has just expressed the desire to go and see someone of her acquaintance. Do you think she's referring to Martin's son Roberto?"

"He's in bed with scarlet fever."

"Then by 'someone', which is a generic and therefore neutral term, could our child be referring to Elisabeth? That sweet, friendly little girl who once saw fit to throw up on yours truly's trousers?"

Annelise had closed the book and could no longer hide her amusement. "I'm afraid Clara and Elisabeth have had a little falling out."

"Stop it, you two!" Clara cried. "I don't like it when you make fun of me."

Confronted by her worried little face, we burst into uncontrollable laughter.

"I'm sorry, sweetheart. It's just that . . . Did I hear correctly? You want to go and see someone? And who might this someone be?"

"A friend."

"A friend?"

"His name is Yodi."

"What kind of name is Yodi?" I said, nonplussed.

"Yodi is very kind. And *very* old," she whispered, "but don't say it to his face. Yodi is like *Nonno* Werner, he doesn't like that word."

"Three very sensitive letters: 'old'."

"What does 'sensitive' mean?"

It was Annelise who replied. "Sensitive means that you get upset about little things. In German, it's *empfindlich*." (We were determined for Clara to grow up learning her parents' three languages.) "In Italian . . ."

"*Suscettibile*," I finished for her.

After a long pause Clara said, "Twelve. Twelve letters, Mamma!"

"Impressive. But you were telling me about Yodi."

"If you like, I can show him to you."

"You have a photograph?"

Clara didn't reply. She ran to her room and came back immediately, giving me and Annelise time to exchange puzzled glances.

"This is Yodi. Nice, isn't he?" Clara asked, handing me a book.

Yodi was a fossil. An ammonite, to be exact.

"Shall we go and see him, Papà?"

"Sure, he's seen lots of people in the course of his" – I read the caption – "280 million years of existence. But where exactly do we go to see our new friend?"

It was Annelise who replied, amused. "I know. In the Bletterbach."

"And what the hell, pray, is the Bletterbach?"

Both Annelise and Clara looked at me as if I'd asked the stupidest question in the world. They weren't far wrong. The fact is that things tend to escape me, especially when they're right under my nose. That's the way I am.

The Bletterbach was all around us, the tourist magnet that pumped money into the veins of the local communities. Not only Siebenhoch, which was in fact the largest beneficiary of that flow of cash, being very close to the Visitors' Centre, but also the villages of Aldino (in German, Aldein), Salorno (in German, Salurn), Cembra and Cavalese (which, being in the Trentino part of the region, escaped the double-name rule), Ora (which was still in the province of Bolzano and so was also called Auer), Nova Ponente (Deutschnofen) and Nova Levante (Welschnofen) and many other tiny conglomerations of houses and small churches (in the local *dialokt, Hittlen und Kirchln*).

The area around Siebenhoch, something like 6,000 hectares of woods, forests and rocks, was part of the nature reserve of Monte Corno. In the centre of the reserve, beneath Monte Corno, that is, the Corno Bianco (Weisshorn, in German), a peak more than 2,000 metres high, was a gorge eight kilometres long and more than 400 metres deep.

Through it runs the stream that gives it its name: the Bletterbach.

The rock that the area, and the rest of the Dolomites, is composed of is a strange mixture of calcium carbonate and magnesium, a crumbly mixture through which the waters of the stream have hollowed a canyon, bringing a great many fossils to light. The Bletterbach isn't just a gorge. The Bletterbach is a movie, an open-air documentary that began 280 million years ago, in the period known as the Permian, and ended in the Triassic, a hundred million years later. From the time of the great extinctions to that of the great lizards.

There's a bit of everything in the Bletterbach. Shells, ammonites (like Yodi), the remains of fauna and beasts that would make your skin crawl and your jaw drop in amazement. A prehistoric zoo concentrated in a lost gorge towards which I headed with Clara, her hair gathered into two delightful plaits and her little pastel-coloured boots on her feet, that afternoon in October when things, I thought, had started to take off again.

* * *

We were greeted by a young woman whom I had met several times in Siebenhoch but whose name escaped me, however hard I tried to remember it. She asked me if I had recovered from the accident. She didn't add anything else and I was grateful for that.

To visit the Bletterbach, there were two possibilities. Ilse – her name was written on the badge on the lapel of her blouse – showed us a route marked on the map by a red dotted line. It was the route recommended for families. An excursion of three or three and a half hours which wouldn't take us too far "into the deep" (I couldn't help noticing that strange use of words) but which would show us quite a lot of shells, the footprints of dinosaurs ("nine letters, Papà!") and ferns crystallised in time and in the rock. The second route was estimated at around five hours and would take us further in, to where the gorge narrowed and the Bletterbach stream became a waterfall. In both cases, Ilse added with a severe frown, it was obligatory to stay on the route indicated, to wear helmets and to remember that the management of the reserve took no responsibility in the event of accidents.

"Enter at your own risk": that was written on a trilingual notice.

Ilse explained, "It's a difficult area, sometimes there are rock falls. You could easily hurt yourself. That's why it's obligatory to wear protective helmets. If you don't have them, we can rent you a couple." She smiled at Clara. "There should be a pink one just your size, signorina."

"My name's Clara," my daughter said, "and I want to see the giant ammonite."

The woman turned to me in surprise. "Your daughter is very precocious."

"I'm five years old," Clara said sententiously. "I can read a little and I can count to a thousand. I like dinosaurs with long necks – brontosauruses – strawberry ice cream and *Nonno* Werner's *speck*. And I don't want a pink helmet, I want a red one. That's my favourite colour, apart from blue and green," she concluded, arousing Ilse's incredulous laughter. "Papà," she added immediately afterwards, "ask her where we can find Yodi."

"Who's Yodi?" Ilse said, disorientated by that riot of words.

"Yodi," I replied, "is the name of the giant ammonite. Where can we see it?"

Ilse regained her professional tone. "You'll find it in the geological museum. Which tour do you prefer? Short or long?"

"Short tour, I'd say. I don't like . . . enclosed spaces."

Ilse tore off two tickets. "Do you suffer from claustrophobia?"

"It's a recent thing."

Ilse made us try on several helmets. Clara wanted me to take at least three different photographs of her, one with the pink helmet, one with the yellow helmet and the third with the red helmet, on which her choice fell. Then, backpacks on our backs, we began our excursion.

It was a nice walk, although more than once, thanks to a breeze that made the leaves on the trees rustle, I seemed to hear that infernal hissing and felt a pressing need to start screaming. But I didn't. Because there to show me the shells in the layers of Werfen, the seaweed of the Contrin, or the prints of some pareiasaur that had made its way over the sandstone, was my daughter, and for Clara I had to be the nearest thing to a hero.

So: I was strong, I was cured. I was Superman. Don't I deserve applause?

By the time we got to the end of the route, I was sweating and my nerves were on edge, but Clara was in seventh heaven. Seeing her so happy was one more step towards the end of my torment. After a well-deserved *speck* and pickled gherkin sandwich, we headed for the museum contained within the glass, aluminium and wooden structure of the Visitors' Centre, to finally meet Yodi the giant ammonite.

Clara really loved the fossils. The stranger they were, the more she enjoyed them. She even made an effort to read out all those Latin names, and woe betide me if I tried to help her. "Papà, I'm *big*." No need to point out that "big" was a three-letter word, written in block capitals.

I wasn't crazy about fossils, there was something disturbing about those pieces of rock that had retained the features of living organisms swept away millions of years ago.

Even the concept of millions of years was disturbing.

I preferred the last part of the museum. It was devoted to the old Bletterbach copper mine, which had been closed down after it collapsed in 1923. I was fascinated by the photographs of those big men, blackened by earth, holding antiquated tools. Those handlebar moustaches, those ogre-like beards and those clothes that seemed to have come out of a Mickey Mouse cartoon were irresistible.

Of course, it wasn't all Disney, the lists of miners engulfed by the rock were horrifying, but I was there with Clara and I had no intention of thinking about death and destruction, I had already had my fill of that: better to concentrate on the plus-fours and the haughty expressions of those men whose D.N.A. ran in my daughter's veins. "That's why she likes fossils so much," I thought, grinning to myself. "It's the call of the rock."

Eat your heart out, Jack London.

At last, Yodi. The 280 million-year-old ammonite. When we came to the star of the museum, Clara started telling me his story. You see, for Clara, the world was a big *a*, the beginning of a multitude of stories that went from *a* to *b* and then to *c*, but which almost never got to *z* because Clara didn't force her stories to an ending, it would be like cutting off their wings. I could spend hours listening to her without getting tired of them because that's the nature of love: listening to stories without ever getting tired of them. And I loved Clara more than myself.

When the moment came to return to Siebenhoch, I took out my camera and framed child and ammonite on the display screen. Clara granted me a smile that could wring your heart, then turned, said goodbye to Yodi with a skip that was also a kind of curtsey and turned back to me, all the while talking, talking, talking. As I bent down to put the camera back in the backpack, I caught a fragment of conversation between Ilse and two elderly villagers, legs uncovered, regulation Birkenstocks over dazzling white socks, varicose veins plainly in view. Just a few sentences, but sometimes that's all it takes for destiny to put the rope around your neck.

"It was 1985, signora."

"Are you sure?"

"I was born that year. The year of the Bletterbach killings. My mother was always talking about it. 'You were born the year of that terrible business, that's why you behave the way you do.' She was still traumatised by it. The Schaltzmanns were her distant relatives, you know."

"Did they ever find the person responsible?"

A pause.

A sigh.

"No, never."

Promises and Lies

There's something you really need to know. On September 15, Annelise and I had made a pact.

* * *

When the doctors and nurses had left and Werner had gently taken Clara's hand and gone with her to the hospital's cafeteria, Annelise and I were finally alone. After a silence that the painkillers stretched to excess, Annelise landed me a slap that almost burst the stiches on my eyebrow.

Then she started crying.

"You have to promise," she said. "You have to promise you'll never. Never. Never again make me . . ."

She broke off. I reached for her hand. She pulled it away.

That scared me. It scared me a lot.

"You could have died, Salinger," she said. "Our daughter would have been without a father. Do you realise that?"

I nodded.

But it wasn't true. I couldn't think about anything but the hissing. That damned hissing.

The hissing of the Beast.

"You have to give up this work. And you have to promise me."

"It's my—"

"*We*'re your life."

Everything was going round and round in my head. The effect of the tranquillisers and painkillers was starting to wear off and behind Annelise I could see the Beast, sneering.

"Mike. I—" I stammered.

"Mike?" she almost screamed, furious. "*Mike*"?

"Annelise—"

"You were dead, Salinger. Dead."

"Anne—"

"When I opened the door and saw my father with that expression on his face, I knew . . . I knew you were dead. And I thought of Clara and I thought, God forgive me, I thought, serve you right. You'd asked for it, that was how you'd wanted to end up, and I . . . I hated myself for that."

"Please . . ."

Annelise hugged me.

I felt her body shaking with sobs. "I know," she said, "I know how much that life means to you. But Clara has a right to have a father. And I don't want to be alone, I don't deserve it, Salinger. I can't live without you, you stupid idiot." She pulled away from me, rubbed her nose, and tried to joke about it. "I don't look good in black."

Smiling gave me a sharp pain. I tried to sit up. I felt dizzy, with all the delicacy of a truck. "You'd be the sexiest widow in Siebenhoch," I replied.

Annelise ruffled my hair. "And you'd be the handsomest corpse in the cemetery. I need a year, Salinger."

"A year?"

In spite of the voice of the Beast, I felt this was an important moment. Whatever I said, or didn't say, would affect my marriage.

My future.

"I can't ask you to stop. That wouldn't be fair. But you have to promise me you'll take a year out . . . a sabbatical year. To decide what to do with your life. Then if you want to get back to it, I'll be with you. Just like before."

"Just like before."

"Promise?"

I was about to answer her when the door was flung open and Clara rushed in, with all the enthusiasm of her five years, followed by Werner, who was trying to apologise with his eyes. I signalled to him to drop it. Everything was fine.

I took Clara's hand. "How many letters in the word 'promise'?"

Clara counted. "Seven," she said radiantly.

I looked Annelise in the eyes. "Seven letters."

* * *

That October day, as I headed for Welshboden, I kept telling myself I wasn't really doing it. I wasn't violating the pact I had made with the woman I loved, a pact sealed by our daughter's words. I told myself it was mere curiosity, nothing more. I'd promised Annelise a sabbatical year and I would keep that promise. I was just going to have a chat with my father-in-law because I needed to get out of the house. That was all.

I wasn't working on any idea.

Ideas? Who?

Me?

Of course not.

Just a little chat by the fire. A cigarette. Coffee with a splash of alcohol. Maybe a couple of innocent questions about what Ilse at the Visitors' Centre had referred to as the Bletterbach killings. You couldn't call that work. And anyway, I thought, continuing the imaginary dialogue with myself as I approached Werner's property, supervising the documentary that Mike was editing was a kind of work, wasn't it? And Annelise hadn't objected to that.

You know something? I was a good liar.

I pretended to have forgotten that Annelise had only given her consent to that on condition that it wouldn't have any repercussions on my mental state (she didn't use the word "mental", she said "emotional", but we both knew what she was talking about) and that Mike would be working on it a long way away in New York. Almost as if the hours spent editing were radioactive. I pretended to have forgotten that Annelise had accepted because Mike had pointed out to her that this footage was part of "Mountain Angels", so technically it wasn't a new idea, it was an old idea that needed to be reworked a bit "in the light of what had happened". Furthermore, "apart from a couple of hours discussing the narrative line, Salinger won't have to do anything else except answer an occasional e-mail. You won't even notice."

Dear Mephistophelean Mike.

"Anyone at home?" I called out, once I had slammed the car door.

Werner's face appeared from behind the curtains. He let me in. We talked about this and that, had coffee and a smoke. I told him about Yodi and the excursion to the Bletterbach, trying to seem as natural as possible, while inside I was seething with curiosity.

Then I threw the bait.

"I heard a crazy story."

"What story?"

"A hint, nothing else. But it struck me as strange."

"The mountains are full of strange stories. And that's a witness to the fact," Werner said, indicating the scar beside my right eye. "Or am I wrong?"

I stroked it with my fingertips. Clara called it "the kiss of the bad fairy". It reminded me of the photographs of the Bletterbach that I had looked for on Google, deleting the search history for fear that Annelise might ask me questions I wouldn't be able to answer.

I didn't want to lie to her.

Not directly, at least.

"No, you're not wrong."

Something in my voice persuaded Werner to change the subject. We had never talked about what had happened on September 15. It had happened and that was it. If he had to refer to the accident, Werner would say, "That nasty day."

Mountain men's natural reserve worked in my favour because Werner now stood up, almost embarrassed, opened the fridge and took out a bottle of gentian grappa. He filled two small glasses. We toasted in silence.

"You were saying . . ."

"I heard a story. Or rather, there were two quite elderly tourists talking about it to the woman who rented us our helmets at the Visitors' Centre. Ilse. Do you know her?"

"That must be Ilse Unterkircher. Here in Siebenhoch we all know each other, even though old people like me are almost extinct now and the new generations . . ." He took a sip of his grappa. "When you're my age, you'll realise something very funny. All faces look alike. Especially the faces of young people. But I bet that's not what you wanted to talk about."

"Ilse called it the Bletterbach killings. And I think she added a name: Schaltzmann."

"I think", my ass.

In the Google search history I'd deleted, there were at least twelve different responses with that name. Of course I remembered it. Except that not even the great oracle of the twenty-first century had given me an answer. I had discovered a Schaltzmann who was a professor at Yale, a hockey player, a photographer in Hamburg, two separate used-car dealers in Bavaria, and an infinite number of Schaltzmans, Saltzmanns and so on. But about the Bletterbach killings? An absolute void. Instead of depressing me, this had rekindled my interest. Curiosity is fed by blank spaces on maps.

Werner poured himself some more grappa. "What did you hear?" he asked, curtly.

"That nobody was ever arrested."

"Nobody. That's correct."

I lit a cigarette and held out the packet.

Werner refused with a distracted gesture. "April 28, 1985. As they say on T.V., I was there."

"*You were there?*"

It was impossible for me to hide my excitement. I had imagined that Werner would be a good source of information, not that he would be an eyewitness.

Werner met my gaze and sustained it for a few seconds.

He put his glass down on the table. My excitement faded in a flash.

"Jeremiah, I've never interfered in my daughter's business. Herta used to say that children should be allowed to fly the nest and I always agreed with her. So I don't like saying what I'm about to say, but I'm also doing it for your sake" – he paused – "and for Clara."

I stopped him with a gesture of my hand. "I'm not planning to make a documentary about it, Werner," I said. "I've given my word. I don't want my marriage to break down because of my . . . shall we call it 'ambition'?"

"Stupidity, Jeremiah. Destroying a marriage, and a family that works, a family like yours, is stupidity, nothing more, nothing less."

"Amen."

"Pass me one of those, will you?"

He lit the cigarette as he always did: using his thumbnail to strike the match. "So you want to hear an old story?"

"Werner . . ."

From my mouth emerged the kind of confession that came from the heart. Maybe that was why, precisely because I was sincere, I damned our souls.

"It's a story I'd like to hear. But I don't want to make a documentary about it. I'm too . . . tired. But I need to have something to *play* with. It's like you with the mountains. When was the last time you had a proper climb?"

"At least twenty years ago, maybe more."

"But you continue to go on excursions, right?"

"If you want to call them excursions," Werner replied bitterly, "Yes, of course. But they're walks fit only for arthritic tourists."

"I'd like this story to be my mental version of your walks. I need an idea to kill time with. I needed to get out of . . . this state."

An alarmed expression on Werner's face. "You mean you're sick again?"

"No," I reassured him, "nothing like that. Annelise and Clara are fantastic medicine. I've stopped having nightmares." Faced with his sceptical expression, I corrected myself. "I've *basically* stopped having nightmares and the ones I do have are . . . manageable. Physically, I've never been better. Clara is tiring me out with all our walks, and I can't wait for it to start snowing to teach her how to sled. Mentally, though . . ."

"You can't just sit twiddling your thumbs."

"Exactly"

Werner dropped a little ash on the floor. "Annelise told me you're working with your friend Mike . . . "

"Actually, all I'm doing is making a few suggestions from time to time. Nothing more. And I won't hide from you the fact that I'm fine with that."

"Remembering hurts?"

"It hurts a lot," I replied, trying to get rid of the lump at the back of my throat. "It's like a wild animal that's hidden inside me, Werner. And it bites. All the time. Maybe one day I'll manage to put a muzzle on it. To master it. To go back to having only good days. But now I need a new . . . toy to keep this thing up here in shape," I concluded, pressing my index finger to my temple.

I didn't add anything more. I was in Werner's hands. Whatever his answer, I would accept it. Even if he kicked me out of the house. I felt drained. But it was a pleasant sensation. Maybe like the one a religious person feels after confessing his sins to his spiritual guide.

Werner absolved me.

And started telling the story.

The Bletterbach Killings

"The story starts in the Tyrrhenian."

"The sea?"

Werner nodded. "Do you know what a multicellular cluster with windward regeneration is?"

"You might as well be speaking Arabic."

"It's a meteorological definition. 'Multicellular cluster with windward regeneration', more commonly known as a 'self-regenerating storm'. Imagine a hot, humid current coming in from the sea. In our case, from the Tyrrhenian. Very hot and very humid. It moves up the coast, but instead of breaking over the Gulf of Genoa it keeps moving northwards."

I tried to imagine the map of Italy. "Over the Po Valley?"

"Without encountering any obstacle. On the contrary, it gathers even more heat and humidity. Are you with me?"

"I'm with you."

"Imagine this current as humid and hot as the tropics slamming into the Alps."

"A snowstorm."

"*Genau.* But just as the humid current is about to collide with the Alps, an icy current comes down from the north, also incredibly heavy with water. When the two currents meet, it's a real mess. A perfect self-regenerating storm. You know why 'self-regenerating'? Because the collision between the two masses of air doesn't diminish the intensity of the storm, but makes it even stronger. Violence that breeds more violence. We're talking about more than three thousand lightning flashes an hour."

"A storm that generates itself," I said, spellbound. "Are they rare?"

"There are a couple every year. Some years three, some years not even one. But nature gives and then takes away. Storms of this kind are miniature apocalypses that don't last long. Not more than an hour or two, three at the most, and they're restricted to a small area." A brief hesitation. "That's the norm."

"And when the general rule doesn't apply?"

"Then we come to April 28, 1985. The mother of all self-regenerating storms. Siebenhoch and the surrounding area were cut off from the world for nearly a week. No roads, no telephones, no radio. The Civil Defence people had to fight their way through with bulldozers. The point at which the storm broke with the greatest violence – and I'm talking about violence equal to that of a hurricane – was the Bletterbach." He passed a hand over his chin, cleared his throat and added, "It lasted five days. From April 28 to May 3. Five days of hell."

I tried to imagine that storm mass shedding its load over the horizon I could admire from the window a short distance from me. I didn't succeed.

"But that wasn't how they died," Werner whispered, shaking his head. "That would have been . . . I won't say fairer, but more natural. It can happen, right? A flash of lightning. A rock. In the mountains, nasty things . . . happen."

My throat had gone dry. Yes, nasty things happen. I knew that only too well.

To get rid of the dryness, I stood up and poured myself another grappa. It went down my throat like hot iron. I poured myself a third, less generous measure and sat down again.

"Those poor kids weren't just killed, what happened to them was . . ." Werner grimaced in a way I'd never seen from him before. "Once, many years ago, I went hunting with my father. Before the reserve was there and . . . You remember our chat about going hungry?"

Of course I remembered it. "Yes."

"I'm hungry, I go hunting, I kill. I try not to cause pain, I kill in a clean, rational manner. Because. I'm. Hungry. Those things can't be judged, can they? They go beyond the normal concept of good and evil."

These words, uttered by a man who had spent years saving other people's lives, made a deep impression. I nodded to encourage him to continue, but there was no need, Werner would continue with or without my approval. It was a concept over which he had spent many hours and he was determined to express it as best he could. I could recognise an obsession when I saw one.

"During the war, people killed other people. Was that right? Was it wrong? Stupid, ridiculous questions. Anyone who didn't go out to kill was shot. Can we assert that the people who refused to use a rifle were saints or heroes? We can, of course. In fact, in times of peace it's right to see them that way. But can we force millions of people to behave like saints or heroes? To sacrifice themselves for an ideal of peace? No, we can't."

I wasn't sure where he was going with this, but I let him continue. If working on factual series had taught me anything, it was that the more freely people talk, the more interesting the words that come out of their mouths.

"In war, people kill each other. It's bad to order them to do so. It's bad to force generations to slaughter each other on battlefields. It's an insult to God. But if you're not a king or a general, what else can you do? Shoot or be shot. And if you shoot, there's a chance you'll save your own skin and get back to the people you love."

He drummed with his fingers on the table.

"In war, you kill. In hunting, you kill. Killing is human, even though we don't like to admit it, and it's right to try and stop it as much as possible. But what was done to those three poor kids in the Bletterbach in 1985 wasn't killing. It was slaughter, and there wasn't much that was human about it."

"Who were they?" I asked in a thin voice.

"Evi, Kurt and Markus," was the brief reply. "Do you mind if we go out? It's starting to get a bit too hot in here. Let's take a walk."

We went out and headed for a path that led to the woods.

The smell of autumn, that sweetish smell that almost upsets the nostrils, was at its height. I had no doubt that winter would soon sweep everything away. After a while, even the most beautiful autumn asks for the right to eternal rest.

I shuddered. I didn't like the turn my thoughts had taken.

"They were good kids, you know?" Werner said, after we had passed a pine tree split in two by a bolt of lightning. "All three born here. Evi and Markus were brother and sister. She was the older of the two. A lovely girl. Very unlucky, though."

"In what way?"

"You know the South Tyrol disease, Jeremiah?"

"No, I have no idea."

"Alcohol."

"Evi was an alcoholic?"

"Not Evi. Her mother. She'd been deserted by her husband, a travelling salesman from Verona, in the '70s or thereabouts, soon after Markus was born. But her life was already a disaster, you can bet on it."

"Why?"

"Different times, Jeremiah. You know my property?"

"Welshboden?"

"You know why I bought it for not much more than peanuts?"

"Because you have a nose for business?"

"That, too. Can you translate the name?"

"Welshboden?"

"*Genau.*"

The local dialect was a fairly twisted version of the *Hochdeutsch* my mother had brought me up on, and I often found it incomprehensible. I shook my head.

"The word *Walscher*, or *Welsher*, and God knows how many other versions there are, is a key word if you want to understand the dirt that's been swept under the rug around here, Jeremiah."

He was alluding to the ethnic clashes that had begun after the Second World War. I'd heard a lot about them. "Italians against Germans and Germans against Italians? Belfast with strudel?"

"*Walscher* means foreign, alien. Someone from outside. But in a nasty, derogatory way. That's why I bought it for a ridiculous figure. Because it was the land of the *Walscher*."

"But the conflict—"

"The conflict is over, thanks to tourism and thanks to God. But deep down, there's always that hint of . . ."

"Resentment."

"I like that, it's a nice word. A polite way of putting it, but that's the way it is. A very polite ethnic conflict. In the '60s, though, when Evi and Markus' mother married that travelling salesman from Verona, the ethnic conflict was being expressed with bombs. In the register, Evi's surname was Tognon, but if you ask around everybody will tell you that Evi and Markus were called Baumgartner, which was their mother's surname. You understand? The 50 per cent of Italian blood was wiped out. Evi's mother had married an Italian: can you imagine what that meant at the time, a mixed marriage?"

"Not a happy life."

"Not at all. Then her husband left and alcohol destroyed what little common sense she still had. It was Evi who raised Markus."

"Is she still alive?"

"Evi's mother died a couple of years after we buried her children. She didn't come to the funeral. We found her lying on her back in the kitchen of her apartment. She was out of her head with booze and asked us if we wanted . . . you know, if we wanted . . ."

I spared him his embarrassment with a question. "She prostituted herself?"

"Only when she'd run out of the money she managed to scrape

together doing a few little jobs here and there."

We walked in silence for a while. I listened to the calls of the loons and the sparrows.

A passing cloud obscured the sun, then headed east, placid and indifferent to the tragedy that Werner was recounting.

"What about Kurt?" I asked to break the silence, which was starting to make me uncomfortable.

"Kurt Schaltzmann. Kurt was the oldest of the three. He was a good kid, too." He stopped to break off a small branch from a dark, gnarled pine. "I know that in such cases people always say that kind of thing. But believe me, they really were good kids."

Werner fell silent and to fill the silence I murmured, "In '85 I wanted to be a pitcher for the Yankees and I was in love with my aunt Betty. She made incredible muffins. I have beautiful memories of that period."

"Around here, that period was the worst since the war, believe me. The young people were leaving and those who didn't killed themselves with alcohol. Just like most of the adults. There was no tourism, there were no subsidies for agriculture. There was no work. There was no future."

"So why did Evi and the others stay?"

"Who said they stayed?"

"You mean they left?"

"Evi was the first. She wasn't just bright, she was also beautiful. And you know what happened in those years to beautiful, intelligent girls around here?"

"They married and became alcoholics?"

Werner nodded. "The first bastard who showed up, and there are plenty here like everywhere else, would make her fall in love with him, get her pregnant, and then slap her with his belt if there wasn't enough beer in the fridge. And after a while, trust me, there's never enough. Evi had seen what happened to women who lost their heads over a bastard."

It was the first time I had heard Werner use that kind of language.

"Evi had a plan. She graduated with the highest marks and won a scholarship to university. Both she and Markus were bilingual, but her mother refused to speak Italian and had taught Evi to call herself Baumgartner, so when she had to choose what university to go to, Evi opted for Austria."

"What faculty did she choose?"

"Geology. She loved these mountains. The Bletterbach, above all. The Bletterbach was where she took her younger brother when things at home got bad and it was in the Bletterbach, or so they say, that she realised she was in love."

"With Kurt?" I asked, already sure of the answer.

"They knew each other, because in a small village everyone knows everyone, but they led different lives. Kurt was five years older than Evi, he was an Alpine guide and an accomplished rescuer. He came from a good family. His father, Hannes Schaltzmann, was a friend of mine." He broke off, and for a moment his eyes were veiled with sadness. "A dear friend. It was Hannes who passed on his love for the mountains to his son."

"Was Hannes also in the rescue team?"

"One of the leading lights. He was the one who raised the money to buy the Alouette. I remember that Kurt was always urging us to use that little machine to fly tourists over the Dolomites for a good price, but, although it was a brilliant idea, we didn't listen. The Alouette was for saving lives, not for making holidaymakers happy. Don't go thinking he was greedy, though. As an Alpine guide Kurt didn't earn much, and as a rescuer he earned even less, given that we were all volunteers. But for Kurt, money wasn't important. His reward was the mountains."

"Was it a happy love story between Evi and Kurt?"

Werner smiled. "The kind you only see in fairy tales. Evi had clear ideas about her future. University, graduating with top marks, a doctorate, then the Natural History Museum in Bolzano, which people were talking about a lot at the time. She was ambitious. Her dream was to become the curator of the geology department. And in my opinion, she would have done it, she was that good. Once she got started at

Innsbruck, she immediately stood out in the classroom. And remember, she hadn't had an easy life. Imagine the girl, a mountain girl speaking our *dialokt*, who starts debating in front of the know-it-alls at the university, some of whom had started their careers in the '30s or '40s. I don't know if I'm making myself clear. In spite of all that, she got excellent marks. She started publishing papers. She was a rising star."

I shuddered. I too had been called 50 per cent of a rising star. It was a definition that brought bad luck. Really bad luck.

"When did she go to Innsbruck?"

"Evi left in '81, leaving Markus behind. He was a minor, and his mother, as people say in such cases, wasn't in her right mind, but Markus could take care of himself. Evi left and Kurt went to live with her the following year, 1982, the year Italy won the World Cup." Werner burst out laughing. "Quite a few long faces around here!"

"Still for ethnic reasons?"

"We supported Germany."

"Not Austria?" I asked innocently.

Werner's immediate response made me laugh, too. "Have you ever seen the Austrian national team play? They might as well have raised a white flag."

"How stupid it all seems."

"Think of it this way, Jeremiah: if you're talking about football, you don't have time to make bombs." A brief pause. "Kurt was in love and so he left. When Hannes told me that his son, his only son, was going to Innsbruck to live with Evi, well, even though I considered myself fairly broad-minded, it was a bit shocking even for me."

"Why?"

Werner cleared his throat, embarrassed. "Around here we've always been a bit conservative, you understand?"

"They weren't married."

"And had no intention of getting married. They said that marriage was a tradition from the old days. I tried to convince Hannes that it wasn't such a bad thing. You see, when Kurt left to live with Evi, he and his father stopped talking to each other, and I didn't like that. And besides, I was fond of Evi, she was a good girl. But Hannes could never accept it. Like a lot of people in Siebenhoch," Werner added bitterly.

"Because of Evi's surname?"

"Evi already had one sin to atone for – being half Italian. Now she was cohabiting with her boyfriend, in a world that still hadn't even coined the word. Cohabitation. Cohabitation was fine for film stars, but certainly not for the hard-working people of Siebenhoch. But do you want me to tell you the whole truth?"

"I'm here to listen."

Werner stopped.

We had reached a point where there was a hairpin bend above a forty-metre drop. We were exposed to the breeze from the west, which was starting to turn into a wind. It wasn't cold yet, though.

"Even though it may make you see Siebenhoch in a new light?"

"Of course."

"Evi had taken one of Siebenhoch's best sons away. He was a good boy and they were a good match, but, as always in such cases, it never occurred to anyone that going to Innsbruck had been his own idea and not a kind of . . . plot on Evi's part to steal one of the most eligible bachelors in the village for herself."

"What sons of bitches."

"You can say that again, although out of love for my country I ought to punch you on the nose. Absolute shits. Then time passed, and, as happens in little villages like ours, Evi and Kurt vanished from memory. If it hadn't been for Markus, I don't think anyone would have gone on talking about them."

"Because Markus had stayed here."

"He'd go to school then spend his days wandering in the mountains. When he could, he went to work as an apprentice in a carpentry shop in Aldino, to earn a little bit of money. Evi and Kurt would come to Siebenhoch just to see him. In spite of my efforts to make Hannes see reason, he and Kurt were still at daggers drawn."

Having spent a good half of my life quarrelling with my own father and the other half realising how like him I was, I immediately understood.

"They didn't come often. No European Union, no reduced prices and above all no credit cards for Evi and Kurt. Travelling cost an arm and a leg. Evi had her scholarship and, knowing her, I'm sure she had a part-time job even up there. Kurt on the other hand found the classic job for an Italian immigrant."

"Pizza-maker?"

"Waiter. They were happy and they had a future. I won't hide it from you . . ." – he stopped and asked me for a cigarette – ". . . That's what I find the hardest to take about this business. Kurt and Evi had a future in front of them. A wonderful future."

We smoked in silence, listening to the wind bending the treetops.

Less than ten kilometres away, the Bletterbach was listening in on our conversation.

"Some people in the village said it was the Lord who had punished them for their sins."

These words struck me like a whiplash. I was disgusted.

"What happened on April 28, Werner?"

Werner turned to me so slowly that I thought he hadn't understood the question. "Nobody knows for certain what happened that day. I can only tell you what I saw and did. Or rather, what I saw and did between April 28 and 30 of that damned year 1985. Let's make a pact, Jeremiah."

He was deadly serious.

"What kind of pact?"

"I'll tell you everything I know, without leaving anything out, and in return you promise me that you won't let yourself be devoured by this story."

He had used the German verb *fressen,* which means eating in the sense used for animals. For men, the verb is *essen,* to eat.

Beasts devour.

"That's what happens to anybody who becomes too involved with the Bletterbach killings."

The hair stood up on my head.

The breeze had become a wind and seemed to me to be hissing.

"Tell me."

At that moment my cell phone rang, making us both jump.

"I'm sorry," I said, annoyed at the interruption.

The line was bad and it took me a while to understand.

It was Annelise. And she was crying.

The *Saltner*

I flung open the car door without waiting for the engine to stop and rushed into the house. Annelise was sitting in my favourite armchair in the middle of the living room.

Without saying anything I kissed her. She smelled of coffee and ironing.

Clara emerged from her room and ran to hug Werner.

"Mamma's screaming," she said.

"She must have her reasons," Werner replied.

"She was veeeery angry," Clara whispered "She said lots of bad words. Lots and—"

"*Clara*." It was rare for Annelise to address our daughter so sharply. "Go to your room."

"But I—" she protested.

"Why don't we go and make a strudel?" Werner cut in, stroking Clara's contorted face. "Wouldn't you like to know how your poor *Nonna* used to make strudel?"

"*Nonna* Herta?" Clara's eyes lit up. "The one who's an angel now? Of course I would."

Werner took her by the hand and headed for the kitchen.

Only now did Annelise speak. "I hate them."

"Who?"

"All of them."

"Calm down."

"*Calm down*?"

I scratched my scar. "I'd just like to know what happened."

She burst into tears. Not the anguished whine that had wrenched my heart the day I had sworn to her that I would take a sabbatical. These were tears of rage.

"I went to Alois', I wanted to get a bit of jam and a few cans of pickles. On the radio they said it was going to snow and" – she sniffed – "I think a kind of hoarding instinct kicked in. Mamma always got in a good supply when the first snows were coming, because you never know. And then . . . "

If she was bringing her mother, who was a taboo subject, into this, the situation must really be serious.

"I was behind one of the shelves. You remember how poky Alois' little shop is, don't you?"

"I go there to buy cigarettes."

"After a while I heard Alois and Luise Waldner—"

"The big woman who brought us a blueberry pie when I got out of hospital?"

"That's the one."

"What were they saying?"

"They were talking."

I closed my eyes. "What were they saying?"

The reply was a whisper. "That it was all your fault."

"And then?" I asked dryly.

"Then? Then I came out from behind the shelf. And I started to insult them. And that bitch said to me that I was the one to speak, seeing as how I was the wife of a murderer."

Murderer.

That was the word. Murderer.

"And . . . ?"

Annelise opened her eyes wide. "What do you think I did? I took Clara and left. God, if I could, I'd have scratched her eyes out. In fact, you know what? I'm sorry I didn't. First her, then that . . . " She burst into tears again. "I'm sorry, I'm so sorry . . . "

"Don't worry. It's nothing. You know how people are."

"Signora Waldner read the eulogy at my mother's funeral."

I remembered Werner's words. What Signora Waldner had said about me was nothing compared with what the dear inhabitants of Siebenhoch had said over the graves of Evi, Kurt and Markus. I hugged her tight.

"How did Clara take it?"

"Can you understand that girl?"

I smiled. "I understand that I love her. And that's enough for me."

* * *

I was very patient, amusing and completely false for the rest of the afternoon.

I helped Clara to mix the dough for the strudel and joked with Werner, who had taken on the task of peeling the apples.

I was really cool that day.

Then, as a delightful smell of sweetness invaded the kitchen and Werner was about to leave, I grabbed the opportunity and offered to drive him back to Welshboden.

"Do you want me to tell you the end of the story?" he asked, once we were in the car.

"I'd like to get back to Annelise as soon as possible. I'll drop by this evening, if you don't mind."

When we got to his house, Werner said, "Don't do anything stupid, Jeremiah."

I said goodbye, reversed the car, left the property and headed at high speed towards Alois' tiny store. I didn't want to do anything stupid. I just wanted to smash his face in.

What stopped me was the flashing of indicator lights in the rear-view mirror.

* * *

The face that appeared at my window was known to me, like that of most inhabitants of the village, and as with almost everyone else, I couldn't put a name to it.

Around fifty, balding, a touch of stubble under his chin. When he asked me for my papers, he displayed small regular teeth.

Behind him, along the road, a black Mercedes slowed down. I saw a figure behind the wheel but couldn't make out anything else. Darkened windows.

Whoever that person was, their curiosity merely increased my irritation.

I handed over my licence, registration and passport, which I always carried with me, to the uniformed man. He studied them absently. They weren't why he'd stopped me, I was sure of it.

"Was I speeding?"

"On these bends? If you were from around here, no."

"But I'm not from around here."

He shook his head good-naturedly. "If you were, I'd already have tested your alcohol level. And if you were over the limit by even just this much" – he showed me a microscopic gap between thumb and index finger – "I'd have confiscated your vehicle, believe me."

"It's the first time," I said, indicating the badge he had on his chest, "that I've been stopped for speeding by a forest ranger."

"That's how we do things around here. Siebenhoch . . ."

". . . is a small community, I think I got that. But everyone keeps repeating it."

The man winked. He seemed like a good uncle. The uncle who dresses up as Santa Claus at Christmas. If it wasn't for the fact that he was hampering my plans for revenge, I'd have liked him. But I was angry.

Furious.

At last I managed to read the name on the lapel of his grey-green jacket. Krün. Annelise had told me about him, calling him "Chief Krün".

I had glimpsed him a few times in that truck of his, flashing his lights behind my car, patrolling the roads or parked outside some bar.

There were quite a few bars in Siebenhoch and they were all always crowded.

"So you're what they call, where I come from," I continued, maintaining a jokey tone, "'the local sheriff'?"

He laughed. "The sheriff? I like that. Yes, that's about right. Traffic cop, police officer, forest ranger. At other times, even paramedic and father confessor. You know how it is, the administration tends to look kindly on anything that saves the taxpayers money. And nobody's ever complained about me. People tend to trust a familiar face. Especially . . ."

". . . in small villages."

Krün sighed. "*Genau*," he said. "In Siebenhoch, we all know each other, for good or ill. Do you follow me?"

"To be honest, no."

"Really?"

"If I was speeding, then fine me and let me go on my way."

"Are you in a hurry, Signor Salinger?"

"I'm out of cigarettes. Alois will be closing soon and I don't want to spend the night dreaming about Marlboros. Is that enough for you?"

"You can always go down to Aldino. There's a service station there that's open twenty-four hours a day, with a bar next to it. Truck drivers go there a lot. I don't recommend the coffee, but they sell cigarettes. Marlboros. Lucky Strikes. Camels. There's an embarrassment of choice. A smoker's paradise."

"Thanks for the information. Now, about that fine . . . "

His face lost the expression of a good uncle coming into the house on Christmas Eve going ho-ho-ho. The face I now had in front of me was the face of the bad cop.

"I haven't finished, Signor Salinger."

"Are you threatening me?"

Krün opened his arms wide. "Me? I'm just giving you directions. We're sociable people here in Siebenhoch. Especially to anyone related to old Mair. You have a really pretty daughter, Signor Salinger. What's her name? Clara?"

My hands tightened on the wheel. "Yes."

"You know what's nice about small communities like this, Signor Salinger?"

I stared at him for a few moments, then the dyke broke. "I don't give a shit," I hissed. "I just want to buy those damned cigarettes and get back home."

Krün's face showed no reaction. "Would you mind getting out of the vehicle?"

I turned my head to him. I felt the tendons in my neck creak. "For what reason?" I croaked.

"I'd like to test your alcohol level. You don't seem to me to be in a condition to drive."

"I'm not taking any fucking test, Chief Krün."

"Please get out, Signor Salinger. And I'd advise you not to use such language with a public official. Tomorrow morning, you can complain as much as you want to the proper authorities, I'll be happy to provide you with the requisite form. But for now, get out."

I got out.

"Hands on your head," Krün ordered.

"Are you arresting me?"

"You've seen too many films, Signor Salinger. Well, it is your job. Hands on your head. Raise your left leg and stay balanced until I tell you."

"This is ridiculous," I objected.

"It's the rules," was the icy reply.

I obeyed, feeling a perfect idiot.

With a theatrical gesture, Krün started timing my performance.

It lasted more than a minute. Passing cars slowed down and I could hear the quips of the occupants over the rumble of the engines. At last, satisfied, Krün nodded.

"You're not drunk, Signor Salinger."

"Can I get back in my car?"

"You can listen to me. Then you can go on your way. If you still want to."

I didn't say a word.

Krün adjusted his cap on his head. "On this road, the limit is sixty kilometres an hour. In less than a kilometre, after three bends, you'll enter what's considered a built-up area. There, the permitted limit is forty. Are you listening to me, Signor Salinger?"

"Thanks for the information. I'll try to remember it."

"To get to Alois' mini-market, respecting the speed limits, will take twelve minutes. Maybe thirteen. The question is: is it worth it?"

I gave a start.

Chief Krün noticed my surprise. "There are no secrets in Siebenhoch, Signor Salinger. Not from me. Not from the *sheriff*." He came a step closer. "Do you know why I stopped you, Signor Salinger?"

"You tell me."

Krün rubbed his chin a couple of times. "I heard about an argument, a somewhat heated discussion this afternoon between your wife and Signora Waldner. An argument that also involved Signor Alois, the owner of the general store down in the village. Nothing much, let's be clear about that. Except that when I saw you driving to the village, I won't say at top speed but, as I'll write in my report, at quite a high speed, I thought maybe you'd felt the pressing need to take the law into your own hands. And that, Signor Salinger, really isn't on."

"I just wanted an explanation."

"Don't take me for an idiot. I know everything about you." A pause, his voice trembled. "Everything you did. Up there."

A twinge behind my neck. An icy needle of pain. "And what am I supposed to have done?"

Krün put his finger on his badge. "Nothing punishable from the point of view of the law."

"Why?" I asked. "Are there other points of view?"

Uniform or no uniform, I was ready to jump on him. He must have noticed because his tone became less unpleasant. The good uncle reappeared.

"We've got off to a bad start, Signor Salinger. Don't you agree?"

"I do," I mumbled, the adrenalin still howling in my veins.

"I don't want you to feel like a stranger. You're old Mair's son-in-law. Werner is a person who's greatly respected in Siebenhoch, and we're all happy that Annelise decided to come back to the village for a while. What's more, your daughter is a delightful child. Frau Gertraud, from the library, adores her. She says she's the most precocious child she's ever met."

"Does that make me a local?"

"Not quite. But you're more than a tourist. You understand what I mean?"

"No," I replied curtly.

"I want to be frank with you precisely because of your status as a . . . welcome guest. In Siebenhoch, there are lots of fights. Lots of them. And my job isn't just to slap a few drunks in gaol or call the doctor to sew them up. My job is to avoid problems. To prevent them. At least that's how I see it." A brief pause, then he continued, "I know what people have been saying about you. Especially since the accident on the Ortles. But it's just idle chatter."

"Do you join in this chatter?"

The good uncle shook his head. "What I think or don't think doesn't count, Signor Salinger. Not here and not now. If you could, you'd already have given me a good kick in the balls. Do you think I'm blind? You're beside yourself with anger. What matters to me now is that you go home. Have a good sleep and forget the gossip of a couple of old people who have nothing to do all day but speak ill of others. It's not worth it. Don't prove them right."

"Prove them right?"

"To do this job, you need to use a little bit of psychology, Signor Salinger. Using your muscles gets you nowhere. And the psychologist in me says that if someone is heading *at high speed* to a shop run by a person who has made a not very flattering comment about him, that comment must have hurt him in some way. Hitting a man who, although he may not look it, is nearly ten years older than your father-in-law,

Salinger, might make you feel better at the time, but it would only prove Alois right – along with God knows how many other people here in Siebenhoch."

However much I hated the idea, in my heart of hearts I knew that's the way it was.

Yes, I felt like a murderer. That's why I wanted to go to that gossip and smash his face in. Not because of Annelise's tears and not because of Clara, as I'd been telling myself all afternoon, but because I felt that all that chatter wasn't without foundation. I would have taken out on him a hatred I actually felt towards myself, and that was the behaviour of a coward.

I hated myself.

I heaved a big sigh. The adrenalin had worn off.

I rested my eyes on Krün and saw him for what he was. A guy in a uniform doing his best to avoid trouble.

"You're a good man. I understand now why they call you Chief Krün. You're right, I admit it. I'd like to buy you a beer one of these days. It seems I owe you a debt."

Chief Krün appeared to relax. He held out his hand. "Call me Max. No debt, just doing my duty."

"Thanks, Max." I smiled. "You can keep calling me Salinger, even my wife calls me that."

* * *

I put Clara to sleep, having first read her a story, kissed Annelise, who was engrossed in watching some romantic nonsense, and said goodbye, telling her that I had promised Werner I would thrash him at chess. I put on my jacket and went out to hear the story of April 28, 1985.

Outside it was snowing.

April 28, 1985

Welshboden greeted me with its reassuring smell of woodsmoke and tobacco. Werner offered me a herb grappa and I gave him a cigarette in return.

"The storm over Siebenhoch," I said. "If you haven't changed your mind."

"Before I start, you have to know one last thing. Self-regenerating storms aren't easy to predict. Even today, with all the electronic gadgetry available, all you know is that it'll rain and there'll be a big storm. You don't know if it'll be a really bad one. That's why they went."

"Evi, Kurt and Markus."

"All three were expert climbers, especially Kurt. Believe me, he wasn't the kind to take risks, but nor was he the kind to get upset about a few drops of rain. And anyway, when they left Siebenhoch it wasn't raining. I want to be clear about this, Jeremiah: none of them could have known what was about to be unleashed. Self-regenerating storms are unpredictable."

"What time did they leave?"

"We were never able to establish that precisely. But it must have been still dark. About five in the morning, let's say. Only tourists take their time when there's walking to be done in the mountains." A brief pause. "In '85 the Visitors' Centre didn't exist, the Bletterbach was a wild place. Have you noticed that even today there are only two practicable routes?"

"And woe betide if you don't follow them," I said, remembering Ilse's recommendations.

"Well, at the time there were no sure routes through the Bletterbach. There were the old hunters' paths, not much more than tracks buried by the ferns, and a few mule tracks used by the woodcutters but which didn't go very far. It was pointless cutting trees down there, in the deep: how would you have carried the trunks back? The stream isn't big enough, and there were no roads to transport them by truck or jeep."

In the deep.

"The rain started around ten in the morning. A decent enough storm, but with not much lightning. If there was any sign of the disaster that was to come, nobody realised. In April, storms are a given around here, and those of us in Mountain Rescue were getting ready to face a long boring day. All day playing cards, while outside it got darker and darker. Around five in the afternoon, I decided to take a break and go back home. I got there in time to hear the storm changing."

"To hear it?"

"It was as if you'd ended up in the middle of a bombardment. The rain was beating down with so much force that I feared for the windscreen of my car. And the thunder . . . Deafening is an understatement. Annelise . . ." A touch of sadness in his voice. "Is she still scared of thunder?"

"Fairly."

I chose not to add that Annelise had found an infallible cure for that phobia of hers: sex. That's not the kind of information a father wants to know about his own daughter.

"I ate, then dozed in front of the television until about nine-thirty, when the electricity went out. I wasn't alarmed, it happened quite often, and with a storm like that it was inevitable. I lit a few candles in the house and stood there looking out of the window. You know, Jeremiah, I don't believe in all that supernatural stuff. Ghosts, vampires, zombies. And I don't want to make you believe that I had a premonition. No, I don't want to say that, but . . . "

He let the sentence hang.

"I was nervous, very nervous. I've never been upset by thunder. In fact, I like it. All that power unleashed on the earth makes me feel, I don't know, as if I'm dealing with something bigger than me. And it's a nice feeling. But that evening, the thunder and lightning drove me crazy. I couldn't keep still. To calm myself down, I started checking my rescue kit. Not the equipment I used when I was on duty with the helicopter, but my old backpack, the one I used for operations on the ground. And when I'd closed the last buckle, there was a knock at the door. It was Hannes, Günther and Max."

"Max Krün?" I asked, surprised. "The sheriff?"

"The head of the Forest Rangers," Werner corrected me. "Have you met him?"

"Let's say we had a little chat."

"What did you think of him?"

I tried to find the right words to describe him. "The good uncle who dresses up as Father Christmas. But don't piss him off."

Werner beat his hands on his knees, as a sign of approval. "You have a way with words, Jeremiah. The good uncle it's best not to piss off. That's exactly it. Did you piss him off?"

"I came close."

"He's a good man. Tough. He has to be, at least when he wears his uniform. But if you ever happen to talk to him when he's not on duty, you'll find he's a pretty sharp person, full of common sense, very amusing"

"What was he doing in '85?"

"He was a simple forest ranger. Chief Hubner was still around, he died four years later, just before the Wall came down. In March he'd had his first heart attack, and even though Max was quite young he'd had to take on all his work. He came in with that little teenage face of his, his eyes like a whipped dog's. Soaking wet. He was also very nervous. There was him, Hannes and Günther. I knew both of them and neither looked as if they were in a good mood. I let them in and suggested a drop to warm themselves. They refused. I know it may sound ridiculous, but it was that refusal that really scared me."

"Why?"

"Max was young, and in the absence of Chief Hubner it was obvious that he was feeling the pressure of a call-out, especially in that bad weather. But Hannes and Günther weren't snotty-nosed kids. We were often called out suddenly in the middle of the night, it wasn't new for us. Woodcutters who hadn't come back home when it got dark, missing children, shepherds who'd ended up in a ditch, things like that. Hannes and Günther had seen it all before. Especially Hannes."

At last my mind made the connection. "Hannes. Hannes Schaltzmann," I murmured. "Kurt's father?"

"That's right."

I closed my eyes, trying to absorb that information. I tried to imagine what Hannes Schaltzmann must have felt finding his son's body. I sat back in my chair, feeling the heat of the fire licking at my thighs.

"And besides, Günther had never refused a drink. Especially not from my special reserve. By the way, would you like one?"

He didn't wait for my reply. He stood up and fetched the bottle. He made the glasses clink.

"Special reserve. Prepared according to an age-old Mair recipe. My ancestors must have been rich once, but all that remains from that time are some excellent recipes. Not that I'm complaining – on the contrary."

"Why do you say rich?"

"Because of the surname. *Mair*. It means landowner. Many German surnames mean something, usually they indicate professions. *Mair* is the local variant of *Mayer*, a landowner. *Schneider* is a tailor. *Fischer*, a fisherman, *Müller*, a miller. Does your name mean something?"

"I'm an American," I said, a sweeter version of Bruce Willis. "Our names don't mean anything."

Werner closed the bottle again and handed me the glass. "Grappa with pepper. Produced, bottled and selected by yours truly, Werner Mair."

"To old stories," I toasted.

"To old stories," Werner echoed. "May they stay where they are."

It was liquid fire. Once the flame passed, the heat turned into a lovely warmth below the sternum, accompanied by a pleasant tickling on the tongue.

Werner cleared his throat, filched a cigarette from my packet and resumed his story.

"It was Hannes who'd raised the alarm. He'd spent all day out of the village, working, and when he got back had discovered from his wife, Helene, that Kurt and the others had gone on an outing to the Bletterbach. They'd taken a tent with them because the idea was to do a bit of camping. At first, Hannes hadn't worried. Even though the two of them hadn't spoken since Kurt had gone to live in Innsbruck, Hannes was aware that his son knew his stuff. He'd been a rescuer and, even though it's not true, we rescuers feel a bit as if we're the elite of the mountains. If for no other reason than because, unlike many people, we know how to predict and avoid risky situations."

"But then I assume the storm had grown worse, a self-regenerating storm, and Hannes had got worried."

"No, not at first," Werner said. "They don't last long. They're powerful, that's true, but they last three hours at most and then die down. But this one wasn't dying down. On the contrary, it seemed as if its strength was increasing from minute to minute."

"And that's when Hannes raised the alarm."

Once again I was wrong.

"*Nix.* Hannes left home and went to the Forest Rangers' barracks because he wanted to talk to Max. The lights had blown and the telephones were dead, but in the barracks there was a shortwave radio for emergencies. Hannes wanted to use it to communicate with Civil Defence in Bolzano and to find out if there was any reason to worry. Max wasn't there, so Hannes went to his house, but couldn't find him. It was the birthday of the girl who would later become his wife, Verena. Hannes turned up in the middle of the party like a ghost at a feast. He apologised for butting in and told Max that he needed the shortwave radio. They went back to the barracks and tried to get in contact with Bolzano."

"They tried?"

"Too much lightning. The communication was so distorted, it was like sticking your head inside a washing machine. They'd never come across anything like it. They got scared. It was only at that point that they decided to organise a rescue mission. On the way, they stopped at Günther's, and the three of them came to my house. As I said, I already had my equipment ready, as if I was expecting them." He shook his head. "A premonition? I don't know. I really don't know.

"It was around midnight," he continued after a slight pause, "when we left in the rescue team's jeep. We left the village and had to stop twice. The first time to move a fallen tree trunk, the second because part of the road had slipped and we had to anchor the jeep to a rock to try and overcome the obstacle."

"The situation was that bad?"

"Worse." Werner stood up and took out a map from a drawer. "This is the point where the dirt road leading to the Bletterbach stopped." He ran his finger backwards several centimetres. "But we only managed to get as far as here."

I calculated. "Three kilometres away?"

"Four. The rest was a quagmire. We knew that in those conditions we'd do better to turn back and wait for the storm to abate."

"But the son of one of your colleagues was out there."

"So it was out of the question. We pressed on. It was raining stones everywhere, we could feel them whistling past our ears. The road was a river of mud and every step might mean a sprain or a fracture. Not to mention the trees and the landslides."

With his thick finger he pointed to a contour line on the map, almost in the middle of the Bletterbach, but slightly to the east.

"They were here, but we didn't know that."

"Was there a path?"

Werner grimaced. "A kind of path. They'd followed it only up until a certain point" – he indicated it on the map – "more or less around here. Then they'd veered west, but still moving in a northerly direction, and then made a second detour and started climbing. As far as here."

"Did you ever understand why?"

"The path must have become impassable by about four in the afternoon, and Kurt must have thought that by bearing west they could walk on the layer of rock, instead of on the clayey, crumblier layer where the path was."

"But why on earth did they then change their minds?"

"I assume, although this is only my speculation, that his initial idea had been to reach the caves, here, you see?"

"Caves?"

"The old name of Siebenhoch was Siebenhöhlen, which means 'seven caves'. He probably hoped to find a dry hole where they could spend the evening. Except that at sunset, having figured out this was no normal storm, he realised they'd never get there and so opted to go east and move up a level. You see here and here? These are little depressions that must have been waterlogged, so the only way to go up was this way. And here, in a clearing, is where we found them. They'd pitched the tent under a rocky spur, with their backs to the mountain, so that the wind wouldn't blow it away." A pause, which I used to calculate how many kilometres they must have trekked. "Kurt was good. And cautious."

"How much later did you find them?"

"The next day," was Werner's brief reply.

"*The next day?*" I echoed, stunned. It struck me as incredible that four well-trained and well-drilled men, long-time mountaineers, could have taken so long to traverse two points that seemed so close on the map.

I thought that because I was a metropolitan idiot with not much imagination.

If only I'd taken the trouble to visualise the inferno of water, mud and lightning that Werner had tried to describe, I would surely not have been so surprised. Besides, I was reasoning with the famous benefit of hindsight, the element of which cemeteries are full. I knew that Kurt and the others were at that point only because Werner had told me, but the rescue team on the night of April 28 and 29 hadn't the least idea.

"It was a nasty night. And a very long one. I repeat: I kept telling myself that we should turn back."

"But you didn't."

"No."

I waited for Werner to pick up the thread of his story.

"The flashlights didn't help us much, but at least they made sure we didn't end up in a crevasse. We just needed to count the white dots. Around three in the morning, Günther was hit by a big stone that smashed his helmet. He threw it aside, muttered a couple of curses and kept on searching, as if nothing had happened. Even though it was completely useless, we became hoarse from shouting. At five, we allowed ourselves a break, not more than half an hour."

Again he indicated the route on the map.

"We made a wrong choice. We'd taken the right direction, north-west, but we assumed Kurt had decided to keep above the tree line."

"Why would he do that?"

"Because that's where you were least likely to be buried in a mudslide. He surely wouldn't have gone and stuck himself in the middle of the gorge between the mud and the water from the stream: that would have been suicide."

"Kurt had gone north-west . . ."

"Yes, but much lower than we were. In addition, he'd veered east, whereas we'd kept straight ahead. But with that noise, the darkness and those stones flying in all directions like shrapnel, we may well have passed right by those poor kids without even realising it. Sad, but true."

"When did you decide to head east?"

"We didn't decide; we got lost."

I opened my eyes wide. "You got lost?"

"We were exhausted. It was seven in the morning and as dark as if it were midnight. We turned right instead of left. And when we realised that we were near the bottom of the gorge we almost lost Max, who was swept away by the stream. He was only saved thanks to Günther's quick reflexes. We decided we weren't going to find Evi, Kurt and Markus, and that if we didn't make a move we ourselves would die in that hole."

He showed me the long curve of the route taken by the rescue team.

"At midday we stopped here."

His finger lingered over an area to the east of the gorge, and I couldn't help noticing that as the crow flies it was less than a kilometre from the spot where they would eventually find the bodies of the three young people.

"We were completely exhausted. I had a painful cough and we were hungry. We rested for about an hour. The visibility was no more than two metres. It was terrible. We were dying of fear, even though we'd never have admitted it out loud. We'd never seen a storm like that before. It was as if nature had decided to attack us. You see, Jeremiah, usually the mountains are . . . The mountains don't give a damn about you. They're neither good nor bad. They're beyond the petty consolations of mortals. They've been here for millions of years and God knows how much longer they'll still be here. To them, you're nothing. But that day, we all felt the same sensation. The Bletterbach had it in for us. It wanted to kill us." He sat back in his armchair and put the map aside. "And now I think I need to take a break."

* * *

Werner decided to smoke one of my Marlboros in the doorway, under the overhanging roof. We stood there looking at the snow falling, in silence, each absorbed in his own thoughts. Finally, as if he were about to be subjected to a further torture session, he motioned to me to come back inside.

It was time to finish the story.

* * *

"By about three in the afternoon, it looked as if the worst was over. It wasn't true, but that little bit of extra light raised our morale. We started searching again. An hour later, we found them. Hannes was the first to spot what remained of the tent. A scrap of red material caught on a branch."

He waved his arm, miming the scene.

"The clearing where they'd camped was a few metres ahead, behind a chestnut tree that obscured my vision. As soon as I saw that scrap of tent . . ." Werner shook his head. "That piece of material, that red on a black and green background, was like the cat in *Alice in Wonderland*."

"The Cheshire cat?"

"It was as if the Bletterbach were making fun of us. There was a nasty atmosphere there. I could feel it just as I could smell the mud in my nostrils. Except that it had nothing to do with the sense of smell. It was a sensation I felt under my skin. A kind of electric current. You know what I mean?"

"Yes."

I certainly did.

Werner stared at my scar. "We went ahead. Hannes in front, Max and Günther behind, and me trying to keep up with them with my painful calf. Then I heard the scream. I've never heard a more frightful scream than that one. The hair stood up on my head. It was Hannes. We were rooted to the spot. Günther in front of me and Max in front of him. I forced myself to move my legs, but they were paralysed. In the mountains we call it 'being in cast iron'. It happens when you have a panic attack or when you have too much lactic acid in your muscles. That was it, my legs were in cast iron."

"A neat metaphor."

"Yes, but it doesn't convey the fear I felt at that moment. Even though the man who'd screamed was one of my best friends, a man I would have risked my life for, knowing he'd have done the same for me, my first instinct was to run. And then . . ."

Beast, I thought.

The Beast.

"What happened?"

"Max threw himself on Hannes, grabbed him by the arms and threw him down into the mud. He saved his life. At the time, I didn't understand, I thought he was having a panic attack. The clearing was only about four and a half metres wide. Above it was a spur of rock, and on the spur what remained of a fir tree. On our side there was the chestnut, as I said, which covered the scene, on the other side more fir trees and then a precipice. If it hadn't been for Max, Hannes would have thrown himself over it. He wanted to kill himself and Max stopped him."

"Christ."

"I grabbed Hannes, and Günther slapped him a couple of times. He was beside himself. I took Hannes and hugged him as tight as I could. I wept. I wept a lot. I wept for Hannes, who was still screaming and screaming, his eyes bulging from his sockets. I wept for what I was seeing. What I *wasn't* seeing, because as I hugged Hannes to stop him from throwing himself into the void, I kept my eyes tight closed. But what little I'd seen was stamped in my brain, very clearly. I don't know how long I stayed in that position. I broke free of Hannes and we laid him under the chestnut, with a ground sheet to shield him from the rain and . . ."

His voice broke.

"The canvas had been ripped by something sharp. A blade. There was stuff everywhere. And they, too, were . . . everywhere. Kurt was in the middle of the clearing, eyes facing the sky, open. He was looking at the clouds, but he didn't have a peaceful expression on his face, I can assure you of that. Both his arms were missing. One was half a metre from his chest, the other in the undergrowth. He had a wound right here" – he beat his sternum – "a clean wound. A blow with an axe or a big knife, the Carabinieri said."

"An axe?"

"Evi had both her legs cut off at the knees."

I felt a wad of bile rise through my oesophagus.

"She had her right arm broken, as if she'd tried to defend herself. And her head was missing."

I had to get up and run to the bathroom. I threw up. It didn't make me feel any better.

I found Werner with a steaming cup of camomile in his right hand. I accepted it gratefully. I lit a cigarette. I wanted to get rid of that horrible taste.

"Go on, Werner."

"Are you sure?"

"Did you find it? Evi's head, I mean."

"We didn't find it, and nor did the Carabinieri. In fact, what the Carabinieri found was much less than what the four of us saw. The storm had taken away quite a bit of stuff in the meantime, but also" – he lowered his voice, almost apologetically – "you know, the animals . . ."

"What about Markus?"

"Same treatment. Except that he was a bit further down. In trying to run away, he'd fallen and cracked his head open. He had a nasty wound on his leg and shoulder, but it was the fall that killed him."

"God . . ."

"God was looking in another direction, that April 28."

"What did you do?"

"All that horror had made us lose all sense of time and the storm had started up again, even stronger than before. It was seven in the evening."

"Four hours? You stayed there four hours?"

"It went inside you, Jeremiah," Werner whispered. "That horror went inside you and you couldn't leave. I don't want to seem morbid to you, but what we saw was so unnatural and bad, just that, bad, that we lost the light of reason. I've often thought about it over the years, you know. I think Max, Günther, Hannes and I left part of our souls in the Bletterbach that day. That day and the following night."

I almost choked. "Are you telling me you stayed there all night?"

"The spur provided excellent cover, the ground all around was sliding and melting like hot wax. There were so many bolts of lightning that it was a miracle none of us was roasted alive. We had no choice."

"But the bodies . . ."

"We covered them with our spare oilskins. We anchored the tent with stones and tried to pile up those poor kids' things to stop the wind and rain from taking them away. We knew we were at a crime scene, we were conscious that the more objects we managed to keep intact, the greater the likelihood that the Carabinieri could catch those who'd carried out that slaughter. But the real reason we stayed there was simpler. If we'd moved, we'd have died. The mountains follow rules all of their own, whether you like it or not." He aimed his finger at me. "In some conditions, exceptional conditions, and these were more than exceptional conditions, all that matters . . ."

". . . is to survive."

Werner massaged one temple. "We waited all night, huddled together. With Hannes praying and screaming and Günther cursing and me trying to calm both of them. The next morning, as soon as there was a bit of light, we set off again. Hannes couldn't have stayed on his feet if God himself had ordered him to, and my calf was gone, so Max and Günther took turns helping him. But even Günther wasn't quite with it. Remember the stone that had smashed his helmet?"

He didn't finish.

There was no need.

"We got back to the jeep. We hoisted Hannes on board and went back to the village. I took a shower and slept for ten hours straight. When I woke up, Herta didn't ask me anything. She'd made my favourite dish and I wolfed it down. Only then did I take in what we'd been through, and I started crying as I hadn't done even at my parents' funeral."

"Didn't you call the police?"

"Siebenhoch was without telephone or electricity lines. The short-wave radio wasn't working. The Civil Defence people took two days to open the road with bulldozers. They didn't have the slightest idea of what had happened in the Bletterbach. They knew Siebenhoch could cope with emergencies and so they'd diverted their resources to places further down the valley that had more people but were less well equipped than us. The Carabinieri arrived on May 4, when the storm was over. There was an investigation, but the killer was never found. In the end, the Carabinieri and the prosecutor said that the three kids had been unlucky to meet the wrong person at the wrong time."

"Is that all?" I asked, shocked.

Werner opened his arms wide. "That's all. I hope that bastard died somewhere in the Bletterbach. I hope that after he slaughtered those poor kids the mountains took him, and every time the stream overflows, I always hope it'll bring to the surface a piece of that son of a bitch. But that's just a hope."

"Didn't they investigate anyone in Siebenhoch?"

"What do you mean?" Werner said, lighting a match and raising it to the tip of his cigarette.

"Someone from the village. It strikes me as obvious."

"You're letting your imagination run away with you."

"Why?"

"Because you're forgetting what Siebenhoch is. It's a small community. Do you think what you're telling me now never occurred to anyone? It was the first thing we thought of. But if anyone had followed those kids to the Bletterbach, we would have known. Believe me. Because everybody here knows everything about everybody. Minute by minute. Besides, with that storm, getting to the clearing, going so far into the Bletterbach, killing them and then getting back without anyone suspecting, would have been impossible."

"But—"

Werner stopped me. "You promised."

I blinked.

"That's the whole story of the killings. And it's over. Don't let yourself be devoured by it, Jeremiah. Don't let yourself be devoured by this story as others have been."

"Which others? People like Hannes?"

"People like me, Jeremiah."

* * *

We were silent for a long time.

"Each of us reacted in a different way. The whole village was shocked, though some . . ."

"Some less than others," I whispered, thinking of the comments on what had happened to Evi and Kurt that Werner had mentioned to me: after Annelise's unpleasant encounter in Alois' store, they seemed to me much more plausible now than the first time I'd heard them.

"We'd seen. We'd felt that . . . nastiness. So I made up my mind."

"To leave?"

"I'd been thinking about it for a while. I already told you I went to work in a printing shop in Cles, didn't I?"

"You told me you did it for Annelise."

"She had a right to a father who didn't spend his days risking his life. What I didn't tell you is that I couldn't stand it here anymore. I saw the people of Siebenhoch go back to normal and I couldn't accept it. The electricity poles were straightened, the telephone lines restored, the roads patched up and, where necessary, explosives were set off to produce controlled landslides. People wanted to forget, and the Bletterbach killings were forgotten in a hurry. I saw all of that and kept telling myself it wasn't right."

"You told me I mustn't let myself be devoured like the others. Which others?"

"A few hours after we got back, when Siebenhoch was still cut off from the world, Hannes aimed his hunting rifle at Helene's head and fired, killing her. They found him next to his wife's body, with the weapon in his hand. He was catatonic. He was arrested and interned in Pergine until his death in 1997. He's buried here, beside his wife and son. The people of Siebenhoch can be hard, and all too often they open their mouths without thinking, but everyone had understood what had happened to the Schaltzmann family. It wasn't Hannes who killed Helene: it was the bastard who slaughtered Kurt, Evi and Markus. Günther is also buried there. Every so often I take him flowers, and I know that if he were alive, the Günther I knew would be really pissed off. I can almost hear him. 'Flowers? Get me a beer, *du Arschloch*!'"

"How did he die?"

"Even before, Günther was someone who could never say no to a drink, but after the Bletterbach it got him completely. He became the kind of alcoholic who picks fights. Often Max had to put him in the barracks overnight, to stop him hurting anyone. When he was drunk, all he could talk about was the killings. He was obsessed with them. He'd got it into his head to find the killer. All this they told me later, I was living outside Siebenhoch by then. In 1989 Günther had a car accident. He was blind drunk. He died instantly. Better for him, he'd suffered enough. You know why I go and put flowers on his grave? Because I feel guilty. Maybe if I'd stayed, Günther would have had someone to open up to. But I wasn't there. And the others had no way of knowing. They couldn't understand. They hadn't seen."

"There was Max."

"True. But even Max was devoured by the Bletterbach. He married Verena, the girl with the birthday, took Chief Hubner's place and does his work with dedication."

Werner looked me in the eyes, emphasising his words.

"With too much dedication. It's his way of making amends. To embody the protector of Siebenhoch, the one who breaks the balls of strangers and tourists because . . ."

"Because whoever killed Evi and the others could only have been an outsider."

Lily's Bar

I took Annelise and Clara to Bolzano to visit the archaeological museum where Ötzi, the oldest natural mummy ever found, was kept.

Ötzi was an old shepherd (or maybe a traveller, a shaman, a metal prospector, a . . . the theories about his identity were legion) from the Bronze Age, killed on the slopes of the Similaun, nobody knows why or by whom.

Seeing him, Clara burst into tears. She said that dried-up little man was a child elf who had lost his mother. Annelise and I had our work cut out to calm her down.

I have to admit that I, too, was moved by that small, 5,000-year-old figure preserved in a kind of giant refrigerator, face contorted in a sad grimace, but for quite other reasons. I was thinking about the Bletterbach killings.

Like Evi, Kurt and Markus, Ötzi hadn't received justice. Or was I wrong? Maybe in 3,000 B.C., there had been someone who had investigated enough to find the poor man's killers. Had they mourned him?

And who had done it?

Ötzi had been a man of advanced years. The old had children and the children had grandchildren, I thought as I admired the skill with which that man, just over a metre and a half tall, had built the equipment that had allowed him to survive in a world without antibiotics or disinfectants, a world in which there was no Dolomite Mountain Rescue to call if you were in difficulty. Had those children and grandchildren mourned him? Had they built him a funeral pyre? Sacrificed a few animals in his memory? To what gods had that ice man turned before the arrows shot him dead? Had God been looking away that day too, to quote Werner?

A lot was known about Ötzi. Modern technology had made it possible to scan his stomach to discover what he had eaten before he was killed. We knew the pathologies that affected him and thanks to this the reason, medical rather than aesthetic, why there were more than thirty tattoos on his body. Ötzi suffered from arthritis, and the tattoos allowed him to inject curative herbs under his skin. Archaeologists had reconstructed his equipment piece by piece: the bow, the quiver, the axe he carried on his belt, his poncho of dried grass and his hide headdress. His techniques of construction had been revealed in detail. We even knew the colour of his eyes (dark) thanks to D.N.A. testing, and through computer graphics they had reconstructed what his face must have been like before he was buried in the ice for 5,000 years. And yet I couldn't help but think that these details were trivial compared with the real questions the mummy aroused in my mind.

Had he dreamed?

Had he dreamed about hunting? Had he dreamed about wolves howling at the moon? Had he dreamed about the outline of the mountain on which he would meet his death? And what had he seen as he gazed at the stars at night? By what name did he know the Great Bear?

But above all, why had he been killed?

And by whom?

* * *

We celebrated Halloween with the obligatory pumpkin in the window, orange lanterns, a plastic skeleton that glowed in the dark, bats on the ceiling, popcorn and a nice horror movie. All according to tradition.

Clara didn't like the movie, she said you could see the zombies were fake. She said it, though, as if she were asking a question. She wanted to be reassured.

Annelise gave me a glance as if to say, "I told you so, genius!" and I spent the rest of the evening showing Clara how they made blood in movies: blueberry juice and honey. With a touch of coffee to make it darker.

"And the zombies' ugly faces?"

I put on my best zombie imitation, my tongue hanging out of my wide-open mouth and my eyes wild. Clara wrinkled her nose.

I kissed her.

A moment of zombie intimacy.

"And those nasty things on their faces? How do they make the nasty things on their faces?"

"Plasticine and cornflakes."

"Cornflakes?"

I demonstrated this too.

Clara was in seventh heaven. We organised a game to trick Annelise, who pretended to be terrified by the miniature zombie (in polka-dot pyjamas) advancing through the living room holding her arms out in front of her and muttering in a cavernous voice (in so far as the voice of a five-year-old girl can be cavernous), "I'm going to eat you! I'm going to eat you!"

It took us quite a while to get her to go to bed, and then we allowed ourselves a glass of wine.

"Your daughter," I joked, as I sipped the excellent Marzemino, "used the word 'brooding' the other day. Eight letters, your honour."

"And where did she hear a word like that?"

"From you."

Annelise lifted the glass to her mouth. "Talking about what?"

"Try to guess."

"Well, you *are* distracted. Admit it."

"Do you want me to see the doctor again? Would that reassure you?"

Annelise took my hand and squeezed it tight. "You're fine. You're O.K. I can see that. Do you still have" – she bit her lip, a gesture I found extremely sexy – "bad dreams?"

Of course I did, as she knew perfectly well. I appreciated her tact, though.

"Sometimes." I bent down to kiss the tips of her fingers. "But don't worry. I'm fine. And I'm not brooding."

"Would you tell me?"

"Of course I would."

* * *

I was lying.

If Annelise had decided to search on my laptop, which had once been white but had turned grey from all the cigarette ash that had fallen on it, she would have discovered that in the folder "Things" there was a file entitled B. B for "Bletterbach".

And for "bastard".

* * *

One afternoon, a few days after my chat with Werner, I went to Trento on the pretext of acquiring a couple of D.V.D.s for my collection.

What I actually did was spend two hours in the reading room of the university library.

No microfiches or digital copies, but a mountain of yellowing newspapers. Between one layer of dust and another, I found just a few references to the Bletterbach killings. The journalists' attention at the time had been focused on the chaos caused by the storm. Interviews, articles that illustrated more or less what Werner had reconstructed for me. Experts explaining the kind of disaster that had afflicted the region and big black-and-white photographs showing the damage caused by that cataclysm of water and mud.

The final count of eleven dead had led to a brief burst of controversy that had soon burnt itself out, overwhelmed by other events.

A mayor had to resign, and various councillors apologised and put in contrite appearances at the funerals of the victims. The Civil Defence were praised by the President of the Republic, a little pipe-smoking man named Sandro Pertini. I found him odd, but gifted with unusual charisma.

About the murders, little or nothing.

An aerial photograph of the gorge, devoid of the glass and aluminium outline of the Visitors' Centre, which had yet to be built. Evi's face, maybe because it was more photogenic than those of her companions in misfortune. A curt "No comment" uttered by the men pursuing the case (whose names would fit on the back of a cigarette packet). An interview with Werner, more blond than white, with fewer wrinkles but just as many rings under his eyes, who talked about a "horrible slaughter". A few days later, the obituary of Helene Schaltzmann. Nothing about Hannes' madness.

I'd also have liked to look for the obituary of Günther Kagol in '89, but by now I'd realised it would be a pointless task. Plus, it was late by now.

I thanked the staff and got home in time for dinner. Roast pork and potatoes. I kissed my wife, I kissed my daughter and asked them what they'd been doing all day.

Before going to bed, I updated the file with what I had found out in the library.

I told myself I was doing it to keep in practice. To keep myself occupied.

Another lie.

* * *

Without realising it, I was following the same method I had used for all my previous jobs. I was, and remain, a creature of routine.

After transcribing Werner's testimony, trying to put down in digital form the emphasis and emotions that his words had conveyed to me, and compiling a dry list of the characteristic morphology, geology, flora and fauna of the Bletterbach, I started searching for a few historical allusions that would give me a broader picture of the place.

My search started one afternoon when Annelise and Clara had gone to Bolzano to do shopping ("Women's things, Papà." "Expensive things?" "Pretty things") with a visit to the geological museum that was part of the Visitors' Centre in the Bletterbach.

There weren't many books. Most of those there were had been put out by tiny publishers subsidised by the province, and they were often useless for my purpose, panegyrics on the good old days (with no mention of either the poverty that had gripped the area until not so long ago or the days of "Belfast with strudel"), but I read them avidly, noting down the paragraphs that most aroused my curiosity.

The best were the – sometimes ungrammatical – accounts of the most amazing feats of Dolomite Mountain Rescue. The names of Werner and Hannes cropped up frequently. Günther's too, a couple of times. In a long celebratory article, there was even a mention of Hermann Kagol, the man who'd had the idea for the Centre.

A photograph showed a solemn Werner, posing by the recently purchased Alouette. The photograph of the flaming red EC135 gave me stomach spasms.

* * *

In the days that followed, I started frequenting one of the bars in Siebenhoch, Lily's, a crummy place with terrible watery coffee, wooden crucifixes that glowered at you and the heads of roe deer, stags and ibex as an insult to animal rights people.

Lily's was a meeting place for Alpine guides and mountain people who wanted a bit of peace and quiet. They served a *Bauerntoast* that satisfied you for days, and the beer was always cold. In addition, nobody squawked into a cell phone or burst into raptures about how quaint this hole in the wall was.

Most of the customers were pensioners, but you mustn't think of it as a kind of old people's home. There were lots of young people there, too, even very young people, all united by mountain life. In short, Lily's was a place where the locals could read the *Dolomiten*, have a few drinks, and curse in two languages without having to worry about offending the tourists.

I was brilliant. My jokes about my countrymen made them split their sides. I learned to play Watten. I had them teach me the local *dialokt*. I bought rounds of beers as if it were water and did everything I could to gain the customers' confidence. Above all, I was very discreet about my true intentions.

I was under no illusions, though. That bunch of mountain people were as pleasant to me as I was to them, but that didn't mean we had become friends. I was nice, amusing, maybe a bit odd, and lent a touch of colour to their evenings, but nothing more.

I was a welcome guest, a bit more than a tourist, much less than a local, as Chief Krün had said.

These ugly mugs – their hands rarely had all ten fingers, either because they'd been lost in the course of some climb (as had happened to Werner) or because they had been mangled by the teeth of a chainsaw or sawn off with a chisel in order to avoid military service – accepted my presence only because of my connection with old Mair, and I was sure that some, if not all, of them reported back to him more or less everything we said to each other. But I was crafty. I had prepared a cover for myself. As Mike would have said: I had a plan.

After the first week spent talking about this and that and losing at cards, I happened to mention that I intended to build a wooden sled for my daughter. A Christmas present, I said. Was there anyone who could give me a few tips? I knew that many of them were skilful woodcarvers, and I assumed that it would be a way of getting into their good graces and diverting suspicion as much as possible.

It worked.

Two in particular threw themselves body and soul into the enterprise of turning me into an artisan: a friendly nonagenarian named

Elmar and his inseparable drinking companion, a seventy-five-year-old with one leg missing (an accident in the woods: a chainsaw that had gone *zag* instead of *zig*) named Luis.

Elmar and Luis explained to me what kind of tools I would have to acquire, how to avoid being cheated by the assistants in the hardware store, and what type of wood to get for each part of the sled. We sketched various designs on napkins that I then left in my pockets and which ended up in the washing machine, arousing their hilarity.

I was just a stupid city-dweller, after all, wasn't I?

Every now and again, with studied casualness, I would ask a few questions.

Elmar and Luis were more than happy to tell me stories that everyone in Lily's Bar had already heard too many times.

I discovered what the books in the museum hadn't had the courage to tell me.

Accidents. Deaths. Absurd deaths, sad deaths, pointless deaths, deaths a hundred years ago. Deaths *centuries* ago. And legends that started out making us sneer but always ended up very badly.

There was one in particular that struck me. It was about the mysterious people of Fanes, and both Elmar and Luis swore it was just a story.

The people of Fanes were an ancient tribe that, according to the legend, lived in peace and harmony. They didn't start wars, and their kings dispensed justice intelligently. Everything went wonderfully until, all at once, they vanished without a trace. Overnight. Fanes was about ten kilometres north of the nature reserve, but Elmar and Luis said they were convinced that whatever had swept that ancient people away came from the Bletterbach. A bad place, Luis had called it. It was there that the blade of the chainsaw had gone *zag*.

That evening, I checked on Wikipedia what the odd couple in Lily's had told me. Much to my surprise, I discovered that the two of them hadn't been lying. The late Bronze Age population of Fanes had indeed disappeared as if by some conjuring trick. Now you see them, now you don't.

Poof!

The most plausible hypothesis was that there had been an invasion by tribes from the south, maybe from the Veneto, who were more advanced and aggressive. But wars leave traces, and nothing had been found to bear witness to such an event. No skeletons, no arrowheads, no broken shields or mass graves. Just legends. Elmar and Luis had earned their Forst.

* * *

Halfway through November, two things happened.

First: Luis brought me a cake that tasted of nothing.

Second: the cake that tasted of nothing acquired a vague taste of blood.

The Cake that Tasted of B

It had been a quiet evening at Lily's. Elmar had left early, because of his arthritis. Luis had been as sociable and talkative as ever. We had played Watten (I was improving, although I suspected that my victories were due more to my opponents' good nature than to any real progress on my part) and drunk a couple of beers.

Outside, the snow was some twenty centimetres deep and the temperature was a couple of degrees below zero. No wind.

"Do you mind seeing me home, *Amerikaner*?" Luis said, indicating the void beneath his knee.

Luis didn't need me to get home. Ice or no ice, he was a sensation on his crutches. No, he wanted to talk to me far from prying ears. And indeed, once we got to his front door, he offered me a little drink, just to warm myself up. I accepted with a mixture of curiosity and excitement.

Luis's place was a mess, as might have been expected of a widower who had spent his life surrounded by woodcutters felling trees. But it was clean, and I couldn't help but appreciate the taste, old-fashioned as it might be, with which it was decorated. The correct term was "welcoming", nine letters.

Judging from the framed photographs on the walls, Luis must have been happy there.

"Are these your children?"

"Marlene and Martin. She lives in Berlin, she's an architect. Martin has a haulage firm in Trento. They're doing well. Marlene's house is a kind of meeting point for artists, not my kind of people, but she's happy. Martin is the same age as you. He has one son."

He handed me an inviting-smelling glass of grappa.

"What's his name?"

"Francesco. He's three years old. They'll be coming to see me at Christmas."

"To your family, then," I toasted.

"To the Bletterbach," he replied.

I froze, my glass in mid-air. Luis grinned, clinked his glass against mine and gulped down the contents without taking his eyes off me.

"Is that why you invited me here?"

Luis nodded. "Maybe you can deceive Elmar, who, thank God, manages to empty his bowels every morning at the crack of dawn and still has good eyesight, but who as far as his head goes . . . I don't know if I'm making myself clear."

My face had turned red. "Does Werner know?" I asked.

Luis shook his head. "If he does, it's not thanks to me. But Elmar and I aren't the only people who drink at Lily's."

I cursed mentally.

"Werner," Luis continued, "is an influential, respected person. One of those people who don't necessarily have to ask."

"I . . ." I stammered.

"You don't have to justify yourself, *Amerikaner*. Not to me anyway. To your father-in-law? Maybe. To your own conscience? Definitely. Unless you're one of those individuals who don't even know what a conscience is. But I don't think you are. Are you?"

"No, I'm not."

L for Liar.

Or almost.

"That's what I thought. That's why I invited you here. I want to give you a piece of advice."

"What kind of advice?"

"People in Siebenhoch are simple. We don't want much, a hot meal in the evening, a job, a roof over our heads and a few dozen grandchildren for our old age. We don't like problems. We have enough headaches living in this area to go and look for others from outside."

"And I'm from outside."

"Almost," Luis replied, echoing what Chief Krün had said. "Half and half."

"I'm allowed a few beers at Lily's, but not to stick my nose into matters that don't concern me."

"Don't take it so hard, son. We're not as prejudiced as all that. We're good people. Almost all of us. I heard what happened to your wife at Alois' store, and I think it was a disgrace. A real disgrace. But what do you expect from someone" – he indicated the packet of Marlboros sticking out of the breast pocket of my shirt – "who sells coffin nails even to little kids?"

"Thanks for the warning, Luis," I said, after a long pause.

"Don't be melodramatic. This is the warning: Werner is keeping an eye on you, and when Werner sniffs you out it's best to be careful. But he likes you and he has a sense of justice. He's not a bad person. When he moved to Cles, many of us felt down. We missed him. But *his* sense of justice isn't *my* sense of justice. You know what my wife always said? That the best way to make a child's mouth water is to forbid him to eat cake."

He laughed.

I felt my heart start to do somersaults in my chest. "Whereas you want to give me the cake?"

Luis sat back in his armchair. He reached out his hand and from a low table took his pipe and tobacco. "This conversation never happened, understood?"

"Understood."

"And stop drooling, *Amerikaner*. The cake I'm about to give you isn't much to speak of. That's why I'm going to tell you a couple of things that nobody at Lily's will ever have the courage to tell you. Because the cake in question is a cake that tastes of nothing."

"You mean empty?"

"*Genau.* Empty. Tasting of nothing. And although my wife brought up two wonderful children, I'm of the opinion that if you let a teenager taste the cake and the cake is disgusting, if nothing else he'll stop wandering around the house like a dog on heat."

I returned his smile.

"I think Werner told you what happened better than I ever could. He's always been good with words. He was someone who could speak to politicians and beat them at their own game: bullshit. I on the other hand am just a woodcutter with one leg, the only book I've read is a collection of unfunny jokes, and if films don't have a few explosions in them I fall asleep. But I can understand what people want. And you want what on television they call the 'word on the street'. Or am I wrong?"

"You're not wrong."

Luis dragged on his pipe. I heard the tobacco sizzle.

The smell was pleasant.

"Who was it?" he said craftily. "That's the question it all revolves around. Who killed those poor kids? Officially, nobody. But in 1987 a guy was arrested, an ex-policeman from Venice who'd killed, at different times, three tourists in the Dolomites between Belluno and Friuli. He'd dismembered them with an axe. He said he was the victim of a judicial plot. He and his lawyer hinted at mental illness. At the trial, someone remembered the Bletterbach killings, so the police investigated and apparently there were some clues that placed this guy around here in April and May of '85. But they were very vague clues and so, without proof or a confession . . ."

"Nothing."

"They accepted mental illness. He was crazy, not stupid."

"Do you think it was him?"

Luis aimed his pipe at me as if it were a gun. "I'll give you the cake, son. The rest is up to you."

"Go on," I encouraged him.

"Then there was the poachers angle. You see, you also fell into the trap of the lone killer. But what if it wasn't only one person who committed that foul deed? After all, no evidence was ever found to suggest that."

"Right," I muttered. I'd overlooked the fact that Werner's was just one version, not the objective truth. A beginner's mistake, I reprimanded myself.

"Hunting is second nature around here. People hunt deer, chamois, ibex, pheasant, woodcock. Sometimes even grouse, and wolves when they were still around. If you go to the back room at Lily's, there's a stuffed lynx. The plaque says 1888, but in my opinion it's much more recent, that's why it isn't on display."

"Bad publicity?"

"Of course, but that's not the point. Even today, not everyone in Siebenhoch has fully digested the idea of the nature reserve. Plus, you have to remember that in '85 the reserve was just a typewritten request on the desk of some provincial official. There were hunters who followed the rules, but also quite a few poachers."

"Why would they have killed those three?"

"Markus. Markus was the target. In '85 he was sixteen, but he already knew his stuff. He was always hanging around Max, who was his role model, along with Kurt. He wanted to join the Forest Rangers. And Max, well, when Markus was around, you should have seen how he acted: chest out and boots all shiny." Luis shook his head. "They were just two kids, but kids have enthusiasm. And enthusiasm makes the world go round. Markus was a big pain in the arse, and not only that, he was an environmentalist, the hard-headed kind. Whenever he heard about some illegal killing he'd go and spill the beans to Chief Hubner. Chief Hubner would fill in endless paperwork, nod and thank him, all the while laughing at the kid. Before his heart attack, Chief Hubner had also been a hunter. Needless to say, all those statements ended up in the stove as soon as Markus left the office. So, that's the second theory."

"Poachers with a grudge?"

"Poachers whose wallets had been hit. Markus had got into the habit of ruining their nests."

"Their nests?"

"Most poachers don't make a living selling stag meat to restaurants. They make their money catching birds. Capturing chicks and setting traps for chaffinches and robins. You can make quite a bit that way."

"And Markus destroyed their traps?"

"That's right."

"Was that a good enough motive for killing him?"

"It depends on your conscience. But listen to this: at the end of the '70s, I caught Elmar with a sack full of small birds. Jackdaws, a dunnock and two white partridge chicks. He told me he knew a guy in Salorno who would buy the two partridge chicks for a whole lot of cash."

"How much?"

"The following week, I went with him to a dealer in Trento to buy an ivory-coloured Fiat Argenta."

"That much?"

Luis shrugged. "It certainly wasn't the two partridges that made him rich, but I'd say a good part of the budget came from the contents of that sack."

"What else?"

"Don't you hear the noise of your jaws chewing air, Salinger?"

"Maybe I like it."

Luis sucked at his pipe pensively. "Evi's father."

"The travelling salesman from Verona?"

"Mauro Tognon. They said he'd gone mad and come back to Sienbenhoch. That he'd killed Evi to play a prank on his ex-wife."

"A prank?"

Luis grinned. "He was a damned *Walscher*, wasn't he?"

"That seems a bit—"

"Far-fetched? Racist? Both? Of course, like all the other stories. They're local rumours, not the truth. Nobody knows the truth about the Bletterbach killing. Just theories."

"Didn't they investigate him?"

"They don't even know what happened to the bastard. But that didn't stop the rumours." Luis drummed his arthritic fingers on the arm of his chair. "Then there's the theory that it was a settling of scores."

"Over what?"

"Drugs."

"*Drugs*?" I said, surprised.

"Markus again."

"He did drugs?"

"It was '85, he had an alcoholic mother, his sister was in Innsbruck, and he had to get up at five in the morning every day to go to school. In my opinion, he had every right to smoke a bit of that grass I even found once in my daughter Marlene's drawer. He got a talking-to from Chief Hubner, and the matter ended there. But not the badmouthing. He was branded a—"

"And yet everyone says he was good boy," I cut in.

"Everyone speaks well of everybody in Sienbenhoch," Luis said, getting heated. "They speak well of Werner although they say it was out of cowardice that he moved to Cles, because he didn't want to help poor Günther. They also speak well of poor Günther, except that when he started howling at the moon, they closed their eyes and ears. The only one who tried to help him was Max, who in the meantime had become Chief Krün, and everyone speaks well of him, right?"

"Max, too?"

"They said it was suspicious that he should go and see Evi and Kurt in Innsbruck, seven hours by train. They forget, though, that Max went to Innsbruck to accompany Markus who was a minor. They forget that minors couldn't go across the border without being accompanied. Especially in those days. And if you point out that detail of the Cold War to them, the border guards, the searches of the passengers, what do they say? They change the subject! They say it was Verena, Max's fiancée who's now his wife, who killed those three poor kids out of jealousy. Even though that's crazy, given that Verena is about one metre sixty tall and Kurt could have knocked her out with one hand tied behind his back. People talk, Salinger, that's all they ever do. And the more they talk, the more hypocritical and inventive they become."

"Inventive?"

"Oh, yes. Because I haven't yet told you my favourite theory," Luis said, his eyes glinting wickedly.

"What's that?"

He leaned towards me and lowered his voice. "*Monsters.* Monsters that live under the Bletterbach, in the caves. The monsters that caused the collapse of the mine in '23, flooding it and killing everyone who worked down there. The same monsters that wiped out the people of Fanes. Monsters in the belly of the mountain who every now and again, when it's full moon, come back to the surface and tear everything they find to pieces."

He sat back in his chair. A small cloud of tobacco smoke rose to the ceiling.

Finally, his toothless smile. "What do you think of your cake that tastes of nothing, Salinger?"

* * *

Scratch beneath the surface of a small village of seven hundred souls and you'll find a nest of vipers.

That evening, I made notes on what Luis had told me and, beginning the following day, I decided to go less often to Lily's. Partly because of Werner, but also because I needed to develop the stories Luis had stuck in my head.

All the same, I didn't spend my time twiddling my thumbs. On the contrary.

Much to my surprise, I'd started really getting to like carpentry. The idea of building a sled for Clara, which had begun as a ruse, had turned into hours spent at the back of the house in Welshboden trying to fashion something decent from the planks that Werner gave me.

Werner himself offered on many occasions to give me a hand (fearing for my safety, I suspect), but each time I refused. I wanted to succeed by myself.

I liked the smell of the wood shavings, the slow sliding of the plane as it smoothed the edges, the pain in my back after a few hours' hard work. I had even bought a can of paint and some high-quality brushes for when I'd finished the sled. I intended to paint it red.

A nice bright red.

* * *

November seemed to rush by. Snowball fights, snowmen with carrots for noses, endless card games with Werner, and the smell of wood at the back of Welshboden. I answered Mike's e-mails, though I refused to open the video files my partner sent me from across the ocean. I immediately deleted them, as if they were infected.

Now and again I'd reread file B, Werner's account, the legends about the Bletterbach, the local rumours that Luis had shared with me, and I invariably found myself biting air. It was just a cake with no taste, but it was still a great story, one of those you tell around the fire, maybe at Halloween, so I kept going back to it.

I also thought about what my next moves might be if I decided to go deeper.

Getting in touch with the officers who had pursued the case, digging up the files, which were buried God knows where. But the idea that Werner was keeping an eye on me made me quite nervous.

All the same . . .

Before going to sleep, I would reflect on how I could tell the story to Mike and persuade him to work on it a little, imagining one of our talks full of ifs and buts. The Bletterbach was the last thought of the day.

I still had nightmares.

I would see the Beast again, hear the hissing. But the Beast was less present, its voice more muffled, as if it belonged to another life. No longer a memory devouring me, but something vague and indefinable. Distant, luckily for me.

There were several nights that passed in deep black darkness. Nights from which I woke happy and full of energy. Those were the best days.

On December 1, Mr Smith and his bunch of super-cool guys with tattoos from the network ruined everything. And yours truly received a nice slice of cake tasting of blood.

My own, to be precise.

South Tyrol Style

In that second half of November, as I said, I rationed my visits to Lily's, but didn't stop going there altogether. I'd grown fond of those lopsided benches and the tables that looked as if they hadn't had a new coat of paint in at least a dozen years.

Every now and then, Luis would make a quip about people who come out with a lot of hot air, but I didn't bear a grudge. Just as I pretended not to know that that sprightly old man he went around with, Elmar, had a past as a poacher.

I had fun showing them photographs of my progress in building the sled and took their advice to heart. At Lily's, I was among people who maybe weren't my people (and wouldn't be even if I decided to spend the rest of my life in Siebenhoch), but in whose company I felt safe. They knew me and I knew them.

That's why Thomas Pircher caught me by surprise.

That and the fact that what happened at Lily's started 8,000 kilometres from Siebenhoch, in the swish offices of the network.

* * *

Mike and I had obligations. Contractual obligations. Mr Smith had a whole army of lawyers paid to make sure that contracts were honoured down to the last clause. To make money, you have to be inflexible.

Mr Smith was interested in maximising his income, not making good or bad television. The network invested in a product and expected to see a decent return. So, since the profits from the "Road Crew" series had grown from season to season, the cheque that Mr Smith had signed for the pre-production of "Mountain Angels" had had several zeroes on it. It was considered likely that the project would get the same reaction from the public as "Road Crew" had. That, for the great emperor of the network, meant advertising space. In other words, money. Simple as that. But then everything had gone to hell. September 15 had happened. No more factual series, Mike had told Mr Smith. In its place, a documentary film. Ninety minutes of pure adrenalin.

Mr Smith had shown cautious interest and in the end, in spite of opposition from various experts in the network, had agreed. But at this point, the odds in our favour had collapsed and the pressure was on.

Pressure? No, what Mike had to suffer – while I was still trying to put my shattered psyche back together – wasn't pressure, it was an avalanche of biblical proportions.

True, I'd co-signed all the contracts, the narrative line of the documentary was mine, the script had me as one of the main characters. But for Mr Smith and the network, there was only one God in heaven, only one captain on the *Pequod*, and only one director for the film: Mike. And it was on his head that all the shit came down. Text messages at all hours of the day and night, constant e-mails and telephone calls, Fed-Ex couriers handing over ever more threatening missives. Mike didn't tell me about any of it. He could have (and in some respects, he really should have), but he wanted to protect me.

And I'm grateful to him for that.

In November, Mr Smith's patience ran out. He had signed a cheque and now he demanded to know where his money had gone. Mike did everything that heroes do at times like these: he wheedled, made up excuses to justify the delays, and bowed and scraped like a Chinese mandarin. He defended me and the project energetically for as long as he could.

In the end, he had to give in.

On the morning of November 30, at exactly nine o'clock, he found himself in a conference room on the top floor of the network's headquarters, as nervous as someone condemned to death, showing a rough cut of "In the Belly of the Beast".

The extremely select audience consisted of Mr Smith, a few experts from the creative team, two executives with hangovers, and a guy from Marketing with horn-rimmed spectacles, tattoos on both arms and a Dolce and Gabbana suit, who was constantly taking notes on an iPad and whom Mike had nicknamed T.A.

Total Asshole.

The screening went better than expected. Mr Smith decided that there was indeed money to be made from it, offered a few words of advice just to keep up appearances (advice that Mike ignored), and even the experts from the creative team and the two executives admitted through clenched teeth that maybe not *all* the money invested had ended up down the toilet.

The man who was most generous with his praise was Total Asshole. He gave Mike comradely pats on the back, shook his hand, said "wow" at least twenty times, and never stopped sniffing. After which, he gathered his notes and went off to talk to the press.

I'll give him this: Total Asshole knew his job. A storm was created that, inexorably, broke on my nose.

Literally on my nose.

* * *

On December 1, after a day spent tidying the house, helping Werner to replace a pipe in the toilet at Welshboden, and trying to explain Darwin to Clara (she had seen a documentary on television and couldn't understand how T Rex had turned into a hen, which obliged me to bring up Yodi), once dinner was over I went down to the village with the intention of grabbing a beer, having a little chat with the Elmar & Luis double act and then burying myself under the blankets and enjoying eight well-deserved hours of sleep.

It was my tiredness that prevented me from noticing the looks when I went into Lily's.

Eyes that stared at me for a frozen moment and then went back to looking somewhere else. No reply to my usual "Hallo!" in a now almost passable *dialokt.*

There were even some who stood up and walked out. Just like in a Western.

I ordered a beer and sat down at the table of my two favourite drinking companions. "Quiet evening, isn't it?"

Elmar clicked his tongue, then raised his newspaper, creating a barrier between him and me.

Surprised, I looked at Luis and raised an eyebrow.

"Hi, Salinger," was his greeting.

I waited for my beer. It didn't come.

I cleared my throat. "What's up, boys?"

"Boys," Elmar croaked. "You can say that to someone else."

Usually, Lily's was filled with chatter, coughing fits, and cursing in two languages. That evening of December 1: silence. I heard someone muttering. A couple of chairs squeaking on the floor. Nothing else, apart from the sensation of having all eyes aimed at me. Luis was stooped over his tankard of beer, now almost empty, as if trying to read the future in the lukewarm dregs.

"Luis?" I said, lightly brushing his elbow.

"Don't touch me, Salinger. Don't. Touch. Me."

I moved back, wounded. "What the hell is going on here?" I snapped.

"This is what's going on," was the gruff reply of someone behind me, who threw a copy of the *Alto Adige* down on the table. Followed by a copy of the *Dolomiten.*

"You can read, can't you?" Elmar said. I had never seen that expression on his face before. Usually, he was a mild old man with dentures that had a tendency to slip out, especially when he had to deal with words of more than three syllables. The scorn with which he uttered that sentence hurt me.

All I needed to see was the headlines.

"But I didn't—"

"You didn't know?"

"Yes, I knew, but—"

"Then you're no longer welcome here."

I sat there open-mouthed. "I can explain."

"What would you like to explain?" Luis almost snarled.

"I'd like," I said, trying to display a calm I didn't possess, "to explain my point of view."

"Have they written crap? Have two different papers written crap? Is that what you're trying to say? A conspiracy against you? Or maybe you'd like me to read you what's written here? Maybe something was lost in translation."

A number of people laughed.

It was nasty laughter. I couldn't believe I was the target of this hostility. Not here, not at Lily's. Not from these people.

"I don't—"

At this point, I felt a hand come down on my shoulder.

"Did you hear what Luis said? Just get out of here."

The blood went to my head. But I resisted the impulse to grab that hand and shake it off.

"I just want to give you my side of—"

"You talk too much," said the bearded man behind the counter: Stef, the owner of Lily's. "I pay the bills in this place and I'm telling you to get lost."

I had no choice. That much was clear. There was a nasty atmosphere. But just like Kurt, Evi and Markus, I, too, took for a simple storm what in fact was a hurricane.

"Listen," I said, "there's been a misunderstanding. Is the film coming out? Yes. Will the film feature the accident? Yes. Will it be a second-rate product? No. Will it make me look like a hero? No. Above all," I said emphatically, looking Luis in the eyes, "will it show the men of Dolomite Mountain Rescue in a bad light?" I paused briefly, praying that they would believe me. Because that was the naked truth and I wanted them to know it. "Absolutely not."

Luis shook his head. "It says here it's going to be called 'In the Belly of the Beast.'"

"That's correct."

"It says that you and your friend are the authors."

"That's correct, too."

Luis looked at me as if to say, *You see? I'm right.*

"But it isn't true that it'll engage in hypotheticals, like it says here. It isn't true that it'll be a . . . " I looked for the sentence and read it out loud, ". . . 'an attack on the failings of Mountain Rescue.'"

Elmar again clicked his tongue.

"You have to believe me. I can have you shown a few clips, I can—"

"How long have you been in Siebenhoch, Salinger?"

"Almost a year."

"How long did it take you to shoot your lousy film?"

"Three months, more or less."

"And you still don't get it?"

"Get what?" I asked, hurt.

"What happens in the mountains stays in the mountains." It wasn't Luis who said this, it was the man whose hand was still pressing down on my shoulder. "Stupid *Walscher.*"

This was the proverbial last straw.

I exploded.

"Get your hands off me," I hissed, leaping to my feet.

The man, an Alpine guide more or less my age, was a good ten centimetres taller than me and his eyes, blurred by alcohol, were no less nasty than mine. His name was Thomas Pircher. I'd even bought him a beer once.

"Or else?"

The man struck. Fast.

He caught me on the nose.

"Or else I'll teach you a new way to shit, *Walscher*. Maybe from the ear, what do you say to that?"

I staggered back, bent double with the pain, while blood gushed onto the floor. Some applauded, others whistled.

Nobody made a move to help me.

Pircher grabbed me by the hair, slapped me twice, and hit me in the solar plexus. I collapsed to the floor and dragged myself behind Luis and Elmar's table.

"You want some more?"

I didn't reply, I was too intent on trying to breathe. He poured a beer over my face. Then he kicked me twice in the ribs.

It was a beating in authentic South Tyrol style. If I hadn't reacted immediately, I'd have left Lily's on a stretcher.

I shook my head and tried to get up. Nothing doing. The world was spinning and it seemed as if it didn't want to stop. The blows increased. Some urged Thomas to hit harder. Others jeered. There was no doubt about it, they were really enjoying it.

"Listen . . . " I mumbled, playing a trick as old as the world.

There was a one in a million chance that it might work, but Thomas Pircher fell for it hook, line and sinker.

He bent down to listen to what I was muttering. Incredible, the innocence of some people.

I lifted my head abruptly and caught him on the chin. The pain on the back of my neck was strong, but bearable. Mitigated by the cry that escaped my attacker. I didn't waste even one second. I got up, grabbed a chair and brought it down on his back.

Thomas went down immediately.

I stood there motionless, challenging everyone there to square up.

"Who else wants some?" I cried.

At this point, I saw my reflection in the window of Lily's. The chair leg in my right hand, my face reduced to a mask of blood, and an insane expression in my eyes. I felt a sense of disgust and futility. I could have yelled my innocence until my throat hurt, but the customers of Lily's would have believed only what was there in black and white in the newspapers.

Maybe the next day, by the light of the sun, some of them would question what the hacks had written, which was taken straight from Total Asshole's press releases. In a week, most of them would listen to me. In six months, I might even be able to exchange a few jokes with Thomas Pircher, who was still moaning on the floor. But not that evening, that evening nobody would pay any attention to me. Whatever I might say in my defence would sound false and empty.

I dropped the chair leg, wiped my mouth with the sleeve of my jacket and went home.

* * *

Annelise was awake. Better that way. I couldn't have justified my swollen nose and the blood anyway. I told her what had happened and she flew into a rage. She threatened to bring in Werner, and it took quite a lot of effort to calm her down. It was pointless getting agitated. When the film was shown, things would sort themselves out. In the meantime we would have to make the best of it.

"But—"

"No buts. What do you want to do? Lodge a complaint? In a place where fights break out even at church bingo?"

"But—"

"I'll have to go to another bar, what's the big deal? There are plenty to choose from."

Annelise treated my wounds and I promised her that I would go to the emergency department of the hospital to get seen to, which I did the following day, accompanied by Werner, who, needless to say, already knew all the details of the fight at Lily's.

At the San Maurizio, it emerged that neither my nose nor my ribs were broken. They both hurt badly and the doctors prescribed some painkillers. I thanked Werner for the ride, said goodbye, and went home. That evening, I had a long conversation on the phone with Mike, who told me he still hadn't quite figured out the "leak" deliberately engineered by Total Asshole to give our documentary an aura of controversy, then, dead tired, I took refuge round the back of Welshboden and worked on the sled I wanted to give Clara for Christmas.

* * *

On the night of December 2, I dreamed about the Beast. Inside. In the whiteness. Between those jaws that wanted to crush me. The sensation of total hostility.

Get out, hissed the Beast.

Get out.

Der Krampusmeister

I'd first heard about it from Annelise, years earlier, and swollen face or not I wouldn't have missed it for the world now that I was in Siebenhoch.

On December 5, the feast of Saint Nicolas (here called San Nicolò, with the stress on the last syllable), Alto Adige celebrated the saint in its usual style, a mixture of the burlesque and the sinister.

Annelise had shown me photographs and YouTube clips of the celebrations, and they'd aroused my enthusiasm. I'd renamed December 5 the feast of the South Tyrolean Devil. A kind of older Halloween, without sexy pussycats to ruin the atmosphere. Annelise had taken offence. It wasn't a feast of the devil, she reprimanded me, it was a feast in which the devil was *chased away*. I'd apologised and tried in every way to earn forgiveness, just so as not to ruin the atmosphere, but I didn't abandon my idea.

The fact that at the end of the celebration the saint chased away the devils sounded to me like a happy ending imposed by a production company lacking in imagination.

On December 5, I woke up early, as excited as a child on Christmas Eve. I was beside myself with joy. Annelise and Clara watched my excitement incredulously. I even phoned Werner to ask if the feast would take place as normal in spite of the snow. Werner pointed out that it hadn't been snowing for a while now, and that maybe I didn't know but, around here, snow wasn't exactly unheard of.

Around six, with Siebenhoch still shrouded in darkness, Werner knocked at our door and found us ready to leave. I didn't want to miss even one second.

Throughout the ride to Siebenhoch, Clara, infected by my enthusiasm, bombarded her grandfather with questions. He did his best to stem that overwhelming tide. No, the devils (which were called *Krampus*) wouldn't carry her away, at most she'd get her nose daubed with coal. No, they weren't real devils, they were local youths disguised as devils. No, in spite of what that precocious child of her father kept repeating, the *Krampus* weren't bad for real.

"They're very bad, trust me, eight letters," I murmured, winking at her conspiratorially.

"Honeybun doesn't trust you," Clara said sententiously, her little nose up in the ear. "Honeybun believes five letters."

"Five letters?"

"*Nonno*."

"And you'd do well to believe me, too, Jeremiah," Werner muttered.

I shut my mouth.

Siebenhoch was a jewel of mountain architecture. Small houses clustered around the little church, behind which was the cemetery, totally white now under a good fifty centimetres of snow.

It was from there that the *Krampus* would come.

The square was packed with people, mostly tourists, all rigged out as if to defy a Siberian winter, their cameras at the ready to immortalise the devils of South Tyrol.

At a kiosk, we bought a cup of hot chocolate for Clara and two beers for me and Annelise and looked for the best place from which to enjoy the spectacle.

Behind the church, we sensed a certain agitation. The local youths were putting the finishing touches to their costumes, swarms of children were running excitedly on the ice. At the windows, the faces of old people started to appear. There was no sign of the parish priest, who would make an appearance only at a later stage, dressed as San Nicolò, to chase away the terrible *Krampus*.

"You see that one?"

Werner was pointing at a man with a drooping moustache sitting on the steps in front of the church, clutching an unlit pipe between his teeth and enjoying the spectacle of the crowd.

"The guy with the red beret?"

"He's a living tradition. The *Krampusmeister*."

"The devil master?" I asked, fascinated.

"He's the man who makes the costumes. *Krampusmeister* is a term we only use here in Siebenhoch and we're very proud of it. For as long as there's been a Siebenhoch, there's been a *Krampusmeister*."

"I thought the young people made their own costumes."

Werner shook his head. "*Nix*, there are rules to be respected, Jeremiah, traditions. You have to be attentive to details when you talk about the *Krampus* costumes. Otherwise he might get angry," he added, amused.

"The *Krampusmeister*?" I asked, looking at the man sitting there so seraphically with his pipe in his mouth. I couldn't place him, but I was sure I'd seen him before.

"No, the devil."

I laughed. "That's crazy."

"What's crazy, Papà?"

I hoisted Clara up onto my shoulders (how heavy she was now!) and pointed out the man with the pipe. "You see that man in the red beret sitting on the steps?"

"Isn't his bottom cold?"

"Oh, no."

"How come?"

"He," I said solemnly, "is the *Krampusmeister*. The devil's tailor."

Clara launched into a long exclamation of wonder.

I winked at Annelise. "Oh, yes. He's the one who makes the clothes for the *Krampus*, isn't that right, Werner?"

"A real *Krampus* must have horns, and they must be real horns, from a ram, a goat, a sheep or an ibex."

"Do they kill them to get their horns?" Clara asked.

For the first time since I had known him, I saw Werner turn red. "Of course not. Their horns just . . . fall off."

"Like leaves?"

"*Genau.* Like leaves. Would you like another hot chocolate, Clara?"

"And doesn't it hurt when their horns fall off?"

"They don't even notice. Are you sure you don't want—"

"And what else are the *Krampus* supposed to have?"

It was the roar of the crowd that rescued my father-in-law from this interrogation.

The *Krampus* arrived in single file, about two metres apart. The one in front was holding a flashlight that he held up like the Olympic flame.

"His horns are sooooo big," Clara said in a whisper.

The procession marched in step, setting a slow, almost funereal pace.

Gradually, the crowd fell silent. Flashes went off, but soon even these abated. Siebenhoch was wrapped in an unreal silence.

Each *Krampus* was different, but they all wore animal skins, had cowbells on their belts and clutched whips in their right hands, some made of sorghum, some from ox sinews. They really were scary.

Especially with that silence.

"They're really ugly, Papà," Clara stammered.

I noticed the tremor in her voice, so I stroked her leg to calm her. "They're fake. It's just dress up."

Clara didn't respond, not immediately. The *Krampus* arranged themselves in a half-moon a few metres from the crowd, which had instinctively retreated. The *Krampus* with the flashlight had positioned himself right in the middle of the formation, his back to the church. His horns danced in the flame.

"They don't look fake to me, Mamma. They don't have cornflakes on their faces."

"That's because they're not zombies, darling. They're *Krampus.* But they're not real. It's just make-believe."

Clara wasn't the only one whose courage had faded. I noticed that almost all the children, and even a few teenagers, cocky up until now, had grown silent and were clinging to their parents' winter jackets.

"How many letters are there in the words 'make-believe', Clara?" Werner asked.

"There are . . . there are . . . I don't know."

Clara slipped into Werner's arms, half her face hidden in the hollow of his neck and the other half turned to the square. I heard Werner whisper words of comfort and saw him give her a little tickle, but also noticed her jump at the first crack of the whip.

I let out a cry of surprise, turning my attention again to what was happening in the square. The sinews struck the ground. A dry crack that echoed through the village. I lit a cigarette.

The first blow was followed by a second. Then a third and a fourth, getting louder all the time.

Crack! Crack! Crack!

At the height of the frenzy, the *Krampus* with the flashlight let out a fearsome cry, guttural and violent. The whips stopped hitting the ground. The commotion died down.

I knew what would happen next. This was the amusing part of the celebration.

The *Krampus* launched themselves at the crowd, emitting feral screams. They scared the couples, yelled at the tourists, waved their sorghum whips over the heads of the people, forced a few young men to dance by whipping them lightly on their legs and smeared soot on the faces of the youngest children, all the while making sure they were being photographed and filmed.

Annelise had told me about it and I had seen it in the clips.

All the same, I was taken by surprise.

The crowd retreated. It undulated, bellowed. A corpulent guy pushed me away from the perimeter of the square, thrusting me against a door.

The *Krampus* were pushing forward, getting themselves into wherever they found space. They were following people, overjoyed at the chaos they were causing.

I lost sight of Werner and Clara, I lost sight of Annelise.

I saw a *Krampus* terrifying a young man of no more than sixteen, who ran off with his girlfriend following, while a second *Krampus*, wearing a mask that made him look like a cross between *The Thing* and Michael Myers with horns, passed so close to me that I caught the goat-like smell of the hides he was wearing and the acrid fumes of the alcohol he had drunk.

This was a detail that both Werner and Annelise had omitted. Before the show, most of the *Krampus* drank their fill in the village bars. According to tradition, buying a drink for a *Krampus* brought good luck.

South Tyrol style, right?

I came out of my hiding-place and went in search of Clara. I was upset by the fact that she'd been really scared. But the crowd was an impenetrable mass of bodies. Many of those present had come from the nearby villages where the feast of the *Krampus* was less spectacular, and Siebenhoch was overflowing with people. I had to make a detour and go down a number of side streets. It was in one of these that a *Krampus* saw me.

He appeared suddenly, against the light. Big ram's horns on his forehead, a wooden mask with dark studs like a ferrous parody of an unkempt beard. He looked gigantic.

The apparition made me jump, but there was nothing to be afraid of. It was just a teenager with an ugly mask. Then the *Krampus* spoke and the affair took quite another turn.

"Hey there, *Amerikaner*."

I recognised the voice.

Thomas Pircher.

"I don't want any trouble, O.K.?" I said, provoking nervous laughter from a group of bystanders.

It was a scene I'd already lived through once, and I didn't feel like repeating it. I stopped.

The *Krampus* advanced.

"You," he said.

"Go fuck yourself," I replied.

I turned, ready to run.

"Where do you think you're going, *Amerikaner*?" said a second *Krampus* who had emerged from nowhere.

"To see my daughter. Let me pass."

"Have you been a good boy, *Amerikaner*, or do we have to take you to hell?"

I've already been to hell, I thought. Not a hell of flames and sulphur, but an ancient, white, frozen hell.

"A very good boy. I haven't yet smashed your face in, right?"

"Right," the voice behind me said.

The sorghum whip caught me full in the face. It wasn't sturdy, but it was flexible and it hurt. It hit me on my nose, which was still tender. I slipped on the fresh snow and fell to the ground, cursing. The *Krampus* bent over me and smeared soot on my face, pressing hard on my nose until it started bleeding again.

"You see what happens to bad boys? You see?"

"Leave him alone!"

It wasn't San Nicolò who saved me. It was the *Krampusmeister*. His presence was enough to persuade the two *Krampus* to slink off, sneering and yelling up at the sky.

The *Krampusmeister* handed me a handkerchief. Still clutching his pipe between his teeth, he was looking at me intently.

"Thanks," I said, as I tried to wipe the mixture of blood and soot from my face.

I didn't want Annelise or Clara to see me so messed up. After all, I'd been the one who'd insisted on going to this damned feast of the devil.

"Are you the *Krampusmeister*?" I asked. "Werner told me you make the costumes."

"*Genau.* I have to preserve the traditions. Drink a little of this." He held out a small bottle.

My head was tilted back to stem the flow of blood, and I made a negative gesture. "No, thanks."

"As you prefer, but it'll do you good. It's on the *Krampusmeister*. That's another one of my duties."

"Tell me, what are the others?"

"Making sure the boys don't cause too much trouble. And if they do, trying to remedy it."

"With clean handkerchiefs and grappa?"

"Cognac."

The blood had stopped flowing, but my nose really hurt. I needed to put ice on it. I made do with a handful of snow.

"Tomorrow it'll be like new. Tell me something."

"Go on."

"Are you planning to lodge a complaint about what happened?"

"No, it has nothing to do with the celebration. There's already a bit of bad blood between me and that guy."

"Excellent choice," the *Krampusmeister* said. "Because, you see, the tradition of the *Krampus* is very important to us. The *Krampus* punish bad people and drive away evil spirits. They take the evil on themselves."

"Then San Nicolò turns up and chases them away."

"Of course, but in any case, after the festival, when people have gone and the priest has taken off his fake beard and his red costume, the young men who have impersonated the *Krampus* are obliged to make confession and get a blessing."

"Best not to play with the devil."

"You say that as if you found it amusing."

"I can't help myself."

"That's why the *Krampus* had it in for you. You like playing with the devil. But even when he laughs, the devil is always extremely serious. I have my personal theory on the subject, it's only natural after so many years spent thinking about him and the best way to present him. Do you want to hear it?"

"I'd love to."

"I think the fact that he can never really laugh is part of the punishment that God thought up for him. The devil is always serious."

I took the handkerchief full of snow from my nose. "It's a paradox.

If I laugh, I'm playing the devil's game, if I don't laugh I *am* the devil. In both cases I've lost."

The *Krampusmeister* nodded slowly. "That's it. Around here, the devil always wins. He always has the last laugh."

We parted company and it wasn't until after I'd rejoined Annelise and Clara that it occurred to me I should have asked him what his name was. I was sure that I'd seen that face before.

And that it was important.

* * *

I had missed the redeeming arrival of San Nicolò. I saw only the *Krampus*, now docile, being taken inside the church – strong halogen lighting emerged through the wide-open door – by altar boys dressed as angels.

San Nicolò was distributing little red paper bags tied with ribbons. Clara was clutching one triumphantly in her hand. She showed it to me.

"Papà, look, San Nicolò gave me this."

"San Nicolò in person?"

"He looks like Santa Claus, but he isn't Santa Claus. He's much cooler."

Indeed, with his white beard and red costume, San Nicolò could have been a leaner version of our dear old Santa Claus. And he didn't go ho-ho-ho.

"In what way is he much cooler?" I asked, more than anything else to delay the moment when I would have to explain the state of my face.

"Because Santa Claus doesn't chase away monsters, does he?"

Unassailable logic.

Annelise took my face in her gloved hands and turned it, first right, then left. "What happened?"

"*Krampus*," I replied. "An epic battle. There were at least thirty of them, maybe even forty. Or a hundred. Yeah, I'd say there were a hundred."

"Papà?"

"Yes, sweetheart?"

"Don't play the clown."

"Who taught you to answer your father back like that?"

"What happened?" It was Werner this time, his eagle eyes narrowing.

"I slipped and fell. A *Krampus* made a fat man jump and in order not to end up under him I slipped to the ground. Then, while he was about it, the *Krampus* painted my face."

I didn't convince Annelise and I certainly didn't convince Werner, but it was enough for now.

I bent over Clara and together we discovered what the saint had given her. Tangerines, peanuts, chocolates and a gingerbread figure in the shape of a *Krampus* that my daughter was quite happy to let me have. Gingerbread wasn't at the top of the list of my favourite sweets, quite the contrary, and perhaps San Nicolò really was cooler than Father Christmas (even though I was certain that my red sled would even up the account), but Jeremiah Salinger wasn't going to let himself be intimidated by a drunk guy, and with horns to boot. I turned the little figure over in my hands, then bit its head off and wolfed it down with gusto.

* * *

It was difficult to get Clara to sleep that evening. It was one of those times when a parent hopes he'll find the *off* button hidden somewhere on the head of his own offspring. The *Krampus*, San Nicolò who "raised his stick all made of gold and said, 'Get out of here, *Krampus*! Leave these good children alone!' And they started stamping their feet and shrieking. Papà, you should have seen how they shrieked! And then San Nicolò pretended he was going to hit them, but it was make-believe, right? And they got down on their knees, then those children arrived with wings and . . ." In other words, enough had happened for her to spend a sleepless night, and us with her.

At about eleven-thirty she started yawning, at midnight she at last surrendered, and within a few minutes I was in the kitchen preparing a midnight snack of matured *speck* and an ice-cold beer.

My nose hurt.

"Are you going to tell me what happened?"

"There were millions of them."

"Oh, shut up."

Still with a piece of *speck* in my mouth, I muttered, "It was that same guy again, that Thomas Pircher."

"He could have broken your nose."

"It wasn't as bad as it looks. A few shoves. That's all."

Annelise touched my cheek where the sorghum whip had scratched me badly. "And these?"

"Grazes."

"It was like a teenage girls' catfight, was it?"

"Look how he ruined my nail polish."

"You idiot. What are you planning to do?"

I crumpled the can and flipped it into the recycling basket. "Nothing at all. I want to finish the present for Clara, buy a tree . . ."

"A plastic one."

I rolled my eyes, I hated plastic Christmas trees, but I realised I was a dinosaur when it came to environmental awareness. ". . . made in China, decorate it as flashily as I can, and spend a lovely Christmas."

"Sure?"

"I love you, Annelise. You know that, don't you?"

"I love you, too. And I bet a *but* is on its way."

"But I hate it when you're such a goody two shoes. The thing about men is . . . We don't talk things over, we just hit each other. It's our way of resolving conflicts."

Annelise folded her arms over her chest. "I didn't mean that."

"In a few months, Mike will have finished. We'll arrange the premiere here, in Ortisei or Bolzano. T.A. says—"

"Who?"

"T.A., Total Asshole. The head of marketing at the network. He says it's an excellent idea. In his e-mail, he used the word 'exciting' twice and 'epic' four times."

"Do you think people will understand?"

"They'll understand," I reassured her, although I was far from convinced myself.

It was possible they wouldn't even bother to see that damned documentary. And to be honest, I wasn't even sure I wanted to see it either. Just the idea of it made me feel like throwing up.

So, to cast it from my mind, I started thinking again about the Bletterbach.

Nine Letters and a Sled

I waited a couple of days. Time enough for my nose to go down a bit. Then, after a rapid search on the internet, taking my courage in both hands and using a trip to the city to buy Christmas decorations as an excuse, I set off for the courthouse in Bolzano.

It was a square building, in pure Fascist style, on the not very imaginatively named Piazza Tribunale. Watched by a bas-relief depicting a Mussolini of cyclopean dimensions making the Roman salute ("Believe! Obey! Fight!" said a caption), I plunged into the arcana of the Italian legal system.

The staff were very kind. I introduced myself and explained what I needed, and they sent me to the third floor, where I waited for the deputy prosecutor on duty to have a few minutes to spare. When he emerged, he apologised for the wait, reproached me for not making an appointment over the phone, and shook my hand energetically.

His name was Andrea Zeller. He was a youthful man, slightly stooped, with fine features and a dark tie. I knew, because I'd read it in the online archives of the local paper while I was waiting for him to arrive, that his almost submissive bureaucratic appearance concealed a shark of the courtroom.

Zeller, too, must have done his research while I was waiting for him, because I didn't need to explain to him who I was. Unlike the inhabitants of Siebenhoch, though, he showed no hostility towards me. On the contrary, when I explained to him that I needed his help for a new project, he proved more than happy to lend a hand.

We made our way to a nearby café, where he secured a discreet table, and once the coffee was served he rubbed his hands, adjusted his glasses and asked me, "What can I do for you, Signor Salinger?"

"I'm working on a documentary about a murder that took place in Alto Adige in 1985, and I'm trying to contact the prosecutor and the Carabinieri captain who carried out the investigation. I think they must both be retired by now. The name of the Carabinieri captain was Alfieri, Flavio Massimo Alfieri, a name fit for an emperor," I joked – he stared back impassively – "and the prosecutor's name was Marco Cattaneo. Maybe you—?"

"I remember Cattaneo well. Unfortunately, he died about ten years ago. As for Captain Alfieri, I don't know anything about him. I can give you the number of the provincial headquarters of the Carabinieri. They may know something. But don't expect too much, they guard the privacy of their own men jealously. What murder are we talking about? In these parts, '85 wasn't a happy time."

"Are you from around here?"

Zeller started playing nervously with a gold-plated cigarette lighter. "I was born in the Oltrisarco district and grew up in Gries, where the Santa Maddalena cellars are. In '85, I'd only just graduated, but I remember very well what it was like in this city. *Ein Tirol* had declared war on Italy, and the tension was tangible. If your documentary's about that, I'm afraid—"

"No, I'm not interested in terrorism. That's not my thing. I'm interested in a murder that took place near Siebenhoch, in the Bletterbach."

The prosecutor made an effort to visualise this. "Unfortunately nothing comes to mind."

"The newspapers didn't talk about it much. They were too concerned with a storm that caused a dozen deaths."

"Now that, I remember. It caused quite a lot of damage. I'm not surprised the crime didn't get much attention. Was anyone ever arrested?"

"Never. As far as I know, the case is still open."

There was a gleam in Zeller's eyes. "Homicide cases are never shelved, at least until the perpetrator is sentenced, but if after, I don't know, thirty years, nobody has been charged, it's possible that the paperwork was transferred to the courthouse records. If you like, I can give you a few telephone numbers that'll save you a bit of time, what do you think?"

I perked up. "That would be very kind."

* * *

The clerk in the records department looked me up and down. "There's nothing here."

"Are you telling me the files have gone missing?" I asked in astonishment.

"No, I'm telling you they're not here."

"Then where might they be?"

"In the relevant police headquarters. Maybe the police are late transferring them to records. They're up to here with paperwork and—"

"Thirty years late? Do you think that's possible?"

That wasn't his problem.

"And anyway," I grunted bad-temperedly, "it wasn't the police who conducted the investigation, but the Carabinieri."

"Then you'll have to ask them," the clerk said, completely unfazed.

I left the records department furious. I'd drawn a blank, and I was late for the decorations. I left my car on Piazza Vittoria, behind the monument, and headed for the feverish bustle of the historic centre of Bolzano, what the locals call I Portici. I bought coloured stars, Father Christmases of various sizes and at least ten kilos of spangles and silver paper. Our home would sparkle.

I shoved everything in the trunk of my car, but before setting off back to Siebenhoch I decided to make one last attempt. I called the Carabinieri headquarters.

At the third ring, a bored voice answered me.

I explained who I was and also mentioned the name of Deputy

Prosecutor Zeller. The voice became less bored and more attentive.

I asked about Captain Alfieri. "Could I speak to him?"

"That would be difficult, Signor Salinger. He's dead."

"I'm sorry."

"A good officer. Now, if you have nothing else to—"

"Actually, there is something else."

"Go on."

The voice showed a touch of nervousness. I tried to be as concise as possible.

"I'm trying to gain access to a file. An old investigation conducted by Captain Alfieri."

"You'll have to ask the records department at the courthouse."

"I've already done that. They say the file isn't there."

"Strange," the voice said. "Very strange."

I had no doubt that, in Carabinieri headquarters, a few butts were about to be kicked.

"Do you want the records number?"

"Yes, please, Signor Salinger."

I dictated it to him.

I heard the man mutter something to himself. Then I heard the unmistakable noise of a keyboard being attacked by hands ill accustomed to navigating it.

At last, an amused exclamation.

"Now I remember, of course. The Bletterbach affair. Mystery solved, Signor Salinger. The file isn't in records."

"Do you have it?"

"That pain in the arse Max Krün has it. In Siebenhoch."

I was stunned. "I beg your pardon?"

"You're from there, aren't you? You told me you're from Siebenhoch."

"I live there."

"Then you must have met him. The head of the Forest Rangers."

"Yes, I know him. But I don't understand why the file is in his hands."

"Because Krün is a big son of a bitch," the carabiniere explained jovially at the other end of the line. "As stubborn as a mule. That business in '85 . . ."

"Were you there?"

"No, in '85 I was having an easy life in Pozzuoli, I was thinking of becoming a mechanic, and girls would smile at me, Signor Salinger. Don't make me any older than I am. But the way Krün managed to piss everyone off around here is the stuff of legend. That's why I remembered. What a character, that Krün!"

"I'm curious. Could you explain?"

"Technically, the investigation was entrusted to us, do you follow me?"

"Yes."

"So for a few years the file stayed here, in Bolzano. Then the case was forgotten about and the paperwork went into records. But, being an investigation for homicide, it wasn't really shelved. It was in a kind of bureaucratic limbo. That happens constantly. Are you still on the line? Try to follow me, because this is where it gets good. Krün doesn't like the way things have gone, so he starts looking through the laws and bylaws. What you need to understand is that in Siebenhoch Max Krün serves as an interim police officer. Now, according to a law dug up by Krün, a code that comes straight from the Albertine Statute and has never been repealed, the public official performing the function of police officer can request the documentation regarding any crime committed in his territory and keep hold of it for as long as he wants, which in this specific case means until the paper rots away."

He laughed so loudly, he almost burst my eardrum.

"Are you telling me," I said, once that weird laugh was over, "that the file is in the Forest Rangers' barracks in Siebenhoch?"

"Precisely, Signor Salinger," the voice on the telephone confirmed, turning serious. "May I add something in confidence? I wouldn't like you to have misunderstood my tone."

"Please."

"We haven't been telling the story of Krün to all the new recruits for the last twenty years to make fun of him. We've been doing so because for us the man is an example. We admire him."

"I don't understand."

"The people who were killed were his friends," the man said. "What would you have done in his place?"

* * *

Each of them had been looking for a way out from the Bletterbach. The members of the rescue team. Werner, Max, Günther and Hannes. And where had they ended up?

Günther had dug his own grave by trying to drown the story in alcohol. Hannes had gone out of his mind. Werner had run away from Siebenhoch. And Max? What was it Werner had said about Max?

Max had turned his uniform into the armour of the defender of Siebenhoch. He had clung to his role in order not to succumb. Now I had proof of that.

Nine letters: "obsession".

* * *

On the morning of Christmas Eve, before the sun had even emerged from behind the mountains, Werner found me round the back of Welshboden. The sled was finished; the paint dry.

"Looks like you have a talent for this kind of work."

I jumped. "I hope I didn't wake you," I apologised.

Werner shook his head, then looked at the sled again. "I'm sure Clara will love it."

I wasn't so sure. All I could see were the defects. "I hope so," I muttered.

"I'm convinced of it."

"What if it doesn't work? I'm afraid I put on the runners too quickly and . . ."

"Even if it was the slowest sled in the world and fell to pieces at the first test drive, you made it. With your own hands. That's what Clara will remember one day."

"You think so?"

"She'll grow up, Jeremiah. She'll grow up quickly and you won't be able to protect her anymore. I know, I've been through that myself. But you know what a father can do?"

I didn't want to reply. I felt a knot in my throat. So I waited for him to continue.

"A father can give only two things to his daughter: self-respect and good memories. When Clara is a woman, a mother, what will she remember of this Christmas? That the sled was slower than a tortoise or that you made it with your own hands?"

I smiled, grateful for those words.

I noticed that his eyes had grown a little moist.

There were too many memories in the air that morning.

"Anyway, there's only one way to find out," he said, dismissing his embarrassment and sadness. "We have to try it out."

I thought he was joking.

But that wasn't Werner's style.

If anyone had seen us, two stout adults taking it in turns to slide down the snow-covered meadows of Welshboden, as excited as little boys and cursing like dock workers every time they ended up with their muzzles in the snow, I think they would have taken us for lunatics. Actually, we were really enjoying ourselves.

By the time the sun peered out, we were breathless but smiling.

"I think it works, don't you?"

"I think I owe you a thank-you, Werner."

* * *

It was Clara who handed out the presents immediately after dinner: a task that she seemed to enjoy as much as unwrapping them.

The house in Siebenhoch filled with exclamations of surprise and joy. It was as if Werner had never wanted anything more than that pink spotted tie ("That way you can have a bit of colour on you, *Nonno* Werner, pink suits you"), Annelise hugged the sweater with the reindeer as if it were an old friend ("Her name is Robertina, Mamma, she likes geraniums"), and as for me, I had never seen anything more beautiful than that pair of gloves, so colourful it hurt to look at them.

As well as the gloves, I received the latest novel by my favourite writer (from Annelise), a toolbox (from Werner) and a photograph of Kiss' road crew with the words "Get better soon, friend!" (from Mike) – which made my eyes a little moist.

"Do you like your gloves, Papà?"

"Each finger has a different face! They're wonderful, sweetheart!" I put them on and strutted about. "Simply wonderful!"

"How many letters are there in the word 'wonderful', Papà?"

"As many as the kisses you deserve, sweetheart."

And although she pretended to object, I whirled her round in the air.

Good memories, right?

When things had calmed down, I spoke up. "I think your present is somewhere here, honeybun. But I'm not sure where . . . "

Clara, who had just finished unwrapping Werner's present (a pop-up book) and the one that Mike had sent her by post from New York (a Kiss T-shirt with the word "Clara" on the back), she turned her head to me, her little eyes looking like two stars.

"'Somewhere', four letters?"

I ruffled my hair, trying to seem confused. "*Papà*'s old. *Papà*'s losing his memory."

"Four letters is lying."

"Maybe," I said. "But something tells me you should put on your jacket and gloves."

In a moment, her jacket half buttoned up and her scarf dangling, Clara was at the door. Before flinging it wide open, she turned to Annelise. "Can I?"

"It's not a pony, sweetheart."

"I don't want a pony, Mamma. Can I go outside?"

"Last year you wanted a pony."

Clara stamped her feet impatiently on the floor. "Last year I was little, Mamma. I know ponies can't be kept indoors. Can I go outside now?"

Annelise barely had time to nod before a gust of wind covered us in tiny snowflakes.

"Papà!"

I smiled. Annelise kissed my cheek.

We went out to admire my masterpiece.

"But it's beautiful! It's all red."

"Bright red, sweetheart, you don't want it to get offended. Bright Red Sled, let me introduce Clara. Clara, let me introduce . . . "

I didn't finish the sentence. Clara had sat down astride her new gift.

"Will you help me, Papà?"

How could I resist that delightful little face? For the remaining two hours, but maybe it was more, all I did was drag Clara up and down the meadow in front of the house, feebly illumined by the moon, until it resembled a battlefield.

Then I threw myself on the ground, defeated.

"Papà's old," I panted. "Clara's sleepy. Tomorrow we'll go to Welshboden and I'll show you how to sled downhill. It's more fun there. And maybe I'll manage to avoid any muscle strain."

"Clara isn't sleepy," she protested. "Papà isn't old. Well, maybe a little bit old."

Annelise took her by the hand. "It's time to go to bed. You can play with your new sled tomorrow." She gave me a glance that meant that it was time for Salinger to unwrap his Christmas present, too. The kind of present forbidden to minors, the kind I liked a lot. "Provided your father is still in one piece tomorrow morning."

I admit it.

I shouldn't have known. It isn't good to know what your presents are before Christmas Eve, I'm aware of that. Nor is it good to go around the house rummaging in drawers like a truffle hound.

No, it's not done.

But curiosity is a nine-letter word that fits me like a glove. Besides, in my defence, I have to add that Annelise hadn't been at all careful in her choice of hiding-place. It had taken me less than half an hour to find it. And I have to say that the words "Victoria's Secret" had whetted my appetite.

* * *

And anyway Victoria's Secret slid away in the twinkling of an eye. A really bad girl, that Victoria, really bad.

Most Things Change

I started thinking again about the Bletterbach around December 28. I read through my notes and once again began pondering over what I had discovered at the courthouse in Bolzano.

On the evening of the 30th I made my move.

* * *

The woman who opened the door was tiny, with dark bobbed hair and big luminous eyes.

"Verena?" I said.

She immediately had me pegged. "You're the film director everyone's talking about, aren't you? Werner's son-in-law."

"Salinger. Not director, screenwriter." I showed her the bottle of Blauburgunder I had bought for the occasion. "May I come in?"

The wind was strong enough to freeze your bones, but it was only now that Verena seemed to realise. She apologised, stood aside to let me in and closed the door behind me.

"I imagine you're looking for Max."

"Isn't he here?"

"He has a meeting in Bolzano. You're out of luck, but take a seat anyway. Would you like a drink?"

"Yes, please."

I hung up my jacket, scarf and hat and followed her into the kitchen. Verena seated me at a table on which stood a hamper crammed with goodies. Fruit, jars of sauce, pickles, jam. All home-made.

"They look delicious."

"The people of Siebenhoch," she explained. "Either they want to say thank you, or they want to apologise. It's fifty-fifty."

I laughed with her. "Werner has also had his fill of Christmas hampers. And I'm at risk of indigestion."

"A pity," the woman said. "I thought I could offload some of ours onto you."

We both laughed.

The tea was scalding hot and I had to blow on it. Verena had made herself a cup, too. I tried to imagine her in '85, which wasn't difficult. She couldn't have been so different from the woman I saw now. Chief Krün's wife looked not much more than thirty, even though she must have been pushing fifty.

"Is that bottle a thank-you or an apology?"

"Both, to tell the truth. I wanted to thank Max for not fining me and—"

Verena interrupted me, raising her eyes to heaven. "So he did his favourite number on you, too."

"What number?"

Verena imitated her husband's severe expression (his bad cop look). "Hey, stranger, make sure you don't stick your fingers in your nose, around here we hate people who stick their fingers in their nose, we hang them in front of the town hall and then we practise clay pigeon shooting with their heads . . ."

The tea went down the wrong way.

". . . using a nail gun," she finished, winking at me.

"Yes, that number. Except in my case it was for speeding."

"So half the bottle is a thank-you, and the other half?" she asked.

I hadn't forgotten that Werner had his eye on me. But nor did I want to miss the opportunity to ask a few questions. So I said, half seriously and half facetiously, "We're friends, right?"

"We've been friends for more than ten minutes."

"Where I come from that's time enough to build empires."

"Then let's say we're friends. So spit it out."

I sipped at my tea. "I'd like to ask Max about the Bletterbach."

Verena's smile turned sour, and a deep furrow appeared in the space between her eyebrows. This all happened in a second, then her face relaxed again.

"Didn't they give you enough brochures at the Visitors' Centre?"

"They were wonderful," I replied cautiously, "but I wanted to know something more specific about the killings in '85. Simple curiosity," I added after a pause.

"Simple curiosity," she repeated, playing with her teacup. "Simple curiosity about one of the nastiest things that ever happened in Siebenhoch, Salinger?"

"It's second nature to me," I said, trying to give the words a light tone.

"Reopening old wounds? Is that also second nature to you?"

"I don't want to seem—"

"You don't seem, you are," she interrupted. "Now take your bottle and get out."

"But why?" I said, surprised by such vehemence.

"Because I haven't been able to celebrate my birthday since 1985 – is that a good enough reason for you?"

"I don't . . ."

April 28. The birthday party.

Everything was clear to me now. I turned red.

I took a deep breath. "Maybe Max doesn't agree with you. Maybe he'd like to tell me the—"

I stopped.

Hatred and pain. That was what I read on her features.

A huge amount of pain.

"It's not up for discussion."

"Why?"

Verena clenched her fists. "Because . . ." she replied in a low voice, wiping away a tear. “Please, Salinger. Don’t talk to him about it. I don’t want him to suffer.”

“Then why don’t *you* talk to me about it?”

Judging by the emotions crowding onto her face, a bloody and hard-fought battle was being waged in Verena’s mind.

I waited in silence for the outcome of the conflict.

“Promise you won’t tell him afterwards?”

“I promise.”

L for liar.

B for bastard.

S for smile.

“You can be sure of it.”

“This isn’t for a film, right?”

“No, it’s a kind of hobby.”

It was an unfortunate choice of words, I admit. But if I’d told her the truth, she would have kicked me out. Not to mention that, by this point, I no longer knew what the truth was.

Was it simple curiosity that was leading me to ask all these questions? Or had the story of the Bletterbach become an obsession for me, too?

“What do you want to know?”

“Everything you know,” I replied avidly.

“What I know is that I hate that place. I haven’t set foot there since ’85.”

“Why?”

“Do you love your wife, Salinger?”

“Yes.”

“What would you feel towards a place where your wife lost a part of herself?”

“Hatred.”

“There you are. I hate the Bletterbach. And I hate the work my husband does. I hate that uniform. I hate it when he goes in search of poachers, I hate it when he does his number on the new arrivals”

– she looked around – "and I hate these damned hampers." She passed her hand under her nose and recovered her breath. "Max is a good person. The best. But that business has marked him, and I'd so much like to get away from here. Let the Forest Rangers, Siebenhoch and this house go to hell. But it's impossible. It's like a scar" – she pointed to the half-moon around my eye – "except that Max's scar is here." She placed a hand over her heart. "You can leave a place, but a scar you carry with you forever. It's part of you."

"I can understand that."

"No," Verena replied, "you can't."

But I could. The Beast was my witness.

"It must have been hard," I said.

"Hard?" Verena snorted. "Hard, you say? I had to build him back up piece by piece. There were days when I wanted to leave him. To get away from here, to drop everything. To give up."

"But you didn't."

"Would you have abandoned your wife?"

"I would have stayed."

"At first he didn't want to talk about it. I begged him to see a psychologist, but he always replied the same way. He didn't need a doctor, he just needed a bit of time. Time, he'd say," she whispered, shaking her head, "it was only a matter of time."

"They say it's the best medicine."

"Until it kills you," was Verena's bitter reply. "And the story of the Bletterbach killings is a curse. Do you know about the others? Hannes killed Helene, Werner left without saying goodbye to anybody. He packed his bags and disappeared. And even before he left, there were more days when you didn't see him around than days when you could say hello to him. He'd become another person. He was grumpy, hardly said a word. It was obvious he couldn't stand being here anymore. Then there was Günther."

Verena passed her hands over her arms, almost as if a shudder had run through her.

"It almost scared me, seeing him and Max sitting talking. They'd sit here for hours and hours, right here, talking and talking, with the door closed. They didn't drink, thank God for that, but when Günther left, Max had a strange light in his eyes . . . " Verena searched for the words. "They were the eyes of a corpse, Salinger. Would you like your wife to have the eyes of a corpse?"

There was only one reply to that question. "No."

"Then the visits grew few and far between. Günther had a girlfriend, someone local, Brigitte, and they started to get serious. He spent less time with Max, and I was happy that he was out of our way. Without Günther around, Max seemed to be better. But every year, towards the end of April . . ."

Verena started fiddling with her wedding ring.

"When it happened the first time, in '86, I was nineteen. When you're nineteen, death is something that happens to your grandparents or to mountaineers who slip and fall. I even thought that a party might do him good. You know, distract him."

"You were wrong?"

"It was the first and only time I've seen him in a rage. No," she corrected herself, "'rage' doesn't do it justice. I got scared and wondered if it was worth fighting for a person who seemed out of his mind. Did I really want to spend the rest of my days with a madman? But then I realised that it wasn't anger he was feeling, it was grief. Evi, Kurt and Markus were his only friends and he'd found them torn to pieces. I forgave him, but I never again celebrated my birthday. Not with Max. The following year, the day before my birthday, he loaded the car and went off to his family's old *maso*, to get plastered and wait for it to pass. Since then it's become a habit, even a ritual. It's a good compromise, and at least Max hasn't ended up like Günther and Hannes."

"Werner also saved himself."

Verena made a face. "Werner's older than Max, and he's a different kind of person. As head of the rescue team, he'd seen all sorts. Max at the time was little more than a boy, although to me, innocent as I was, he seemed like a grown-up. Plus, Max had the telegram to keep the wound open."

Seeing the bewildered look on my face, she laughed.

"You don't know about that, do you?"

"A telegram?"

"Do you want to see it?"

"Of course."

Verena left the kitchen and came back with a photograph: Kurt, Max, Markus and Evi with the wind in their hair. She took it out of its frame, and a yellowed telegram slipped out with it. Verena put the telegram on the table and smoothed it with her hands.

"This is the reason Max can't resign himself."

"What does it say?"

Verena showed it to me.

Geht nicht dorthin!

"Don't go down there," I murmured.

The date at the bottom was April 28, 1985.

"Who sent it?"

Verena sighed, as if she'd heard that question many times before. She turned the telegram over. "Oscar Grünwald. He was a colleague of Evi's, a scientist."

"And how . . . ?"

"One of the first duties that Chief Hubner was only too happy to hand over to Max was going to get the telegrams and the urgent mail down there in Aldino. Siebenhoch was too small to have its own post office, and the postman was an old man who had to go back and forth on a pre-war moped. Max hated having to do it: he said it wasn't suited to his role." Her expression became distant. "The uniform meant a lot to him. And he was right. It gave him a lot . . . " She dismissed the thought with a gesture of her hand. "It was a kind of informal agreement between Chief Hubner and the postal service. Whenever something important arrived, a member of the Forest Rangers would go down to Aldino to collect it and then deliver it."

"Isn't that illegal?"

Verena snorted. "People trusted Chief Hubner, and Max too, for that matter, so what was the problem?"

"No problem," I replied, while all my concentration was focused on that rectangle of paper.

Don't go down there!

"That morning, Max went down to Aldino to fetch the mail. Evi had already left for the Bletterbach, and Max slipped the telegram into his pocket and almost immediately forgot about it. That day was a real mess, even before the killings. Max had a lot on his plate."

"Such as?"

"It was raining, and there were a couple of landslides. Max had to check them out. He was on his own, Chief Hubner had had a heart attack and was in the San Maurizio hospital in Bolzano. Then, towards evening, there was that truck that overturned and Max had his work cut out. It was a nasty accident and Max was afraid he wouldn't get to my birthday party in time. He managed, though, because when he promises something, you can be sure he'll do everything he can to keep his word."

"What about the telegram?"

"I found it in his jacket pocket when he got back from the Bletterbach. If I'd known what the consequences would be, I'd have burned it. Instead, I showed it to him and Max made a face I'll never forget. It was as if I'd stabbed him in the heart. He looked at me and said only, 'I could have.' Nothing else, but it was clear what he meant. He could have saved them. That was how his obsession began."

"That doesn't make any sense."

"I know that, and you know that. But Max? In that situation? After he'd seen the bodies of the only friends he had here in Siebenhoch cut to pieces like that? I told you, he changed. He started pissing off the Carabinieri, bombarding them with phone calls night and day. He even came to blows with that captain . . . "

"Alfieri."

"Who never lodged a complaint, but there you are. Max kept saying that nobody was doing anything to find the person who'd killed his friends. It wasn't true, but if you told him that he'd lose his temper. When he realised that the investigation had come to a standstill and would soon be shelved, he started investigating by himself. He's never stopped since."

"I heard that the case file is in the barracks in Siebenhoch."

"No. Max has it, in his grandparents' house. The old Krün family home, where he grew up. He has everything there."

By now the tea was cold. I drank it anyway, because I felt the need to smoke and that seemed like the one way to get rid of the craving. It didn't work.

"Have you ever asked him about this Oscar Grünwald?"

"He's never wanted to let me see his records, those he keeps locked up in the family home, but I'm convinced that Max has a file on every single inhabitant of Siebenhoch."

I shuddered.

"It's the only way he has of keeping going," Verena said. "Keeping the anger alive. Max is an orphan. His parents died in a car accident when he was just a few months old. He grew up with his grandmother. Frau Krün. A hard woman. She was nearly a hundred when she died. Her husband was killed in the mine collapse in '23, and from that day on Frau Krün never wore any other colour apart from black. With the death of her husband, she'd lost everything, there was no insurance at the time. They were very poor, maybe the poorest people in the whole area. Max was a shy, gentle child. He was very good at school, but Frau Krün wouldn't have accepted anything other than the best marks anyway. The only friends Max had were Kurt, Markus and Evi. With them, Max didn't have to be the toy soldier Frau Krün was trying to bring up, he could let himself go. Their deaths condemned him to solitude."

"Thirty years of anger. Isn't that self-destructive?"

"That's why I'm here, isn't it?"

We fell silent, lost in thought.

"What about you?" I asked.

"What about me?"

"What's your idea about what happened?"

Verena toyed with the photograph, drawing small circles with her fingers around the face of a beardless, carefree Max. "You're going to think me just a superstitious mountain woman, but I'm not. I trained as a nurse, and I consider myself a good one. Conscientious, well-prepared. As many people here in the village can testify. I like reading, I was the one who insisted with the local council on getting broadband installed in Siebenhoch. I don't believe in fairy stories, in monsters under the bed, or that the earth is flat. But I'm certain that the Bletterbach is a cursed place, just as I'm certain that smoking is bad for your health. There have been too many deaths down there. Shepherds who vanished into thin air. Woodcutters who've told stories about strange lights and even stranger footprints. Legends, myths, will-o'-the-wisps. Look at it however you want, but behind even the most absurd legend there's a small element of truth."

I thought about the people of Fanes.

"I bet," Verena continued, "that after hearing all the nasty things said about you, it won't be hard for you to believe me if I tell you that in the past there were a good few summary trials in this area. Witches above all, but no burnings. Siebenhoch had its own system of administering justice. Those poor women were taken and left alone in the Bletterbach. None of them ever returned. There are tons of rumours about that place. And not even one that the people in the Visitors' Centre would like."

"Horror attracts," I said.

"Not that kind of horror. Have you been there?"

"I took my daughter."

"And did you like it?"

"Clara enjoyed it a lot."

"I asked you."

I thought about it for a few moments. "No, I didn't enjoy it. And I know it's crazy to say this, everything in the world is old, but you feel the weight of time down there."

Verena nodded. "The weight of time, yes. The Bletterbach is one huge graveyard. All those fossils, they're bones. Corpses. Corpses of creatures that . . . I'm not a fundamentalist, Salinger. And I'm not a bigot either. I know that Darwin was right. Species evolve, and if they don't evolve when their habitat changes they become extinct. But I believe in God. Not a God with a white beard sitting up there in the sky, that's a vision I find reductive, but I believe in God and in his way of running the machine that we call the universe."

"Intelligent design."

"Yes. And I believe there must have been a reason why God decided to wipe out all those creatures."

The kitchen seemed to have become darker and narrower. I felt a stab of claustrophobia.

Verena looked at the clock over the sink and her eyes opened wide.

"It's late, Salinger, you have to go. I don't want Max to find you here."

"Thanks for the story."

"Don't thank me."

"Then I hope the bottle is worth the price I paid for it."

Verena seemed relieved by my joke. The interrogation was over. "I'll let you know."

We stood up.

"Salinger?"

"No, I won't tell Max."

Verena seemed calmer. Not too much, but enough for that furrow between her eyebrows to have disappeared.

She shook my hand. "He's a good man. Don't hurt him."

I was looking for the best way to take my leave when we heard the door open, followed by Max's weary footsteps.

"Salinger?" he said, surprised to see me. "To what do we owe this visit?"

Verena showed him the bottle of Blauburgunder. "He said something about avoiding a fine, Mr Sheriff."

Max laughed. "You shouldn't have."

"I'm almost one of the locals now," I joked. "Anyway, it's late, I was hoping to have a drink in company, but Annelise will be getting worried."

Max looked at his wristwatch. "It's not so late. It'd be a pity if you went home thirsty." With long strides, he walked through the living room. "I'll get the corkscrew and . . ."

He didn't finish the sentence. He stood frozen in the doorway of the kitchen. I saw Verena take a step towards him, then stop and raise her hand to her mouth.

Max turned and hissed icily, "What's *this* all about?"

He was pointing to the photograph and the telegram on the table.

"I was careless, Max, I knocked over the frame and—"

"Bullshit," Max said. His eyes were pinned on mine. "A heap of bull-shit."

"It's my fault, Max," I said.

"Who else's would it be?"

"I wanted to have a chat with you. That's why I came."

"But you weren't here," Verena cut in, almost falling over her words, "and I thought it would be best if I talked to him."

"It's my fault, Max," I repeated emphatically. "Verena had no intention of—"

Max took a threatening step towards me. "Of doing what?"

"Telling me the story."

Max was shaking. "And does Verena know why you're so interested in that story?"

"What do you mean?"

He gave a contemptuous laugh. "That you want to make a pile of money."

I stood rooted to the spot.

"Did this son of a bitch tell you," Max said, addressing his wife, "that he wants to make money with a film about the Bletterbach killings? Take a seat, Mr Director. Take our corpses and show them off to half the people in the world. You can even spit on their graves. Isn't that how you earn a living, Salinger?"

"What the newspapers have published is a lie. I'll demonstrate that as soon as the documentary on the Ortles is finished. And I can assure you I have no intention of making any kind of film about the story of Kurt, Evi and Markus."

Max took a second step towards me. "Don't even dare speak their names."

"It's best if I go, Max. I'm sorry I bothered you. And thanks for the tea, Verena."

I didn't have time to turn to the door before Max grabbed me by the neck and shoved me against the wall. A wooden crucifix fell to the ground and broke.

Verena let out a scream.

"Show your face here again," Max snarled, "and I'll see you end up in a whole heap of trouble. And if you have any common sense, you dickhead, make sure you get out of here. We don't need vultures like you in Siebenhoch."

I grabbed his two hands and tried to break free. His grip was strong, and all I could do was gain enough oxygen to say, "I'm not a vulture, Max."

"I assume that's how things work in Hollywood, that you're used to this kind of mean trick. But here in Siebenhoch, we have something called morality."

He let go of me.

I gasped for breath.

Max hit me. A hard, accurate right to my cheekbone. There was an explosion of lights and I crumpled to the floor. When I looked up, Max was towering over me.

"Take that as a first instalment. And now clear off, if you don't want more."

Aching, I grabbed my jacket and left.

* * *

Fortunately, Clara was asleep.

I tried to make as little noise as possible as I entered the house. I took off my shoes, cap and winter jacket. The house was shrouded in darkness, but I didn't need to switch on the light to find my way.

I managed to slip into the bathroom and rinsed my face. One side of it was the colour of an aubergine.

"Salinger . . ."

I felt my stomach heave.

Annelise's hair was ruffled and her expression alarmed. Even without make-up, I thought she looked beautiful. She took my face in her hands and examined the bruise.

"Who did this to you?"

"It's nothing, don't worry."

"Who was it? That guy from Lily's?"

"It's not as bad as it looks," I said, giving a couple of stupid grins in an attempt to calm her down.

The pain was making my eyes water.

"This time he won't get away with it. I'm calling the Carabinieri."

I stopped her. "Let it go, please."

"What's going on, Salinger?"

She wasn't angry. She was scared.

"It was Max."

"Chief Krün?" Annelise seemed shocked. "Was he drunk?"

"He wasn't drunk, and in a way I deserved it."

Annelise pulled away from me.

I'm convinced that part of her had already guessed what I was up to. The hours shut up in my study in front of the computer. The sudden excursions. They were all clues her brain couldn't have helped but register. Except that she didn't want to admit it. At this point, though, she had to have understood.

"What are you working on?"

Her voice was flat and monotonous. I would have preferred it if she'd screamed.

"Nothing."

Annelise put her index finger on the bruise and pressed. "Does it hurt?"

"Fuck, yes."

"Your lies hurt even more. I want the truth. Now. Immediately. And at least try to be convincing."

"Can we go in the kitchen? I need a drink."

Annelise turned and disappeared without a word into the shadowy corridor. I followed her. First, though, I peered into Clara's bedroom. She was sleeping curled up on her side. I adjusted the blankets. Then I went down to the kitchen.

Annelise already had a beer ready for me on the table.

"Talk."

"First of all, I want you to know it isn't work."

"It isn't?"

"No. It's a way to keep my brain active."

"Getting yourself beaten up by half the village?"

"That's collateral damage."

"Am I also collateral damage?"

I noticed that her voice was shaking. I tried to take her hands in mine. I barely managed to touch them. They were icy. Annelise pulled them away and laid them in her lap.

I started to tell her everything, somehow avoiding the word "obsession".

"It isn't work," I finished. "I need it to . . ."

"To?"

"Because otherwise I think I'd go mad." I bowed my head. "I should have told you earlier."

"Is that what you think? That you should have told me earlier?"

"I—"

"You promised. A sabbatical year. One year. Instead of which, what? How long did you last? A month?"

I didn't say anything. She was right.

L for liar.

"God, you're like a child. You throw yourself into things without a thought for the consequences. You can't even—"

"Annelise—"

"Don't say a word. You promised. You lied. And what will you tell Clara tomorrow morning? That you bumped into somebody's fist?"

"I'll make up a funny story."

"That's what you always do, isn't it? Make up stories. I should leave, Salinger. Take Clara and leave. You're dangerous."

These words came as a shock.

I felt my guts contract. The pain had disappeared.

"You can't be serious, Annelise."

"I am."

"I made a mistake, I know. I lied to everyone. To you, to Werner. To everyone. But I don't deserve this."

"You deserve far worse."

I tried to articulate a defence, but Annelise was right. I'd demonstrated that I was a terrible husband and an even worse father.

"You're sick, Salinger." Annelise's tone had changed. There was a hint of tears in her voice. "You need those drugs. I know you're not taking them."

"The drugs have nothing to do with it, I just wanted—"

"To prove to yourself that you're still you? That you haven't changed? You nearly died on that glacier. If you think that hasn't changed you, then you really are an idiot."

I closed my mouth abruptly. My palate felt dry, my tongue reduced to a leather flap.

Get out.

"It's pointless pretending it isn't so. You've changed. I've changed. Even Clara has changed. It's only natural. There are some experiences you don't emerge from unscathed."

"No, you don't emerge unscathed."

"Do you think I haven't noticed? I see you. I know you. I see that look."

"What look?"

"The look of an animal in a cage."

"I'm almost out of it."

Annelise shook her head bitterly. "Do you really think that, Salinger? I want you to look me in the eyes. I want the truth. But if what comes out of your mouth isn't the truth, and nothing but the truth, I'll call my father, take Clara and spend the night at Welshboden."

"It's just that . . ."

I didn't finish the sentence. It suddenly happened. Something broke inside me.

I burst into floods of tears.

"The Beast, Annelise. The Beast is always here, with me. Sometimes it's quiet, sometimes it shuts up, there are good days, days when I don't think about it even for a second. But it's always inside me. And it hisses, it hisses, its voice, I can't, its . . ."

Annelise hugged me. I felt her warm body press against mine. I sank into that warmth.

"I'm always afraid, Annelise. Always."

The woman I loved cradled me as I'd so often seen her cradle Clara. Gradually, the tears abated. Only the sobbing remained.

Then not even that.

Annelise gently pushed me away. "Why didn't you tell me?"

"Because I don't want to take those damned drugs."

Annelise stiffened. "You need them."

Now even I realised that. "Yes. You're right."

Annelise heaved a deep sigh. "Promise."

I nodded. "Whatever you want."

"The sabbatical year. It starts now."

"Yes."

"You'll forget about the Bletterbach killings."

"Yes."

"And you'll start taking the drugs."

"Yes."

She looked me in the eyes. "Will you do that?"

"Yes," I lied.

The King of the Elves

On December 31, I went into Clara's room and woke her. Frowning, she looked at me with eyes full of sleep.

"Papà?"

"Wake up, lazybones, we have to go."

"Where?"

"To the castle of the King of the Elves," I replied radiantly.

Clara's little eyes sparkled with curiosity. She sat up in bed. "Where does the King of the Elves live?"

"On a distant mountain. A very beautiful mountain."

"Are you really taking me to see the King of the Elves?"

"Cross my heart, sweetheart," I replied, winking. "How many letters in 'heart'?"

"Five."

Clara leapt out of bed and ran to the kitchen, where Annelise had already prepared a little snack. In less than half an hour, we were ready.

I'd organised everything with the complicity of Werner and a couple of people I'd met during the filming of "Mountain Angels". It was a gift. Not for Clara. It was a gift for Annelise. I wanted her to start trusting me again. I wanted her to look at me again the way she'd looked at me before September 15.

That's why, when we got in the car, I was as excited as Clara. I started the engine and very soon turned onto the main road.

Apart from a few trucks and a couple of cars, we had the road all to ourselves. I switched on the stereo and started singing Kiss' greatest hits at the top of my voice.

Clara put her fingers in her ears, while Annelise followed my performance with a mixture of doubt and amusement.

It was supposed to be a surprise, and I'd kept her in the dark as to what I had in store for our South Tyrolean New Year, but without being so secretive as to make her suspicious about what I was doing.

No Bletterbach, in other words.

I don't know how much she trusted me, but there she was, with me, and that was enough to fill me with energy and hope. The year that was about to start, 2014, had to be a turning point.

A year of healing.

"Will it be cold?"

"Quite cold."

"Clara will get sick."

"Clara won't get sick."

"Then you'll be the one to catch flu."

"Don't jinx it."

"Are you sure you don't want to tell me where we're going?"

I didn't reply.

I hadn't made all that effort just to ruin the surprise at the last moment. So, lips sealed. Above all, I made no reference as to how we would get to the castle of the King of the Elves. Annelise would have refused, I knew. Presenting her with a fait accompli was a dirty trick, but it was for a good cause.

I turned up the volume on the car radio and started squawking my way through "Rock and Roll All Nite".

We got to Ortisei, the first stop on our journey. The village was wrapped in a blanket of snow, but was buzzing with activity.

I left the car in the centre and devoured an enormous breakfast. Clara put away a slice of pie that seemed as big as she was. Once we'd eaten our fill, I looked at my watch.

"We're late for our special coach."

Annelise looked around. "I thought this was the surprise."

"Ortisei?"

"Was I wrong?"

"It isn't cold enough."

"It seems perfectly cold to me, Daddy Bear."

I took in a lungful of air. "For Daddy Bear, this isn't cold. This is warm."

"The thermometer says minus seven."

"Tropical heat."

"Papà, if we arrive late, will the special coach turn into a pumpkin?"

"We'd best hurry up. You never know. But Mamma has to promise something, otherwise no special coach."

"What does Mummy Bear have to promise?" Annelise asked, dubiously.

"She has to keep her eyes closed."

"For how long?"

"For as long as Daddy Bear says."

"But—"

"Mamma! Do you want the special coach to turn into a pumpkin? I want to see the castle of the King of the Elves!"

Clara's intervention was crucial. We set off again and less than fifteen minutes later reached our destination.

"Can I?"

"Not yet, Mummy Bear."

"What's that smell?"

"Don't think about it."

"It's like kerosene."

"Mountain air, darling. Concentrate on that."

I helped her out of the car and walked with her arm in arm to just in front of the hangar.

"Mummy Bear can open her eyes now."

Annelise obeyed. Her reaction was exactly as I'd expected.

She folded her arms and said, "Forget it."

"It'll be fun."

"I said, forget it."

"To fly is humanity's dream. Icarus. Leonardo da Vinci. Neil Armstrong. A small step for a man . . ."

"Icarus came to a bad end, genius. If you really think I'm getting into that thing, dear Jeremiah Salinger, you don't know me at all."

"But why?"

"Because it won't stay up. It doesn't have wings."

I knew her. Oh, yes, I knew her. That's why instead of coming back at her, I took Clara in my arms and walked over to the helicopter.

"It's a B3," I said to her, "it's a kind of flying mule."

"Does it eat straw?"

"Straw and kerosene."

"Is it the kerosene that makes that stink?"

"Don't say that too loud or the B3 will be offended."

"I'm sorry, Mr Flying Mule."

"I think he's forgiven you."

"How do you know that?"

"Papà," I said gravely, "always knows everything."

I wondered how much longer a sentence like that would be able to put an end to arguments.

"Are we going to use the flying mule to go to the castle of the King of the Elves?"

"Of course. You see that man there?" I said, pointing to the pilot of the B3, who was coming towards us. "He's going to drive the flying mule for us."

Very excited, Clara started clapping her hands. "Can I ask him how he's going to stay up?"

"I'll do my best," the pilot replied. "How would you like to sit next to me? That way you can help me drive."

Clara sat down in the cockpit of the helicopter without even answering.

I turned to Annelise. "Darling?"

"You're a bastard," she said.

The flight lasted less than a quarter of an hour. There was no wind at that altitude and no clouds to obstruct our view. From up there, the landscape was worthy of Clara's little screams. Even Annelise, once accustomed to the noise of the turbines, had to admit that it was enchanting. As for me, I was too engrossed in enjoying my daughter's expressions of wonder to think about the Beast.

Or all the gorges hollowed by streams down there.

We landed in a swirl of snow and ice. We unloaded the backpacks, I said goodbye to the pilot, and the helicopter set off again, leaving us alone. At an altitude of 3,000 metres.

"Is this the castle of the King of the Elves?"

The Vittorio Benedetto refuge on the Sasso Nero was a slice of history made up of bricks, stone and lime. It was built by the pioneers of Alpine mountaineering and bore the marks of time. Those walls had saved God knows how many thousands of lives in the course of their 120-year history. Soon, they would be knocked down because the melting of the permafrost had undermined the foundations. It was sad to think that this place would no longer exist.

Now that the helicopter had disappeared over the horizon, the silence was unreal. Around us, there was only sky, snow and rock. Nothing else. Annelise's eyes were sparkling.

I gave her a pat on the cheek. "Minus 25, darling. This is what Daaddy Bear calls 'cold'."

"Shall we go, Papà?"

A black-clad old man had peered round the door. His eyes were little more than cracks and there wasn't much hair on his head. A slight smile appeared on his weasel face.

"You're Signor Salinger," he said, taking my backpack. "And you're Annelise, Werner Mair's daughter, aren't you?"

"That's right."

"And you must be Clara. Do you like my house, *du kloane* Clara?"

Clara stared for a few moments at this strange character, who really did look like an elf, then, instead of replying, she asked a question. "Do you live here?"

"I've lived here for more than thirty years."

"So you're the King of the Elves?"

The man looked with delight first at me, then at Annelise. "I think this child has earned herself a double ration of dessert. Come, please."

Apart from the King of the Elves and a couple of attendants – goblins, according to Clara – there was nobody else there. The castle was all ours. Clara was very excited, and Annelise no less so.

I was proud of myself.

We ate early, as you do in the mountains. A gigantic portion of polenta and mushrooms, *speck*, sauté potatoes and the purest water I've ever drunk. Maybe it was the altitude, or maybe the joy of being up there with the people I loved most, but that water went to my head. What happened after dinner was interminable, but in a good sense. We stayed on, talking to the manager of the refuge and his helpers.

He was lavish with his anecdotes, each more incredible than the last. Clara hung on his every word. Often, she interrupted the narrative to ask for more details, and instead of becoming rattled, the manager seemed happy to have such an attentive audience. At eleven, we toasted with grappa and got ready for the final part of my surprise.

I made Clara and Annelise put on a double layer of sweaters and padded jackets and, equipped with flashlights, we went out into the night.

A few steps were enough to project us into another world. A world of absolute vastness and beauty. We sat down on the snow. I took the thermos of hot chocolate and passed it to Clara.

"Would you like to see something magic, sweetheart?"

"What kind of magic?"

"Look up there."

Clara raised her head.

No light pollution. No smog. Not even a cloud. We could have grabbed the stars one by one.

Annelise leaned on my shoulder. "It's wonderful."

I didn't reply. There was no need. But I recognised that tone. It was the voice of the woman who had chosen me as her partner. Not diffident, not on the defensive.

Simply in love.

"You know something, Clara?"

"If you don't tell me, I don't know."

"What you're looking at is the treasure of the King of the Elves. He has no money, he doesn't even have a car. He only has two suits in his wardrobe, but he's the richest elf in the world. Don't you think so?"

"Is this where the stars hide, Papà?"

"It could well be, sweetheart, it could well be."

We sat there looking at the stars until my watch showed it was midnight.

We toasted again and hugged one another. Clara gave me a big kiss on my cheek and laughed at the echo the kiss set off. She said it was the mountain wishing us good luck.

We went back into the castle much richer than when we had left it.

* * *

Annelise never noticed anything. The trick was simple: take the sleeping pills every evening before going to bed. That meant no nightmares, no screams, nothing suspicious.

In the meantime, I made an effort to be the most caring husband in the world and a father worthy of the name. I continued lying to Annelise about the drugs, but I did intend to keep my promise. I would forget about the Bletterbach killings, I would enjoy my sabbatical year, and I would get better.

It was important. For me. For Clara and Annelise. And for Werner. My wife's father didn't say anything, but I could see reproach in his eyes from a distance of kilometres. I don't know how much Annelise had confided in him – I think little or nothing, knowing her – but there was no way of escaping his eagle eyes.

Ever.

I spent the first week of January sledding with Clara. I won't hide the fact that, at my age, I was enjoying myself like a schoolboy. Behind Werner's house was a sloping open space over which the bright red sled ran like a rocket. It wasn't dangerous, because the slope ended in a gentle undulation that made it possible to brake quite safely.

The eastern side of Welshboden, on the other hand, was another story, and I was categorical with Clara: no sledding on that kamikaze trail. There the slope was steep and ended in the forest, where big trunks asked for nothing better than to make mincemeat out of my princess. Even I was afraid of that descent. So: *verboten.*

The days at Siebenhoch passed in a joyful routine. I played with Clara. I slept soundly. I had a good appetite, and the bruise on my face was a fading yellowish stain that would soon disappear. I made love with Annelise. Yes, we'd started again. Cautiously at first, then with increasing passion. Annelise was forgiving me.

I went down to Siebenhoch as little as possible, just to do shopping. I bought my cigarettes from the petrol station in Aldino. I never again set foot in Alois' store.

Every now and again, I would think about the Bletterbach, but I would force myself to dismiss the thought. I didn't want to lose my family. I knew that Annelise's threat wasn't dictated by momentary fear or anger. In any case, I had no intention of putting it to the test.

On January 10, I made the acquaintance of Brigitte Pflantz.

* * *

There was no lack of choice on the shelves. There were various kinds of brandy, cognac, bourbon, vodka and grappa. I've never been much of a one for vodka, and as for grappa I could count on the special reserve at Werner's house, so I'd ruled them out from the start. Annelise didn't like cognac, and I wasn't crazy about it either, but bourbon every now and again . . .

I heard a woman's voice, but not what she'd said.

"I beg your pardon?" I asked, turning.

"Am I disturbing you?"

She had stringy blonde hair falling on both sides of her face. The make-up around her eyes was smudged.

"No, I was lost in thought."

"It happens," she said.

She kept looking at me. I noticed she had big, nicotine-stained teeth. Her breath smelled of alcohol, and it was only ten in the morning.

"What can I do for you?" I asked, making an effort to be nice.

"You really don't know who I am?"

"I'm afraid not," I replied, embarrassed.

She held out her hand and I shook it. She was wearing leather gloves. "We've never met in person. But you know who I am."

"I do?"

The intensity of her gaze made me uneasy.

"Of course you do. I'm an important person. From your point of view, Salinger, I'd say I'm central."

The dark gloves went back into the pockets of an overcoat that had seen too many winters.

"Can I call you Jeremiah?" she asked.

"You'd be the only one, apart from Werner and my mother."

"It's a beautiful name. It comes from the Bible. Did you know that?"

"Oh, yes . . ."

"'Why criest thou for thine affliction? Thy sorrow is incurable for the multitude of thine iniquity: because thy sins were increased, I have done these things unto thee.'"

"I'm not a great fan of religion, Signora . . ."

"Signorina. Call me Brigitte. Brigitte Pflantz."

"All right, Brigitte," I said, grabbing a bottle at random and laying it in my trolley. "Now, if you don't mind . . ."

Brigitte blocked my path. "You shouldn't talk to me like that."

"Or what? The wrath of the Lord will come down on me for a thousand years?"

"Or you'll never know what happened in the Bletterbach."

I froze.

She nodded. "That's right."

Something clicked in my brain. "Günther Kagol's fiancée. *That* Brigitte."

"Some people say you're planning to make a film about it."

"No, I'm not," I replied brusquely.

"A pity. I know lots of things. Lots and lots of things."

For a moment, I was tempted. But I resisted. "Nice to have met you, Brigitte."

I rerouted my trolley and left.

* * *

That evening, after dinner, I replied to a couple of e-mails from Mike. Then I opened the folder marked "Stuff". I moved file B over to the recycle bin. I stared at it for a few moments.

Then I put it back in its place.

It didn't mean anything, I told myself. But I didn't want to delete it.

I wasn't ready yet.

* * *

Sledding. Snowball fights. Trying new recipes. Making love with Annelise. Taking sleeping pills. Sleeping without dreaming. Then all over again, from the top.

On January 20, I decided to do without the sleeping pills. No more nightmares.

The same on January 21. And 22, 23 and 24.

I was in seventh heaven. I felt strong. Refusing to play along with

Brigitte Pflantz had made me more aware of the struggle. Every morning, I would wake up and say to myself, “You can do it, you’ve done it once, you can do it again.”

On January 30, one of the coldest days of the year, there was a knock at my door.

The Krün Family Home

It was Annelise who opened the door. I was busy tidying the kitchen. Mike would have called it "work for queers", but washing dishes is one of the few occupations that have the ability to calm me down.

"There's someone to see you."

I knew at once that something wasn't right. Annelise's tone was icy.

I turned, detergent foam up to my elbows. "Who . . . ?"

Standing in my kitchen, with his hat in his cold-reddened hands, was the last person in the world I'd have expected to see.

"Hello, Max," I said, letting the water run over my hands. "Would you like a coffee?"

"Actually," he replied, "I'd like to offer you a coffee. And I'd like to show you a few things concerning that business we . . . spoke about. It won't take long."

Annelise's face turned red and she left the room without a word.

Max looked at me, embarrassed. "I hope I didn't . . ."

"Wait here," I murmured.

Annelise was sitting in my favourite armchair. She was looking at the blanket of snow and at Clara, who was building her umpteenth snowman.

"What more does he want of you?" she hissed.

"To apologise."

Annelise turned to look at me. "Do you take me for an idiot?"

She was right. What was that "business" Max wanted to talk to me about if not the Bletterbach killings?

"If you want, I'll throw him out without a second thought. But I also owe him an apology." I kissed her on the forehead. "I'll keep my promise. I don't want to lose you."

Was I really convinced I'd be able to keep a safe distance?

That Max and I would shake hands like two civilised people and when he brought up the subject of the Bletterbach I would cut short the conversation, thank him and return home with a clear conscience?

I think I was.

I was sincere, and that's what persuaded her. But wasn't there a voice inside me, a bothersome voice that, as Annelise lightly stroked me, implored me to kick Max out of the house and get on with washing the dishes?

"Do what you have to do, Salinger. But come back to me. Come back to us."

* * *

"Let's take mine." Max pointed to the Forest Rangers' Land Rover.

"Max," I said, "if you want to apologise, I accept your apology. And I want you to know I'm really sorry I stuck my nose in your business. That was a mistake. But I have no intention of talking to you about the killings. I promised my wife I'd forget all about it, O.K.? It's water under the bridge."

Really?

Then why did I feel my heart pounding? Why couldn't I wait to get in the vehicle and start listening to what Max had to tell me?

Nine letters: "obsession".

Max kicked a heap of snow and shook his head. "I hit you that night because I realised you're in this Bletterbach business up to your neck. And if you got to the point of having to make promises to Annelise, that means you're in it worse than I feared. Don't lie to me, Salinger. I can see it in your face, as clear as day."

There wasn't a single word that didn't correspond to the truth. Part of me was still hooked on the Bletterbach killings. Sooner or later I'd start to dig, to investigate, to ask questions.

And what would happen to my family then?

Was it at this point that I gave in?

No.

I continued lying to myself.

"You're wrong."

"Don't talk bullshit, Salinger. It's what you're hoping for, that I'll give you more information, gossip, clues." Max approached and pointed a finger at me. "And it's what I intend to do. I'll show you so many blind alleys I'll put you off once and for all, so that you don't end up like Günther." A sigh. "Or like me."

"I promised, Max."

A weak protest. The troublesome voice was muffled. Distant. Almost like weeping.

"Come with me and you'll be certain you won't break that promise."

I turned towards the big windows of the living room. I raised my hand to wave at Annelise's silhouette. She did the same. Then she disappeared.

"Why?" I asked in a thin voice.

"I want to spare you thirty years of pain, Salinger."

* * *

There wasn't much traffic, just a couple of jeeps and a black Mercedes going in the opposite direction. We passed Welshboden, and at a crossroads Max turned onto a dirt road that climbed between the trees.

It was just after two in the afternoon when we got to the Krün family home.

"Welcome to the land of my ancestors."

"So this is where you grew up?"

"Did Verena tell you that?"

"She told me something about your childhood. She told me about Frau Krün."

"For me she was *Omi*, Grandma. She was an inflexible woman, but she was also fair, and she was very strong. We were poor, and to make sure I lacked for nothing *Omi* had to be hard with everybody. She was a widow bringing up an orphan. In the village, they took her hardness for arrogance. It wasn't easy to see that there was something different behind that attitude. My grandfather's death had broken her heart, but what remained was full of love. She had a huge heart, my *Omi*." Max granted me a smile. "Come."

The Krün family home was a mountain *maso* with a tiled roof that could have done with decent maintenance. Beneath the eaves you could see the remains of swallows' nests. A twisted apple tree framed the front door, which squeaked a little on its hinges.

The interior was devoid of light.

"No electricity," Max explained, lighting an oil lamp. "I have a generator, but I prefer to keep it for emergencies. I'll make some coffee, if you're O.K. with that."

Once lit, the house took on a less spectral aspect. Above the fireplace was a damp-stained photograph.

"Little Max and Frau Krün," Max said, as he made the coffee. "Please sit down."

Apart from the table and a couple of chairs, the only other furniture in the room, the *Stube* – which was what they called this kind of all-purpose large room in Alto Adige (kitchen, bedroom, living room, all gathered around the ceramic stove that gave its name to the space: the *Stube* itself) – was a pair of metal filing cabinets.

Max saw where I was looking. "Thirty years of investigations. Testimonies cross-checked. Evidence collected. False leads. Possible suspects. Thirty years of a life spent collecting nothing. Thirty wasted years."

"A nice slice of cake that tastes of nothing."

Max raised an eyebrow. "You spoke to Luis?"

"I guess the style is unmistakable."

"Here's something that not even Luis has the courage to say: Kurt, Evi and Markus aren't the only victims of the Bletterbach. There's also Günther and Hannes. Verena. Brigitte. Hermann. Werner. And me."

I stared at the flames in the fireplace. I followed the trail of the sparks, which Clara called "little devils", until I saw them burn themselves out on walls blackened by God knows how many years of smoke and flames.

Max sighed. "I'd close my eyes and hear Kurt's voice. Or Evi's footsteps on the floor, or Markus's laughter. And when I opened them again, I'd see them. They were accusing me. You're alive, they'd say."

I shuddered.

You're alive.

I lit myself a cigarette.

"I'd been left alone. Who could I have talked to? Verena wouldn't have understood. Werner left, Hannes . . . Hannes did that terrible thing to his wife. There was only Günther. He wanted to know. And he drank. I also wanted to know. I wanted to find the son of a bitch who had condemned me to solitude and do away with him. I'd decided that I would strangle him. Time passed. Günther had his accident. I got married. Chief Hubner died. Verena didn't want me to accept his post, but I wanted to become Chief Krün. I saw myself as the *Saltner* of Siebenhoch, you know what that is?"

It was a word I'd never heard before.

"In the old days every village had its *Saltner*," he explained. "He was chosen from among the strongest young men to watch over the vineyards and the stables. It was a prestigious office. Everybody had to trust him: if even a single vote was cast against him, the young man was ruled out. There was too much at stake. If the *Saltner* had wanted, he could have come to an agreement with the outlaws and plundered a whole year's harvest, condemning the community to certain death. I felt like the *Saltner*."

I threw my cigarette into the flames. I'd smoked less than half.

It was making me dizzy.

"The *Saltner* protects his people," I said, "and you wanted to do the same for the inhabitants of Siebenhoch."

"I've done it all these years, but today . . ." His voice cracked. "The people who died down there were my best friends, Salinger, people I loved. But if I could turn the clock back, I'd take Verena and leave without turning round. To hell with the *Saltner*. To hell with Evi, Markus and Kurt. Does that sound cruel? It isn't. I'm sure that when you've heard the full story, you'll realise it isn't worth it."

"You could leave any time you wanted. What keeps you in Siebenhoch?"

Max paused for a few seconds. "The Bletterbach killings have become the purpose of my life." A bitter grimace crossed his square face. "That's the kind of obsession I'm trying to save you from. If thirty years ago someone had shown me the contents of those records, if someone had warned me . . . then maybe everything would have been different. For me and for Verena."

I remembered his wife's words. The anguish they had conveyed to me.

I thought of Annelise. And of Clara. I saw her growing up with a father who was ever more distant, and sick.

Come back to us.

"Tell me."

Max stood up. The filing cabinet opened with a clatter. "Let's start with the official investigation," he said.

"It was the Carabinieri in Bolzano who carried it out."

"Captain Alfieri and Deputy Prosecutor Cattaneo. I never met Cattaneo. He was just a voice on the telephone. Captain Alfieri was a good man, but you could see he'd have preferred to be dealing with something else. From an investigative point of view, the Bletterbach killings were a major hassle. Starting with the scene of the crime."

He showed me a yellow folder. It was as thick as a dictionary. He drummed on it with his fingers.

"This is the final forensics report. It's more than 400 pages long. I had to ask the doctor in Aldino to help me figure out some passages. Wasted effort. No organic traces, no fingerprints, nothing. The rain and mud had washed everything away." He put the folder back in the filing cabinet. "And anyway, by the time the report was ready, both Cattaneo and Alfieri had already figured out that nobody would be arrested for the murders."

"But you," I said, "you wanted to find the bastard."

"I became insistent. Quite insistent. But it was like beating my head against a wall. Nobody wanted to hear about the Bletterbach. I even laid my hands on Captain Alfieri."

"Luis told me about a few suspects . . ."

"We're getting there. First I want to show you something else."

He pulled out a file. He turned it without opening it and slid it towards me.

He gave me a sign of encouragement. "The scene of the crime. Open it. Look."

The first photograph was like a kick in the face. The others were no less so. Most were in black and white, a few in colour. All were revolting.

"God . . ."

Max took them gently from my hands. Then, like the most obscene of conjurers, he started showing them to me one by one.

"This is the tent. Kurt had chosen this point so that . . ."

I remembered Werner's words. "So that the wind wouldn't blow it away."

"Would you like something strong to drink? You look pale."

I dismissed the idea with a gesture. "Who did this backpack belong to?"

"Markus. As you can see, it's torn. We reckoned Markus had thrown it at the attacker to defend himself. He was the only one who tried to run away. Look at these."

Another photograph.

More horror.

"These are Markus' boots. His body was found barefoot. He was wearing a sweater. No jacket. And Kurt, too. Actually, Kurt was in his vest. You see this? It's his backpack. It's possible they'd only just gone to bed when they were attacked." Max stopped for a second. "I was the one who identified it. The backpack was a gift from me. You can't see them, but I'd had his initials sewn on just here."

He jabbed at the snapshot.

Then another photograph. And another.

"Kurt. Kurt. Kurt."

Every time he uttered his friend's name, he slid another photograph across the table.

"The pathologist said the killer wounded him without killing him immediately. Kurt was probably the first to react and the killer didn't want the others to get away. Or else, and this is another possibility, he wanted to punish him for his heroism. Rendering him harmless and leaving him time to see what he was about to do. He hit him, then killed Evi, followed Markus and came back."

"Followed?"

"Markus managed to run away. Just for a short time."

I stared at the photographs on the table.

I pointed to the wounds on Kurt's body. "Did he torture him?"

"According to the pathologist, by the time the killer came back to him, he was already dead. These marks were inflicted post mortem. He kept attacking the corpse."

"As if he were the intended victim?" I ventured.

Max gave a half smile. "That's what I thought too, Salinger. Then I began to think the intended victim was Evi. Then Markus. It's a bloody roundabout." He stopped and stared at me. "The photographs of Evi are . . ."

I nodded. "Go ahead."

"Evi."

I think I screamed. I stood up, ran out and buried my face in the snow. I threw up everything I had eaten for lunch. Then I screamed some more, that much I remember.

I felt Max lift me up and take me back inside the house. He sat me down on the chair next to the fire. He slapped me once, twice. I got my breath back.

"I'm sorry, Max."

"It's only human."

I pointed at the photographs. "But this isn't."

"I meant your reaction."

I lit a cigarette. "Why did he cut her head off?"

"Of all questions, Salinger, that's the most pointless. There's no answer."

"There *has* to be."

Max sat down. "Supposing you found the killer. Supposing you had him in front of you and you could ask him: why? What do you think he'd say?"

"I'm not a psychiatrist. I don't know."

"And what if that was his reply? 'I don't know.' What if there wasn't a reason? Or if there was a reason it was so stupid as to seem ridiculous? What if the killer replied: I did it because I didn't like the rain. Or because my dog told me to. Or because I was bored. How would you react?"

I understood what he was saying, but I didn't agree. "Finding a motive means finding the killer."

"That may be so. But without any leads? It's pointless racking your brains about the motive. That's what I thought. Find the culprit and the motive will come by itself. Better to concentrate on the suspects."

"How many?"

"*All of them.* Nobody ruled out."

He opened a door in the filing cabinet and took out yet another file. On the cover were the words: "M KRÜN". "This," he explained, "is the investigation into the suspect Max Krün." He opened a map on the table. "Look. I've marked everything. Our route. Kurt's possible route, or rather, three different routes that Kurt could have taken. Possible escape routes."

"And these numbers?"

"The timetables. Those in red are the possible timetables of Kurt, Evi and Markus. Those in black are more precise because they refer to our rescue team. These on the other hand are photocopies of a report into a road accident. As you can see, there isn't only my signature on it. The other one's the signature of the fire chief."

"The accident before the birthday party?"

"A truck overturned just below Siebenhoch." Max indicated the road that led out of the village, two kilometres below the Despar, in the direction of Aldino. "It was carrying weedkiller. It took us three hours just to straighten it and free the carriageway: if the load had spilled it would have been a real mess. I was in a hurry, I didn't want to miss Verena's party, but we did everything with the utmost care. We took a Polaroid for the insurance. This is it."

It showed an overturned lorry, the registration number perfectly recognisable.

"Nineteen and twenty. The date and hour on the back weren't written by me, but by the fire chief. We parted company around eight. A few minutes later, I was in the barracks, doing other paperwork. Around nine, I went home, changed and rushed to Verena's birthday party. At ten-thirty, we cut the cake. You see?"

A group photograph. The clock behind the cheerful faces clearly showed ten-thirty.

"Did anyone see you when you were in the barracks?"

"No. The two alibis confirmed are eight o'clock and ten-thirty."

"A gap of two and a half hours. What time was established as the time of death of Kurt and the others?"

"According to the coroner, between eight and ten. Now look."

Max drew my attention back to the map of the Bletterbach. He took a ruler and started measuring.

"As the crow flies, it's about ten kilometres from Siebenhoch to the murder scene. Ignoring the lack of roads, the difference in altitude and that hell of water and mud, a good walker could have got to the spot where we found the bodies in two hours, two and a half. How long to kill them? The report doesn't say, and nobody knows. But we do know that Kurt tried to defend himself and Markus ran away. Shall we say ten minutes? Twenty? Plus another two hours or so to get back. How long is that?"

"Five hours, more or less. Not to mention the self-regenerating storm and all the rest. The defendant Max Krün is acquitted."

Max nodded.

"It's absurd," I added, with a shudder.

"Absurd?"

"That you subjected yourself to such a trial."

"That's what I'm trying to save you from, Salinger."

I didn't think I would ever get to that degree of paranoia. It did occur to me, though, that Max had had thirty years to dig that pit for himself. Whereas I, in less than three months, had already come close to breaking up my marriage.

Max had piled more files on the table. "The serial killer angle. Did Luis tell you about that?"

The file contained a few newspaper articles. A few faxes. Crumpled maps. Pages written in nervous, barely legible handwriting.

"What are these?" I asked.

"Notes. Transcripts of telephone calls, to be precise."

"Who with?"

"The prosecutor's office. I helped them to look for a connection with the Bletterbach."

"Did you find one?"

"The man in question wasn't in Siebenhoch but in Nova Ponente. Close, therefore plausible. But in December '85. A two-week skiing holiday with his wife and children."

"He had a family?"

"Does that seem so strange?"

A wife and children. I absorbed that, too. "No, I guess not."

Max closed the file. "Guilty, but not of the Bletterbach killings."

The next file was much thicker. He took out an A3 sheet to which some ten numbered passport photographs were attached. Each number corresponded to a caption referring to annotations on other papers.

"And these?"

"Poachers active at the time. Markus was a big pain in the arse. My fault, I suppose. I was twenty-three, practically a child. To make myself look good in his eyes, I invented a whole lot of adventures chasing poachers. Bullshit to impress the boy and feel stronger than I was. In reality, the hunt for poachers began and ended in Chief Hubner's office."

"No stakeouts in the woods or anything like that?"

"Nothing like that," Max said, amused. "Chief Hubner would pick up the phone, call the poachers and ask, 'Catch anything last night?' That's all. But I knew who they were and I investigated all of them. And got nowhere. They were poachers, not killers. There's a big difference between killing a stag and murdering a human being."

"And the drug story?"

Max showed me another file. "Not much. Markus was caught with a little hash in his pocket. Not even good quality. One of his schoolmates had sold it to him. Chief Hubner gave him a slap on the wrist and dismissed the case. Do you think it's possible to kill someone for a few grams of hash?"

"But you investigated anyway."

Max scowled at me. "Obviously."

He didn't need to say any more.

"Verena?" I asked doubtfully.

"These are her movements that day. A trip to the hairdresser's. Two errands for her mother, here and here, then home to make the cake with a few friends."

"And besides, she's too delicate."

"You never know."

I thought of Annelise. Where was she in April '85? In her cradle. She was a few months old. A solid enough alibi.

But was it enough for Max?

"Werner? Here he is," Max exclaimed, opening a drawer in the cabinet. "Günther? Here you go. Brigitte? Of course. Hannes? I had a good motive for Hannes, too. Since Kurt had moved to Innsbruck, the two of them had stopped talking to each other. I ruled him out, too, though. He'd spent the day outside the village, for work. It's all written here, you can help yourself if you want. I also investigated Evi and Markus's father, Mauro Tognon."

"You tracked him down?"

"Of course," Max replied, as if it were the most obvious thing in the world. "A real piece of shit, if you want my opinion. And it isn't only my opinion. I have his criminal record. His business card said he was a 'travelling salesman', but he wasn't. Tognon was a con man and a card shark, with a history of violence. Especially to women. And that was his luck."

"How do you mean?"

"In '85, he was in prison. Attempted murder. Of one of the many poor women he'd seduced and then had fun mistreating."

"A real son of a bitch."

"You can say that again."

From his shirt pocket he took the telegram. The one Verena had shown me.

Geht nicht dorthin!

Don't go down there!

I hadn't forgotten it and I hadn't forgotten the name of the man who had sent it.

"Who is Oscar Grünwald?"

"I knew Oscar Grünwald. I met him a couple of times when I took Markus to Innsbruck to see his sister. A retiring, solitary character. Evi liked him a lot. I thought he was a bit odd. She introduced him to me as an important scientist, but I later discovered he wasn't that at all. He'd been thrown out of the university and scraped a living as best he could. Dishwasher, gardener, tourist guide. He was a geologist, but he also had a second degree. In palaeontology."

"He studied fossils," I said, thinking of Yodi.

And of the Bletterbach.

"You've also made the connection?"

"The Bletterbach is a vast open-air fossil collection."

"That's what I thought, too."

"Why on earth had he been thrown out of the university?"

"Academic differences, let's call it that. It took me a while to find out. Innsbruck University is very secretive about its internal affairs. Plus, apart from the telegram, I had nothing to go on."

"What did Captain Alfieri say?"

"Alfieri didn't know about the telegram."

"How is that possible?"

"The telegram could have been evidence for or against, depending on how you looked at it. Or else a coincidence. It didn't mean anything."

"That's not true," I retorted. "To me, it seems obvious. Grünwald knew someone would kill them in the Bletterbach and tried to warn them. It says clearly: *Geht nicht dorthin!* Don't go down there!"

Max was unfazed. "Or it could have been a threat. Don't go down there or else . . . Have you thought of that?"

"Anyway, it was worth investigating, don't you think? Maybe the Carabinieri . . ."

Max clenched his fists. "Nobody was interested in finding out who killed my friends. It was obvious from the start. Those were the years of bombs. The Carabinieri had other things on their minds. If I'd taken the telegram to Alfieri and told him about Grünwald, it would have been a waste of time. Only one person could find the murderer. Me. The telegram was my reminder to myself. My sentence. Because if instead of forgetting all about it and putting it away in my pocket, I'd paid attention to it, I might have saved them."

"That's what torments you, isn't it?"

"That, too. As I see it, this telegram makes me guilty of dereliction of duty. In other words, I'm an accessory to murder."

"That's ridiculous, Max."

"I looked for Grünwald. I looked for him everywhere. I spent a whole lot of money. I couldn't find anything. He'd vanished. The telegram is the last proof of his existence."

"A person can't just vanish like that. He must have had friends, acquaintances, someone."

"I was dealing with the most solitary person in the world, Salinger. More so than me," he murmured. "At least I had three ghosts to keep me company."

* * *

It had grown late. Max put the files back in the cabinet and locked it, and we got back in the grey Forest Rangers' Land Rover, the heat turned all the way up.

"It isn't true," I said, once we were inside. "You weren't alone. Verena was with you."

"Verena's something else. Verena's the reason I didn't end up like Günther."

He started the engine and we set off. We said nothing more until we got to our destination.

Max parked and switched off the headlights.

I listened to the engine ticking over.

"Verena would have liked children," Max confessed, looking straight ahead of him. "She would have been an excellent mother. I said we couldn't afford it, even though it wasn't true. I said the time wasn't right for it. I kept putting it off. The real reason was fear. I was scared that what happened to Hannes would happen to me. One fine day, you wake up and go to the woods to recover your son's body."

I saw Clara waving at me from the living-room window. I waved back.

Time to get out.

I made to open the car door.

Max stopped me. "That day, I called you a murderer. You're not a murderer. I know what happened on the Ortles. It wasn't your fault."

I didn't reply. Not immediately, at least. I was afraid my voice would crack.

"Thanks, Max."

It was good to hear myself say that.

"You have that child, Salinger. You can be happy. These aren't your people. This isn't your place. Don't you think" – he pointed to my daughter in the window – "you have something better to fight for?"

* * *

That night I was *inside* again. Inside the Beast. In spite of the sleeping pills.

I didn't scream. I woke weeping, with the feeling I had lost everything that was worth living for. Beside me, Annelise was sleeping peacefully, with a placid expression I found enchanting.

I embraced her, clung to her. By the time my heartbeat slowed, I'd even managed to stem the tears. Trying not to disturb Annelise's sleep, I got up. In the bathroom, I opened the cabinet and looked through the blister packs of drugs I was pretending to take every morning. Those pills weren't my salvation, they were only a chemical substitute. I closed the cabinet again. I didn't want to have anything to do with them. I would double the dose of sleeping pills, if necessary. But I wouldn't let chemistry decide my emotions.

I can do it, I thought. I can do it all by myself.

The First of February

On the first of February, three things happened. There was a blizzard, I nearly killed someone, and I had a phone call from Mike.

* * *

The cold days (the days of the blackbird, as they're known) wouldn't let go. That damned little bird, I'd heard Werner say, wanted to kill us all.

If in December the temperatures had conformed to the local average, cold enough to freeze the tips of your fingers even in gloves, but not enough to make you miss the warmth of your house (at least it was that way for me, but I love the cold), January had opened wide the doors to a Siberian low pressure area that seemed intent on turning north-eastern Italy into a kind of Arctic tundra inhabited only by bears and other furry animals.

Siebenhoch glittered under a layer of ice as hard and treacherous as armour plating.

The locals were used to it, but the village didn't only contain natives and there were lots of tourists damaging arms and femurs. Even I fell a few times.

I started to think that walking on the ice isn't a mere skill, but a genuine art that's transmitted in the genes. That would explain how Clara and Annelise could walk solemnly with the grace of two ballerinas while yours truly seemed like a clumsy cross between a one-legged goose and a clown with chilli peppers up his backside.

At night, the reflection of the moon on the mountain glaciers made the use of lamps pointless. Everything was illumined with a ghostly bluish light. Sometimes it was a bewitching spectacle, at other times it verged on the terrifying.

Especially when, in my half-waking state, my mind wandered to the black hole of the Bletterbach.

* * *

When I woke that first of February, my tongue numb from the sleeping pills, I found myself alone, without the touch of Annelise's body beside me.

I stretched and waited for my mind to clear, then calmly got out of bed and went to the window to gaze out at the landscape. The snow-shrouded forest, the pointed roofs of Siebenhoch blurring into the mist generated by a violent wind raising slivers of ice. The sun was a mere speck on the horizon, to be imagined rather than seen.

A good coffee brought me back to the land of the living.

Annelise had been up for a while. Cleaning day in the Salinger household. Not that I was crazy about some chores (I was the one who washed the dishes, put clothes in the washing machine and ironed, while Annelise changed the sheets and vacuumed – that was how our agreement worked), but after a quick shower I set to work. By midday, the house was gleaming like a mirror.

At one o'clock, Annelise's hoarding instinct kicked in. She had that look of hers as she uttered anxiously, "We're going to starve to death."

In the cupboard, there were kilos of pasta of various shapes, sugar both refined and cane, sea salt and rock salt, tinned goods (peas, beans, soups of various kinds, tomato paste), a lot of beer, dried fruit (walnuts, hazelnuts, peanuts, figs, prunes, apples, pears, even dates) and everything that a regiment would need to survive a winter twice as long as the one we would have to live through.

"Darling," I said, "don't you think you're exaggerating?"

"Don't joke, Salinger."

"I'm only saying that this house won't turn into the Overlook Hotel until at least 2030."

"Salinger—"

"Seriously, Annelise. Now you can tell me. Where have you put my axe, darling?"

"Don't joke about these things."

I started rolling my eyes and gnashing my teeth. "Wendy, darling, my axe. Where's my axe?"

Annelise glared at me. She hated that film.

"Isn't my performance convincing?"

"No."

"Do you want me to make it better? Then give me my axe."

"Drop it."

"O.K."

I kissed the tip of her nose, took pen and paper and resigned myself to an excursion I hadn't reckoned with.

It took me at least ten minutes to jot down everything that Annelise wanted me to buy, and forever to get to the supermarket. An S.U.V. had overturned in the middle of the road, paralysing the traffic.

When I was a few metres from the vehicle, I saw Max among the road rescue team. I hooted my horn. He turned with the expression of someone ready to bite. When he recognised me, he relaxed.

I lowered my window.

"Salinger," he said, touching his hat.

"A bit chilly, isn't it?"

"So they say."

"Will it last?"

"All week, at least."

"Is anyone hurt?"

"Tourists," Max muttered. "They'd be capable of causing an avalanche just by sneezing. You know what's worse than city people?"

"I have no idea."

"City people who are convinced they aren't city people."

I laughed with him.

We hadn't had occasion to see each other since Max had opened the filing cabinets in the Krün family home for me. I'd have liked to thank him. But I felt not so much embarrassment as a kind of reticence that prevented me from saying the right thing at the right time.

I missed my moment, as we say in such cases.

"Are you going shopping?"

I showed him Annelise's list. "My wife's afraid it's going to be a long winter."

"She's not wrong there."

"At least I have an excuse for standing still and wasting gas."

"Get out of here now before I slap a fine on you. You're blocking the road."

We shook hands and I closed my window. It really was cold.

Maybe, I thought as I passed the breakdown truck lifting the overturned S.U.V., it was better this way.

Maybe what I had seen in the Krün family's *maso* should remain something not spoken about, one of those things it's best not to dig up. Not in the light of day, at least.

And anyway, the Bletterbach was the last thing on my mind that day. I can swear to that.

That's why what happened took me by surprise.

* * *

I left the supermarket with three bags full to bursting, put them in the trunk and got in the car. I switched on the heating and lit a cigarette.

I opened the window just enough not to die of suffocation.

I leaned my head back against the seat and half closed my eyes. I let myself be cradled by the rumbling of the engine and dozed off. Cleaning the house had tired me more than I'd realised. My siesta didn't last long. The embers of my cigarette touching my fingers startled me awake, cursing. I opened the door wide and threw out the glowing cigarette end.

I didn't see it vanish into the snow. I looked around, disconcerted. I couldn't see the luminous sign of the supermarket to my left. I couldn't see anything. For a moment, I thought I'd gone blind. Above and below were identical.

"Just snow," I said aloud, trying to calm my heartbeat.

The old ticker had started taking big leaps. I raised a hand to my chest.

"A nasty blizzard, nothing more. Take it easy."

Werner had told me about the blizzards. The blizzards weren't just snowfalls. Snowfalls are to blizzards as summer downpours are to self-regenerating storms. Blizzards arrive silently and are worse than fog. They blind.

I felt a clenching in my stomach. Everything was white.

I closed the door, gasping. I knew what was about to happen, but I didn't want to accept it. Nevertheless, I had to eat the whole dose of shit that first of February had in store for me.

It came. And how.

P.T.S.D. Post-traumatic stress disorder.

The hissing.

The voice of the Beast.

It started like a rustling, a radio tuned to a dead station. Within a few seconds, it became as solid as the wheel I was gripping with all my strength. I tried to struggle, controlled my breathing, did everything the doctors advise those who are about to have a panic attack. It didn't help at all.

Total paralysis.

Get out.

That voice. And its smell. The smell of the Beast. A metallic smell, which left a patina of numbness in the mouth. An ancient smell. So ancient as to turn the stomach. Because the Beast was ancient. So ancient that . . . At last, I screamed.

With my left hand, I found the safety catch on the car door. I threw myself out, banging my knees on the ground. The pain was a blessing.

The hissing faded.

I stayed there motionless on all fours on the asphalt while the snow got into the folds of my clothes. The icy contact helped me to regain control.

I shook my head. I wiped away my tears. I stood up.

"I'm alive," I said.

Alive and in the middle of a blizzard. Visibility was down to less than two metres.

I got back in the car. I switched the headlights on. I started the engine and set off, hearing the tyres skid.

She emerged out of nowhere.

Her mouth was open wide, her arms outspread like Christ on the cross. She was wearing a blue jacket, completely unsuitable for that cold. I slammed on the brakes less than ten centimetres from her legs.

Brigitte Pflantz looked first at me, then at the sky.

Then she fell to the ground.

* * *

I rushed to help her. She was groggy, more from alcohol than from the fall.

I had to drag her into the car, she couldn't stay on her feet.

"Brigitte? Can you hear me, Brigitte?"

She clutched my wrist. Her eyes were feverish. "Home."

"I have to take you to hospital."

"Home," she repeated.

"I don't think that's a good idea. You need help."

"The only help I need, Salinger, is the Lord's. But He abandoned me a long time ago. Help me to sit up straight. I'll guide you."

I fastened her seat belt. We left.

Brigitte lived in an old house with peeling walls. The rolling shutters were off their rails, swollen by damp.

The interior was even worse. It was the home of someone in the last stages of alcoholism, I told myself, as soon as Brigitte, after ferreting in her handbag, managed to push the keys into the keyhole. There were bottles everywhere. On every surface there was a layer of grease and dust. The place smelt like an animal's cage.

I laid Brigitte down on the couch. It was only then that I realised she was wearing a pair of spring shoes. I gently took them off. Her feet were blue, as were her hands and lips. Her teeth were chattering. Her eyes were yellow, jaundiced, and her dilated pupils followed every one of my movements. From somewhere I managed to dig out a pair of blankets stained with what could have been dried vomit. By now, I was used to the stench and didn't pay much attention to it.

I covered her and started rubbing her.

"Are you sure you don't want me to call a doctor?" I asked after a while.

"I'm feeling better. You can stop now, or God knows what your wife would say."

I left the blankets on her and lit a cigarette. I realised that I was bathed in sweat. Now that the fear had passed, I was angry. I could have killed her. "What the hell were you thinking!" I exclaimed. "Coming out dressed like that in this weather. You could have died, dammit!"

"I'm an alcoholic, Salinger," she murmured. "Haven't you noticed? This is what alcoholics do. We're a danger to ourselves and others."

She smiled.

That's what rooted me to the spot. It was a sweet smile.

"If you want a drink, help yourself," she said, her face gradually regaining colour. "There's plenty to choose from. And thank you for not running me over."

"There's no need to thank me," I muttered.

Brigitte sat up, smoothing the blankets as if they were an evening dress. "Oh, but there is. There's always a need to say thank you. The night Günther died, I wish I'd said thank you to him, but I didn't. Sit down."

An insistent buzzing started up in my eardrums at these words.

I discovered a chair half buried under a layer of old newspapers, cleared it and sat down.

"You know Günther killed himself, don't you? It wasn't an accident. He knew the roads around Siebenhoch better than anyone. He could have taken those bends with his eyes closed. And that evening, he hadn't drunk any more than usual. I know. I was there. I was with him before he ended it all."

"And why do you wish you'd thanked him?"

"He said he wanted to have done with the story of the Bletterbach and with alcohol. Because he was ruining my life. He was trying to tell me that he was going to kill himself. But I was too drunk to understand. He felt guilty about that, too, he thought it was because of him that I hit the bottle. He loved me, you know."

She stared at me, defying me to contradict her.

"Were the two of you very much in love?" I asked.

"Not like Kurt and Evi, no. We" – she laughed – "we weren't Kurt and Evi, unfortunately. But it worked. We loved each other and when we were drinking there were even moments when we were happy. Unfortunately, as the years passed, those moments became few and far between. Pass me that, will you? I'm thirsty."

"Better not."

"It's my medicine, Salinger. Give it to me."

I could have refused. I could have got up from that rickety chair and left without saying another word. She was feeling better, the risk of her dying of exposure had passed, I had no more responsibility towards her. I didn't do it, though. I didn't leave.

As usual, I lied to myself.

I told myself I was doing it for her. As long as I was there, as long as she felt it her duty to speak, she wouldn't get drunk. I would grant her a drop only to warm herself. She was still numb with cold, after all.

B for bullshit.

But I didn't do it to discover new details about the Bletterbach killings. I did it to ward off the Beast. If I concentrated on the story of the

Bletterbach, I wouldn't think about all that whiteness the blizzard had brought down on Siebenhoch and the speed with which my mind had gone to pieces. One worry drives out another.

I was scared. Scared of what had happened to me in the supermarket parking lot.

What if the attack had come while I was with Annelise? Would she have realised that I was still refusing to take the drugs? What would she have done? Would she have left me as she had threatened to do? And what if the attack had come while I was with Clara? How would my child have reacted?

I handed Brigitte the bottle of beer that was on the table. She knocked it back in a moment.

The eyes of a wounded animal.

"Do I disgust you, Salinger?"

"I feel sorry for you."

"Why?"

"Because you have a big problem with that stuff."

"I'm fine, my dear. Now that Günther isn't here, I'm really fine."

"Didn't you love him?"

"Love isn't as simple as it's depicted in films. Not in Siebenhoch anyway. I only realised I was really in love with Günther when he killed himself."

She burst into a guttural laugh and threw her head back.

"He did it to save me, don't you see? That's what he was trying to tell me. That he was going to take his own life because he knew he was killing me. And I'm not just talking about the booze. I'm talking about the Bletterbach. It was that story that he was killing me with. Killing *himself*. That's why I'm sorry I didn't thank him."

Brigitte stood up, letting the blankets fall on the dirty floor.

Stumbling a little, she walked over to a dark wooden dresser. She opened a drawer, causing a couple of empty bottles to fall. She didn't even notice.

She sat down and I passed her the blankets. She laid them in her lap.

She held out an old photograph album with a leather cover.

Ever since Max had shown me the pictures taken at the scene of the crime, I'd had a difficult relationship with photographs.

"Take it, it doesn't bite."

I took it and placed it on my knees. It took me a while to open it.

"Is this you?"

"It *was* me," Brigitte corrected me. "They said I could have been an actress."

The woman I had in front of me was light years from the splendour of the blonde girl winking from the album. The hand placed on the pelvis, the defiant look. The long hair, the shorts accentuating a pair of legs that wouldn't have looked out of place on any catwalk.

"That's from 1983. I'd only just turned twenty. I was working as a waitress in Aldino. I'd had a seamstress shorten the skirt of my uniform. Only by a few centimetres, but it was an excellent investment. The customers would compete over who would leave me the biggest tip. After closing hours, some of them tried to get into my knickers."

"And did they succeed?"

I immediately regretted the question, but Brigitte took it as a compliment.

"Some yes, some no," she replied coquettishly. "I wasn't an easy girl, but if you were nice enough to me, didn't have nasty scars on your face, and had all your marbles, then you might just possibly get to the finishing line. And to think that up until I was ten, my mother made me study with the nuns. The only thing that's still with me from that period is the Bible quotations. If she could hear me . . ."

She laughed, and tried to drink from a bottle that was now empty. Her face clouded over.

"There should be something cold in the fridge," she said, pointing to a door.

The smell in the kitchen was nauseating. The shutters were closed and when I switched the light on, surprised that the electricity was still working, I thought I saw the tail of a mouse disappear into a crack in the wall. The refrigerator was humming quietly. Inside, apart from some leftovers, there was only beer and spirits.

I took out a can of Forst and went back into the living room.

"Drinking alone is a crime," she said.

"I'm fine as I am."

"Thirty years ago, Salinger, I'd have turned you on just by looking at you. And now you refuse to have a beer with me?"

"Maybe thirty years ago, just like today, I'd have been married."

"Married men are a myth. Do you really think no married man ever got it on with me?"

"I don't doubt it."

My tone must have bothered Brigitte, who contemptuously ordered me to turn the page. I obeyed.

The second photograph showed Brigitte hugging a girl I couldn't help recognising. Brown hair, blue eyes and freckles on her upturned nose.

Evi.

"She was my best friend," Brigitte said. "Even though we were like night and day. She was so sweet, adult, intelligent, while I" – she shook herself – "was that slut Brigitte Pflantz."

"Your definition?"

"Siebenhoch's definition."

"Did it bother you?"

"It was Evi who consoled me. We were seriously inseparable. I was an only child and she only had Markus. We both would have liked to have a sister, so we adopted each other. We spent our days laughing over nothing. We tried to spend as much time as possible together, even though I had my work and she had her mother." Brigitte darkened. "That bitch."

She fell silent.

I waited.

Brigitte looked at me, then drank from the can and burped. "She was an alcoholic. And she was mad. I used to hear her screaming. We all heard her screaming. And we knew perfectly well that when she went down into town, all scented and shiny, she was going to prostitute herself."

"Did Evi know?"

"You can bet on it. Of course she knew. As the Lord is my witness. But you know something? Nothing made her lose her smile. It seems like a joke: your mother is a first-class alcoholic whore and you still have the strength to smile? But that's how Evi was. She always managed to find the good side of things."

"And what would that be?"

"You'd have to ask her, I'm the spitting image of that bitch mother of hers. But at least I had the good sense to have my tubes sewn up. No children for me, my dear. Not even dead ones. I wanted to be free. Brigitte Pflantz would get on a plane and go to Hollywood to be an actress, she would fuck all the handsomest actors in the world, and nobody would ever try to order her about. Nobody."

"Not even Günther."

"Günther came later. Before Günther, there was Kurt."

"I didn't know," I said, embarrassed, "that you and Kurt . . ."

Brigitte stopped in mid-air the movement of raising the can to her lips. "I didn't mean *that.* I never fucked Kurt, although I wouldn't have minded, he was a good-looking boy. Tall, with intense eyes. I meant that Evi fell in love with Kurt and I was cut out of the picture."

She was silent for a while, brooding.

"Like a forest fire. One spark and everything goes up in flames. Well, it was the same with Kurt and Evi. It was round about then that this photograph was taken, in '81. The year Evi graduated and moved to Innsbruck."

"Were you O.K. with the idea?"

"Of her leaving?"

"Yes."

"Everybody talked about leaving, she was actually doing it. I admired her."

"What about Kurt? How did he take it?"

"He followed her. I think that's answer enough."

"And you felt cut out of the picture? Your words."

"Do you suspect me, Salinger?"

"I don't suspect anyone, I'm not playing detective."

"That's not how it looks to me. And anyway, yes, I was upset. Because it all happened very quickly. One day, Evi and I were inseparable, the next day all she could talk about was Kurt. Kurt this, Kurt that. Then she started standing me up. Brigitte had dropped off the radar, my dear. A fire, and it's every man for himself. And the place the fire started was the Bletterbach. Fate has a strange sense of humour, doesn't it?"

"So it seems."

"Would you be kind enough to get a drink for a lady, Salinger? This one's finished."

"Isn't it a bit soon?"

Brigitte shrugged.

"The last one," I said to her, when I got back from the kitchen.

"Or what will you do? Spank me?"

"I'm leaving now."

Brigitte leaned towards me. "Don't you want me to tell you about Kurt and Evi? Everything revolves around them, doesn't it?"

"You tell me."

"Kurt was five years older than Evi. He was a handsome boy, there was a queue at his door." A wicked gleam. "With or without wedding rings on their fingers, women would eat him up with their eyes."

"Did Kurt take advantage?"

"If he did, he was clever enough not to get caught. But if you really want to know, he wasn't the type. The only thing Kurt cared about was the mountains. His role model was his father, Hannes. He wanted to be like him, a rescuer. And he was, at least until he moved to Innsbruck. Those two were very similar, even though they quarrelled like cat and dog and ended up not speaking to each other." She gulped her beer. "Evi spent quite a lot of time in the Bletterbach. Did you know she was studying geology?"

"So I've been told."

"Her passion started there, in the Bletterbach. Whenever she had free time and I wasn't available, she'd grab her backpack and go off to look at fossils."

"You didn't go with her?"

"With all those brambles? Are you joking? Have you seen the legs I had?"

I smiled. "No brambles for Miss Siebenhoch."

"There was nothing like that around here, but I bet I would have won first prize. Anyway, it was during one of those hikes that Kurt and Evi's paths crossed. I mean, they were acquainted, but up until that moment they'd never really looked at each other. But then the spark, and the fire. You know what Kurt liked about Evi? The way she had of always seeing the good side of things. Kurt was a grumpy character. Just like his father. But Evi was sunny. You could never be angry with her. And she was incredibly intelligent. Go to the last page."

There was a voluminous plastic folder.

"What's this?"

"My scrapbook of Evi's triumphs. Have a look."

They were mostly press cuttings. Sometimes short items. Evi Baumgartner (or rather, Tognon, I noticed) has won the prize for . . . Deserves congratulations for . . . Local scientist . . .

"Scientist?"

"She was the closest thing to a scientist we'd ever had around here," Brigitte replied. "Carry on. There you have the proof of what I'm telling you."

There were a number of little pamphlets. The heading was that of the University of Innsbruck.

"Papers she published," she said.

"But Evi hadn't yet graduated when . . . it happened."

"When she was killed, you mean?"

I nodded.

"I told you she was good. She stood out. It didn't take her teachers long to realise that she had potential. Evi wasn't seen very often in Siebenhoch in the last three years of her life. Too much research, too much studying. She would have had a career, believe me." She took one of the pamphlets from me. "Look at this. It's her first paper. She was really emotional when she told me about it on the phone. Actually, I thought it was pretty much of a scam, but she said I was just being cynical as usual."

"Why a scam?"

"It's a refutation of a thesis by another researcher at the University. All a bit technical and complicated, but that's not the point. To me, it was obvious that Evi had been manipulated. Her teachers had persuaded her to publish this in order to demolish that other guy. It wasn't her idea. You see what I mean?"

"They were using her to get at him."

"But that's not the end of it. The guy showed up at Kurt and Evi's place. He was furious. The thing had been a real blow to him. But after two hours spent with Evi, they became friends. I mean, you destroy my work and I become your best friend? Impossible for everyone else, but not for Evi. That's how she was."

My mouth was dry.

I had just found a motive.

"Do you remember the name of the researcher?"

"No, but it's written there."

I looked for it, already knowing what I would find.

Oscar Grünwald. The man who sent the telegram.

Geht nicht dorthin!

"You look like you've seen a ghost, Salinger."

"Is that offer of a beer still open?"

Brigitte pointed to the kitchen door. "One for you, one for me."

I came back, sat down and sipped from the bottle. Then I lit myself a cigarette. I pondered for a while, and Brigitte sat there silently watching me.

"What's the matter?" I said.

"You."

"What about me?"

"Why on earth you are interested in this story? Do you really not want to make a film about it?"

"I'm not a director."

"Then why?"

"It's none of your business."

Brigitte blew through her teeth, producing a kind of shrill whistle. "You know who you remind me of?"

"I don't think I'd like to know."

"Günther. You also want to find out who killed them."

It wasn't a question.

There was no answer.

"Günther used to say he knew quite a few secrets about the killings. Things he couldn't admit to. Stuff that would have blown the whole of Siebenhoch sky high. He used to say that when he was very, very drunk. One time, I tried to get him to talk. I made him drunk deliberately. It was getting on my nerves, all that going on about secrets without ever coming out with them. I didn't think he was being very respectful."

"Respectful?"

"I was the one who wiped his vomit, bought the aspirins for his hangovers, made excuses for him when he stayed away from work. I was the one who cradled him in my arms when he had one of his nightmares. He never told me anything. Anything. When he died, I thought for a few days it was murder."

"You mean someone might have killed him to keep him quiet?"

"Yes. But it was a stupid idea."

"Why stupid?"

"He was already killing himself. A little more patience and he would have died anyway."

"You were there to protect him."

"But who would have protected me?"

I said nothing.

"Sometimes I still think it," she resumed. "It'd be more heroic, wouldn't it?" Her voice shook. "Günther murdered just as he was about to shed light on the Bletterbach killings."

She was crying now.

"I'm sorry, Brigitte."

Brigitte looked up abruptly, her eyes shiny. "Get out, Salinger, get out and shut the door behind you."

I didn't want to leave her alone, not in that condition. But I did. I left her alone with her booze and an army of demons.

* * *

Outside, the blizzard was still covering Siebenhoch in snow and ice. I drove the kilometres separating me from Clara and Annelise, in the grip of a thousand thoughts.

Just before getting within sight of home, I stopped and switched off the engine. I grabbed my cell phone and waited for Mike to pick up on the other side of the ocean.

After the seventh ring, I heard his drowsy voice. "Salinger? Do you know what fucking time it is?"

"For you, it's always too early. Is she a blonde?"

"A redhead, sergeant," Mike joked. I heard him closing a door. "So," he said with a hint of anxiety in his voice, "how's it going, partner?"

"So-so. How about you?"

So-so meant half shit and the other half wasn't much better.

"Mr Smith is trying to crucify me and I screwed up the sound tests twice running. Partner, seriously, is everything O.K.? Are you taking the magic pills?"

"How did you know?"

"Mike McMellan always knows everything."

"Have you been talking to Annelise?"

"Yep. We're worried about you, shithead."

I screwed up my eyes. I didn't want to be moved.

"I need a favour."

"Annelise told me you've become obsessed with the story of a murder."

"More than one," I corrected him without even thinking.

"Whatever. Is it true?"

"Yes."

From the other side of the ocean, silence. And a noise that I couldn't define at first. Then I realised Mike was chomping on nachos.

"She told me that if I dared help you, she'd cut off my . . . you know."

"She'd be quite capable of that."

"Have things gotten so bad, partner?"

This time, I was the one to be silent.

"I need to know."

"Who committed a murder thirty years ago? Have you gone completely crazy?"

"I'm not so stupid," I replied, even though a part of me was convinced of the opposite, especially after what Brigitte had told me. "I just want to find out if I'm still capable. If I'm still able to tell a story the way it should be told."

"But it's obvious that—"

"Not after the Ortles."

"Shit, Salinger, do you want me to massage your ego? Do you want me to tell you you're the best writer around? If that's what you want, I'll do it. I'll get on a plane today and come there and sing you a lullaby, but I want you to know that if that's your real problem, then you're as crazy as shit."

"There's no way you could understand."

I'd offended him. I knew that even before I'd finished the sentence.

"Because I wasn't there, right?"

"That's not the reason."

"You're an asshole, Salinger."

"If you'd been in my place, nothing would have happened."

"That's not true."

I'd thought a lot about it. I'd spent nights on end thinking about it.

"You wouldn't have been so dumb as to go down into that crevasse. Right now, 'Mountain Angels' would be the latest series from the McMellan–Salinger stable, Mr Smith would be sitting happily in his office counting his money and we'd be thinking about the second season. Or making a movie."

"We already are," Mike murmured. I'd never heard him sound so depressed.

"I hate it."

A sigh. "So do I. But we have a contract."

"I know. Now listen carefully," I said, again pretending a normal voice, "because I need your help."

"Shoot."

"I want you to find any information you can about a particular person."

"Who is he?"

"Do you have pen and paper?"

"*Of course.*"

"His name is Oscar Grünwald. He used to be some kind of researcher at the University of Innsbruck. I want to know everything there is to know about him. Unleash your inner 007."

"Salinger?"

"Do you want me to spell it for you?"

"Are you sure this is a good idea?"

"Just do it."

Silence.

Then Mike's voice: "Is it a good story at least?"

I smiled, and for the first time that afternoon I was sincere. "It's a great story, Mike. As soon as I have a little time, I'll tell you the whole of it."

"Then I owe you one."

"'Bye, man."

"Partner?"

"Yes?"

"Be careful."

* * *

Clara was dressed in red. Dark red. Blood red. She had her hands behind her back and she was pale, her lips blue. Her eyes wide open and fixed. I crouched and opened my arms. I wanted her to come to me and hug me. I wanted to warm her up.

I wanted to warm myself up.

"Why won't you come to me, sweetheart?"

"Can you hear it, Papà?"

I couldn't hear anything and I told her so.

Clara bowed her head.

"Why are you crying?"

"The voice says it's coming to get you. It says that this time . . ." Clara sniffed, her breath rising in little clouds. It was cold. It was so cold. "It says that this time I have to come, too."

I would have liked to go to her. To hug her, console her.

I couldn't move.

"Five letters, Papà."

"Stars?"

"Five letters, Papà."

She was barefoot, I only realised it at that moment. And her feet weren't blue. They were black.

Like the feet of a corpse.

"Five letters, Papà."

"No, sweetheart, *no*." The kilometres separating me.

Clara raised her head abruptly. Someone had gouged out her eyes.

She screamed.

I screamed.

* * *

Five letters. "Beast".

The Devil's Workshop

It was already February 5 when I knocked on Hermann Kagol's door. The blizzard was now just a memory and, even though the sun didn't break through the ice even at the warmest times of day, it was pleasant strolling in the open air.

The creator of the Visitors' Centre lived in one of the oldest and most beautiful houses in Siebenhoch. But the two-storey building wasn't ostentatious, its richness lay in the details. Elegant ironwork, a wall that must have been an explosion of wisteria in the spring, sober but luxurious finishing touches everywhere. The one concession to vanity, standing beneath a snow-covered slate canopy, was a black Mercedes, the latest model.

I was greeted by a woman of about fifty.

"Signora Kagol?"

"I'm the housekeeper. Are you Signor Salinger?"

"Yes, I am. I have an appointment. And I'm sorry for the blunder."

I followed her to a *Stube*, where she sat me in a leather armchair. The *Stube* here was very different from the one in which Max had spent his childhood, and the stove, set into the wall, was a masterpiece of masonry. I was no expert, but judging by the skill with which the majolica had been worked it must have been made by a great craftsman. On the panelled walls were carvings that must have cost a fortune. Everything here exuded money and power.

"I'm sorry to have kept you waiting, Signor Salinger." Hermann's handshake was firm and decisive. "Can I offer you a drink?"

"I'll have whatever you're having."

"I'm teetotal," Hermann said, almost apologetically. "Do you mind mineral water?"

"Mineral water will be fine."

The housekeeper left us.

When she returned carrying two glasses with slices of lemon at the bottom and a jug of what looked to me like very pure crystal, Hermann thanked her and dismissed her. As soon as we were alone, the door properly closed, he served the water.

"They say toasting with water brings bad luck," he said, raising his glass. "I hope you're not superstitious."

"I'm many things, Signor Kagol," I replied, clinking my glass against his, "but not superstitious."

"You intrigue me, Signor Salinger, tell me how many."

"I'm a father. A husband. A T.V. writer. And a very bad skier."

Hermann laughed politely and smoothed his droopy iron-grey moustache. "And are you here as a T.V. writer, Signor Salinger?"

"No, as a writer pure and simple."

"We've had various woodcarvers around here," Hermann stated, indicating the works on the walls, "a couple of bishops, a few witches, quite a few mountaineers and lots and lots of troublemakers, but not a single writer. I'm intrigued."

I tried to be convincing. I'd prepared well. I'd had four days to absorb what Brigitte had told me. I'd made notes. Above all, I'd done a lot of thinking, and had prepared a nice little story to con Hermann Kagol. Hoping he wouldn't then go and spill it all to Werner, in which case I'd be screwed.

"As you know, I'm here in Siebenhoch as a visitor. After that terrible accident—"

"I know the details. I'm sorry such a tragedy should have happened to you. I hope you're not still suffering the after-effects."

"It was hard at first, but I'm much better now. So much better that I'm getting quite bored."

Hermann nearly choked on his mineral water. His laughter made him lose his veneer of elegance in favour of what he must have been like before making his fortune.

A mountain man with big ambitions.

"I admit," he said, recovering his composure, "Siebenhoch isn't New York."

"But the quiet of Siebenhoch is what I needed. And besides," I added, feigning an embarrassment I wasn't feeling at all, "it's here that I discovered my . . . vocation."

"As a writer?"

"I always thought that writers were serious people, Signor Kagol. People with lots of degrees, real nerds. Instead of which, I woke up one day and told myself: why not write a book about this place? About its myths, its legends. A biography of Siebenhoch."

"A biography of Siebenhoch? I wouldn't want to dampen your enthusiasm, Signor Salinger, but there are already quite a few books about this region. Not to appear immodest, but several of them were financed by my foundation."

I'd expected an objection like that. "I've read all of them, Signor Kagol. From first to last. But nobody has ever treated this place like a living being. As if it were a person who was born, had a childhood and then grew up."

"It's an unusual point of view."

"Isn't that why you would read the book? Curiosity."

Hermann raised his glass. "It's an excellent idea. But I don't quite see how I can help you. Are you asking me to finance the publication?"

"No, I'm not looking for a publisher. Never put the cart before the horse, as my *Mutti* used to say. First I write it and then I sell it."

"An excellent philosophy. But I still don't—"

"According to lots of people, you saved Siebenhoch from a slow, painful death."

"That's an exaggeration."

"But I think you had exceptional foresight. And I'm not just referring to the Visitors' Centre. You've kept Siebenhoch's traditions alive. That's what interests me."

Hermann's eyes gleamed.

I'd nailed it.

He nodded passionately. "Without its traditions, what would Siebenhoch be, Signor Salinger?"

"A tourist village like any other. With the Bletterbach instead of a beach. Entertainers in Tyrolean costumes and songs in the elevators. Look, you're the *Krampusmeister*. I'd like to start the book with the man who makes the devil's clothes."

"The man who makes the devil's clothes. I like it. May I call you Jeremiah?"

"Whatever you prefer, although everyone calls me Salinger. Apart from my mother and Werner."

"So be it. Come with me, Salinger."

* * *

He led me down a steep staircase to the basement. There was a strong smell of glue in the air. When he switched the light on, all became clear.

I smiled, surprised. "Is this where the magic is born?"

"The devil's workshop, Salinger, to paraphrase your words."

It was a huge room that must have extended under the whole of the house. The indisputable centrepiece was a gigantic table heaped with *Krampus* costumes and masks and various types of sewing machine.

All around the walls was an impressive array of cupboards and shelves filled with all kinds of objects.

"Extraordinary."

"I try to use traditional materials. These are all natural dyes. Iron for blue, for example. Mercury. Silver. Nothing that can't be found locally."

I pointed at a box filled with shells. "These, too?"

"Let me show you one of my treasures."

He took a book from a cupboard. It looked very old. I noticed that every page was protected by a layer of cellophane.

"What's this?"

"The notes of a schoolmaster. From 1874. He was sent to Siebenhoch by the Emperor. The Austro-Hungarian Empire cared a lot about the education of its citizens. The dream of the Habsburgs was to build an enlightened monarchy in which nobody was illiterate and everything worked to perfection. Herr Weger lived here for fifty years. He married a local girl and you can see his grave behind the church, a simple iron cross, as he requested in his will."

"Weger . . ." I said. "I don't know of any Wegers in Siebenhoch."

"He had a son, who died of diphtheria. A sad story. Weger didn't deserve it. He was an intelligent person and his ideas were quite advanced for his time. This" – he tapped his index finger on the cover of the book – "is proof of that. At the end of the nineteenth century, Europe was in the grip of positivism. People thought science would solve all problems. A kind of Enlightenment attitude raised to the *n*th degree. Everywhere, factories and railway lines were being built. Soon, there would be electric lighting in every street. The Habsburgs were infatuated with the writings of the great thinkers of the day, and Weger had studied them, too. But then he'd put them aside."

"How do you mean?"

Even though I'd come to the Kagol house with the intention of extracting information about the dead brother of the wealthiest man in Siebenhoch, this story fascinated me.

"Because he'd realised that some things can't and shouldn't be done away with."

"Such as?"

Hermann opened his arms in a gesture that was meant to take in the whole of his workshop. "The old traditions. So many people had tried to eradicate them, Salinger. First, the Catholic Church, then the men of the Enlightenment, Napoleon, and finally the Habsburgs. But a simple schoolmaster had understood that if the ancient traditions disappeared, not only would strange customs and a few proverbs be lost: the soul of the people would die. So he started keeping this."

He showed me a few pages. Weger had close, elegant handwriting. He wrote in a refined German, full of words I couldn't translate. But above all, this brilliant schoolmaster showed himself to be an artist manqué.

"These drawings are remarkable."

"As precise as photographs, aren't they? But Weger didn't only transcribe old stories and draw traditional costumes. He started collecting them."

He led me to the far end of the room.

"Naturally," he explained, opening a large wall cupboard, "these aren't the originals. They're faithful reproductions. Same fabrics, same ornaments. As you can see," he added, shaking an inlaid belt so that it jangled, "these are shells."

I was fascinated. "Are these also copies?"

"They're real. I paid for them out of my own pocket."

They were *Krampus* masks. Hermann put on rubber gloves and placed the masks carefully on the table, revealing their detail in the harsh fluorescent light.

"This one's the oldest. According to estimates, it probably dates from the end of the fourteenth century. Extraordinary, don't you think?"

I couldn't stop looking at it. "It's a masterpiece."

"Does it scare you?"

"To tell the truth, no. I'd call it curious, amusing. Certainly not scary."

"Because things change, Salinger. People modify their concept of what's horrible according to the flow of history and changes in customs. But at the time, believe me, this mask was meant to instil fear."

"No movies. No television and no Stephen King."

"Only the Bible, translated badly and understood even less. And long winter nights."

"With the Bletterbach behind the houses."

I didn't even realise I'd said it. I was hypnotised by the *Krampus* mask. By those empty eyes, above all.

"Does the Bletterbach scare you?"

"Can I be honest?"

"Please," Hermann said, putting his treasures away.

"I do find it frightening. It's a prehistoric graveyard."

Hermann turned to look at me. "Those aren't your words, are they?"

"Actually no," I replied, embarrassed. "But I find them fitting. They're Verena's, the wife of—"

"The wife of Chief Krün. But she was quoting someone else as well."

"Really?"

Hermann sighed. "These aren't things to talk about down here, Salinger. Unpleasant memories. I'd prefer to continue our conversation in daylight, if you don't mind."

* * *

Hermann was examining a photograph, an aerial shot of the Bletterbach that hung next to a stag's head carved out of pinewood.

"Do you see anything unusual in this picture, Salinger?"

"The Centre isn't there."

"That's right. Do you know who took this?"

"No."

"The same person who called the Bletterbach 'a prehistoric graveyard'."

"Your brother Günther?"

"That's right. He was on board the rescue team's Alouette when he took it. He gave it to me for my birthday. He said only a fool like me could think of making money from that terrible place. He was convinced nobody could possibly like the Bletterbach."

"He was wrong."

"A lot of people were wrong at the time. But I was sure of it. I was convinced." He turned to me, and in his eyes I saw a determination

I'd rarely seen in my life. "I knew it would work. The question wasn't whether or not people would be interested in the Bletterbach, but whether or not I'd be the one to monopolise that treasure."

"I'm afraid I don't follow."

"Tourism was taking off everywhere. In the Val d'Aosta, in Switzerland. In Austria. But around here it was as if nobody had noticed because everyone was too busy planting bombs or demanding special laws. Sooner or later, though, someone else would get the idea."

"And you wanted to be the first."

"I wanted the Bletterbach, Salinger. I felt I was the right man in the right place at the right time."

"And time proved you right."

Hermann nodded smugly. "Yes, it did. Time proved me right. My family wasn't rich. Nobody in Siebenhoch was rich. Not in those days, anyway. The young people were leaving, the old did nothing but complain, and those in the middle? Either they left or they complained about the fact that they couldn't leave. My family had four cows. Four. Maybe that's how your book should begin, with four cows. Because it was with those four cows that the rebirth of Siebenhoch started."

"You'll have to explain."

"There's not much to explain. My father died and I inherited everything."

"And Günther?"

"It's the law of the closed *maso*. The eldest son inherits everything, but has to make sure he gives half of the value of the property to the second born, in cash. Half," he said, "or a third or a quarter, depending on the number of siblings. The important thing is that the land and property shouldn't be divided."

"Why?"

"Because dividing the barren land in Alto Adige meant destroying a family. Reducing it to starvation, if not worse. When my father died, I sold the cows. Günther didn't make a fuss. He said I had all the time in the world to give him his share of the inheritance. He thought I was crazy, but he trusted my abilities. The proceeds of the sale I invested in my first company. A construction company."

"To build the Visitors' Centre?"

"That was already in my mind, but it wasn't the first thing I built. The foundations of the Centre weren't laid until 1990. Kagol Construction started in 1982, the day I turned thirty, a date I chose because I was young and idealistic and it seemed to me quite . . . symbolic. It brought me luck, anyway. The first order Kagol Construction got was to repair the roof of a henhouse in Aldino. I found myself up to my ears in chicken shit, but believe me, I was overjoyed."

"Four cows and a pile of shit. I could use it as a title."

"That would be wonderful, but I don't think it'd sell many copies."

"Did Günther work with you?"

Hermann's face clouded over. "It's the second time you've mentioned my brother, Salinger. Why's that?"

"I'm curious," I said, choosing my words as if I were walking on eggshells. "From what I've heard, a lot of people here miss Günther."

Hermann looked surprised. "Really?"

"People have often spoken to me about him."

"In relation to his drinking?" he asked, his face registering no emotion.

"In relation to the Bletterbach killings."

"Are you planning to write about that business?"

"I don't think so," I replied without batting an eyelid. "Maybe a few hints, just to give a slightly sinister feel to the Bletterbach."

"I don't know if I like the idea, Salinger."

"The book will be about the village and that event is part of its story."

Hermann nodded, although there was a touch of suspicion in his eyes. "A lot of nasty things happened that day. And in the days that followed."

"Werner told me about that. He also left."

"In a hurry, yes. One night he just upped and left. So I've been told."

"Weren't you here?"

"I was away."

"On business?"

"In '85, Kagol Construction became Kagol Construction Ltd. I had an office in Rovoreto, I was constantly travelling throughout the north of Italy. I had ongoing projects in Friuli, in the Veneto, and was about to seal a major deal in the Tyrol. The building of a skiing centre. I wasn't on my own now. The previous year I'd hired, in addition to the usual office staff, two young architects with very innovative ideas. One of the two still works for me, the other emigrated to Germany. He's designed several stadiums and a skyscraper in the Arab Emirates."

"That's impressive," I commented.

"In '85 I was hardly ever in Siebenhoch. Nor the following years. I came for the feast days and even then I wasn't around much." He sighed. "Do you have regrets, Salinger?"

"Lots."

"Then you'll understand why I'm so hostile to the idea of seeing that horrible story in print."

"No problem," I replied. "I'm interested in the *Krampus* and the legends. The rest is background. I can easily leave it out. I don't want to write a book that's going to upset anyone. Knowing me, I'll probably never finish it anyway."

"How can I thank you?"

"By allowing me to smoke in here."

Hermann opened wide a window. "I'd be glad to keep you company, Salinger, but I quit."

We were interrupted by a sudden scratching at the door. Hermann's face lit up.

It was his dogs. Two Dobermans that sniffed me and then ran to fete their master. Hermann returned their affection with genuine love.

"Ulysses and Telemachus."

"Heroic names."

"They're all I have."

"You don't have any family?"

"I have my business. I have the Visitors' Centre. Three hotels, two of them in Siebenhoch, and I'm the *Krampusmeister*. But no children. No family. I didn't have time."

"Too much work?"

Hermann again stroked the heads of the two Dobermans lying at his feet. "Too much work, yes. That's why I lost Günther, too."

Hermann sat back in his armchair. He drank a glass of water while I savoured the taste of the Marlboro.

The cold coming from the window had numbed half my face.

"Even though I was away, I knew everything that was going on in the village. I knew about Günther and his problem."

"The drinking?"

"Of course, but Günther was" – Hermann assumed a dark tone – "a weakling. Does that strike you as cruel? Please tell me the truth."

"Yes, it does."

"He was my brother, but to me he was a source of embarrassment. I was living proof that you can make your dreams come true by yourself, just through force of will. I'd turned four cows into an empire that was growing day by day. I had a nine-figure turnover, Salinger. Politicians came and licked my arse. I attracted envy as if I were a nice juicy piece of shit in the middle of a swarm of flies. And I would swat those flies away. One word from me and a haulage firm lost half its orders, one sign and building material companies collapsed like sandcastles. I had innovative ideas, and those ideas bore fruit. The world was mine." He raised his fist. "Günther, on the other hand, was a weakling. Like our father. He also drank like a sponge. He died of cirrhosis of the liver."

"But Gunter had seen that—"

"That carnage? What of it?" Hermann cut in, contemptuously. "You know how many dead workers I've seen in my career? Bricklayers drowned in cement or falling off scaffolding, technicians blown up by explosives. An endless number of dead people. But do you think I started drinking and feeling sorry for myself?"

"Maybe Günther wasn't made of the same stuff as you."

Hermann sighed. "No, Gunter wasn't made of the same stuff as me.

He was too sensitive. As big and fat as a bear, language that would have made our poor mother faint, and yet he had a heart of gold. I only realised that later, when the euphoria of those years passed. For me the '80s and '90s were a kind of festival. I was working eighteen hours a day, seven days a week. I never stopped to think about important things."

"Things like a family?"

"And Günther. I often told people I was an only child. His death was merely the fitting end to a wasted life. One less drunkard, I told myself, and went back to signing contracts, supervising projects and having my backside kissed by some local councillor as if nothing had happened. But when it comes down to it, we were similar, Günther and I."

"Why do you say that?"

"Because Günther had his drinking and I had my work. It was my drug. And when I started to slow down, I began looking back. And thinking about Günther. I realised I'd behaved like a real arsehole. I wondered if I could have saved him."

"But how?"

Hermann looked at me as if I had just landed from Mars. "I was rich, and I still am, Salinger. I could have taken him to some specialist clinic to be cleaned out, I could have paid for him to travel around the world, and have as many whores as he wanted. Whatever it took to get that demon out of his head, I could have bought it. Instead I left him alone. Here. This is the house we grew up in, and this is where Günther lived. I had it almost completely refurbished."

"Almost?"

"When it dawned on me what I'd done to Gunter, I went crazy. I don't know why, but I took it out on these four walls. I wanted to raze them to the ground. But it was my house. Our house. So I decided to refurbish it from top to bottom. I didn't have the courage, though, to touch his room, it stayed exactly as he'd left it the last time he was here."

"I'm no specialist, but that strikes me as pretty insane," I couldn't help saying.

"Sometimes, I think that, too. Do you want to see it?"

I followed him upstairs.

While the rest of the Kagol house was furnished with care and with furniture of great value, the room that Hermann showed me was a dump.

The planks on the walls were black with soot, the bed was worm-eaten and the windows were of an opaque glass that almost entirely blocked the light.

There was a bottle on the cupboard next to the unmade bed. And under the bottle, two 1,000-lire banknotes.

"What do you think, Salinger?"

He was about to add something, but a voice interrupted him. It was the housekeeper. An urgent phone call from Berlin. Hermann cursed.

"Business," he said. He apologised and ran downstairs two steps at a time.

I was left alone, with that time capsule in front of me. I couldn't resist. Even though I could hear Hermann's voice muttering in the distance, I walked into Günther's room.

* * *

What I was doing was wrong. In a way, it was a kind of desecration. I was looking into the cupboards (and under the bed and in the bedside table and . . .) of a man who had been dead for twenty-five years. A man who had lived a brief, unhappy life. Günther didn't deserve what I was doing.

The thought didn't stop me even for a moment.

I had just this one opportunity to establish whether or not what Brigitte had told me had a basis of truth. I had been under the illusion that talking to Hermann might yield some new information. But Hermann had said nothing to help me clarify my thoughts.

I panted as my fingers moved quickly amid boots with holes in them, drugs long past their expiry date, pyjamas, underwear. There was also a mirror, but I preferred not to look at my own reflection. I searched. Time was passing.

One second. Two seconds, three seconds . . .

Quick. *Quick.*

If Günther really had had his suspicions, it was here, in this unhoped-for treasure, that I would find the right clues. I could sense it, just as I could smell the dust of decades prickling my nostrils. I felt in the jacket pockets, the trouser pockets, rummaged through prescriptions and postcards. I searched in a couple of mountain backpacks. I searched in a leather bag devoured by worms. I searched in every damned nook and cranny in that room. Without finding anything other than old bills, dirty handkerchiefs and a few out-of-date coins. I was bathed in sweat.

Then I saw it.

Behind a wardrobe. A music box. It seemed to vibrate, it was so promising. Holding my breath, I lifted it.

I stopped and pricked up my ears. I could still hear Hermann's monotonous voice from the foot of the stairs.

Move.

I turned the music box over and found the battery compartment. I opened it, using my nails as a picklock. It was a pointless precaution: the acid from the batteries had spilled out, turning them into little sponges with an acrid odour that hurt the nostrils. No music would betray what I was doing.

And what I was doing was desecrating the grave of Günther Kagol.

I opened the box. It emitted a squeak and nothing more. Inside were a few official-looking typewritten papers. I unfolded them and tried to read them. There were stamps and a few rings. Beer, I thought. Or maybe tears.

I read.

What I read took my breath away.

It was the dogs that saved me.

I heard them barking, then Hermann's voice calming them. I put the papers in my pocket, replaced the music box, closed the wardrobe and pretended to be interested in the window frame.

"It's lead, isn't it?"

I hoped he wouldn't notice the breathlessness in my voice.

"That's how they used to make them," he said. He looked at me, smoothing his moustache. "Do you want to ask me anything else, or . . . ?"

"I've already taken too much advantage of your hospitality, Hermann. I'd like to photograph your workshop one of these days. If you don't mind."

"With pleasure. But I meant . . . " he said, letting his eyes complete the sentence.

"No Bletterbach. Let the dead rest in peace."

The typewritten papers were burning a hole in my trouser pocket.

* * *

The following minutes spent in the company of Hermann have faded from my memory. Wiped out. All I can remember is my longing to get out of there and devote myself to my treasure.

Four pages. The paper was yellow and crumbly to the touch. The date at the bottom was April 7, 1985. Three weeks before the killings.

I reread them quickly. Then again. I couldn't believe what Günther had discovered. For a moment, I put myself in his shoes, and what I felt was indescribable. I understood why he had drunk himself to death.

Those typewritten sheets were a hydrogeological risk assessment. A report that in a few lines, with a couple of graphs and several references to ordnance maps, demonstrated how the building of the Bletterbach Visitors' Centre would prove not only damaging to the ecosystem in the gorge, but also dangerous.

The foundations of the Visitors' Centre were laid in 1990, five years after a young geology student, in filing these four pages, had made herself an enemy that not even her smile could win round. The signature at the bottom of this document opposing the construction of the Centre was Evi's.

I could still hear the contemptuous way Hermann had spoken about

Günther. But was a man who refused to accept his brother's alcoholism also a murderer?

Maybe not, I told myself, as I reread the report for the umpteenth time.

And yet Hermann Kagol had shown the world that he was someone it was best not to mess around with. Especially back then. To use his own words, Günther had had his drinking and Hermann his work.

But there was much more to him, in my opinion. Those four cows he was so proud of were not only four animals left to him by an alcoholic father. They were a symbol. The symbol of his social redemption. And the Visitors' Centre was the outward mark of his success.

Jaekelopterus Rhenaniae

The following morning, I updated the file on the computer, putting down everything I had discovered, attaching a scan of the document signed by Evi and noting all the hypotheses, questions and leads that I could think of.

There were a lot of them.

Then I went for a long walk in the cold, hoping a bit of movement might chase away that sense of impending menace. It didn't help. At lunch, I picked at my food and answered Annelise's questions with monosyllables, until she got fed up and stopped talking to me.

All I could think about was Evi's report. With those few pages, she had held up work on the Visitors' Centre for five years. Given the competition in the tourism field, five years are as long as geological eras.

It also occurred to me that if Evi hadn't been killed on April 28, 1985 and had been able to continue her battle for the conservation of the Bletterbach, of which she was obviously very fond (wasn't it there, as Brigitte had told me, that her love for Kurt had blossomed? Wasn't it there that Evi found peace when her mother flipped out?), maybe Hermann Kagol's Centre would still have been nothing more than a plan in its creator's mind.

No Centre, no money.

Money.

A major motive, as old as humanity. When it came down to it, even Rome had been built on the scene of a crime.

Romulus killing Remus over a simple land dispute.

"Papà?"

I didn't even look up from my plate to answer her. "Yes, sweetheart?"

"Did you know that scorpions aren't insects?"

"What?"

"Scorpions aren't insects. Did you know that?"

"Really?"

Clara nodded. "They're spiders," she exclaimed, excited by the discovery. "They said so on television."

I didn't even listen to her. "Eat your potatoes, sweetheart," I muttered.

Clara went into a sulk. I didn't even notice. I was too busy following the thread of my thoughts.

I tried to calculate what the annual turnover of the Visitors' Centre must be. If the statistics I had found online were to be believed, the annual number of tourists paying the entrance fee was somewhere between 60,000 and 100,000. A decent figure, from which the running expenses, maintenance and all the rest had to be deducted. But that wasn't the only source of income. Because at least half the visitors who opened their wallets to gaze in awe at the Bletterbach stayed at hotels in Siebenhoch.

And they also ate their meals in Siebenhoch, bought souvenirs, basic foodstuffs and other things.

"Papà?"

"What is it, sweetheart?"

"What are we doing this afternoon?"

I made an effort to eat a little stew, just to please Annelise. It was very good, but my stomach was closed. That sensation under the skin was still there.

"I don't know, sweetheart."

"Shall we go sledding?"

In my mind, the money circulating around the Visitors' Centre was becoming a river of gold.

"Of course."

Who was the main beneficiary of that fortune? The community, but above all Hermann Kagol. The man who had sold four cows to become . . . what?

"Promise?"

I ruffled her hair. "Promise."

Four cows and the roof of a henhouse as stepping stones towards becoming, to all intents and purposes, the boss of Siebenhoch. He owned the Visitors' Centre, and he owned the two main hotels in the village.

He had the biggest slice of the earnings.

Hermann Kagol.

I cleared the table. Then I sank into my favourite armchair and switched on the T.V. My eyes saw, but my brain didn't register.

Clara followed me like a puppy, her little face turned towards me. "Papà?"

"Tell me, ten letters."

"What are you thinking about?"

"I'm watching the news."

"It's finished, four letters."

It was true.

I smiled. "I think four letters needs to clear his head."

"Shall we go out and play with the sled?"

I shook my head. "Later."

"When?"

"I have something to do first."

"But you promised!"

"A couple of hours, no more." I stood up.

"Where are you going?"

"I have to go to Bolzano. But when I'm back, we'll go on the sled, O.K.?"

* * *

I needed evidence. And the only place I could find it was the provincial land registry. There, I would be able to reconstruct the story of the Visitors' Centre.

And then?

Then, I thought just before the phone rang, I would think of an idea.

* * *

"Did I wake you, partner?"

"It's two in the afternoon and I'm driving."

"I always get confused with the time difference."

"Did you do your homework, Mike?"

The line was very poor. Mike's voice kept cutting out.

I cursed.

Fortunately, I noticed the exit to a service station. I put on the indicator light, found an empty space and parked. I switched off the loudspeaker and raised the phone to my ear.

"First of all, it was a lousy job you gave me. Second of all, the whole thing's a real mess. What kind of business have you gotten yourself mixed up in?"

I struck a match and breathed in the afternoon's first mouthful of cigarette smoke. It made me cough a little. "A weird story."

"I'll start with the conclusion. Grünwald. Nobody knows what happened to him. One day he just disappeared."

"When was this? In '85?"

"April or maybe May 1985."

"What do you mean April or maybe May? Can't you be more specific?"

Mike's voice turned shrill. "Why don't you do all this stuff yourself, if you're so good at criticising other people's work?"

"Because you're a genius, Mike. And I'm just a humble hack."

"Keep going."

"And you're the only person in the world who can help me get the chestnuts out of the fire."

"And?"

"And nothing, this isn't phone sex."

"If it was, I'd save my money: do you have any idea how much an intercontinental call costs?"

"You're using the network's phone, aren't you?"

"Do you want me to read you your horoscope, while we're about it?"

"I want you to start telling me the story. April or May 1985."

"Oscar Grünwald disappears. He was supposed to be giving a lecture in Ingolstadt, which is a place in—"

"Germany."

"But he never showed up. The lecture was meant to be on May 7, to be exact. He was replaced by a certain Dr Van der Velt, a Dutchman. Judging from the credentials of this Van der Velt, they won out on the deal. Grünwald was discredited, Salinger."

"What does 'discredited' mean?"

While Mike was talking, I had dug out a notebook and a ballpoint pen from the dashboard. I placed the notebook on my thigh and started scribbling.

"It means that the universities had started denying him funds."

"Tell me something I don't know."

"Grünwald's academic credibility began to come crashing down in '83. There were many attacks from the universities."

"Innsbruck?"

"Innsbruck, Vienna. Two papers from the University of Berlin and one from the University of Verona."

"How come?"

"The important question is: who was Oscar Grünwald really?"

"A geologist and palaeontologist," I replied.

"Correct, but reductive. Oscar Grünwald," Mike's voice had taken on the boring cadence of someone who was reading, and I did my best to transcribe everything he said, "was born in Carinthia, in a suburb of Kla—"

"Klagenfurt."

"That one. October 18, 1949."

"In '85, he was thirty-six years old."

"Thirty-six years old, with two degrees and a research doctorate. Palaeobiology. He was good, let me tell you."

"Good?"

"A genius, in my opinion."

"What do you know about geology and palaeontology?"

"I've learned a lot in the last couple of days. The real question is: how much do you know?"

"I know geology's the study of rocks and palaeontology's the study of fossils."

"Have you ever heard of the Permian?"

"It's the period of the great extinctions, isn't it?"

And it was also the deepest stratum of the Bletterbach. The pieces of the puzzle were starting to come together.

"The Permian was roughly between 250 and 290 million years ago. In that period, there was the greatest mass extinction in the history of the world. Almost half of all living species disappeared. Half, Salinger. Doesn't that send a shiver down your spine?"

"Yeah, a big shiver."

"There are various theories about what happened. An increase in cosmic radiation, which means they ended up like hamburgers in a huge microwave, a decrease in the productivity of the seas, an inversion of the magnetic poles, an increase in the salt level of the oceans, a decrease in oxygen, an increase in hydrogen sulphide in the atmosphere caused by bacteria. Then there's my favourite, the one that everybody knows."

"The asteroid?"

"A huge, wonderful, apocalyptic bowling ball that hit the planet and almost split it down the middle. Hollywood to the *n*th degree. And without any body doubles, partner. But Grünwald soon got tired of these studies."

"Why? Did you manage to find out?"

"The chronic lack of funds that's afflicted big brains like him since time immemorial. Grünwald wasn't the kind to sit still. He wasn't content with formulating theories."

"He wanted proof."

"Except that in palaeontology, finding proof is a little bit expensive. Nobody gave him enough money to organise his research trips. I know I shouldn't say this, given that he's a guy I don't even know, but I quite like him. Who doesn't like a madman? Except he should have been a screenwriter, not a scientist, believe me."

"Why?"

"All those who study the Permian ask themselves: ball of fire or mega earthquake? Farting micro-organisms or volcanoes on heat? But Grünwald asked himself a much more interesting question. Why did some survive and others not? Genetics? Luck? And so we arrive at the theory of ecological niches. That's the theory that brought about his downfall."

"What the hell are they?"

"Physical places affected by the apocalyptic conditions of the Permian but in a version that was kind of softer, allowing the species living there to escape the cataclysm. They slaughtered him."

"How do you mean?"

"Grünwald's theory was that there might still be places today where it was plausible that biological specimens that didn't evolve but survived the great mass extinctions were still alive."

"Didn't evolve but survived? And still alive today? 'Jurassic Park' without all that stuff about the toads and the D.N.A.?"

"Exactly." I could see him shaking his head sadly. "He had a research post in Innsbruck and they fired him. Nobody wanted to have anything to do with him. No more papers, no more books."

"How did he earn a living?"

"As a geologist. He organised trips to the Andes, where he had a few local contacts. He worked as a consultant, and even earned a bit of money as a tourist guide or a street vendor. He got by on what he could find. Then, in '85, he vanishes."

"Didn't anybody look for him?"

"Not as far as I know," was Mike's curt reply.

I thought about Brigitte. About her album of Evi's triumphs.

"Evi Baumgartner," I muttered.

"Pardon me?"

"Evi Baumgartner," I repeated, staring at a bird of prey, perhaps a falcon, drawing slow spirals in that day's clear sky.

"Who's she?"

"If you look at the papers that demolished Grünwald's academic credibility, I'm sure you'll find her name."

And a motive.

I heard Mike tapping on the keyboard of his computer.

"Nothing."

I'd been a fool. "Try Tognon," I said, remembering that this was Evi's official surname.

Another burst of gunfire.

"Bingo. University of Innsbruck. And not *one* of the papers that demolished our friend's credibility, but *the* papers that all the others drew on. Who is this Evi?"

"One of the victims of the Bletterbach."

"What did you say?"

"I said she was one of the victims of the Bletterbach. The story I'm trying to reconstruct."

Mike muttered something. More noise of fingers moving frenetically over the keyboard.

"Is that written with c and h at the end?"

"Bletterbach? Yes, why?"

Mike imitated the baritone voice-overs on film trailers. "A major twist, partner."

"Will you stop playing the fool?"

"I'm not playing the fool. You're bang in the middle of an ecological niche."

"Impossible. That kind of stuff is science fiction."

"Oh, yes?" Mike said. "Let me give you a short rundown on our friend Grünwald's book. Alto Adige has its own microclimate. In theory, it should have a continental climate, but it's in the middle of the Alps. So no continental climate. But since it has the Alps, then the climate should be Alpine, right? Wrong. The Alps protect it from winds from the north, the Alps protect it from the influence of the Mediterranean, but the Alps don't dictate the climate of the region, they create a different one: a microclimate. Which, as a point of information, Grünwald considered the primary condition for the development of an ecological niche. And now hold onto your hat, because this is really funny."

"Shoot."

"In Alto Adige there are varieties of ginkgo plants that became extinct in Europe hundreds of thousands of years ago. Yet there they are, under the Dolomites, making nonsense of our scientific beliefs, and they're in good company. For example, the nautilus. In theory, it became extinct 400 million years ago. In Alto Adige, they've found fossil remains going back to *200* million years ago."

"Are you telling me that while the nautilus was extinct in the rest of the world, here it was still swimming around for another 200 million years? Science fiction, Mike."

"No, ecological niches. I've checked this out."

"But—"

"Listen. In one of Grünwald's last papers, there was a mention of the Bletterbach. In a magazine halfway between 'The X-Files' and 'Doctor Who'. You know, the kind that predict the end of the world every two weeks."

My heart beat faster. "And?"

"Grünwald had identified the Bletterbach as one of the possible sites in which living biological material that had survived the Permian could be found. A very specific species. And I'm not talking about a little fish like Nemo, dammit. I'll send you a scan."

I waited until my cell phone emitted a beep.

I looked.

And sat there staring at the screen open-mouthed.

A kind of scorpion with a mermaid's tail. An elongated body covered with a shell that made it look like a lobster. I had never seen anything so hostile.

That was the word that came into my mind at that moment: "hostile". Seven letters.

"What the hell is it?"

"*Jaekelopterus Rhenaniae.* Forgive my pronunciation."

I tried to imagine the kind of world that could have hosted a creature like that. A planet swarming with monsters devoid of any emotion beyond an urge to hunt, a world that God decided one fine day to sweep away.

Mike continued. "A gigantic ancestor of our modern spiders, or rather, of scorpions." Something lit up in my brain, but when I tried to grab it, it had already faded. "An arthropod. But a marine arthropod. It lived in water. It was two and a half metres long. The claws were fifty centimetres long."

"And Grünwald was convinced that one of these things was still alive and living in the Bletterbach?"

"*Under* the Bletterbach. He talks about underground caves and lakes. That thing lived in fresh water. And it was a predator it was best to keep well away from."

I almost didn't hear this last comment of Mike's. Siebenhoch, I was thinking.

Whose old name was *Siebenhöhlen.* Seven caves.

"Are you still there, Salinger?"

"Do you have pen and paper?" I croaked. "There's someone else I'd like you to investigate: Hermann Kagol. He's a local businessman."

"When did he die?"

"I talked to him yesterday. I want to know everything you can find out about him. Concentrate in particular on what he's worth."

"Is he rich?"

"Stinking rich."

"But what's this guy got to do with *Jaekelopterus Rhenaniae* and Grünwald?"

"Thanks, Mike."

* * *

The interior of the land registry in Bolzano was pleasantly lit and very modern. Luckily for me, the staff were very kind, even when I tried to explain what I needed.

I had to wait half an hour, which I spent trying to get what Mike had discovered about Grünwald into some kind of perspective. The man had certainly had some weird theories. Things better suited to a movie than to the stuffy world of academia.

I realised that Grünwald was the only protagonist of this story I didn't have a photograph of. I imagined him as a kind of mad scientist, dressed like a mixture of Indiana Jones and a nineteenth-century bureaucrat, only much more awkward. I don't know why, given that this was a man who had conducted research in the Andes, but I couldn't see him coping with a steep rock face: I saw him more as a guy who tripped over his own feet, maybe with a bow tie around his neck.

Clearly, Grünwald had been a man obsessed with his work. He had sacrificed everything for his theories. Mike hadn't mentioned any wife or girlfriend. The fact that he had vanished from one day to the next without anybody becoming suspicious suggested a social life that was close to non-existent. A lone wolf with one sole purpose. Finding the ecological niches and thereby redeeming his lost honour.

I shook my head in bewilderment.

Obsessed enough to kill the woman who had destroyed his career? Maybe. What was the meaning of that telegram? Had Evi wanted to go down into the caves under the Bletterbach to refute Grünwald's theories once again, and had Grünwald been unable to bear yet another humiliation?

Maybe the sweet Evi had actually been a bitch, blinded by her rapid rise in the academic world and eager to confirm how ridiculous Grünwald's theories were, just to show off to the big shots at the university?

I couldn't see her like that, not with those limpid eyes and with everything I'd been told about her. On the other hand, I told myself as I paced back and forth along the corridor of the land registry, people always speak well of the dead.

There was another possibility.

Maybe Evi, who loved the Bletterbach so much and knew it better than anybody else, had had second thoughts. Maybe she had realised that Grünwald's theories about ecological niches weren't so crazy after all and had decided to explore the caves under the Bletterbach, hoping to find evidence that would restore Grünwald's academic credibility, which she had helped to demolish.

It was certainly a possibility.

But giant scorpions from the Permian?

Come on, now.

And yet . . .

I had a fleeting vision. The photographs Max had shown me, the ones taken at the scene of the crime. The amputations. The twisted, broken arms.

The wounds.

The decapitation of Evi.

Could those horrible mutilations have been caused by the half-metre-long claws of the *Jaekelopterus Rhenaniae?* What if . . . ?

A voice brought me back to reality.

The assistant who led me to a kind of reading room with a very high ceiling had a beard that tumbled down over his shirt and eyes concealed behind big glasses. He pointed me to an ugly but functional metal desk on which lay several piles of folders.

"Good luck."

I sat down, making my ribs creak. I sighed. And started reading.

* * *

This is what I discovered: the Bletterbach Visitors' Centre was opened on September 8, 1990. The work had gone well and without disruption.

The design had been entrusted to a highly regarded Austrian architect, who in bringing the project to fruition had tried to "preserve the natural beauty of the location, while combining it with modern technology and functionality" – whatever that meant.

I didn't find Evi's report. It wasn't there. Or rather, it was mentioned in the index to the file, but someone had taken it. And I knew perfectly well who that had been.

Nevertheless, increasingly puzzled, I checked the rest of the documentation from top to bottom.

One year after Evi's report, in 1986, a geologist named Dr Rossetti brought out a counter-report, a much longer and more structured one, demonstrating – to cut a long story short – that the Visitors' Centre was a more than feasible project.

In particular, Dr Rossetti suggested, "there is no risk of landslides, given that the upper stratum of the site is composed of granite materials that adapt well to the capacities of the structure presented for review by Kagol Construction." Four cows transformed into an empire.

In '88, there was a third report, compiled by an engineer named Pfauch, again favouring the construction of the Visitors' Centre. It was an exact copy of the one produced by Dr Rossetti two years earlier. Strange, I told myself.

Something about the fact that two favourable reports had been presented within a couple of years of each other aroused my curiosity. I rushed to the municipal library.

I wanted to figure out the reason for all that effort.

* * *

By the time I got there, I was out of breath and starting a migraine. Not even half a kilo of aspirin could have got rid of the pain.

It didn't stop me. What I had discovered at the land registry had been mouth-watering.

I filled in request forms, waited, discovered that my phone was out of batteries, waited some more. At last I got down to work. More pages of my notebook, more notes.

For once, though, answers.

In '86, a few months after signing off on the report in favour of Hermann Kagol's project, Dr Rossetti had been arrested. A nasty case of bribery.

You wanted to build a huge seventy-storey hotel on a sandy beach, a place where marine turtles reproduced? All you needed was a few tens of millions of lire and Dr Rossetti was the man who would do what you wanted.

Rossetti's arrest must have put a spoke in the wheels of Kagol Construction, and so Hermann, finding himself in a difficult situation financially, had had to turn to another expert, the engineer Andreas Pfauch.

I couldn't find any stain on this man's résumé, no bribes, no shady deals, but I felt justified in asking myself a question.

When he produced this crucial final report, Pfauch was ninety-three years old. Could a near-centenarian really be considered reliable? Anything was possible, even that monsters with shells and claws lived in the Bletterbach, but the story reeked to me of fraud.

I said goodbye to the staff of the library and set off for home. Along the way I stopped in a pharmacy. My migraine had become a miniature Permian.

* * *

I don't remember anything about the ride from Bolzano to Siebenhoch, only the darkness and the wild stream of my thoughts. I didn't concentrate on the road, only on Hermann Kagol, the Visitors' Centre, and what had happened to those poor young people.

I had remembered a detail that Mike had discovered while investigating Grünwald, one that hadn't struck me at the time. Now it assumed quite a whole other significance.

When Grünwald had been cut off from the academic world, cut off above all financially, how had he managed to earn his crust? Among other things, Mike had said, by doing consulting work. And what kind of consulting work could a geologist do?

Risk assessments.

Poor Grünwald. There were no monstrous creatures under the Bletterbach. The real monsters lived *above* the Bletterbach, they walked on two legs and didn't have claws.

I even hazarded a guess that Evi, driven by a sense of guilt, had entrusted the report on the feasibility of the Visitors' Centre to Grünwald, to help him make ends meet, simply putting her own name to it. That way, working together, they had ruined Hermann's plans. Which would also explain Grünwald's mysterious disappearance so soon after the Bletterbach killings.

Mike would have said that this part of the theory was a bit shaky. Above all, I had no proof. But that was a detail I could remedy by digging further. The main point remained.

The report had cost Hermann a lot of money. Of that there was no doubt.

And then what had happened?

Hermann had waited for the right moment, and luckily for him the self-regenerating storm had provided an ideal cover for the murders. He had killed Kurt, Evi and Markus. Then he had got rid of Oscar Grünwald.

Once again, Mike's voice inside my head contradicted me.

What about Chief Krün?

True, Max also had a file on the richest man in the village and had crossed him off his list of suspects, but rich men can buy alibis easily. Alibis everyone must have believed, even that paranoid obsessive Max, but not Günther. Günther had reached the same conclusions as me. But he hadn't had the courage to denounce his own brother.

These were the serious allegations he had hinted at to Brigitte when he was drunk.

It all made sense.

The man who had transformed Siebenhoch into one of the main tourist centres in the region was actually a vicious murderer. The money that every inhabitant of the village handled every day dripped with the blood of three innocents. Evi, Kurt and Markus. One question remained.

What to do?

Go and have another talk with Brigitte, I told myself. Maybe some detail or other would come back to her. Maybe Günther had hinted at something that she had dismissed. Yes, I told myself, Bridget might be the key to everything.

When I got home, I didn't notice that the lights were off. I parked and hid the notebook in the inside pocket of my winter jacket. Then I took out the key.

"Where have you been?"

Werner's voice.

I jumped.

"You startled me."

"Where were you?"

I had never seen him in that state. He had dark rings under his eyes, skin so drawn as to appear almost shiny and red eyes as if he had been crying. He was clenching and unclenching his fists as if he wanted to hit me.

"In Bolzano."

"Have you checked your phone?"

I took it out. It was dead. "Oops."

Werner grabbed me by the lapel of my jacket. In spite of his age, his grip was like steel.

"Werner!"

"Hermann called me," he snarled. "He told me you're planning to write a book. You asked him a whole lot of questions. You lied to me. You lied to your wife."

Where my stomach should have been, I had a hole.

No lights in the house. No voices. That could only mean that Annelise had carried out her threat and left.

I felt myself sink.

"Does Annelise know?"

"If she does, I didn't tell her."

"Then why isn't there anyone at home?"

Werner released his grip. He took a step back and looked at me in disgust. "They're at the hospital."

"What happened?" I stammered.

"Clara," Werner said.

The Colour of Madness

They wouldn't let me see her. I had to be patient. Sit down, read a magazine. Wait for the arrival of God knows who. Ten letters: "impossible."

I started yelling.

They told me to calm down.

I yelled even louder and punched an orderly. To defend himself, he pushed me against a wall. I hit my head on a fire extinguisher.

Someone called security. Nine letters: "pointless".

Not even the sight of the uniforms made me recover my self-control. I cursed the two officers who grabbed me as if I were a criminal. I wasn't, but I belonged to the most dangerous of living species: I was a father driven mad by fear.

They had no choice.

They threw me to the ground and handcuffed me. I heard the noise of the metal closing and went wild. They gave me a couple of well-aimed punches to the kidneys and finally forced me onto an uncomfortable plastic chair.

"Mr Salinger . . ."

"Take these handcuffs off."

"Only once you've calmed down."

A small crowd had gathered around us. A couple of male nurses, a cleaner who kept sniffling. A few patients.

"My daughter," I said, trying to contain my anger. "I want to see my daughter."

"That's not possible, signore," a nurse said, more to the officers than to me. "The child is in intensive care with her mother. The doctor says that—"

I raised my head, drooling from the mouth. "I don't give a fuck what the doctor says, I want to see my daughter!"

I started crying.

Crying did me good.

Maybe it helped to soften them. I certainly calmed down.

In the end, the officer who had handcuffed me spoke to me, "If you apologise to the nurse, I think my colleague and I could forget what happened and let you go. But only if you assure me you won't fly off the handle. Got that?"

I felt them taking off the handcuffs. They gave me some water.

It was lukewarm, but I drank it all.

"When will I be able to . . . ?"

It was the male nurse I'd almost strangled who replied. "Soon, you just have to be patient."

"Patient. Seven letters," I muttered. "That's a lot, seven letters."

"Pardon me?"

"Nothing, I'm sorry."

I waited. And waited.

There was a strong smell of disinfectant in the air. It was a smell Clara hated. I remembered the year before, when she'd been hospitalised with food poisoning and, as usual, I wasn't there with her because I was heavily into the editing of 'Road Crew'. By the time Annelise had managed to contact me, Clara had already had her stomach pumped. I'd rushed to the hospital. Clara was a little creature, not much more than a metre long, lying on a bed that seemed too big for her, as pale as the sterile gown they had made her put on. She stared at me with a look I would never forget.

Why didn't you protect me? her eyes said.

Because I had things to do. I was far away.

I was an asshole.

And now here I was, my head in my hands, ever more terrified, waiting for someone to tell me what had happened. With that smell in my nostrils growing stronger with every passing minute.

Two hours later, a weary Annelise came towards me. I stood up and ran to hug her, but she pulled away and when I tried to kiss her she took a step back.

"How is she?"

"Where were you?"

"How is she?" I repeated.

"Where were you?"

It was a game that could go on ad infinitum. Her accusing me and me trying to find out what she was hiding from me. I felt my anger becoming uncontrollable again.

"For fuck's sake tell me how my daughter is!" I screamed.

Out of the corner of my eye, I saw the male nurse get up from his post. "Is everything all right, signora?"

"Yes, fine, thank you," Annelise replied automatically.

"Answer me, dammit," I whispered, grinding my teeth.

I was beside myself.

As if what was happening were her fault.

"She took the sled and had an accident."

"What kind of accident?"

"She went to Welshboden," Annelise said, staring into the distance. "I didn't even notice. I thought she was playing in the garden. Instead, she took the sled and went to Welshboden. She dragged it behind her, can you imagine? A five-year-old."

I could imagine the scene. Clara making her way to her grandfather's place. A determined five-year-old panting at the side of the highway, observed by passing motorists, obstinately dragging a wooden sled as heavy as she was.

Why had she done it?

Because I had promised that we would play together that afternoon. And she had grown angry because I'd broken my promise. Yet another promise. I'd had to go to Bolzano, to dig into Hermann's past.

Then . . .

"Werner lost sight of her for a moment, he was in the attic. And Clara . . ." Annelise closed her eyes. "The east side, Salinger. At top speed."

The side I had forbidden her to use. The one that led straight to the forest.

"How is she?"

"Cranial trauma. The doctor says she's lucky to be alive. I saw the sled, Salinger. It's all smashed up . . ."

I tried to take her hand. She immediately shifted.

"Will they have to operate?"

"Her whole head is bandaged. She's so small. So helpless." Annelise's voice was a lament without tears. "Do you remember when she was born? Do you remember how frail she seemed?"

"You were scared of breaking her."

"Do you remember what you said to reassure me? Do you remember, Salinger?"

I remembered. "That I would protect you. Both of you."

"I tried to call you. Your phone was off and I . . ." She shook her head. "I didn't know anything. There were the doctors, and the ambulance. My father crying and telling me Clara was strong and would be all right. And there was" – she stammered – "there was the snow, Salinger, the snow was red. So red. Too red."

For the second time I tried to hug her. For the second time my wife retreated.

"Where were you?"

"In Bolzano. My telephone was out of battery. Mike called me. We spent a bit too long talking. I kept forgetting to recharge the battery and . . . and . . ."

I couldn't continue.

Red. The red snow.

Snow.

The Beast, I thought. The Beast kept its promise.

Just like in my dream.

"Why did you go to Bolzano?"

"I wanted to buy you all presents."

"You're a *liar*."

"I beg you."

"You're never there. Never."

"Please."

Her words hurt like punches.

"You're never there," she repeated.

Then she withdrew into a silence more painful than a thousand words. We sat down.

We waited.

At last, when I'd lost all sense of time, a doctor approached us.

"Signor and Signora Salinger? Clara's parents?"

* * *

My daughter's skull.

I was looking at the X-rays of Clara's cranium attached to a luminous display screen. "In two hundred millions years this will be her fossil," I kept telling myself. I couldn't stop staring at it, which prevented me from listening to what the doctor was trying to explain. The doctor had circled a darker area with a felt-tip pen. It was here that Clara had crashed against a damned red fir tree. The trauma. It looked like such an insignificant stain. No bigger than a ladybird. All that anxiety for a tiny little stain.

I didn't understand.

"Doctor," I said, tapping the X-ray with my fingers, "it can't be so serious, can it? Just a little stain. A ladybird. Eight letters."

The doctor stood up, approached the luminous screen and, using a pencil, went over the mark made with the felt-tip pen.

"If this haematoma is reabsorbed by itself, as I just said, the child will be able to go home without any need for intervention. If the opposite happens, she'll have to be operated on."

I went from being stunned to being dismayed. "Are you telling me you'll have to open my daughter's head?"

The doctor retreated. He withdrew towards the desk, as if to put as much space as possible between my hands and his neck.

I was sure that he knew about what had happened in the corridor with the two security guards and the male nurse.

He cleared his throat, trying to maintain a detached, professional tone. "Signor Salinger," he said, "if the haematoma isn't reabsorbed by itself, a surgical intervention will be necessary. I don't want to alarm the two of you, but the risk is that because of the trauma your daughter may lose her sight. Perhaps partially, perhaps totally."

Silence.

I remember the silence.

Then Annelise's weeping.

"Can we see her?" I heard myself say.

I walked behind the doctor, a frightening emptiness in my head.

* * *

She was alone in a room. She had little tubes everywhere. Complicated equipment was humming. A few beeps every now and again. The doctor glanced at the medical chart.

I looked at the tiles under my feet, studied the cracks in the plaster on the walls, stared at the shiny metal of the bed on which Clara was sleeping. Then, at last, I managed to find the courage to look at my daughter. She was so small. I would have liked to say something. A prayer. A lullaby. I didn't say anything. I didn't do anything.

They walked us out into the corridor.

I remember the fluorescent lights. The plastic armchairs. Annelise trying to stop the tears. I remember finding myself in front of a mirror, in a bathroom that stank of bleach. I remember the anger I saw in my eyes. It was making my stomach clench, forcing me to look at the world from behind a red, animalistic veneer that I didn't recognise as mine.

What I was feeling was the worst kind of anger. The kind of obscure sensation that drives you to commit the unthinkable.

It was anger caged inside a prison of powerlessness. I couldn't do anything for Clara. I wasn't a surgeon. I didn't even have any real faith, which was why my prayers sounded empty. Just like my curses. Who should I curse if my concept of God was so nebulous as to be evanescent? I could curse myself, and I did so a thousand times. And I could try to comfort Annelise. But the words coming out of my mouth were thin and tasteless. As tasteless as the coffee we drank at three in the morning, sitting at a table in the cafeteria on the first floor of the hospital in Bolzano.

I had to give vent to my feelings, or I would explode. I thought again about the dream. Clara with her eyes gouged out. Clara in danger of blindness.

Three letters: "red". Six letters: "yellow". Four letters: "blue". Five letters: "black". Another six letters: "purple". Another four letters: "pink". And green and all the shades in the world, lost. Vanished. No more colours for Clara.

No colour except one. I was sure of it.

Five letters: "white".

White would pursue my daughter to the end of her days. Blindness was white. It transformed the world into a palette of mist and ice.

As I saw Werner looking around for us and raised my arm to attract his attention, I realised that it was all the fault of white.

Of the Beast.

It was a crazy thought, I was aware of that. But far from running away from that madness, I threw myself into it headfirst. Better madness than the nightmare I was living.

I trusted the madness.

If I could track down the Bletterbach killer, I would defeat the Beast. And in doing so I would save Clara's sight.

A Tree is Murdered

I left the hospital at dawn. I tried to persuade Annelise to come with me. I told her she needed to rest and to eat some decent food. To get as much of a grip as she could. She looked like someone about to have a nervous breakdown. She was squeezing a handkerchief between her fingers, tormenting it according to the flow of her thoughts. She had aged ten years in a few hours. She replied that she wouldn't leave without her daughter. I kissed her lightly on the forehead. She didn't even look at me. I wanted to tell her that I loved her.

I didn't do so.

I left her in the company of Werner and went back to Siebenhoch alone. Once through the door, I felt a pang in my chest. The house was dark, ghostly, without Clara's voice to light it up. I wept a little, standing there, the wind ruffling my hair. I didn't even have the strength to close the door. I stayed there, motionless. When the dawn finally turned to morning and I had lost all feeling in my hands because of the cold, I summoned up the strength to confront the silence and went in.

I filled my stomach with a couple of eggs and made myself an abundant dose of coffee that provoked a spasm but at least woke me from my lethargy. I smoked two cigarettes in quick succession, watching the wind shake the tree tops. I switched on my computer almost without realising it and typed in everything I had discovered about Hermann and about Grünwald. The two reports. The *Jaekelopterus*. Everything. After a while, I realised I was pounding on the keyboard as if trying to destroy it. I put even more energy into it. By the end, my eyes were full of tears.

The Bletterbach killings were poisoning my soul. But I couldn't stop thinking about them. I called Werner.

No, no news. Yes, Annelise was O.K.

"Are you sure?"

"What do you think, Jeremiah?"

"That you'd really like to smash my face in."

"Not right now, son. I just want the doctors to tell me that Clara will get better."

"She'll get better."

I was sure of it.

Clara would get better because I would defeat the Beast.

* * *

The wind had driven a big weather front from the Balkans over Alto Adige. It would snow, crackled the car radio. More whiteness, I thought, and I switched it off. I parked just behind the cemetery in Siebenhoch.

I lingered in a bar, where I had a coffee and a croissant. Finally, trying not to be too conspicuous, I headed for Brigitte's house. I walked with my head bowed, like the few people I passed along the street.

The icy wind brought the smell of snow. I cursed it, and in doing so felt even more determined. Anything to save Clara.

I stopped.

A black Mercedes, the latest model, was parked outside. A kind of gigantic shiny cockroach with darkened windows. It looked harmless, a car like many others. But it wasn't. I knew that car. I'd seen it many times since I arrived in Siebenhoch. It was Hermann Kagol's car.

I withdrew behind a porch.

I waited, as the first snowflakes started falling from the pearl-grey sky.

He appeared.

He was wearing a camelhair coat with the collar pulled up and a wide-brimmed hat covering half his face. But it was him, I recognised him immediately. I noticed that, as he came out, he double-locked the door. He had a key to the house and acted as if he were the master of it. Was I surprised? Not at all.

I clutched to my chest the plastic bag I had brought with me. If I had ever had any second thoughts about what I was about to do, seeing Hermann coming out of the house swept them away.

The Mercedes manoeuvred. A white puff from the exhaust pipe, then it glided silently away.

I counted to sixty. A minute was more than sufficient. With big strides, I reached Brigitte's house and rang the bell. Once, twice, three times.

There was no need to ring a fourth time.

* * *

My smile was as fake as a three-euro coin, whereas the expression of surprise on Brigitte's face was genuine enough.

"Hello, Brigitte."

She was wearing a pink and white check dressing gown. She pulled the sides across her chest, maybe to protect herself from the cold.

She shifted a lock of hair behind her ear.

Her voice came out hoarse.

"Salinger," she said. "What are you doing here?"

"I came to have a little chat."

I didn't wait for her to invite me in. I simply walked in of my own accord. After a moment's hesitation, she closed the door.

The interior was the usual mess, but Brigitte must have made an effort to tidy a little. The bottles on the shelves had disappeared and a few items of furniture showed marks of a clean-up. The little table in front of the couch was clear, no crushed cans, no bottles of Forst. The old newspapers, instead of being scattered everywhere, were piled in a corner. I noticed the blankets with which I had saved her from exposure. They were carefully folded, the album with the leather cover propped on them like a trophy.

I held up the plastic bag and offered it to her. "I brought you some breakfast."

"You have Four Roses for breakfast?"

"Not me," was my reply.

In the kitchen I found a glass. I held it under the tap and then dried it as best I could and went back into the living room.

Brigitte had sat down on the couch, a blanket around her shoulders. Her legs bare. And shaved, I couldn't help noticing. She had cleaned the house and shaved her legs.

Hermann.

I poured the liquor into the glass and held it out to her. "Cheers."

Brigitte turned her head away. I approached and put the glass in her hands. Then I squeezed them hard. Brigitte yelped.

"What do you want, Salinger?"

"To talk."

Brigitte gave a little laugh. "What about?"

"Evi's death." A pause. "And Günther's."

"Don't speak his name, Salinger. I'm not drunk enough to bear it."

"You've had a visitor, haven't you?"

Brigitte didn't reply. She tightened her hands around the glass. "That's none of your business."

"You're right. But I have this."

I took out the report. I didn't give it to her. I held it tight between my index and middle fingers, like a playing card.

"What's that?"

"The evidence that Günther never let you see."

"Where did you find it?"

"That's the wrong question."

"What's the right question, Salinger?"

"Are you thirsty?"

"No."

"I had a friend," I said. "His name was Billy, he was a roadie for Kiss. He had his personal recipe for breakfast. Three parts milk, one part

Four Roses, a raw egg and powdered chocolate. Add two spoonfuls of sugar and stir well. Then the sun will shine again. Wouldn't you like a little sunshine, Brigitte?"

"You son of a bitch. Tell me what those papers are."

I could see it in her eyes. Brigitte was dying to have a drink. She was an alcoholic. A chronic alcoholic. Alcoholics can't resist a drink. And I didn't want her to resist. I was a bastard, but I didn't feel any remorse.

"The motive for Evi's murder."

Brigitte started shaking. "You found it?"

"Günther found it," was my reply. "I'd never have got there without him."

Brigitte's chin trembled. She started crying. Only then did I notice that she had made herself up. The eyeliner began running in dark rivulets. I found her pathetic. Worse. I hated her. She was nothing but a drunken slut who had lied to me.

Hating her, I found the strength to rub salt in the wound. "Let's talk about Evi, shall we?"

"Get out."

"I'm not a policeman, Brigitte. I'm not into interrogations. Lamp pointed at the face and all that stuff you see in movies. I'm not like that. I've learned to listen to people. I would interview them, have long chats with them. And I always managed to get them to say what they never imagined they would tell a stranger. It was part of my job."

Brigitte bared her teeth. "Sticking your nose into things that don't concern you?"

"Listening to people. Observing them. Realizing when they're telling the truth. And you lied to me. Drink. It'll be easier for you to clear your conscience. I know you're *dying* to do it."

Brigitte flung the glass at me. I dodged it by a whisker, but I couldn't stop her throwing herself at me. She stank of alcohol and sweat. But she was weak. Her body had been destroyed by all those years of abuse. It didn't take me long to overturn the situation. I lifted her off me and forced her to sit down on the couch. Then I let go of her wrists. Brigitte huddled up, her legs under the blanket, in a foetal position. Her expression was filled with hate.

"Give me the bottle, you piece of shit. I might as well take advantage."

God forgive me, but as I passed her the Four Roses I was smiling.

* * *

Two swigs were enough to calm her. By the time she'd had four, the anaesthesia of the alcohol had made her eyelids heavy, her jaw slack. I grabbed the bottle from her hands.

"Give me that."

"You hated Evi, didn't you?"

"Give me the bottle."

I gave her back the bottle, but was careful that she didn't drink too much. I didn't want her lifeless on the floor. I granted her a last gulp, then took it back.

"How do you know that?"

"That album isn't an album of Evi's triumphs. It's an album of Brigitte's wasted life."

"You're a real gentleman, Salinger," she said sarcastically.

"And you're someone who's sleeping with the brother of your dead fiancé."

Brigitte looked me up and down. "You don't understand a damned thing, Salinger."

"Then help me to understand."

"Pass me the bottle."

I gave it to her. Then I lit myself a Marlboro.

"I didn't always hate her," Brigitte said, staring at the clear liquid in the bottle. "She was my best friend. We got along well. We completed each other. She was day, I was night. We had our great plan."

A dribble of Four Roses ran down her chin. She wiped it with a listless gesture.

"During her last year at school, all we did was talk about it. We liked having a secret that was all ours. It was something adventurous and . . . exclusive. It made us accomplices. We'd saved up. Everything was ready. We wanted to leave. To get out of here. And we wanted to do it together."

"What about Markus?"

"He would join us when he turned eighteen."

"What was the destination?"

"Milan. It was the capital of fashion, the papers were always saying that. I'd be a model and Evi would study to become a geologist."

"Evi would have left her mother alone?"

"She was an alcoholic bitch, Salinger. There was no choice. And besides, Evi had said that after graduating, with the money she earned from her work, she would pay for her to go into rehab. She always had a solution, dear Evi," she added with a certain bitterness.

"Was it an excuse or did she really believe it?"

"She really believed it. She was a daydreamer, but she wasn't a liar. And that made her even worse, you know? But I only realised that later. At the time we were excited, happy. Then she met Kurt and fell in love with him."

"And you were cut out."

"You have a good memory, Salinger," Brigitte sneered, and poured herself another dose of bourbon.

"It's my job."

"When she left, I hated her. I hated her with all my might. I felt abandoned, don't you see? She told me she'd write to me and that we'd phone each other every day. And for a while, the first year at least, we did. Then . . . It couldn't last. She had Kurt and her new life in Innsbruck, and me?"

"And you?"

"I'd lost control. I became Brigitte the slut. But I didn't give a damn what other people said. I drank as much as I wanted and fucked anyone who had a cock between his legs. I was angry, furious with the whole world. I lost my job in Aldino, but found another one that was much more lucrative. A nightclub in Bolzano. I moved my arse on a stage, rubbed my tits in the faces of those perverts, and got them drunk. I took 10 per cent on their orders and my tips ended up in a common chest that we divided at the weekend between us girls." A pause. "Plus the extras, but those were personal."

"Extras?"

"I started prostituting myself. In '84, I'd begun using cocaine. The magic medicine that wiped out every nasty memory and left me bursting with energy. I didn't feel anything. Just euphoria."

"Cocaine costs money."

"A lot of money."

She closed her eyes. A grimace as the white-hot flame of the bourbon descended from her throat to her stomach.

"When Evi died, I was *happy*. My best friend had been torn to pieces and how did I react? I took the car and went down to Bolzano. I did so much coke, it was a miracle I didn't end up in the cemetery. I gave it away to anyone who wanted it. After a while, I found myself naked on the floor, surrounded by at least five guys who were drinking and fucking me. Then someone gave me another line of coke and I don't remember anything more."

"And Günther?"

"Günther was an angel. He was the one who got me off coke."

"But not off booze."

Brigitte shook her head. "You're wrong. The first months were hell. I wanted my magic powder. I wanted to get high. Günther took time off work. He was here night and day, in the house, keeping guard over me. Whenever he went out, he'd lock me in. If I could, I'd have killed him, but inside me there was a little voice that understood what Günther was doing. And also understood that this was my opportunity to change my life. To become . . . "

"Better?"

"Normal, Salinger. And for a time I was."

Brigitte bit her lip until blood showed. When she noticed, she wiped it with her hand and then sat staring at the little red spots on her fingers.

"Günther started investigating Evi's death."

"Did he tell you?"

"No, I figured it out for myself. And I started looking at him differently. He was no longer the man who'd picked me up from the street and given me a new life. My knight in shining armour. Günther had gone over to the enemy. He'd become . . ."

"A photograph in the album of Brigitte's defeats?"

"Evi," she said contemptuously, "Evi, always Evi. But she was dead. Dead and buried. That bitch was six feet under. And with her, that blasted Kurt who'd taken her away from me. And yet even when she was dead, she kept tormenting me. Can you believe it? It was a kind of curse. Günther just kept repeating how unfair what had happened was. Hours and hours discussing who it could have been and how and when and . . . Fuck!" She screamed. "Fuck! I couldn't stand all that talking anymore. There was only one way to keep Günther close to me."

"By getting him drunk."

Brigitte nodded.

Her expression turned from angry to desperate.

She raised her hands to her face. "God will never forgive me for that, will He, Salinger?"

"You certainly haven't."

I listened to Brigitte weeping softly, saw the make-up trickling down over her chin. I lit a cigarette, feeling a dull pain at the back of my neck.

Suddenly I realised what I was doing. I realised I'd forced a ruin of a woman to confess her pain, using her demon as bait. I became clear-headed again, at least for a few moments. Clara was in the hospital and instead of being with her and my wife, I was torturing a victim with this terrible business. Torturing, that was the word.

Disgusted with myself, I stubbed out my cigarette and walked over to the couch.

I stroked Brigitte's forehead. I took the Four Roses out of her hand.

She didn't even notice. She continued crying and moaning like a wounded animal. I flung the bottle at the wall. It shattered into a thousand pieces, inundating the room with splinters.

Brigitte looked up at me.

"I'm sorry," I said.

"I deserve it."

I felt the urge to embrace her. She must have noticed because she shook her head.

"You don't need to console me, Salinger."

"It's just that . . ."

Brigitte nodded. "I can see it in your eyes. You're angry. Why?"

"My daughter. My wife," I gesticulated, realising that I was incapable of explaining the confusion in my head. "This story," I said. "I . . ."

I couldn't utter another word.

"I'm not a whore, Salinger. Not the way you mean it."

I stared at her, without understanding.

Brigitte pointed at the front door. "Hermann. We aren't lovers."

"I saw him come here. I thought—"

"You thought wrong."

"I couldn't figure out where you found the money to—"

"To drink?" Brigitte said, disconsolately.

"To pay the bills," I corrected her. "I thought wrong."

Brigitte didn't reply immediately. She let her eyes wander for a while. She lay back on the couch and smoothed her hair.

"The Bletterbach killings, Salinger," she said. "When it comes down to it, what is that story all about?"

"A murder," I replied.

"You can do better than that, Salinger."

"Evi, Markus and Kurt?"

"Wrong. It's about guilt. My guilt. And Hermann's. Did you know that when Günther was alive he and his brother never spoke?"

"Hermann was too absorbed in his work. His business was growing and he didn't have time for anything else."

"They hadn't got along even before that. Did he tell you about the four cows? He always does that. He says that's where his empire was born."

"Isn't it true?"

"Yes, it is. Except that Günther didn't agree. On the contrary. He thought it showed a lack of respect for the family. But Hermann was stubborn and one fine morning without saying anything to anybody he rounded up those four cows and took them away. Günther never wanted a cent from him. He said he was a social climber who'd forgotten his roots."

A gesture to sweep away the world.

"Then when Günther died, years after his funeral, Hermann shows up here with a bunch of flowers. Dressed like a dandy. He says he wants to talk to me. He says 'talk' and I think 'fuck'. And I say to myself, why not? Let's see if his cock is as big as his brother's. But Hermann wasn't interested. He wanted to make amends. He'd heard that Günther loved me. And a rich man only knows one way to get rid of a sense of guilt."

"Money."

"Every week he came here with an envelope. We talked a little, and when he went away he left the envelope in full view. If he was away on business, I'd get a cheque in the post. Never enough money for me to get out of here. Otherwise he would have lost his way of clearing his conscience. He was using me, don't you see? It would have been better if he'd fucked me."

"Didn't he ever do it?"

"Sometimes, I provoked him. I'd let him find me naked or I'd start to play dumb. Hermann would leave the money and go. He never touched me, not even once. Even now, after all these years, he comes here, leaves his money and goes. In a way, I am his whore after all, Salinger."

I thought of how disgusting such behaviour was. Hermann had used Brigitte to ease his own conscience. With that money, he thought he was honouring his dead brother. Wiping his conscience clean by using Brigitte and her demon.

I showed her the pages of Evi's report.

Brigitte stared at them, eagerly.

"This is a hydrogeological risk assessment. Look at the signature, do you recognise it?"

"Evi."

"She hadn't graduated yet, but at the time they didn't split hairs about such things. All you needed was a diploma in surveying. Besides, she had good academic credibility. At least around here, that was enough, wasn't it?"

"What are you trying to tell me?"

"This was Günther's death sentence."

Brigitte read it. When she looked up at me, I saw a deep black well of despair in her eyes.

"He kept it inside . . . for all that time."

"It must have been hard for him."

"His brother," Brigitte murmured. "His brother. And I . . . "

She couldn't go on.

Brigitte slumped against the back of the couch, prostrate.

"Get out, Salinger," she said.

* * *

I left, appalled at myself.

I almost didn't see it.

Hermann's black Mercedes.

* * *

Werner's telephone call reached me as I was looking for a parking spot in the underground garage of the hospital in Bolzano. I arrived in a flash. Annelise ran to meet me. The whiteness wouldn't be taking my daughter's sight. My nightmare hadn't been a premonition. An operation wasn't necessary, the haematoma was being reabsorbed.

The corridor spun around me.

Annelise pointed to the room. "She's waiting for you."

I rushed in.

This time I didn't linger over the green tiles, on which the rubber soles of my shoes squeaked, or the cracks in the plaster on the walls. I wasn't afraid to confront reality.

Clara was pale, her blue eyes circled with a purple tinge. She still had all those damned tubes coming out of her arms, but at least I knew she was out of danger.

She called to me. "Papà." It was wonderful to hear her voice again.

I hugged her. I had to make an effort not to crush her. Clara clung to me with all her might. I felt her bones sticking out. I could put my hands around her pelvis. I chased away the tears.

"How are you, ten letters?"

"I have a headache."

I stroked her. I needed to touch her. I wanted to be sure it wasn't a dream. "The doctor," said Werner's voice behind me. "He says she has a hard head."

"Like me," I replied, still stroking Clara's waxy face. "Do you have a hard head, sweetheart?"

"I did a bad thing, Papà."

"What?"

"I broke the sled," she said. Then she burst into tears.

"We'll build a new one. You and I."

"Together, Papà?"

"Of course. And it'll be even more beautiful than the last one."

"It was already beautiful."

"That doesn't matter. What colour would you like the new sled?"

Clara broke away from me again, smiling. "Red."

"Aren't you fed up with red? What about pink?"

"I like pink."

For a moment she looked as if she wanted to add something else, but she must have had second thoughts because she shook her head and lay back on the pillow, with a moan of pain that didn't escape me.

"When will they discharge her?"

"In a few days," Werner replied. "They want to keep her under observation for a little while longer."

"I think that's sensible."

Clara half closed her eyes. She moved her hand. I took it in both of mine. It was cold. I blew on it. Clara smiled. Her breathing slowed.

At last she fell asleep.

I stood looking at her. And let my tears flow.

"How's Annelise?"

"She doesn't want to go home. She's very tired. But she's fighting like a tigress."

My Annelise.

"What about you?"

Werner didn't reply immediately. "I need your help, Jeremiah."

I turned, puzzled.

Werner was a ghost of himself.

"Whatever you want."

* * *

I didn't understand until the last minute. Not even when Werner took a very sharp axe, tried the point with his thumb and lifted it. He went out into the snow and I followed him.

When we got to the bottom of the east side of Welshboden, I felt faint.

Even though it had snowed, you could still glimpse Clara's blood beneath the layer of fresh snow. All that red, Annelise had said.

I had to make an effort not to vomit.

Werner knelt, the axe propped next to him. He put his hands together and bowed his head. He was praying. Then he grabbed a handful of snow, snow dirty with my daughter's blood, and flung it at the trunk of a fir tree. Not just any fir tree.

The fir tree that had tried to kill my daughter.

I approached it. About four centimetres from the bottom, you could see the point of impact. The scraped bark, a dark stain that could only be blood. And a clump of hair. I tore it off and gently rolled it around my finger, next to my wedding band. I exchanged a sign with Werner. I had understood why he had brought me here. Werner passed me the axe.

"The first blow is yours by right."

I held it in both hands. The weight was well distributed. "Where?"

"Hit it here," Werner said, expertly. "We need to give the direction of the fall."

When I struck the trunk, the reverberation went up from my wrists to my neck. I groaned. But I didn't let go. I waited for the pain to pass, then struck again.

Werner stopped me. "Now the other side. Let's knock this son of a bitch down."

We went around the fir.

And I struck.

Chips flew everywhere, some almost ending up in my eyes. It didn't matter. I struck again. And again. Werner stopped me. He pointed to the cut, which was oozing resin.

I found the smell disgusting.

"It's my turn."

Werner took the axe from my hands. His feet well planted on the ground. The fluid movements of someone who had performed this operation thousands of times. He lifted the axe. The blade glittered in a sinister fashion. Then he yelled with all the breath he had in his body.

And struck.

And struck.

And struck.

* * *

The tree fell to the ground in a swirl of snow. A chip as sharp as a razor, perhaps the fir's last attempt to defend itself, whistled past me, a few millimetres from my ear.

The snow settled. A mountain chough emitted its lugubrious cry. Then all was still.

I looked at Werner. He was sweating and he had a cruel, desperate gleam in his eyes.

I planted the axe in the trunk and took out my packet of cigarettes. "Would you like one?"

Werner shook his head. "I'm dying to smoke, but in this condition I'd be risking a heart attack. Maybe I should quit."

"Right," I said, taking my first long drag.

In my nostrils, the smell of resin.

"We should protect our loved ones," Werner said. "Always."

I looked at him. "You're right."

"Are you doing that?"

I shook my head. "I'm. . ."

For a moment I felt the impulse to tell him everything. My suspicions about Hermann. The turbulent history of the Visitors' Centre. The reports, including Evi's. I thought of blurting out everything about Grünwald, too. His wild theories, the connection with Evi. And Brigitte. Yes, I would have liked to tell him how, in my madness, I'd used that woman's alcoholism to dig into the past of Siebenhoch. Just to confide in someone. Because the story of the Bletterbach killings was tearing me away from my loved ones. To use the guide's words, the Bletterbach was forcing me to descend into the deep.

I would even have liked to tell him about the Beast. To explain to him what had happened in the supermarket parking lot. All that damned whiteness. And the hissing.

I almost did so.

I was stopped by his reddened face, his breathlessness. His weary arms dangling by his sides, the lines around his eagle eyes.

Werner looked like an old man. A weak old man.

He wouldn't have understood.

Some Die and Some Cry

"It's wrong," I murmured, as I sank into her sweetness.

Annelise raised her fingers to my lips. I licked them. They were salty. My excitement grew. With it grew the sense of unease.

Something wasn't right. I tried to tell her. Annelise silenced me with a kiss. Her tongue was dry and rough. It didn't stop moving.

I lightly touched her breast. Annelise arched her back.

I pushed further in.

"It's wrong," I repeated.

Annelise stopped. She looked at me with eyes full of accusation. "Look what you've done."

And at last I saw it.

The wound. It was horrible. A gash from the throat to the stomach.

I could see the throbbing of her heart, covered by a spider's web of light blue veins.

From Annelise's lips came a scream that was the cry of a tree as it fell.

* * *

The sleeping pills had stopped working. I threw them in the garbage.

* * *

At five in the morning, bathed in sweat, I slipped under the boiling jet of the shower. I was hoping that the water could chase away the cold I felt in my bones.

I tidied the house, swept the ice from the drive in spite of the pain in my back muscles, and by seven-thirty I was ready to go to the hospital.

I had two objectives for that day. To buy the biggest teddy bear I could find and persuade Annelise to come back to Siebenhoch.

She'd now been in Clara's hospital room for two days. She needed to get out of there or she would collapse. The warning signs were all there. Trembling hands, red eyes. When she spoke it was in a shrill voice I found it hard to recognise. She expressed herself in monosyllables, without ever focusing on the person she was speaking to. I had no doubt it was partly my fault. We still had a lot to talk over, Annelise and I.

Would I tell her the truth? I asked myself.

Yes.

But only once I'd written the words "the end" at the bottom of the Word document that was saved in my laptop and now numbered several single-spaced pages. Only then would I take her aside and reveal the outcome of my inquiries. She would be angry, of course, but she would understand.

That's why I loved her.

Nor did I doubt for an instant that this interpretation of mine was totally wrong. Because Annelise wasn't stupid and what I was telling myself as I grabbed my jacket and went out to get the car wasn't the truth. It was a partial (and stupid) version of the truth.

In other words: "shit".

Four letters.

Add two and you'll have "square".

Put on it a good thirty centimetres of snow now turned to ice, the tall thin bell tower and a crossroads: "Siebenhoch". Add lots of confusion. Words that fly from mouth to mouth, contrite faces, some dazed, others that simply shake their heads. And a car coming from the north.

Mine.

Eight letters: "Salinger".

* * *

I saw the flashing lights of a Carabinieri patrol car. And those of an ambulance. My throat went dry.

The ambulance was parked, its siren off, outside Brigitte's house.

I parked where I shouldn't.

"What happened?" I asked a woman tourist buried in a gaudy woollen scarf.

The woman lowered herself to the height of my open car window. "Apparently there was a gunshot."

"Who . . . ?"

"A woman. They say she killed herself."

I barely heard the last part of her sentence. I was already out of the car. The onlookers had formed a small crowd. I made my way through it until a carabiniere pushed me away.

I took no notice, stood my ground. There was a paramedic outside Brigitte's door, talking on his cell phone. I could see his breath condense in light blue clouds. The crowd pushed me forward. I just kept staring at the paramedic, dazed, until he put his phone in his pocket and went back inside.

I tried to peek in.

I couldn't see anything.

When the paramedics, their phosphorescent overalls gleaming in the ghostly February light, came out pushing a stretcher with a sheet under which the outline of a body could be glimpsed, the crowd fell silent, holding its breath.

I had to take my eyes away from the stretcher as it was shoved into the back of the ambulance. I clenched my fists, digging my nails into the flesh.

"You."

A voice I recognised instantly.

Hermann. He looked shaken. His camelhair coat hung open over a rumpled shirt half in and half out of his trousers. He wasn't wearing a tie and he had a day's growth of beard.

He raised his arm and pointed at me. "You!" he roared.

Everyone turned in my direction.

It took Hermann a moment to reach me. He stopped less than two metres away. From the inside pocket of his coat he took out a wallet.

He didn't take his eyes off me. There was hate in them.

He took out a banknote, crumpled it and threw it at me. I felt it slide to the ground.

"Here's your money, Salinger."

A second banknote landed in my face.

"Isn't that what you want? That's what films are for. To make money. Do you want some more?"

The third hit my chest. Finally, Hermann, shaking, flung his wallet at me.

Stunned by his attack, I didn't react.

"I saw you leaving her house, Salinger. Yesterday."

The carabiniere looked first at me then at Hermann, unsure what to do. We both ignored him. A void had been created around us.

Hermann took a step forward. "You killed her, you lousy worm."

He made to rush at me, but the carabiniere held him back. A grey-green uniform appeared. Chief Krün.

He took me by the arm.

"It wasn't me who killed Brigitte, Hermann," I screamed, before Max could drag me away. "It was you, you fucking asshole. And we both know why."

Max dragged me into a side street from which I could see neither the house nor Hermann. Only the gleam of the flashing lights on a barber's sign.

I closed my eyes. "Is she really dead?"

"Suicide."

"Are you sure?"

Max nodded. "She used a hunting rifle. She shot herself."

"When?"

"The neighbours heard a shot just before dawn. They were the ones who alerted me. The door was ajar. I saw her and called the Carabinieri and the ambulance."

"It wasn't a suicide."

Max looked me up and down. "That's a very serious accusation, Salinger."

"Hermann killed her."

"She killed herself."

"How can you be so sure?"

"She was drunk . . ." – a slight hesitation, as if he'd wanted to add "as usual", but had had second thoughts – "and there were bottles everywhere. Signora Unterkircher met her last night. Brigitte was already out of her head then."

"And what did Signora Unterkircher do for Brigitte?" I asked bitterly.

"What we all did for years, Salinger. Nothing."

I couldn't sustain his gaze. "Brigitte didn't kill herself. She was murdered. By Hermann."

"I repeat: these are serious accusations."

"I'm aware of that."

"Do you have any proof?"

I lit a cigarette. I offered him one. "No."

"Then keep your mouth shut. This is hard enough as it is."

"Tell me the truth, Max, did you notice anything strange? Anything that could—"

"Nothing at all."

"You said the door was open."

"Brigitte was a drunk, Salinger. Drunks leave children in cars in July, they forget to switch off the gas and then light one of those."

He was right.

But I knew he was also wrong.

"Maybe I shouldn't tell you this," Max said, "but Brigitte was holding a photograph in her hand."

"A photograph of Evi?"

"Of Günther."

"You think that's a clue?"

"I think it's a suicide note, Salinger. Nothing more, nothing less."

We exchanged a few more words, then said goodbye. He went back to the scene of the suicide and I walked back to my car. When I sat down behind the driving wheel, I realised I had a crumpled 50-euro banknote inside my jacket.

I threw it out the window.

I started the engine and drove away.

* * *

I got to Bolzano at nine o'clock. I couldn't find the biggest teddy bear in the world, but the one that made its appearance in Clara's room halfway through the morning was close enough.

"How are you, sweetheart?"

"My head hurts."

"But not as much as yesterday?"

"Oh, no, not as much as yesterday."

Clara stroked the hairy muzzle of the teddy bear and turned serious. It was the same expression I had seen the day before. As if she had something important to tell me but couldn't find the courage to spit it out.

I smiled.

I stroked her chin, forcing her to look at me. "What is it, sweetheart?"

"Nothing."

"Five letters," I said.

"Mamma?"

"No."

"Heart?"

I shook my head.

Clara shrugged. "Then I don't know."

"Truth," I said.

She passed a hand over her head, looking for a hair to twist round her finger, the same gesture Annelise made when she felt under pressure.

She didn't find anything, because her head was still wrapped in a heavy layer of bandages. Her hand fell back in her lap. She had again shifted her gaze away from me.

"You know you can tell me everything?"

"Yes."

"Do you think I'm angry about the sled?"

"A little."

"But there's something else, isn't there?"

Clara again made to touch her hair, but I took her hand and kissed it. Then I tickled her. Clara laughed, burying her face in the belly of the teddy bear.

"When you want to, you'll tell me," I said.

Clara seemed relieved by that proposition. With a solemn expression, she held out her hand. "It's a deal."

"What are you two up to?"

It was Annelise, accompanied by Werner. I stood up and hugged her. Annelise returned the gesture, but in a cold, detached manner. Beneath the scent of soap, I could smell the sweat on her skin.

"You should get some rest."

"Did you buy that bear?" she asked. "It wasn't here before."

That was her tactic. Changing the subject.

"Yes, it's a present. And you need to sleep in a real bed."

"I'll stay here until Clara has finished her treatment. Then we'll go home. Together."

She walked past me and sat down on Clara's bed.

"O.K.," I said.

We played together for a while.

I made an effort not to think about Brigitte's death and concentrated on Clara. She was weak and pale, but at least she could see us. Soon, I would put her in the car and take her home.

To safety.

Never again, I swore, would I allow anything bad to happen to her.

It was a vow destined to be broken. That's always the way it is when we swear that nothing will ever spoil the lives of our loved ones.

All I could do for Clara was give her good memories.

Werner's words echoed loudly in my head. Just like the crash of the red fir tree brought down by the pain of two broken men.

Around eleven, along with the male nurse who brought Clara her food, the doctor also made his entrance. He recognised me and held out his hand. I shook it, embarrassed.

"You were right, Signor Salinger," he began, after greeting Annelise.

"It was only a ladybird," I murmured, turning red.

"Eight letters aren't so many, when it comes down to it," he said, bursting into a loud laugh that included both me and Annelise.

Clara, he told us, was reacting well. They had administered drugs that would ease the reabsorption of the haematoma. It had been touch and go, but the danger had passed.

"We'll give her a C.T. scan, and on the basis of the results we'll decide whether to discharge her, or keep her in a little longer."

"What's a C.T. scan, Mamma?"

Clara had already finished eating. I was surprised by her appetite, it was a good sign. I helped her to clean her mouth with a white napkin, something I'd stopped doing the year before and really missed.

"It's like radar. You remember what that is?"

I had explained it to her during our flight to Europe. I had no doubt she still remembered. She had a prodigious memory.

"Yes, it's a kind of radio that helps planes not to crash."

"Well, a C.T. scan is a kind of radar that helps to see inside people."

"How's it done?"

"Well . . . " I turned to the doctor.

"It's like a huge washing machine," he said. "You'll lie on your bed and we'll tell you to keep still. Are you able to keep still?"

"For how long?"

"A quarter of an hour. Maybe half an hour. No more than that."

Clara was silent, thinking about this. "I think I can do it." Then, to me, she said in a low voice, "Will it hurt, Papà?"

"It won't hurt at all. It'll just be a bit boring."

Clara seemed relieved. "I'll make up a few stories."

I kissed her and just then my cell phone rang. I gave Annelise a mortified look and made as if to cut off the call. My thumb lingered over the red button.

It was Mike.

"Excuse me."

I went out and answered.

"Partner?"

"Wait," I said.

I went into a toilet that I hoped was deserted.

"You'll have to hurry."

"What's going on?"

"I'm in the hospital. It's Clara. She had an accident. She's better now."

"What kind of accident? Salinger, don't kid around."

"She crashed into a tree with the sled. But she's out of danger now. She's fine."

"What the hell does 'out of danger' mean, Salinger? What . . ."

I closed my eyes and leaned against an immaculate washbasin. "Listen, Mike, I don't have any time to waste. Tell me what you found out. A whole lot of things have happened here in Siebenhoch."

"I made more inquiries about Grünwald, but apart from more details about his theories, there's nothing. Nothing about his death, I mean."

"His disappearance," I corrected.

"Do you really think he just disappeared, partner?"

"I don't think anything."

"Are you sure you're all right?"

"No, I'm not all right, but please go on."

A brief pause. Mike lighting a cigarette. I would have done so, too, but it wouldn't be wise to set off a hospital fire alarm just for a Marlboro.

"You remember that Evi? She came up again."

"In connection with Hermann Kagol?"

"Precisely."

"The report opposing the building of the Visitors' Centre."

"You already knew that?"

"Yes. What else have you found out?"

"Little or nothing. The report was refuted, and five years later the Visitors' Centre opened its doors."

"Shit." I banged my fist on the wall.

"What's happening, Salinger?"

"What have you found out about Hermann Kagol's annual turnover from the Centre?"

"Including the hotels and other properties in the area?"

"Yes."

"Several million euros."

I felt the bile rising into my mouth. "Do you think Hermann could have killed Evi?" I whispered.

"What reason would he have had?"

"Because she held up his Visitors' Centre project."

"You're way off track, Salinger."

It was a reply I hadn't expected. "What are you saying?"

"I'm saying that if I'd been that Hermann, I'd have kissed the ground that Evi walked on."

"But . . . the report . . . "

"The report blocked the Bletterbach Visitors' Centre project. Only, the first project wasn't Hermann Kagol's."

Dizziness.

There was too much white in here.

"What the hell are you saying, Mike?"

"The first project for a Visitors' Centre in the Bletterbach didn't come from Kagol Construction. It was from a consortium in Trento, Group 80. The same consortium that built a whole lot of ski lifts in the area."

I felt myself sinking.

The floor beneath my feet shook. And buried me.

"Salinger? Are you there?"

"Evi's report *helped* Hermann?"

"Precisely. According to my calculations, Hermann would never have been able to afford such an ambitious project in '85 anyway. Evi gave him a hand, quite a hand. Why would he have killed her?"

No reason in the world.

"Thanks, Mike," I muttered. "Speak to you soon."

I hung up without waiting for his reply.

I turned on the tap in the washbasin. I rinsed my face.

I breathed.

Hermann hadn't killed Evi.

I looked at my image in the mirror.

Now, I thought, now you know what a murderer looks like.

I had Brigitte's murderer right in front of me. It was me.

"'Are the dead restored?'" I murmured. "'The books say no, the night shouts yes.'"

It was a quotation from my favourite book, the one that went with me everywhere. John Fante's words took on a new meaning in the mouth of the murderer whose contorted face was looking at me in the mirror.

I couldn't stand it. I bent double, crushed by the awareness of what I had done. I ended up hitting my head on the ceramic washbasin. The pain was a relief.

* * *

It was a male nurse who revived me. Behind his concerned face, Annelise's bloodless one. As soon as she saw me open my eyes, she walked out of the toilet, slamming the door behind her.

"When you didn't come back, your wife got worried. You must have had a blackout."

He helped me to sit up. I was breathing with my mouth open. Like a thirsty dog.

"I can do it, I . . ."

"You had a nasty knock. It'd be better if . . ."

Feeling dizzy, I grabbed hold of him and struggled to my feet.

"I'm fine. I have to go. I have to . . ."

He objected. I didn't even listen to him.

When I was outside the door of Clara's room, I didn't have the courage to go in. I could hear Annelise's voice and my daughter's chatter. I stroked the door.

Then I kept on walking.

I couldn't face them.

* * *

Back home, I headed for the kitchen. I dug up a bottle of Jack Daniels and started drinking it. The first sip was like acid going down through my oesophagus. I coughed and spat. I held out. Stoically, I stopped the retching. Another sip. More acid. All I could think of was Brigitte's head split in two by the rifle shot. The blood spreading over the floor. I took a deep breath, trying to ease the nausea. I didn't want to throw up, that wasn't my aim. I wanted to get drunk. I wanted that total dreamless blackness that I'd experienced after banging my head in the hospital toilet. Before Annelise . . . The thought of Annelise was unbearable to me.

I drank some more.

This time, the Jack Daniels went down without burning. I wiped my mouth with the back of my hand. I headed for the living room and sank into my favourite armchair.

I took out a cigarette.

I had lost feeling in my hands. It took me a while to get the lighter to work, and when I succeeded I found myself staring at the flame like an idiot, wondering what it was for and why it seemed so important to move it closer to that white tube sticking out of my mouth. I flung the lighter across the room and spat out the cigarette.

I kept on drinking. My head grew as heavy as lead.

I tried to lift the bottle of Jack Daniels.

I couldn't do it. It slipped through my fingers.

And then there was darkness.

When I came to, I was lying on the bed. I looked around, lost. I was plunged in darkness. How had I got here? Judging by my confusion, I must have dragged myself here all on my own. My last memory was the noise of the whisky bottle smashing on the floor.

I stared in front of me.

I tried to move.

"What did you imagine you were doing?"

I trembled.

I didn't recognise the voice that had emerged from the darkness.

"Who are you?" I said. "Who are you?"

The voice turned into a shadowy figure. It looked gigantic. It moved jerkily. The dead, I thought, the dead move like that.

The shadowy figure switched the light on.

Werner.

Using all my strength of will, I got up off the bed.

"I've had a bad day."

Werner didn't comment. "You need to fill your stomach. Can you get downstairs on your own?"

"I can try."

Getting down the stairs was laborious. Every movement reverberated in my cranium like a hammer blow. I accepted the pain. I deserved it. I was a murderer.

Twice a murderer.

First the men on the Ortles, and now . . .

Werner cooked some eggs, which I forced myself to swallow. I ate bread, and a slice of *speck*. And drank a lot of water.

Werner said nothing until I had finished. Only then did I notice his posture. He was rigid on his chair, his face contracted.

He struck me as being in pain, but above all embarrassed.

"I'm not keeping an eye on you," he said. "I dropped by to ask for something. It's my back. All my life I've boasted I never took anything stronger than an aspirin, but now . . ."

"Does it hurt?"

"I'm not a boy anymore," he said regretfully.

"Why don't you see someone about it?"

"Forget it, Jeremiah, I've never liked doctors. Don't you have anything for the pain?"

Everything in him, the tone of his voice, the words he chose, clashed with what I read in his eyes. People like Werner hate two things: appearing weak and asking for help. I stood up, went into the bathroom and grabbed the box of painkillers that had been prescribed for me after September 15.

"Vicodin," I said when I went back into the kitchen.

Werner reached his hand out for the box. "Can I take two?"

"One will be enough."

He popped the capsule into his mouth.

"Annelise won't be home this evening," I said. "She may never come back."

Werner took my packet of cigarettes. He lit one and I did the same.

"In a marriage, there are bad times and good times. They both pass."

"What if they don't?"

Werner didn't reply.

He sat staring at the smoke rising to the ceiling, where it flattened out and became invisible.

When he'd finished the cigarette, he stubbed it out in the ashtray and stood up, using the table for support.

"I should be getting back to Welshboden."

"Take the pills with you, they may help."

"I'll be fine tomorrow, you'll see."

"Take them anyway. I don't need them."

Werner put them in his pocket. I helped him on with his jacket.

Outside, it was dark.

"Jeremiah . . ." Werner said. "Can you hear it?"

I pricked up my ears. I tried to figure out what he was referring to.

"I can't hear anything."

"The silence. Can you hear it?"

"Yes."

"Ever since Herta died and I was left alone, I've hated the silence."

Two Conspirators and a Promise

Brigitte's funeral was held two days later, on February 10.

The post-mortem had been little more than a formality and the pathologist's report predictable. Brigitte had committed suicide. Max came to tell me in person that morning, as I was trying to clean the house in preparation for Clara and Annelise's return.

"She had three times the normal level of alcohol in her veins. She was blind drunk, Salinger."

"Right."

Max noticed the bruise on my forehead, where I had hit it in the hospital. "What's that?"

"It's nothing."

We had a coffee in silence. The weather was grey and gloomy.

"I heard Clara's coming back today."

"Did Werner tell you?"

"I ran into him in the pharmacy. He didn't look good."

"His back is playing him up."

"He should see someone about it. Five years ago, I sprained a muscle. It hurt like hell. Then Verena dragged me to see a physiotherapist. Two sessions and I was like new."

"Did you tell Werner that?"

"It just goes in one ear and out the other. He's stubborn, but you'll see, when he realises he can't lift Clara any more he'll come round."

"Let's hope so."

Max played with his empty cup, then stood up. "Well, anyway, I just wanted to let you know."

"Thank you."

"Will you be coming to the funeral?"

"Will Hermann be there?"

"He paid for it all."

"I think I'll give it a miss."

Max put on his hat with the Forest Rangers' badge. "You're a good man, Salinger."

I wasn't. I was a murderer.

* * *

I listened to the mournful tolling from the bell tower until I couldn't stand it anymore. I switched on the T.V. at full volume.

At three in the afternoon, Werner knocked at my door.

I already had my jacket on.

"How's your back?"

"It's fine."

"Are you sure?"

"Look." He bent forward then straightened up again like a soldier at attention.

"All the same, a check-up wouldn't go amiss."

"Let's go," he said, pointing to the car. "Our baby is waiting for us."

They were already in the street when we arrived. Along the highway, there had been an accident that had slowed us down. Our bad mood vanished as soon as we saw Clara.

She was wearing a red hood and a beret pulled down over her eyes to protect her and hide the small bandage the doctor had said would have to stay on for a few days. Under her arm, the bear.

She signalled hello to us with her free hand.

Annelise barely smiled.

It was a delight taking Clara home. She was excited, couldn't stop talking until after dinner, which I had made with care. Her favourite dishes plus at least half those that Annelise liked. I'd given full rein to the entirety of my culinary talents.

"The lady doctor said I was really brave."

"Really?"

"She said she'd never seen a child so brave."

She puffed out her chest proudly.

The female doctor who had given her the C.T. scan must have impressed her quite a bit. She kept quoting her.

"She showed me my brain. It was all full of colours. The doctor said you could see my thoughts. But all I could see were coloured bits. Do you think the doctor can read thoughts, Papà?"

"A C.T. scan isn't for reading thoughts. It shows the electricity in the brain. You can see the emotions."

"Electricity? Like a light bulb?"

"Yes."

"And with that the doctor can understand my emotions?"

"Of course."

"You know what the doctor's name is?"

I knew it, but pretended I didn't. "I have no idea, sweetheart."

"Elisabetta," she said. "How many letters are there in Elisabetta?"

"Ten."

"It's a beautiful name."

"I think so, too."

"Do you think I could become a brain doctor when I grow up?"

"Of course, sweetheart."

We carried on like this until we noticed that Clara's reflexes had become slower. She was starting to mumble her words and sway her head. She was pale.

Werner got up from the table. "I think it's time for *Nonno* Werner to go to bed."

"*Nonno*," Clara said, opening wide her eyes (which, I noticed, were red and weary-looking), "stay a while longer."

Werner kissed her on the forehead. "Aren't you tired?"

"I'm not tired."

"Are you sure?"

"Well, just a little."

Werner left and I carried Clara to bed. I barely had time to switch out the light before she dozed off. I left the door ajar and went down into the kitchen.

I found Annelise sitting stiffly. She had a can of Forst in her hands.

I didn't like her expression and I didn't like the way she gulped the beer down in one go.

"We have to talk," she said.

I knew what about, and I knew how it would end up.

Not a happy ending.

So I took her hands and opened my heart to her. "I know what you're going to say. But don't. Give me a month. If in a month you still want to tell me what you have in your mind, then I'll listen to you. A month. No more. Do it for me."

Annelise put a strand of hair between her lips. "A month."

"No more than that. Then, if you want . . ." I didn't have the courage to go on.

"For Clara," she said. "For Clara." She stood up. "But I'll sleep in the study. I" – her voice broke – "I can't stand it."

* * *

The two conspirators did their job with great skill. Neither Annelise nor I noticed anything up until the last moment.

Around six-thirty, Werner appeared laden with provisions, said hello and, without a word of explanation, shut himself in the kitchen with Clara. Annelise went back to watching television, I withdrew into what had become my den, the little study where I spent hours looking at the ceiling or trying to read something.

Impossible. My mind would wander. I felt like a tightrope walker. Beneath me gaped the abyss of solitude. Werner was right: silence didn't suit me. I didn't want to spend the rest of my life sprawling on a camp bed (just as I was doing now) listening to the noises of a house devoid of life.

How long was it since I had last heard Annelise laugh? Too long.

Lost in these gloomy thoughts, I didn't notice the passing of time. Around eight, there was a knock at the door. It was Clara. She was wearing an elegant flame-red dress with a headband holding in her hair. I noticed that she had make-up around her eyes. A charming mixture of the ridiculous and the lovable.

"Hello, sweetheart."

"Signor Salinger," she said, all prim and proper. "Dinner is ready."

I opened my eyes wide. "I beg your pardon?"

"Dinner," she repeated impatiently, "is served, Signor Salinger."

"Dinner . . . " I said, as if stunned.

"And ties are to be worn."

"I don't have a tie, sweetheart. And I don't understand what . . . "

In a few steps, Clara was ten centimetres from me. Since I was sitting, her eyes and mine were at the same height. I saw in hers a determination that could have come from only one person. Annelise. By her sides, her fists were clenched. I found her incredibly pretty.

"You do have a tie, Papà. You have five minutes. Get on with it."

She walked out, imperiously.

And I found a tie.

Going downstairs, I realised that Werner had done things in style. There in the middle of the living room, my favourite armchair had been replaced by the dining table, set for two. Shining white tablecloth, wine in a cooler (I looked at the label, a 2008 Krafuss, it must have cost a fortune), even a candle that flashed glimmers into the semi-darkness in which the room was shrouded.

Sitting at the table, Annelise.

She took my breath away. She was simply stunning.

She had put on a black sheath dress that reminded me of the first showing of "Road Crew 2", the evening that she had dubbed "our debut in society" (when we had made our entrance into the cinema on Broadway, everyone, even Mr Smith, had stood there open-mouthed and Annelise, terrified, had whispered to me, "Don't leave me alone, don't leave me alone, don't you *dare* leave me alone"), and a string of pearls that brought out the beauty of her sinuous neck. Her hair was gathered at the back of her neck in a flawless bun.

She stood up and lightly kissed my cheek. "Is this a surprise for you, too?"

"Yes," I replied, unable to take my eyes off her.

I was dazzled.

God, how I had missed her.

"Ladies and gentlemen . . ."

It was Werner. He was wearing a cook's hat, he had shaved, and in his white apron he looked like a cross between a French chef and a polar bear. We burst out laughing.

Werner didn't lose his composure. "Dinner . . ."

Lamb cutlets, potatoes with sour cream and chives, an assortment of cheeses and salami to turn your head, *canederli* with butter and dozens of other little culinary masterpieces. The wine lived up to its reputation.

It was hard to break the ice. It was as if Annelise and I were on our first date, a blind date to boot. All it needed was for me to ask, "What about you, what you do for a living?"

But then, gradually, we loosened up. We talked about Clara, because she was what still kept us together. We talked about the weather, because that's what grown-ups do in the Western world. We talked about Werner. We praised the excellence of the dishes that Clara, in that delightful red dress, with a serviette over her arm, served us (and every time I felt a cold sweat: "Please don't spill it, please don't spill it").

I was on my third glass when I realised the reason for this evening. "Today's . . ."

"Hadn't you realised?"

I shook my head. "I'd forgotten."

February 14.

For dessert, Werner had prepared chestnut hearts with whipped cream.

It was the chef in person who served it to us.

"Papà?" Annelise said.

"Madame? Is the food to your taste?"

"It's delicious. But I didn't know you such were a skilled cook. Where did you learn?"

"A chef never reveals his secrets."

"You're not a chef, Papà."

"Let's say that when an old mountain man meets that horrible monster you city people call 'free time', either he finds something to do or he ends up in the loony bin."

It was an unforgettable evening.

The chef also acted as makeshift babysitter and, while Annelise and I savoured an *amaro* and I allowed myself a cigarette, Werner put Clara to bed.

Then he said goodbye.

We were alone. As I gazed at the soft curve of Annelise's bare shoulders, the silence didn't weigh on me. On the contrary.

For a moment, I was very close to happiness.

Annelise stood up and blew me a kiss. "Good night."

She climbed the stairs. I heard her go into her room and close the door behind her.

I hadn't expected anything different, but all the same I felt a pang.

And yet there was no sarcasm in my words when, raising a glass to the ceiling, I said, "Happy St Valentine's Day, my darling."

* * *

Day by day, I saw Clara get better. To understand that, I didn't need the opinion of doctors, even though we were always punctual when we had to take her for check-ups. The bags under her eyes disappeared and she also put back on a little of the weight she'd lost after the accident.

We resumed our walks. The mountains were impassable, but Werner taught us to use snowshoes and it was nice to spend time like that, in the middle of the woods around Siebenhoch. Walking in the snow, talking, watching the birds flit from one branch to another, and trying to discover some squirrel's dens (we didn't find any, but Clara confided in me that she had seen a gnome's house). I tried not to exhaust her because I had suddenly discovered the anxious parent in me. I was afraid she would slip, that she would sweat, that she would get tired. Clara liked all this attention, but after a while, when I became too stifling, she would give me one of her glances and I would realise that I'd become worse than my *Mutti* with her obsession with draughts. So I tried to make amends.

My relationship with Annelise didn't improve. We were civil with each other, so there were no scenes, no smashed plates, but there were too many silences and tense smiles. Every now and again, I would catch her staring at me and my world would sink into anguish. I knew what she was thinking.

What do I feel for this man?

Can I forgive him?

Do I still love him?

I would have liked to put my arms around her and yell, "This is me! This is me! You can't abandon me, because this is me and if we leave each other we'll never be happy again in our lives!" But I didn't. That wasn't the way a Salinger behaved, or a Mair. So, either I would pretend I hadn't noticed those looks, or else I would raise my hand and wave at her. She'd usually shake all over, blush in embarrassment and return the wave.

Better than nothing, I thought. Better than nothing.

I put all my commitment into it, but every evening, when I went to bed, alone, I remembered so many little gestures performed during the day and couldn't help but reproach myself. Maybe I should have bought her a bunch of flowers; not roses, daisies. Maybe I should have taken her out for dinner somewhere. Maybe I would have got even that gesture wrong.

I would fall into an agitated sleep after hours spent tossing and turning between the sheets. Did I have nightmares? Yes. Lots. The Beast, though, wasn't part of them. I dreamed that I was wandering, blind and incapable of expressing a sound, around the house in Siebenhoch, a house empty and devoid of furniture. I dreamed about silence.

* * *

"Papà!"

Clara was in the garden. Her cheeks were red and her jacket was open. She was smiling.

"Come on, Papà! It's warm! The wind is warm!"

I smiled, joining her.

"It's the *Föhn*, sweetheart." The wind had the same name as the German word for hairdryer.

"Like the thing for the hair?"

The warm air caressed my face. It was pleasant.

"In some ways, yes. Except that this was there long before they invented hairdryers."

"It's strong."

"But you have to be careful."

"Why?"

"You know what the old inhabitants of the Alps called it?"

"What?"

"The devil's wind."

Clara leaned towards me. "Why?"

"Because it gives you flu," I said, buttoning up her jacket.

Never were words more prophetic. Within half a day, I noticed that Clara had turned sluggish and taciturn. You didn't need a degree in medicine to understand what was happening.

"Fever," I pronounced, after taking her temperature: "38 and a half."

The flu lasted five days. Then the fever passed and gradually Clara regained her normal colouring. I didn't dare take her outside, though, in spite of her complaints.

February came to an end.

On March 1, I decided that the time had come. Some say you

become an adult when you bury your parents; others, when you become a parent yourself. I didn't agree with either of these two philosophies.

You become an adult when you learn to apologise.

* * *

The Kagol house still looked magnificent, but I wasn't in a state of mind to appreciate it. I stood stock still outside the front door, summoning up the courage required to utter the five most difficult letters in the world: "Sorry."

I wanted to do it, I even needed to do it. Above all, I needed to regain my self-respect. I hadn't forgotten what had happened.

There was Brigitte.

There was Max saying, "She killed herself, Salinger."

There was Hermann throwing the banknotes at me.

Me accusing him of being Brigitte's murderer.

I had to apologise to Hermann. Without that apology, I felt that I would never get Annelise back. Because in order to save my marriage, which was as shaky as one of Clara's snowmen, I first had to find myself again. Not the Salinger who had taken advantage of Brigitte's demon to make her talk, but the Salinger who was making an effort to be the best husband in the world.

I took a deep breath.

I rang the bell.

Instead of the usual housekeeper, it was Verena, Max's wife, who opened. As soon as she recognised me, she made to close the door, but I stopped her.

"What are you doing here, Salinger?" she asked.

"I'd like to see Hermann."

She shook her head. "Impossible. He's ill."

"I think I owe him an apology," I said.

"You certainly do, but now's not the time."

"When do you think I can come back?"

Verena looked at me for a long time with those big girlish eyes of hers. "Never, Salinger."

She tried again to close the door. Once again I stopped her.

"Salinger!" she cried, astonished at my stubbornness.

"What's the matter?"

"This isn't something that concerns you."

"I just want to apologise for my behaviour."

"That's rich," she said, looking at me angrily. "Just an apology, is it? You're a liar, Salinger."

"I—"

"Nothing to do with the Bletterbach killings, is it? You promised me you wouldn't talk about it with Max, but you did. He took you to the Krün family home, didn't he?"

"Yes," I admitted. "He was the one who took me there, I—"

"I suppose he had to handcuff you."

"I—"

"That's all you can say, Salinger. I. I. I. What about us? Don't you ever think of us? You know how I discovered that Max took you to that godforsaken hole? Because his mood changed. He started being grumpy and silent again."

A pause. A sigh.

Her anger was tangible.

"Some evenings, he comes back late, stinking of alcohol. That hadn't happened in ages. Are you pleased, Salinger?"

I stood there with head bowed, silent.

Verena's fury showed me how pathetic and pointless my attempt to make amends with Hermann was. Some things can't be cancelled out. And if they are forgiven, that only happens after several years. Not after a couple of weeks.

Idiot.

"Drop this business, Salinger. The Bletterbach is just a graveyard for monsters."

"That's what I'm doing."

"And get out of here." Verena's eyes glittered like those of an inquisitor. "Get out of Siebenhoch and never show your face here again. Never," she said emphatically, "again."

She was about to say something else. Another drop of poison, for sure, but just then Hermann's baritone voice reached us from inside the house.

"It's all right, Signora Krün."

Verena turned, confused and embarrassed.

I was no less so.

"Signor Kagol, why are you out of bed?"

"It's all right, Verena. You can go."

"You have to rest, you know."

"I will. But first I have to have a few words with Salinger."

"No," Verena cried. "I forbid it."

Hermann smiled. "I appreciate your concern, Signora Krün, but you're my nurse, not my doctor."

"Just be careful," Verena hissed, giving me a filthy look.

She said goodbye to Hermann, walked past me and disappeared round the corner.

Hermann motioned to me to come in. I followed him. His two Dobermans watched me attentively. He didn't offer me a drink. Just a seat.

I noticed that he had shaved off his moustache. His face seemed naked and emaciated.

"How are you, Salinger?"

"I'm here to—"

"I know."

I cleared my throat. "How are *you*, Hermann?"

"Being the devil's tailor, sooner or later you prick yourself," the *Krampusmeister* said. "I have a little heart problem. Nothing serious. Rest and a few injections should get me back in shape. Signora Krün is a highly professional nurse. Thanks to her, I'm already much better. It's been a stressful time for everyone."

"I said some horrible things, Hermann. I'm sorry."

He made no comment. He bent down to stroke the heads of the two big dogs.

I handed him Evi's report.

He studied it, gravely.

"She would have had a splendid future. She was right, you know? The consortium from Trento had to capitulate. They were old school. They thought bricks and reinforced concrete would never go out of fashion. But bricks and reinforced concrete are heavy. And not only in a literal sense, I mean also in a figurative sense. Glass, steel, aluminium, wood . . . those were the materials of the future. I knew that."

I thought of the Visitors' Centre, with its slender modern lines.

"When I found out that others had had the idea of exploiting the Bletterbach, I thought I'd die. I didn't have enough liquidity, you see. Too many ongoing projects and not enough cash. There'd be cash in my pocket eventually, but when? If I'd started selling roast chestnuts on the highway, I'd have earned more money in a day than there was in my bank account. I was desperate, the thing I'd struggled so much for looked like it might collapse."

He shook his head.

"Then I remembered Evi. She was brilliant, intelligent. And ambitious. Plus, she was respected in Siebenhoch. Everyone knew about her mother, and how Evi had basically brought up Markus on her own. I didn't contact her in person. If I had, she would have felt duty bound to refuse. I dropped a few hints around. The rumour that someone would be building a Visitors' Centre on the Bletterbach, and that they would do it using the old invasive methods, soon reached her ears."

Hermann clicked his fingers.

"She drew up the report in a very short time. She knew every single rock in that place by heart. The Trento consortium was hit hard. They went to court, and court cases last forever. Long enough to restructure the debts of Kagol Construction and present my own project."

"Glass, aluminium and wood."

"Exactly."

"But . . ."

"I also thought of that at the time. I wondered if the consortium members were so angry they'd want to kill Evi. All you did, Salinger, was retrace my steps."

"Not yours, Hermann. Günther's."

Hermann half closed his eyes and sighed. "I discovered that when it was too late. Günther never spoke to me about it. He discovered the report and got it into his head that I was the murderer. His own brother, can you imagine? If he'd spoken to me . . . if he'd confided in me, maybe . . ." Hermann shook his head. "Let's leave the dead where they are. They're happier than us."

"Sometimes I think that, too."

We were silent for a while, listening to the breathing of the two Dobermanns and the *Föhn* making the shutters creak.

"I called you a murderer, Hermann. I'm sorry. I shouldn't have."

"The past is the past. And anyway I did the same to you."

"You were right, I am the murderer."

"You haven't murdered anyone, Salinger."

"I talked to Brigitte about the report. I told her that Günther knew about you and that . . ."

I couldn't hold back a sob. I could still see Brigitte's expression when she threw me out. It was the expression of someone who has lost everything.

"Brigitte told me what you two talked about, Salinger. I won't hide from you the fact that I'd been keeping my eye on you for a while. I'd realised that you were actually investigating the Bletterbach killings. I knew you'd talk to Brigitte sooner or later. I knew the business of Evi's report would come out sooner or later. For me, she was dead and buried. I think you saw me coming out of Brigitte's house that morning. I certainly saw you. It was written on your face. You'd found the report and were going in the wrong direction. So I thought I'd straighten things out."

I remembered seeing the black Mercedes.

"You had years to get rid of that damned report," I said, incredulously. "Why did you leave it in that music box all that time?"

Hermann raised his eyes to the ceiling, in the direction of Günther's room. "Because I thought it was safe there. And because it would have been *wrong*."

"So after I left, you told your version to Brigitte."

"Not my version, the truth. The Trento consortium, Kagol Construction's financial difficulties. And how I'd got a few words to reach Evi's ears so as to put a spoke in my competitors' wheels. I didn't want Brigitte to get the wrong idea. In the end, she told me she felt better."

"But it wasn't true."

"No, it wasn't true. I realise that now, but believe me, nobody could have stopped her. It was the third time the poor woman had tried."

"To kill herself?"

"Yes. She didn't commit suicide because of Gunther or Evi, Salinger. She committed suicide because she hated herself, and when a person hates themselves to the point of wanting to die . . ."

* * *

Halfway through March, I took Annelise aside and said, "I want to go back to New York. This place has torn us apart. And I don't want to lose you. Not for anything in the world."

We hugged and I felt something melt inside me.

That night Annelise left the door of her room ajar.

We made love. A bit awkwardly, as if we were afraid of hurting each other. At the end, we lay there listening to our breathing growing calmer.

I fell asleep under the illusion that the nightmare would soon be over.

Heart-Shaped Box

Werner was on the second floor of Welshboden, lying on the floor, face up. Eyes empty, one hand on his chest, the other bent behind his back in an unnatural position.

Motionless.

* * *

I had found the door open and had gone in, calling his name without getting an answer. I wasn't worried. I'd assumed he was keeping his promise to tidy the attic. So I'd gone upstairs.

Annelise had asked me to drop by to see how things were going. For the past two days, the only contact we'd had with him had been over the phone. He said he was busy clearing the attic, and that he had a bad headache. Nothing serious, but he didn't feel like coming down to see us. If it was flu, he might pass it on to us.

The six-pack of beer I'd brought with me fell from my hands. I searched for my phone. I needed help, an ambulance, someone.

"Werner. . ."

I placed my hand on his neck.

His heart was beating. His eyes came to rest on me.

"Hurts," he murmured.

His back.

"Dammit, Werner," I said, finding my phone. "You need to go to hospital."

He shook his head. It must be giving him a lot of pain to speak.

"No ambulance," he said. "You take me."

"Did you fall?"

"I can make it. Just give me a hand."

"How long have you been here?"

"A few minutes. Don't worry."

He tried to get up by himself. He let out a groan.

I helped him.

It was like carrying a dead weight.

We went downstairs. I made him put on a jacket, and had to lay him down on the back seat of the car because he couldn't sit up. His face was red, the veins sticking out. I feared a heart attack.

"I'm calling Annelise."

He raised a hand. "Later."

I didn't so much leave Welshboden as blast off in the direction of Bolzano. The rise in temperature had melted the ice on the roads and I went full throttle.

Reaching Emergency, I got a few nurses to help me. Werner refused a wheelchair, but when we went in he felt faint and they forced him onto a stretcher. Then they took him away.

I sat waiting for him, while the waiting room filled up and emptied like the systolic and diastolic movement of a beating heart. In the meantime, I thought it my duty to inform Annelise. A couple of times, I was about to call her. But what could I tell her? That Werner had fallen because in spite of his back pain he had decided to sort out his damned attic? And his condition? What was his condition? I had no idea. I decided I would call her when I had more information to convey to her.

Hoping that it was good news.

* * *

"Papà?"

I had just started reading Clara her favourite fairy story ("Tom

Thumb") when she interrupted me gravely. I closed the book and put it down on the bedside table.

"Why was Mamma crying?"

"Mamma wasn't crying. She was just a bit sad."

"But her eyes looked bad."

"She's worried about *Nonno* Werner."

"What's the matter with *Nonno*? Why did he go to hospital?"

"*Nonno* had a fall. His back hurts a little, that's all."

"And is that why Mamma's sad?"

"Yes."

"But did you tell her that all *Nonno* has is a pain in the back?"

I smiled despite myself. Clara had the ability to show me the world through her eyes. A simple, uncomplicated world in which everything worked like a charm.

"Of course. And *Nonno* told her as well."

"But she's still sad. Why?"

"Because *Nonno* is old. And old people are a bit fragile. Like children."

"Is it horrible to become old, Papà?"

It was hard to answer that question. Especially when the person asking was a child who, however precocious, was only five years old.

"That depends on who's around you. If you're alone, it's horrible, but if you have children, or lovely grandchildren like you, then it's not so bad."

"Are you afraid of getting old?"

That was a question that took me aback. I replied as sincerely as I could. "Yes."

"But I'll be with you, Papà."

"Then I'll be less afraid."

"I was very afraid, you know."

"When, sweetheart?"

"The snow," she said, and her eyes clouded over with anxiety, as if she were reliving those moments. "It ended up on my head. It was all dark. I didn't know what was up or what was down. And then my head hurt so much."

I said nothing.

I had a knot in my throat. I stroked her until I thought she was asleep. But, as I was getting ready to tiptoe out of the room, Clara called to me. "Papà," she said, opening her eyes wide. "Were you afraid, too?"

I made an effort to keep a calm tone of voice. "It's natural to be afraid, sweetheart. Everybody feels afraid sometimes."

"Yes, but when you had your accident. Were you afraid?"

"Yes. Very afraid."

"Were you afraid of dying?"

"I was afraid of losing all of you," I said, kissing her on the forehead. "I was afraid I would never see you again."

"Were you angry?"

"Who with?" I asked, surprised by the question.

"I was angry."

"With me?"

"With you, too. But especially with *Nonno*."

"*Nonno* Werner? Why?"

Clara's hand automatically rose to look for her hair. She rolled a strand of it around her index finger and started twisting it gently. "Do you think I should apologise, too? Now that he's ill, maybe I should."

"How can I tell you that if I don't know what happened?"

"I wanted to play with the doll in the heart-shaped box. It was beautiful."

"The heart-shaped box?"

Clara's little head went up and then down. Twice. "There was a doll in it. In the attic."

"And *Nonno* got angry?"

It was as if I had said nothing.

"The box was this big." She mimed the dimensions with her hands. "And it was full of old things. Horrible photographs and the doll. But the doll was beautiful."

Horrible photographs.

"What kind of photographs?"

"Pictures from films. Halloween films," she said solemnly, faced with my puzzled expression. "Pictures from zombie films. Except that the zombies were on the ground. Maybe they were broken zombies, what do you think, Papà?"

"Of course," I said, while my brain tried to translate what Clara was trying to tell me. "Broken zombies."

Broken zombies.

A doll.

The heart-shaped box.

Zombies.

Broken zombies.

"*Nonno* said I could hurt myself and I told him it wasn't right for him to keep the doll. He's not a child, I am. And then I was angry because everyone treats me like a little child. I'm not a little child."

"So as soon as he was distracted, you took the sled."

Clara's eyes filled with tears. "I knew you'd forbidden me, but I wanted to show that . . . "

"That you're a big girl."

"Do you think I should apologise to him? For getting angry?"

"I think . . . " I said in a hoarse voice, "I think there's no need to apologise." I smiled. "I'm sure *Nonno* has already forgiven you."

* * *

Why hadn't Werner told me? Why hadn't he told me he had yelled at Clara just before she went and crashed her sled? Maybe in the excitement following the accident, he had forgotten. Or maybe he felt guilty and was keeping it to himself. Werner was good at keeping secrets, I thought.

All the same . . .

A heart-shaped box?

A doll?

What most upset me and stopped me from getting to sleep that night were the photographs of broken zombies. What else could they be if not corpses? Why did Werner have photographs of corpses in his house? And who did they belong to? I was afraid of finding out.

There was worse. Not a fear, though.

A certainty.

Werner was hiding something from me.

* * *

That evening, I reopened the file.

I updated it.

Then I went to bed.

The hunt was on again.

* * *

I waited for the right moment. I was patient. The opportunity presented itself a couple of days later.

Werner would be going down to Bolzano for a check-up on his back. We were having lunch together when he announced it. Annelise offered to go with him. I offered to go with him.

Werner rejected both offers, he could perfectly well drive himself. We said we were upset and annoyed.

Only Annelise really was.

I calculated the timing to the split second. From one of the drawers in the kitchen, I took the spare keys that Werner had given us. I waited for Clara to go to bed for her afternoon nap and told Annelise that I was going out for a quick walk.

I sneaked into Werner's house at three in the afternoon.

At six minutes past three, I was on the second floor, slightly out of breath.

At seven minutes past three, I climbed the narrow staircase that led to the trapdoor to the attic. A few seconds later, I felt the typical smell of a place that has been closed for too long.

At ten past three, I lit the small lamp that hung from a beam. I started searching. Even though I knew there was nobody about and that even if I started dancing nobody would hear a thing, I did everything in absolute silence.

Twenty minutes later, I found the heart-shaped box. I held it up to the light.

There were recent prints in the dust.

I opened it.

The Wasps in the Attic

When I was a child, I spent more time with my head in the clouds than my feet on the ground. My father always told me that. He was the perfect example of a man with his feet on the ground. At the age of eighteen, he had escaped a destiny that was all laid out for him.

For two hundred years, the Salinger family had been born and died in the same village of some two thousand souls in Mississippi. My grandfather had been a peasant, my great-grandfather had done the same work and so on back to the obscure ancestor who had decided he'd had his fill of Europe and set sail for the New World.

Just like that Salinger two centuries earlier, my father had dreams of something better for himself. He dreamed of the thousand lights of New York City. But he wasn't the kind to have crazy ideas. He didn't want to become a Wall Street broker or a Broadway actor.

He had simply heard that in the Big Apple people didn't have time to make lunch or dinner for themselves, and so it had occurred to him that the best way to wipe the soil of Mississippi off his shoes was to open a hamburger stand and erase the southern drawl from his speech.

With time and sweat, the stand had turned into a little snack bar in Brooklyn, a place where you got a lot of food for not much money, but the accent stuck to him like chewing gum to the soles of the orthopaedic shoes his doctor forced him to wear at work.

In 1972 he had met a young German immigrant, my mother, they liked each other, they married, they set up house, and in 1975 I was born, the first and only child in the Salinger family of Red Hook, Brooklyn.

Among the neighbours, there were those who made fun of me. They said I was the son of a redneck, but it didn't upset me. The nice thing about the United States is that in one way or another we're all the children or grandchildren of immigrants. The snack bar was a snug little world that kept my father and mother busy fourteen hours a day, and I had a lot of free time to lose myself in my daydreams. Above all, I loved reading and walking around the neighbourhood.

At the time, Red Hook was in a bad way, there was heroin everywhere, along with the violence that came with it, and at night even police cars didn't venture into the harbour area. A little boy who was all skin and bones could be a target for junkies and crazy people in general.

My *Mutti* (she, too, never lost her German accent, something she often regretted) would beg me to stop my walks. Why couldn't I stay home and watch T.V. like all good boys my age? Then she would give me a kiss on my head and rush off to work.

What else could she do?

And anyway, I was very careful, I wasn't a stupid boy. Curious, yes, but stupid? Never. I read lots and lots of books, for heaven's sake. Nothing bad could happen to me. I believed that up there, in heaven, there existed a deity that protected book lovers from the ugliness of earthly life. My mother was a Protestant with Marxist tendencies, as she liked to say, my father a Baptist whose only tendency was the as-long-as-there-are-no-priests-bothering-me kind, and the neighbours were Lutherans, Hindus, Muslims, Buddhists. There were even a few Catholics.

My idea of heaven was vague and democratic.

So, feeling the hand of the God of readers on my head, I would reassure my *Mutti*, wait to see her walk out the front door of the red brick apartment block in which I'd been raised, then slip out and resume my wanderings. "This boy wears out more shoes than a team of marathon runners," my father would mutter whenever my mother informed him that it was time to buy a new pair, brandishing what remained of the last All-Stars purchased. I was obsessed with All-Stars.

Anyway, I liked walking.

I was especially drawn to the older part of Red Hook, the harbour, the grain warehouses. Sigourney Street, Halleck Street and Columbia, where Puerto Ricans glowered at you, an area that ended in the ocean, like the curled tail of a scorpion.

Or of a Hook, of course.

Walking meant imagining. Every corner a mystery, every building an adventure. In my head, everything became as glamorous as in a movie.

Nothing scared me, I had the God of readers on my side, right? Wrong.

I was ten years old, the best age to enjoy freedom without realising the weight it carries with it. The warm air coming in from the ocean had blown away a lot of the smog and I was walking in the area around Prospect Park, delighting in the rays of the sun. I sat down on a bench, a burrito in one hand and an ice-cold Coke in the other.

I was the master of the world until I heard the noise. A buzzing. Deep, cavernous.

I raised my head to heaven.

I didn't see any deity intent on reading some novel between the branches of the maple tree above me. I didn't even see the spring sky. I saw a nest. Ugly, square, and as gnarled as a potato. And dozens of wasps buzzing around it, looking at me. The sensation I felt, when one of them detached itself from what looked like a paper fruit (the image that had come into my mind as soon as I had seen it), came to rest on my hand and sucked a little of the grease from the burrito, was horrible. That thing that was moving was real, it was bad. And soon it would hurt me.

It would hurt me a lot.

And it did.

Like the stupid boy I was, instead of letting it be, keeping my nerve, waiting for it to finish its lunch and then running off, I started waving my hand and threw myself on the ground. It stung me three times. Twice on the hand and once on the neck. The sting on the neck swelled so much that my *Mutti* thought she needed to take me to hospital. It didn't get to that, but from that day on I stopped believing in the God of readers. I started fearing any insect that happened to be in my vicinity, and the memory of the hate-filled looks of all those wasps comes back into my mind every time I realise I've done something stupid.

Like that day in March.

It was the wasps I was thinking about as I opened the heart-shaped box.

* * *

I staggered back, letting out a cry.

No wasps. Only a heap of dust and yellowed photographs. Photographs of broken zombies. The zombies were Markus. Evi. Kurt.

The broken zombies of the Bletterbach.

Pure horror.

Those photographs must have come from the rolls taken by the forensics team at the crime scene. Presumably Werner had stolen them, and not even Max had noticed . . . Or maybe Max knew? The question occurred to me and quickly went away, as the adrenalin rushed into my veins.

Close-ups of gashed flesh. Muscles severed like offal. Amputated limbs lying in the mud. Those pictures were a branding iron plunged into my guts. And yet I couldn't stop looking at them.

The *faces.*

The faces assailed me with particular ferocity.

The face of Markus, slashed by the brambles into which he had fallen, with deep furrows that seemed to bear the nail marks of some animal. The terrified expression of someone who knows he is facing death.

The face of Kurt, twisted into an expression that was the quintessence of despair.

Evi.

The headless body thrown amid the knotted roots of a chestnut tree. And the dark mud all around, like a demonic halo.

"Hello, Evi," I heard myself saying. "I'm sorry for all this," I sighed. "I haven't told you this before, but I'm really sorry."

There were two more objects in the heart-shaped box.

The doll. It was a rag doll, stuffed with cotton. The doll Clara had told me about. The kind that are made at home using old cloths and a lot of patience. It had no face. Maybe the face had been drawn on with a felt-tip pen and time had erased it. The blonde hair was gathered in two plaits. I stroked them. It looked like my daughter.

Then I noticed a detail. It was stained. The doll was wearing a kind of long ballerina's dress, a white apron in the Tyrolean style. The apron was stained. Big, revolting stains. The colour was dark, like tan. I knew instinctively what it was. I let it slip from my hands.

When it fell, it produced no sound.

I was already shuddering, but now I felt nauseous. I rubbed my fingers on my jeans, trying to rid myself of the sense that I had touched something infected. I started breathing through my mouth, panting like an animal. The other object was something I couldn't bring myself to touch.

An axe.

The handle was broken into two pieces tied together with frayed string. The edge of the blade shone in the light of the naked bulb hanging over my head. I took off my shirt and used it as a glove to move the axe. I would burn that shirt, I thought. The idea of putting it on again disgusted me as much as the thought of admitting what the stains on the faceless doll were.

At the bottom of the box, packed in under all the rest, was an envelope that must once have been yellow, but which was now the colour of a fish's belly.

I took a deep breath and picked it up. I turned it over in my hands, unable to make even the simple gesture of opening it and looking at the contents. It was light. I took an eternity to make up my mind.

Two photographs, a small rectangle of paper and a sheet folded in four.

It was then, I think, that I lost all sense of time.

* * *

Once – it was right at the beginning of our relationship but I was already madly in love with her – I took Annelise to see the neighbourhood in which I had grown up. I did it with a certain trepidation and only because she insisted.

It was no longer the Red Hook of the '80s, with junkies in the doorways of the apartment blocks and dealers leaning on the lamp posts smoking, but I was still a little ashamed of those peeling walls and dirty sidewalks.

I showed her the harbour, the warehouses dating back to the nineteenth century, what remained of the bars my mother had forbidden me from entering, and bought her a scorching hot coffee from the Mexican from whom I'd purchased at least half the snacks of my childhood and many of those in my teenage years.

Annelise loved the neighbourhood to bits. Just as she loved my *Mutti* when, that same evening, I took her to the old apartment for dinner.

She had done things in style, my *Mutti.* When she opened the door to us I noticed she had put on her best skirt. She had even made herself up.

My father was dead by now, killed by a heart attack as he was preparing one of his fantastic hamburgers with onions, and she'd found herself a widow, having to handle both the running of an eatery and the artistic ambitions of a reckless son.

The day I had told her that I had a girlfriend, she'd been unable to contain her joy. Naturally, she wanted to know everything about her. Naturally, I had to bring her to dinner. To introduce her. Was she really so beautiful? Was she really so sensitive? Was she really a good girl?

Naturally she would prepare that dinner weeks in advance. And so she had.

Annelise had been more than happy to converse with her in her mother tongue, and it was nice to hear my mother laughing as she hadn't done in a very long time.

She submitted Annelise to a polite interrogation.

I was fascinated by my beloved's stories. The *Krampus* with their whips, the snow-capped peaks of the Dolomites. The refuge at Cles, made entirely of wood, the elementary school with the windows that looked out on vineyards as far as the eye could see, the vacations in Siebenhoch and the excursions in the mountains with Werner, the decision to move back there, to the place where her parents had grown up and where Werner was not only her father, but Werner Mair, the great man who had started Dolomite Mountain Rescue. Christmas with the snow so high as to force them to stay home all day, the friends she went shopping with in Bolzano, and the decision to leave for the United States.

Above all, my *Mutti* was delighted to hear her talk about the landscapes. She asked her to describe them so many times, I began to feel embarrassed. Maybe she had reached the age when migrants dream of settling again in their country of origin, even though they know that what they want to go back to no longer exists.

Annelise talked about her parents, how they had spoiled her, as the only child of a couple who, because of their age, had given up hope of having children and for that very reason had been especially protective towards her.

She talked about the time her father quarrelled with the schoolmistress about a punishment that in his opinion his daughter didn't deserve (actually she had deserved it, Annelise said, pigeons don't drop firecrackers on someone's head, right?), and she went into great detail about all the recipes that her mother had tried to teach her.

"It must have been wonderful to grow up in a place like that, Annelise."

"I had the most beautiful childhood in the world, Mrs Salinger."

And how to contradict her?

The snow, the meadows. The sparkling air. Two loving parents.

Siebenhoch.

A pity it was all lies.

* * *

I didn't hear him coming. I had lost all sense of time, and maybe not only that. I didn't hear the car parking in the drive and I didn't hear his steps coming up the stairs. I felt only his hand grabbing me.

I screamed.

"You," I said.

I tried to articulate something sensible. Nothing came out.

Werner waited.

He got down on one knee with a moan of pain and grabbed the doll. He blew on it and stroked it. Finally he put it back in the heart-shaped box.

I followed each of his gestures.

He took the two photographs out of my hands. He did so gently, without looking me in the eyes, wiped them on the sweater he was wearing and put them back in the envelope. Then he also put back the two pieces of yellowed paper, the large one and the small one.

He laid the envelope, the blade of the axe and the broken handle in the heart-shaped box. Finally he closed it, took it in his hands and stood up.

"Turn off the lamp when you come down, will you?"

"Where . . . where are you going?" I asked, as a shudder went through my body.

"To the kitchen. We have to talk and this isn't the most suitable place."

He disappeared, leaving me alone.

I went down the stairs, clutching the handrail. I was afraid my legs wouldn't support me.

I found him sitting in his usual chair. He had even lit the fire. He motioned to me to sit down. He had put the ashtray on the table, next to two small glasses and a bottle of grappa. A picture of normality. If it hadn't been for the box in his lap, I would have thought it had all been a hallucination.

The axe. The doll.

The photographs . . .

A figment of my imagination.

"Is that all?" I asked.

Werner seemed at least as surprised by my reaction as I was by his. "Sit down and drink."

I obeyed.

"I think you have a good few questions, right?"

Once again I was struck by his tone of voice. He didn't seem agitated or frightened.

It was the usual Werner telling me an old story. I don't know what I was expecting, but certainly not all that normality: two glasses of grappa and the fire crackling.

Werner looking at me, his expression unreadable.

He held out the glass to me.

"I need answers, Werner, or as God is my witness, the first thing I'll do when I walk out that door is call the police."

He withdrew his hand. He put the glass down on the table and stroked the box. "It isn't that simple."

"Talk."

Werner sat back in his chair. "You have to know that I loved her. We all loved her."

"You're a liar. A murderer."

Werner worked at a hangnail on his thumb until it started to bleed. He lifted it to his lips.

"We loved her as if she were our daughter," he said after an eternity.

The contents of the envelope. The photographs of Kurt and Evi embracing. Kurt and Evi waving. In both, in Evi's arms, a baby.

A baby girl.

Blonde.

The name of that baby was written on the sheet of paper folded in four. Annelise Schaltzmann, it said. Mother: Evi Tognon, unmarried, January 3, 1985. A birth certificate issued by the Austrian Republic. A birth certificate that said the unthinkable.

"Evi and Kurt had a daughter."

"Yes."

"You kept her."

"Yes."

"Annelise?"

"Yes."

I passed my hand over my face. Then, from a distance, I heard my voice formulate the most horrendous of questions.

"Is that why you killed them?"

The Truth about the Bletterbach Killings

"She was so small. She didn't even cry. We thought she was dead. She was sticky with blood. You should have seen her eyes, in the middle of all that slaughter. Those blue innocent eyes."

"Who else was with you?" I asked.

"Hannes, Max and Günther."

I felt the blood rush to my head. "Stop lying."

"You don't understand, Jeremiah. Annelise . . . was in his arms."

"Whose arms?"

"The killer's," was Werner's reply.

His eyes darted from side to side. From the heart-shaped box, he took the yellow envelope.

He unfolded the photographs. Then the birth certificate. Then the small thin rectangle of paper. It was an Austrian driving licence. In the name of Oscar Grünwald.

He showed it to me.

"He killed them."

"Why?"

"I stopped asking myself that many years ago."

He put the licence down on the table. He was silent for a moment.

"You're lying," I said.

When Werner resumed speaking, his face was twisted into a cruel grimace.

"It was the first thing we saw when we came out into that damned clearing. Grünwald covered in blood. With the axe in his right hand and that little creature under his arm."

I could imagine the scene.

The driving rain. The mud sliding beneath everyone's feet. Stones whistling past. The treetops bent by the fury of the elements. The dull howling of the self-regenerating storm. The shattered corpses on the ground.

Everything.

It took my breath away.

"As soon as he saw us, he started screaming, 'Monsters! Monsters!' Max and Günther froze. Hannes saw Kurt and he also started . . . Have you ever heard a madman shriek? I have, that day in the Bletterbach. But I went crazy, too. We all did. Hannes rushed at Grünwald, and I went after him. With a terrifying scream, Grünwald ran to meet him. He was clutching the child to his chest and holding the axe above his head. *This* axe."

He indicated the blade I hadn't dared touch.

"I saw the trajectory, I saw it only in my mind, with extreme clarity. It was as if time had stood still. I didn't hear anything. Someone had turned down the volume. But never in my life have I had such a distinct awareness of reality."

Werner's hands waved in the air in the kitchen at Welshboden. In spite of the fire, I could feel the cold in my bones.

The cold of the Bletterbach.

Of the storm.

The spartan house in Welshboden with its attic full of mysteries and the table with the grappa on it had gone. That was just a stage set, made of cardboard. Werner's words had opened a breach in time.

The smell of mud mingled with the odour of blood. I could feel the electricity in the air.

The crash of thunder.

And Hannes' screams.

But it wasn't Hannes screaming, Hannes had died after blowing his wife's brains out, driven crazy by the horror of the Bletterbach. What my senses perceived was the *fossil* of Hannes' scream. Imprisoned in Werner's mind for more than thirty years.

"The blade was dirty with blood. Big dark clots of it. God knows how long he had been standing there like a statue, with the child clutched to his chest and the muddy axe he used to kill those three. Hours, maybe. I don't know, I don't want to know. All I saw at that moment was the arc of the axe swinging through the air and Hannes' frantic run. Grünwald would have added a fourth victim to his slaughter. So I threw myself at Hannes and grabbed him by the leg. He collapsed to the ground. The axe missed him by a whisker. Grünwald's face, Jeremiah. His expression . . ."

Werner passed the palms of his hands over his trousers, rubbing them hard.

Reality ripped apart a little more.

I smelled the smell of mud, mixed with that of fear.

"He advanced towards us. In slow motion. Grünwald was waving the axe like a war trophy, with the child still clutched to his chest. Clutched so tight, I was afraid he would suffocate her. Hannes had banged his head and had a cut on his forehead. The sight of blood made the sound come back." Werner shook his head. "I don't know why."

A drop of sweat slid down from his temple to the curve of his jaw.

Then it disappeared.

I thought it looked red.

"I thought Hannes' blood would mix with his son's. I found that horrible. Then Grünwald was on me. He seemed ten metres tall. A giant, a creature of the woods straight out of a legend. His eyes were popping out of their sockets, he had blood on his face, blood on his clothes."

Werner grabbed the bottle of grappa and took a long swig. Then another.

"I've seen wounded people, dead people, in my life. I've seen broken limbs. I've seen a father bring his son's leg down the mountain, I've seen children beg me on their knees to save fathers who'd had their skulls opened by a rock. I've seen what the force of gravity does to a body after a fall of 400 metres. I myself have risked death many times. I've felt it coming. Like a fast-moving wind that sweeps you away. But that day in the Bletterbach, death was a giant with an axe in his hand looking at me with wild eyes."

Werner stared at me.

"It was the *Krampus.* No whips or horns, but it was the *Krampus.* It was the devil. And . . . I heard him speaking."

"What was he saying?"

"It sounded like a magic spell. Or a curse. I don't know. I didn't understand, lightning had just brought down a tree less than ten metres away. My ears were whistling, my eardrums were destroyed. But it was a meaningless sentence, maybe just the cry of a madman. I've thought about it for years."

Werner passed his hand through his snow-white hair. I felt an emptiness in my stomach. I knew what it was. It wasn't a meaningless sentence. It was a name in Latin.

My hands made stiff by that cold from another place and another time, I searched in my pocket and took out my phone. I looked in the memory for the image that Mike had sent me, and at last showed the screen to Werner.

"What's that?"

"*Jaekelopterus Rhenaniae.* Were those the words Grünwald was saying?"

Werner repeated them to himself, several times, like a mantra, like a prayer. His eyes were light years away from Welshboden.

"Yes!" he exclaimed all at once. "That's it. *Jaekelopterus Rhenaniae.* How did you know?"

"Grünwald was convinced they still existed in the Bletterbach. The *Jaekelopterus Rhenaniae* was an ancestor of the scorpion that became extinct in the Permian, the very era that the deepest strata of the gorge go back to. That's the monster he was talking about. The monster . . ." I shook my head, incredulous. "Evi had destroyed his career with a paper that demolished his theories. Grünwald had become the laughing stock of the academic world. A pariah."

I remembered Max's words.

"He was a loner. He had nobody. Only" – I pointed to the creature on the phone's display – "his obsessions. He went in search of monsters, and when Evi stood between him and them he became a monster himself."

I examined Grünwald's face on the licence. The high forehead, the incipient baldness. The short hair, the dark, narrow eyes, as if he were short-sighted but too vain to wear glasses.

I picked up the photographs of the killings. I put them down on the table, one next to the other, pieces in a mosaic of horror.

I passed my finger over them. My fingertip burned.

"The severed legs. The arms. The decapitation. That was how the *Jaekelopterus* hunted. 46-centimetre claws as sharp as blades." I sat down. "He was mad. Mad."

I didn't want to believe it. It struck me as absurd, but at the same time it all hung together.

Suddenly, the story of Grünwald became a perfect sequence of points united by a single line that went from *a*, past *b*, until it became red with blood, in the Bletterbach. The evidence was all there, in front of me.

And even if the evidence wasn't enough, part of me was in the Bletterbach, in April 1985. My back was numb with cold.

I could see him.

I could hear him mutter that curse from millions of years ago.

Jaekelopterus Rhenaniae.

"What happened then?"

"Grünwald let out a terrible cry. But Günther was quicker than him. The lightning had roused him from the shock. He threw himself at Grünwald like a fury. He grabbed him by the waist and flung him to the ground. The baby fell in the mud and if it hadn't been for Max's reflexes she would have rolled over the precipice. She started to cry. It was the cry of a kitten, not a child. Günther in the meantime was wrestling with Grünwald. I stood up and went to help him. He was hitting out blindly.

I was the one who tore the axe from his hands. I lifted it up and screamed so loudly I almost destroyed my vocal cords. It was a reaction that didn't belong to me, it was something animalistic. Then I realised that the handle was sticky with blood. I screamed again, but this time in horror."

He pointed to the two pieces of handle tied together.

"I smashed it against a rock. I hit it and hit it until I made my fingers bleed. When I'd finished, Günther was still punching Grünwald. He'd reduced his face to a shapeless mass of bruises. He's killing him, I thought. But you know something, Jeremiah?"

He let the question hang in the air.

"I also wanted that beast to die."

Beast, he said.

"But," Werner continued after an eternity, "I didn't want Günther to become a murderer. Günther was an instinctive person, very pure-hearted. If I'd let him kill Grünwald, he would have been riddled with remorse. I cried out. He stopped, his hands dripping blood, Grünwald under him, moaning softly. Bubbles of blood were coming out of his lips. I didn't feel any pity. I ordered Günther to stop. And, maybe just out of habit, he obeyed me."

A sigh.

"Max in the meantime had cleaned the baby's face. She was no longer crying, but she was shivering from the cold; we warmed her as best we could. Hannes meanwhile had knelt by the body of his son, sobbing as if he really couldn't stop."

Werner took a deep breath. It was almost interminable.

"I knew that if I stayed there in the middle of that slaughter, I'd go mad. Just like Hannes. We had to come to a decision. I made a suggestion."

"What suggestion?" I whispered.

"There are three kinds of justice, Jeremiah. There's God's justice. But God was looking away that day. No angel came to speak to us, to show us the way to follow. There was only a baby dying of cold, Hannes weeping, that madman's wild eyes, and all that blood.

"Then there's the justice of men. We could have tied Grünwald up and taken him down to the valley. Handed him over to the police. But I'd had dealings with the justice of men, and I hadn't liked it. You remember the birth of Dolomite Mountain Rescue?"

"The expedition where your friends died?"

"I was put on trial. They said it was my fault. Since I was the only survivor, they decided it was my negligence that had killed them. How could that judge know? How could he know how it feels when you have to cut the rope tying you to a colleague with a broken back? What did his laws know about what happens in the mountains? Nothing. All that mattered to him was that I was alive and the others weren't. So I had to be punished."

"Beware of the living," I said.

"I was acquitted on a technicality. The same law that had charged me released me over a comma inserted by God knows who, God knows why." Werner shook his head forcefully. "Forget about the justice of men."

"What's the third kind of justice?"

"The justice of our forefathers."

He crossed his arms over his chest, waiting for my reaction. There wasn't one. I sat motionless until he continued his story.

"Our forefathers knew the mountains. Our forefathers worshipped the rocks and cursed the ice. In their day, there wasn't the justice we think we celebrate today. They were born slaves and died slaves. They suffered hunger and thirst. They saw their children die like animals. They buried them in the hard ground and gave birth to others, hoping that at least these would be saved."

He looked up, towards the ceiling and beyond.

Beyond the sky.

Beyond space.

"Our forefathers knew how to wipe away the blood of the living."

I realised I was holding my breath. Werner's words were hitting me in the chest like so many nails. Big, thick coffin nails. I breathed out.

In the meantime, Werner had stood up and unfolded the map on the table.

"This is where we found him, tied him up and hoisted him on our backs. There was no need to say anything. We all knew the justice of our forefathers. We took turns, Günther, Max and I. Not Hannes, Hannes could only cry and call to his son. He begged his forgiveness for not having understood him, for never having told him how proud he was of him. But the dead are deaf to our entreaties, so we tried to console him. In vain. He wouldn't even listen to us, maybe" – he sighed – "maybe because we, too, as we dragged that bastard to the caves, we, too, were dead."

I turned to stone. "The caves."

Werner tapped on the map to show me the exact spot. "Since forever, our forefathers had thrown murderers, rapists and troublemakers in there. Anyone who had shed blood, anyone who had tried to destroy Siebenhoch ended up there. No matter if they were rich or poor, nobles or peasants. The caves are big and dark. They welcome everybody."

Did I see a sneer on his face?

I prayed it wasn't true.

"Witches," I murmured, remembering what Verena had told me. "Witches also ended up down there."

"Yes."

"The witches were innocent."

"Those were different times. We knew Grünwald was guilty. And we threw him down there."

"Weren't . . . weren't you afraid he might escape?"

Werner made a contemptuous sound. "Nobody's ever got out of the Bletterbach caves. It's hell down there. You remember the mine? Every now and again, the miners would knock down the wrong wall and drown. There are lakes under the Bletterbach. Some say also pits of sulphur. There's a whole world."

"And you threw him there."

"It was where he belonged. It was Max and I who went down, with

Günther shouting down to us from the surface every now and again. When his voice was little more than a sigh, we found a shaft. I've never seen such impenetrable darkness. It was like a huge evil eye."

"Was Grünwald still alive?"

"He was breathing. Wheezing. He was alive, yes. Günther wasn't a murderer. Before throwing Grünwald down the shaft, I took his licence, the only document he had on him."

"Why?"

"For two reasons. Because if the underground streams brought up his body, we didn't want his identity to be discovered. He didn't deserve a name on a gravestone. And then because I wanted something to remind me of the anger I felt at that moment. I knew that sooner or later, it would fade. And I wanted it to stay alive. Whenever I feel it wearing off, I go up into the attic, open this box and look that son of a bitch in the eyes. The anger comes back and with it also the feeling I had when we threw Grünwald down the shaft. The feeling that I'd administered justice."

"The justice of your forefathers."

"By the time we got back out in the open air, Hannes had an absent look in his eyes, while Günther was shaking like a leaf." Werner crossed his arms and looked up at the ceiling. "Years later – it was just before that road accident – I met him by chance, blind drunk."

"Here in Siebenhoch?"

Werner shook his head. "No. In Cles, where I was living. He wanted to get something off his chest. He kept cursing and hitting himself with a bunch of keys. He was bleeding. It was like he was crazy. Günther had been the last to leave the mouth of the cave, and he said that when we were down there, already some distance away, he'd heard voices, women's voices. They were asking for help. It was a chorus, that's what he said, a chorus."

"Christ."

"We were mad that night."

"What happened to the child?"

Despite the birth certificate, I still couldn't bring myself to call her by her name.

"We found a shelter, however wretched. We lit a fire. We took turns cradling her. She was hungry. All we had for her was water and sugar. She needed a doctor, but the storm still hadn't abated." Werner started pounding on the table. "It was a bombardment of rain, lightning, thunder. It lasted ages. Ages I spent thinking."

"About what?"

"The child. She'd been born in Austria, after Kurt and Evi moved there, but nobody in Siebenhoch knew."

"They weren't married."

"Precisely. Kurt was afraid of his father's reaction. Markus knew about the child, but Markus had died trying to escape the madman we had just thrown into the caves. Who could that child be entrusted to? There were only two possibilities. Kurt's family and Evi's mother."

"An alcoholic."

"Precisely."

"Weren't there any other relatives?"

"There was Evi's father, but what had become of him? And anyway, would you have entrusted that child to a man who had deserted his wife after turning her into a drunken whore? Plus, he was violent."

I shook my head. "So you decided to keep her?"

"*Nix.* I decided I would help Hannes to get custody of her. I thought Günther might even be able to get his brother Hermann involved."

"Why Hermann?"

"Hermann knew how to deal with the bureaucracy, and at the time was starting to make a few friends in politics. All things that could be useful to us. A risk, but . . . that's what I decided that night. Then we went back. It was dark and cold. Siebenhoch was cut off from the rest of the world. We entrusted Hannes to Helene: they were both devastated about Kurt's death. But I couldn't imagine what Hannes would do in the next few hours . . ." A sigh. "For a few days, I would take care of the child.

Max and Günther were bachelors, I was the only one who had a wife, don't you see?"

"You took her home."

"Herta . . . you should have seen her face. She was scared, terrified, furious with me because I'd risked my life, but the sight of the child turned her into another person. She took her in her arms, changed her, cleaned her, gave her food and, while Annelise was sleeping, had me tell her the whole story."

"Even about the caves?"

"She said we'd made the right decision."

From somewhere, I heard the call of a crow.

The flames in the fireplace had turned to embers.

"That night, Hannes killed Helene. They found him with the rifle still in his hand, catatonic. It was Max who told me. He rushed to my house like a fury, almost knocking down the door. Soon the streets would be cleared, Hannes arrested and the child would be handed over to social services."

"That was when you decided to keep her?"

"We decided it together, Max, Günther, Herta and I."

"What gave you the right?"

"The child didn't deserve to grow up in an orphanage. Nobody deserves that." Werner wriggled in his chair. He seemed angry. "We would bring her up, surrounding her with the love Evi and Kurt could no longer give her. The love someone" – he almost yelled – "had decided they could no longer give her. By tearing them to pieces! To pieces!"

He grabbed the handle of the axe and flung it to the floor.

"It was still abduction. Of a minor."

"Think what you want, Jeremiah. But try to see it as we saw it then."

"How did you do it?"

"We had to wipe out the traces. We went back to the Bletterbach. We combed through the clearing in search of anything that could have alerted the police to the existence of Annelise. The doll, a baby bottle. We took everything away. We also took away the pieces of the axe. We were afraid the police would find fingerprints and screw up everything."

I thought of what Max had shown me about the forensics investigations.

"A wasted effort."

"We know that now, but then? We got back to the village just in time for the Civil Defence bulldozers to make their triumphal entry."

"Annelise. . ."

"I stayed at home, waiting for the end of the preliminary investigations. I only went out to go shopping in Trento, and I was scared I'd be seen with a bag full of baby food and nappies. I saw policemen ready to arrest me everywhere. I was even afraid of the dark. As soon as the investigation was declared closed, Herta, Annelise and I left. In the middle of the night, I put them in the car and we got out of there."

"You went to Cles?"

"That's what people think. No. That wouldn't have been wise. Hermann helped us. Yes, Hermann knows, too. He had a property in Merano, a little apartment. Far enough away for nobody to recognise us. We hid there for nearly a year. It was Hermann and Max who produced the false papers. They never told me how they'd done it, and I never asked. But they did it, and it worked. It was only then that we moved to Cles."

Werner lit himself a cigarette. He was pale, his forehead furrowed with deep lines.

The story was coming to an end.

"In the meantime, Max and Günther had spread a few rumours. Herta was pregnant: a difficult pregnancy that had required treatment and caused me to abandon the rescue team because I was scared of leaving my daughter without a father. Time passed and people stopped thinking about us. When we came to the village for a short holiday, everyone called Annelise by her name, as if they'd known her all their lives." Werner shrugged. "That's how rumours work. But there's something else you ought to know."

"Günther's death."

Werner crossed his arms over his chest, eyes shiny. "Günther, yes. The last time I saw him, in 1989, he was completely out of control. He'd found Evi's report and had got it into his head that his own brother had been in cahoots with Grünwald. He wanted to kill him, he told me in so many words. I tried to dissuade him. To make him see how crazy that was. But a few days later . . ."

"The car accident."

"His mind couldn't hold out. And he killed himself. Günther was the last victim of the Bletterbach."

He had finished. He filled a glass with grappa and held it out to me.

This time I took it.

"And now?" I asked.

"Now it's up to you, Jeremiah. You have to decide. What kind of justice do you believe in?"

I didn't know, so I replied with a question. "Why have you never told Annelise?"

"I thought of doing so at first. I told myself I'd wait until she was eighteen, when she was mature enough to understand. That's why I was keeping the heart-shaped box. I knew that without proof, my words would only confuse her. Maybe she'd think her old man had gone mad. Then I realised that eighteen meant nothing. She was still a child, even though she was taking driving lessons and dreaming of America. I talked to Herta and together we decided that only a mother could accept what she and I did in '85."

"And by the time Clara was born . . ."

"Annelise was on the other side of the ocean and Herta was dying. Was there any point in telling her then?"

"No."

"And now, Jeremiah? What would be the point in telling her this whole story now?"

There were at least a thousand answers to the question Werner had loaded on me like a million-ton burden.

"As far as the law of men is concerned, Annelise ought to know that her father died in that gorge and that the man who took his place" – I said this with bowed head – "is a murderer and a kidnapper. As for the law of God" – I raised my head again – "I'm not very knowledgeable on the subject. But I think that as far as the law of God goes, none of this matters in the least, and if it does, bringing up Annelise in a loving family, rather than abandoning her to an institution or worse, was the right thing to do."

Werner nodded.

I forced myself to smile. "So one vote for and one vote against."

"And the justice of our forefathers?"

Sadly, I opened my arms wide. "Look at me, Werner. I'm the son of immigrants, I don't even know who my forefathers are, and frankly it's never bothered me. I only have one father. A poor man who slaved away all his life making hamburgers at fifty cents a go to get me through school and pay for braces." My voice broke for a moment, then I continued, "But I can speak for myself. I don't know if what you've said is bullshit, or if you've told me the truth. I do know, though, that you spoke from the heart and I know you believe this story, mad as it is. Although madmen can also be very convincing."

Werner stared at me for a few moments. He took a drag on his cigarette, coughed and threw it in the fire. "Whatever you decide to do, do it quickly," he said, leaning towards me, his eagle eyes going right through me. "Because I'm dying."

"What—?"

"The backache. It isn't backache. It's cancer. And it's inoperable."

I was speechless.

"Annelise . . ." I managed to say.

"She won't hear it from you."

"But . . ."

"What do you intend to do, Jeremiah?"

* * *

When I left Welshboden, the March air still smelled of snow, but further down you sensed the stench of decomposition. I was aware of a kind of weariness in nature around me, a weariness that I shared.

I sat down behind the wheel. My arms felt as heavy as if I'd been carrying logs all afternoon. My head was echoing with the screams of the Bletterbach.

During Werner's account, I had clenched my jaws so tightly that now they hurt. I had the feeling I had been biting into a poisoned fruit. Somewhere, a snake was laughing at me.

Now you know, I said to myself.

No, now you don't know a fucking thing.

I clutched the wheel, exhausted.

I was torn. On the one hand, I felt it would be only right to talk to Annelise. To tell her everything Werner had just told me. On the other hand, I told myself I didn't have the right. It was up to Werner. I hated him for confronting me with that choice. It was an unbearable burden that belonged to him, not to me. I struck the wheel with what little energy I still had left in my body. It wasn't right. But what was right in this business?

Evi's death? Kurt and Markus's death?

And what about Grünwald?

Hadn't he been entitled to a fair trial? The justice of men, as Werner said contemptuously, is fallible and inclined to punish the weak, but it's what distinguishes us from the beasts of the jungle.

Did I really think that?

Would I really have acted any differently if I'd been in Werner's shoes? If Annelise had been handed over to social services or an alcoholic grandmother, would she be the same Annelise I loved? Would she have had the same dreams that drove her into my arms? Or would she have been condemned to a lifetime of humiliation?

What distinguished the woman I loved from Brigitte, for instance?

Little or nothing.

I heaved a deep sigh.

It wasn't over yet.

I started the engine and put my foot down on the accelerator.

* * *

This time I was neither kind nor understanding. I pushed Verena aside, almost knocking her down. I had eyes only for Max, who was standing there. It was the first time I'd seen him in civilian clothes.

"We have to talk," I said emphatically. "Come with me."

"You two have nothing to talk about," Verena screamed, beside herself, "and I want you out of my house."

She would have gouged my eyes out if Max hadn't intervened and held her back. Putting his arms around her, he said to me, "Wait for me outside, Salinger."

I went out and closed the door.

I heard Verena yelling and Max's voice trying to reassure her. Then silence. At last the door opened. A chink of light that immediately disappeared. Then Max, his hands in his pockets, an extinguished cigarette between his lips, waiting for my words.

"You know all about it, don't you?"

He looked at me for a long time. "All about what?"

"Annelise."

Max turned pale, or so it seemed. The light was dim, and I couldn't swear to it. What's true is that he gave a start, grabbed my arm and pushed me away from the door.

"Let's walk."

"Werner told me everything."

"Everything?"

"Grünwald. The caves. Evi and Kurt's daughter. And Günther."

Max stopped by a lamp post. He lit a cigarette. "What else do you want to know?"

"How did you and Hermann manage to wipe out all trace of the child?"

Max smiled. "In those days, computers were useless. And who had them anyway? Not us. The bureaucracy worked with paper. It was a big, blind, stupid pachyderm. And don't forget the Iron Curtain."

"Austria was a friendly country."

"True. In fact, if Annelise had been born in East Germany or Poland I'd have saved myself a lot of hassle. But that's politics, and you're interested in the practical details, aren't you?"

"I'm interested in everything."

"Why?"

I went closer and looked him in the eyes. "Because I want to know if you're all feeding me bullshit. Because I want to know whether or not I have to ruin the life of the woman I love."

Max looked around. "You're making a spectacle of yourself."

I brushed him aside and lit myself a cigarette. The flame from the lighter blinded me.

"Carry on."

"Think of the world we were living in. Cold War. Spies. Here, there was terrorism. It was said that the terrorists had bases across the border, then it turned out to be true, in fact some of them are still living there, in Austria. To get to Innsbruck, you had to go through customs. You didn't need a passport, there were already international agreements, but there were a lot of police." With his left hand, Max mimed a barrier going up and down. "On one side, the Italian police, and on the other, the Austrian police. Getting through the Brenner Pass took time. But both countries had one thing in common: bureaucracy. When we decided that the child would be brought up by Werner and Herta, I realised that Hermann and I might be able to pull off a conjuring trick. Günther was never the brightest spark, and Werner was too scared and too well-known to try anything so . . ."

"Illegal?"

"*Delicate.* It was like open-heart surgery. Have you seen Werner's hands?"

He smiled.

I remained impassive. I was registering every one of his words. As soon as he stumbled, as soon as he contradicted himself . . .

"Go on."

"We had to get hold of a death certificate for a child Annelise's age. An *Italian* death certificate for an *Austrian* child. I dealt with that. It was easy, I remembered a little girl who had died beneath the Marmolada. I amended it with Annelise's details. I dirtied it, as if the fax machine wasn't working properly. I sent it to the Austrian embassy and waited for it to be recorded and sent back to the home country. I had to gain time. Time to answer the questions of that idiot Captain Alfieri."

"You were never interested in his discovering the culprit, were you? You just wanted to throw him off the scent."

"That's right. I became a joke, but jokes don't kill, they make people laugh. I'd already killed the culprit, what I was doing was protecting the innocent. Werner, Günther, Herta and Annelise."

The archive in the Krün family home took on quite another significance in the light of these revelations.

"That's why you got rid of the files as soon as you could."

"At first, I thought of burning them. Then I told myself it would be better to keep them. In case. . ."

"In case someone stuck his nose in?"

"Someone like you, yes."

I didn't reply. I took a deep breath and waited for Max to continue.

"I went to Austria, I went there in uniform. In a Carabinieri uniform. I'd bought it specially and I threw it in the garbage before crossing the border on the way back. I asked for Annelise Schaltzmann's death certificate. I said I needed it for an official investigation. I lied, of course, but nobody noticed. They gave it to me and this time it was a genuine death certificate. Annelise Schaltzmann had died of kidney failure at the hospital in Belluno."

"It's like a cat chasing its own tail."

"It's bureaucracy. Then came the most dangerous part."

"Annelise had to be reborn. She had to become Annelise Mair."

"Yes. The only moment when they could have discovered us. Hermann had contacts, he knew his way around. That's why, apart from the fact that he was Günther's brother, we turned to him. So, on September 9, 1985, a clerk at the register office in Merano close to retirement pocketed a decent amount of money, turned a blind eye and inserted Annelise in the register of births. The child of the Bletterbach was born a second time. Nobody noticed a thing. If it hadn't been so tragic, you'd have split your sides laughing. We'd led the entire bureaucratic apparatus of two countries by the nose. And we'd got away with it."

"Until today."

Max half closed his eyes. "What are you planning to do?"

"I'm wondering that, too, Max."

* * *

It was Clara who told me what to do. Her desperate voice, that night, in a dream.

* * *

The house lights were off. To light my way, there was a spectral aura, a phosphorescent glow. I groped my way around, trying to orientate myself.

The walls, although I sensed their presence, were so far away that I could have walked the rest of my days without touching them. And yet I knew it was the house in Siebenhoch.

In the logic of the dream, that's how it was.

I felt an indescribable anxiety. I didn't know why, I knew only that if I stopped, everything would be lost. I wasn't running away. It wasn't one of those dreams in which faceless figures lie in wait, ready to clutch at you. No, I was searching.

But I didn't know what for.

I only realised when I began hearing Clara's voice calling me desperately. I tried to respond to her call, but in vain. My lips were sealed. So I started running to get to where the voice was loudest. It was a circular room, with rock for walls. White rock oozing blood. In the middle of the room, a shaft.

I leaned over.

Clara was there.

So, as my daughter continued calling my name, I threw myself into that vast dark eye.

The Thing from Another World

The next day was a beautiful sunny day. At ten o'clock, I presented myself at Welshboden, ready to face the last chapter in the story of the Bletterbach killings.

Ready to question the dead in order to answer the living.

The Werner who opened the door to me looked like someone who hadn't slept a wink all night. His breath smelled of grappa. I didn't want to go in. I didn't have time.

He just had to glance at my outfit to realise what I was thinking of doing. "You're crazy," he said.

I hadn't expected him to say anything different.

I held out my hand. "Give me the map."

"You'll die."

"Give me the map."

It was my determination that made him give in. He handed it over to me and as I drove away, I saw him in the rear-view mirror, standing there in the doorway. An old man bent beneath the weight of too many secrets.

* * *

The Visitors' Centre was deserted, mine was the only car in the parking lot. I took my backpack out of the trunk and checked my equipment. I hadn't touched it since September 15. I didn't think about that. September 15 was a date like any other.

My movements were slow and precise, as I had learned they had to be at times like this. Everything was there. I unfolded the map and checked that I had memorised it as best I could. Then I climbed the fence and began my walk towards the caves.

While engaged in the shooting of "Mountain Angels" I had learned a few rudiments of mountaineering, but it was mostly a matter of theory, apart from a few climbs in my free time, just to experience the exhilaration, and always under the expert eyes of a guide. I'd enjoyed myself and had become skilful enough not to get into trouble when I was on my own.

Now, though, in the Bletterbach, the game was a lot harder. And more dangerous. I remembered from my excursion with Clara the notices along the marked trail warning about the lack of a signal. In other words, phones were useless down here. And no phones meant no rescue. If what Werner had told me was true, I couldn't even trust my compass.

Did these considerations stop me?

Not for a second.

I didn't follow the route taken by Werner, Hannes, Günther and Max's rescue party. If I had, I would have wasted a great deal of time and energy. 1985, with its tracks made by woodcutters and animals, was archaeology, today there were well-kept paths, even though they were covered in snow right now, and I would exploit every possible advantage for as long as I could. At least until the point where the present met the past.

Before saying goodbye to the tourist trails and going *into the deep*, I granted myself a brief halt. I drank some water and ate a little chocolate. My muscles were hurting, but I could feel in my legs the strength necessary to complete my journey back through time.

Refreshed, I set off down a slope, taking great care not to get caught in the branches of the fir trees.

The slope grew steep, and a couple of times I almost fell. Given how sharp the rocks were, falling could have had serious consequences.

But then, if I'd really thought about the possible consequences of my descent into the Bletterbach, I would have stayed home.

At the bottom of the gorge, the rock was covered with a layer of ice. Beneath it, I could hear the flow of the stream.

I didn't wait even an instant. I climbed up the opposite side.

A rustle of branches: some animal alerted by my presence, or else a little snow yielding to the warmth and the force of gravity. Ice-cold air. Sweat.

And nothing else.

Following Werner's directions, I reached the track along which the men of the rescue team had dragged Grünwald's body and followed it. Not without effort. The snow was deep and I had to lift my knees as I walked.

I cursed the fact that I hadn't thought of snowshoes.

At last, exhausted, I arrived.

Around me, there were red firs, larches and a few pines. All covered in snow. But no caves. Maybe, in my eagerness to get here as quickly as possible, I'd lost my way. So I took off my backpack to check the map.

Which proved I was right. There was no mistake.

This was the place.

Had I made a pointless journey? Had Werner lied to me? The answer was much simpler, and it took me a moment or two to get there. I was a stupid city boy. If as a mountaineer I was a beginner and as a caver not even that, as an explorer I was rubbish. I couldn't even read the terrain.

The Bletterbach caves weren't a cross between Tolkien and a National Geographic documentary, spectacular chasms you could enter easily. They were little holes in the rock that were obstructed by snow from October until the thaw: that was the reason there was nothing waiting for me at the infamous point *x* marked on the map.

Cursing loudly, I started digging with my hands, panting and sweating.

I found it.

An opening no more than eighty centimetres in diameter, from which emerged a smell that made you turn up your nose. I lit the flashlight on the top of my helmet.

Then I took a deep breath and went in.

* * *

I proceeded on all fours, breathing in the damp air, which was warmer than the air outside and imbued with an oppressive graveyard smell. The cave wound its way down between the crumbly rocks of the Bletterbach. I tried to imagine how Werner and Max had managed to drag Grünwald. It must have taken incredible determination.

The same determination that I had now.

A couple of bends, then a small flight of steps in the rock. Beyond it, the tunnel rose again, opening into an enormous space. I stood there, staring at that vastness, hypnotised by the spectacle of stalactites and stalagmites interwoven in bizarre shapes.

I walked, keeping to the right-hand side of the perimeter. In some of the cracks in the wall, there were tufts silky to the touch. Mould, or maybe moss. It seemed incredible to me that even down here, where the sun hadn't shone for 300 million years, there was life. Incredible and terrifying.

I looked at my watch and realised to my surprise that I had lost all sense of time. I knew it was a natural phenomenon, one that professional cavers take for granted, but the speed with which it had happened knocked me back.

I continued, and at last I saw it: the dark eye.

I bent to lean over and look down. It wasn't the way I'd imagined it. More than anything else, it looked like a chute, very steep and very viscous, but I had no doubts that this was the shaft into which Max and Werner had dropped Grünwald. The vaguely circular opening really was like a dark eye.

It was as if there existed various shades of black, and this shaft had decided to show me the darkest shade possible. I was scared, of course.

But I didn't turn back. I wanted to see, I wanted to know. Only then would I be able to figure out what to do.

Whether to tell everything to Annelise or let the whole story fall into oblivion.

I planted a couple of pitons and secured the rope that I had brought with me. I passed it through the abseiling device that I had attached to the harness and began my descent.

I immediately understood why Werner and Max had chosen this spot to carry out their death sentence. Without the requisite equipment, it would have been impossible to climb back up.

The rock was slippery and almost completely devoid of footholds.

I suppressed my claustrophobia and went faster.

When, after several metres, I felt the ground flattening out again, I unhooked myself and looked around, trying to orientate myself. The flashlight on my helmet didn't help much.

The darkness down here was almost solid.

I risked a step, supporting myself on the damp wall. The first step was followed by a second, and so on, until I found myself a long way from the point at which I had descended.

From time to time, an insect would crawl over my hand, provoking a shudder of disgust. They were spiders, white and spectral, with very long legs and a body the size of a one-euro coin.

Revolting.

Just as I was shaking one of them off, I felt something brush against my calves and I stopped to point the flashlight. Water, I discovered to my surprise. I was walking alongside an underground lake. I dipped my fingers in it to test the temperature. It was cold, but not as cold as I'd expected. My surprise didn't last long, because a sudden crash caused me to let out a scream that the echo divided into infinite reverberations.

Something big had fallen in the water. My heart missed a beat.

Everything's fine, I told myself. The mountains are in a state of constant metamorphosis: why shouldn't it be the same for their internal organs, too? Collapses in a cave of this kind must be quite common. So everything's fine. Everything's fine.

Above all: no panic.

Caving, like mountaineering, isn't just a question of skill and muscles.

During the shooting of "Mountain Angels", I'd seen people who spent their days in climbing gyms, people who were technically well trained and physically in much better shape than I could ever be, break down halfway up a not especially difficult wall. How could that be? They couldn't answer the question. In front of the television cameras, they stood there bewildered, empty-eyed, muttering about contractions or cramps.

Bullshit.

The truth is that technique and being in good physical shape are important, but they're only 50 per cent of what's required. The rest is a matter of nerves: it's fear that fucks you up. Suddenly, your fingers feel the texture of a crumbly rock, an insect buzzes around your head, and there it is: the wall you're dealing with becomes the concrete embodiment of all your fears.

The mind gives way.

I knew that perfectly well. It had happened to me, too, in that damned crevasse.

So: no panic.

I had brought a big halogen flashlight with me, a much more powerful flashlight than the one on my helmet. Light helps to chase away fear. Or at least, that's what I hoped deep down.

Cautiously, I took it out of the backpack and lit it. At last I could get an idea of exactly how big the space I was in really was. The underground lake was enormous. I turned the beam of light to the ceiling to calculate how high the vault of the cave was.

And I saw it. The Beast.

* * *

It was white.

It was fierce. It was motionless. But then I realised it was only ice.

I shifted the beam of the flashlight, drawing silvery scimitars on the surface of the water. With each wavelet, it seemed as if the underground lake were smiling. It wasn't a friendly smile, believe me.

I followed the waves until I located the epicentre, about ten meters from me. A kind of white iceberg in miniature was floating placidly, bobbing up and down as if nodding at me.

Come here, it was saying, *come to me.*

I tried to calm down and look for a plausible explanation. It didn't take me long to find one.

The layer of ice above my head gave way from time to time and marble-like blocks fell into the water. That's all it was. Maybe the heat from my body had generated that reaction. Simple physics.

The problem was that this made me think of the cave as being a living creature.

With me inside it.

In the whiteness.

I felt an acid taste in my mouth. My mind, which since a tender age I had trained to tell me stories, started doing its dirty work. Going from *a* and getting to . . . to Grünwald's cries as he woke up, alone, in that darkness.

His frustrated attempts to climb back up to the opening of the eye.

Broken nails, blood, entreaties and cries.

The decision to find another way out. Going round in circles. Arriving here.

What then? Had he gone forward? Had he tried to swim? I wouldn't have, but Grünwald was a lot more expert than I was, maybe he'd taken the risk and gone into that . . .

Niche.

That was the word.

Five letters.

An ecological niche. Protected from external agents. A world in which the hands of the clock had no meaning. Just like in Grünwald's theories.

I took a deep breath. I relaxed my shoulders, rotating them slowly. They were as stiff as strips of steel. I opened and closed my hands to restart my circulation. I was starting to feel cold. I had to keep my muscles warm and relaxed, or I would stay here forever. Like Grünwald. Like . . . How many? How many people had ended up in here? The justice of our forefathers, Werner had called it. Lynchings, more like.

Barbaric acts.

Five letters: "death".

If I hadn't lingered over these macabre thoughts but had retraced my steps, I would have avoided what happened subsequently, because it was pure chance that I saw the body huddled in a crack in the rock.

The old-fashioned clothes hung limply on what remained of the body. The knees under the chin. The right leg broken in two places.

The bones shining in the torchlight.

"Hello, Oscar," I said.

The lake responded with a splash.

I was face to face with the remains of Oscar Grünwald.

The backpack clutched to the chest, the arms wrapped around the knees, the head tilted to the side, the jaw wide open. A child punished. A man defeated.

Condemned to the eternal darkness deep inside the Bletterbach.

I imagined how much he must have suffered down here, all alone, with his broken leg, dragging himself in search of salvation. I imagined the darkness choking him, the hallucinations, the madness. A slow, wretched agony. And at last, death.

The empty eye sockets of the skull told of a despair that went beyond anguish. A man driven mad, imprisoned in the most terrible of cells.

Yes, he was a murderer, but nobody deserved such a dreadful punishment. I felt sorry for him.

And horror at what Werner and the others had done.

I don't know how long I stayed there beside Oscar Grünwald's body,

I only know that when a twenty-centimetre-long centipede emerged from those same eye sockets that had hypnotised me, I leapt back in surprise and disgust and lost my balance.

I fell in the lake and lost hold of the flashlight. The water closed over me with a stifling sound. I gasped for air, but only managed to swallow water. I was blind and deaf.

Above and below became as one.

I waved my arms and legs in senseless movements dictated by panic and sank even deeper, my lungs burning and my stomach filling with a poison that tasted of bile.

Everything was black, everything was dark.

I acted on instinct, and it was instinct that saved my life. I freed myself of the backpack and let the force of gravity clutch at it. I felt it go down. Then I pushed with all my might in the opposite direction. A few metres that were nearly fatal to me.

Once on the surface, I gasped and spat for a while, but instead of continuing to struggle I let myself float.

One thing at a time, I told myself. In the meantime, breathe. Look around you. Find the shore. And get out of here as quickly as you can.

The lamp on my helmet was working intermittently. It must have hit something as I was falling. It sent brief flashes (light, dark, light, dark) that illumined the still, dark waters with a flicker that didn't help my pupils to get used to the gloom, quite the contrary. But during one of those precious seconds of light, I thought I saw the shore and tried swimming in that direction. Slow, methodical strokes.

But it wasn't the shore. It was cold and slippery. Ice, I thought. Only ice. Then the ice *moved.* And something under the water brushed against my knee.

Light, dark. Light, dark.

The object I had touched was big and white and when a sudden flash lit it up, *it went back under the surface.* In the darkness, I felt the lapping of the water closing over it. As if it had been some big albino fish.

Or else . . .

My screams became a chorus of sounds, a thousand superimposed voices that seemed to mock my fear. The screams of the women condemned by Siebenhoch. The laughter of the witches buried down here. That's what Günther said he had heard. What Oscar Grünwald must have heard before he died, huddled in that crack in the rock as if . . . As if he had seen something terrible moving in the water. Something big and cold. And for the second time, I felt something touch my foot. With greater insistence. I jerked my leg up and ended up with my head under the surface of the water. At that moment, the flashlight came on.

Light.

It was white. It was huge.

Jaekelopterus Rhenaniae.

I kicked.

I found the surface, oxygen. I took wheezing breaths. I swam. Away from there. Without thinking about the white, slippery thing with the Latin name that had grabbed my boot. About its 46-centimetre claws. About its unnatural size. Two and a half metres of marine scorpion. About its perfectly round, black eyes, eyes so inhuman they verged on the unthinkable.

A predator millions of years old.

Don't think, I ordered myself.

How did *Jaekelopterus Rhenaniae* hunt? Were its attacks quick and lethal, like those of sharks, or else were they more like those of crocodiles? Would it grab my leg? Would I feel its claw breaking my bones and cartilage, or would it drag me down, drowning me?

Worse still: where had it gone?

Why hadn't it attacked me yet?

"Don't think, dammit!"

There was no monster down there. It was impossible. I wasn't really sure I had seen it. The white monster in the ink-black lake. I *thought* I had glimpsed it. The key to not going mad was in those seven simple letters: "thought".

The taste of bile in the water was making me nauseous. And I was cold.

I swam, trying to keep to the same direction. It was an underground lake, not an ocean. Sooner or later, I would find something to cling on to. I swam until my fingers hit solid rock. Wearily, I hoisted myself onto dry ground.

I had no idea where I was, but I knew I had to move. I was so wet, there was a risk I might die from exposure. So I had to move, but in what direction?

One was as good as the other.

I walked.

The darkness entered into my skin, swallowed me up.

The sound of my breathing became the breath of the Bletterbach.

Time frayed until it disappeared completely.

At last, exhausted, I collapsed to the ground. Maybe I was just a few steps from an exit, but without light I would never know. It was pointless. I was in a labyrinth.

I raised my hands to my face.

I thought about Clara. About Annelise.

"Forgive me," I said.

The witches sneered. At my stupidity.

Maybe I slept, I don't remember.

I was woken by a terrifying sound. A roar that made me leap to my feet, shaking.

It wasn't a hallucination. It was the sound of something moving implacably on the surface of the water, beating what could only be a tail.

A long tail covered with a shell. Eyes like black wells. Claws like blades.

It was coming.

Jaekelopterus Rhenaniae.

This is how the pathetic story of Jeremiah Salinger ends, I told myself.

Devoured by a monster as old as the world.

I started laughing and couldn't stop.

It was the most ridiculous death I'd ever heard of.

"Come on, you scumbag!" I cried.

The noise was rapidly coming closer.

It had followed me. It had spied silently on my every move. It had waited for me to lose energy. For me to despair. Patiently, inexorably. And now it was attacking.

It was clever, the bastard.

"Come on, you son of a bitch!"

I leaned against the wall, looking for some stone or other to pull out and use as a weapon of defence. I wouldn't go down without a fight. When the *Jaekelopterus* charged, I would let it know that now was no longer its time. It was extinct. It was dead. Gone.

My fingers found something much more precious than a stone. They found an inscription.

A few straight lines, carved into the bare rock. Three triangles with the points turned upwards. Human, without a shadow of a doubt. Geometrical. Nothing in nature could have cut into the stone so precisely. Destiny wasn't providing me with a weapon, it was offering me something better.

Hope.

Frantically, I touched it.

The roar of the *Jaekelopterus* seemed closer now. Five metres. Maybe less. A few centimetres from the inscription, my fingers grasped a metal hook.

The noise became thunder.

One metre.

Drops of fetid water on my face.

I screamed and darted to one side, clutching the protruding metal with all my might. I must have pulled a muscle in my back. The pain shot up to my neck. I stumbled, bounced back, lost my balance, held on even more grimly. I knocked my helmet against the rock and the lamp started working again.

Wonderful, blinding light.

What did I see?

A huge block of ice, floating on the water. Nothing else.

* * *

It must have been the miners who had planted the hook and carved the three triangles. The ones who worked in the copper mines that had collapsed in the 1920s. It was their method for indicating exits or bends, so that they wouldn't lose their way in the chasms they themselves were creating. Usually, they were little crosses. At other times, initials or symbols that in some way referred to the identity of those who made them, or the villages from which they came. It didn't matter. Those marks in the rock were *hope.*

I continued to feel my way until I found the entrance to a tunnel, over which the same symbol was carved. I couldn't restrain my joy. I went in without hesitation.

I had to proceed on all fours, my helmet touching the rock, the lamp continuing to blink on and off. I didn't care. Hope gave me new energy. Besides, I could sense that at last I was moving upwards.

Nothing could stop me now. And nothing did.

All at once, I felt fresh air.

When I saw the light, a little hole high up above, I started crying. I clambered up, slipped and fell, hurting my hands. I tried again and again. I broke my nails, cursed and spat. At last, gripping the knotted roots of a chestnut tree, I hoisted myself towards the source of light.

When I emerged onto the surface, I did so with a scream that echoed throughout the gorge.

I rolled in the snow, sinking into the ice, which seemed so pure it went to my head. The air I was breathing was as sweet as honey. The sun was blinding. It was pale and crepuscular, and I was surprised to see it. When I checked the time, I realised that my wandering in the bowels of the mountain had lasted hardly any time at all. And I started to feel the bite of the cold.

I came back to earth.

I was without my equipment, soaking wet, and my body was starting to fall apart. I had to move. I hoisted myself with difficulty onto the chestnut tree whose roots had saved me. I reached a sturdy fork and sat down astride it. I scrutinised the horizon and it didn't take me long to see the tourist trail through the Bletterbach, with its fine white and red signposts, its warnings of danger. Common objects, made by some local carpenter.

They struck me as masterpieces worthy of a museum.

* * *

I turned onto the drive, surprised by how prodigious that banal act seemed. From the windows came a soft warm light. I switched off the engine.

Tears rose to my eyes, and at that moment Clara drew back the curtains and waved at me. I returned her wave. Behind my daughter, I could see Annelise.

She was very beautiful.

I got out of the car.

It was Werner who opened the door. He looked at my scratched and bruised face. Then my swollen, ruined hands. He opened his eyes wide. He tried to say something. I gestured to him to be quiet.

I reached out my hand and he responded to the gesture.

No words were needed.

I passed him and walked towards Annelise. She was as frozen as stone. She looked like a corpse.

"I love you," I said.

* * *

That night, I waited for Annelise to go to sleep, then slipped out of bed, went to my study and closed the door. I switched on the computer and updated the file.

Then I dragged it across to the recycle bin.

It was over.

Parents

I spent the last days of March in bed, brought low by a fever that reduced me to a shadow of my former self. The pills I took were no use: my condition was only partly physical. My descent into the bowels of the Bletterbach had wiped me out, and I needed time to recharge my batteries and start over again.

I didn't sleep much, and then only fitfully. In those brief periods of sleep, I would return to those caves. I would see again the dark eye, Grünwald's body, and the monster that emerged from the water wasn't a block of ice: it had a mouth, claws and a Latin name. I would wake up disorientated and scared, but safe.

At home.

Home was Clara who would put her worried little face round the bedroom door, bringing me a fruit juice that tasted disgusting in my sick state, but which I drank to the last drop to make her happy.

"Is it good, Papà?"

"It's wonderful, sweetheart," I said, struggling not to throw up.

"Would you like me to take your temperature?"

"I'd like a kiss, honeybun."

I always got plenty of those.

Every now and again, when Annelise went shopping, Clara would tiptoe in and sit down on the edge of the bed. She would tell me fairy stories and stroke my hair, almost as if she was the grown-up now and I was the child to be looked after. Lots of times, she'd just sit there and look at me.

Can you imagine a nicer picture of love?

Annelise never asked me anything. She was caring, attentive and anxious. I knew the questions were only being postponed, I could see it in her eyes, but first I had to get better.

And that's what I did.

* * *

The fever passed. I still had dizzy spells, still felt as I'd been driven over by a steamroller. But my eyes no longer filled with tears whenever I tried to read a newspaper, and the headache wasn't much more than a dull ache at the back of my neck. I began to get my appetite back. Annelise would provoke me with incredible quantities of food I simply couldn't refuse. It was so good to feel something that wasn't pain.

After a couple of days spent mooching about the house in my dressing gown, I decided to venture into the outside world. I needed fresh air. And, don't be angry with me, I also needed a Marlboro.

I put on thick jeans, a sweater, a scarf and my padded winter jacket and walked out, as determined as Harrison Ford in pursuit of the Holy Grail.

With unsteady steps, I reached the garden gate. I touched it with my fingertips. Satisfied with my achievement, I turned back, sat down on the front steps and granted myself a cigarette.

The sun was high, brighter than I had seen it in months, and I let the wind waft the smell of the woods to my nostrils. Spring was finally coming. There were still patches of snow on the ground, above all at the sides of the roads, where the snowploughs had heaped it in dark dirty mounds, but nature was waking up again.

And so was I.

Suddenly I became aware of Annelise standing behind me.

"I think I owe you an explanation," I said.

She gracefully slid her skirt under her legs, sat down next to me and leaned her head on my shoulder.

The off-key call of a blackbird could be heard, then a rustling of wings. A bird of prey was flying high in a sky dotted with slow-moving snow-white clouds.

"Tell me just one thing, Salinger," Annelise said. "Is it over?"

I turned.

I looked her in the eyes.

"It's over."

She burst into tears. She hugged me. I looked up at the clouds.

I could have touched them with my finger.

* * *

Two days later, I had a consultation with the same specialist who'd put me back on my feet after the accident of September 15. When I confessed to him that I hadn't taken the drugs he'd prescribed for me, he was furious.

I suffered his anger in silence, with my usual hangdog expression, until he calmed down, then I told him I'd decided to resume the treatment I'd actually never begun: that's what I was there for.

I had to pull myself together, I told him. So far, I'd gone my own way and it hadn't worked.

I had no intention of taking drugs that would make me a happy idiot (and here his face turned red), but now it was time to say farewell to nightmares and panic attacks.

You could say we bargained, and it's almost funny to think about it that way, because he wasn't trying to sell me a used car or a cable T.V. subscription, he only wanted to make my life better.

He prescribed some mild tranquillisers and new sleeping pills to make my nights less restless. When he said goodbye, he had a big question mark on his face.

I understood his doubts, but I couldn't tell him the real reason for my determination. It was because the story of the Bletterbach, the story of the Bletterbach killings, was now just a file in the recycle bin on my laptop. A finished document.

I had succeeded.

I had told the story of Evi, Markus and Kurt. And of Werner, Hannes, Günther, Max, Verena, Brigitte, Hermann, Luis and Elmar. The biography of Siebenhoch.

Nobody would ever read it and I would never make a documentary about that ill-fated excursion, but what did it matter? I had proved to myself that I was still able to do what I loved most: tell stories.

Now it was time to turn the page.

* * *

"Frau Gertraud will look after you," Werner said. "You like Frau Gertraud, don't you, Clara?"

Clara looked first at me then at Annelise, then nodded shyly. "She's read every book in the world."

Werner opened his arms wide. "You see? No problem. So, are you coming to dinner at my place?"

Annelise tried to hide her surprise at the invitation with a "Why not?"

"Good girl," he said and gave her a hug.

Then he drove off in his jeep.

"What do you think that was all about?" Annelise asked me when we were back inside the house.

"I have no idea."

"You've spent a lot of time together."

"That's true."

"I thought you talked."

I put my arm round her shoulders. "How many times do I have to tell you, darling? Men don't talk. Men grunt and drink beer. Sorry, they drink grappa."

She didn't laugh. "He loves being with Clara. It strikes me as strange that—"

"Instead of asking yourself so many questions," I cut in, "why not just look forward to an evening off?"

Werner hadn't told me anything, but I had a pretty good idea what he was planning to do that evening, and I admit I was scared. But I pretended I had other things on my mind.

I was cheerful and talkative. I helped Clara to choose the dress she would wear during the time Frau Gertraud, Siebenhoch's librarian, would act as her babysitter. By the time the loden-clad woman arrived, at around seven in the evening, my daughter had changed her mind at least three hundred times (jeans and T-shirt were too casual, the green skirt was for having dinner out, maybe the red one . . .) and I, in spite of my affable facade, was as tense as a violin string.

What Annelise and I were going to wasn't a simple dinner, it was a farewell that would add a couple of lines to the face of the woman I loved.

I held firm.

* * *

Werner opened the door to us and shook our hands. He searched for my eyes and I avoided his.

We chatted about New York and Siebenhoch. We talked about Clara, who would start school in September. About Frau Gertraud.

I was my normal self.

Werner had lost weight, that was obvious, and yet, when he went to the kitchen to fetch the dessert from the refrigerator, I pretended to be surprised by my wife's comments.

"Werner?" I said. "I think he looks very well."

As lively as the broken zombies in the photographs in the heart-shaped box.

I only thought it, but I did think it.

Once dessert was finished, Werner handed Annelise a little gift-wrapped package. "This is for you. From me and Herta."

She batted her eyelids in embarrassment. "What is it?"

"Open it."

Annelise looked at me, clearly wondering if I was aware of the contents of the package. I knew nothing about it: Werner's move had caught me by surprise, too.

Annelise undid first the ribbon, then the tissue paper, to reveal a little box. Inside it was a pocket watch with a simple round white dial. The casing was silver, scratched in places. The hours were in Roman numerals, the hands were Gothic arrows.

Annelise stared at it in bewilderment. "What am I supposed to do with this, Papà?"

"It's yours," Werner said gravely.

"Thank you, but . . . " At last, Annelise noticed her father's solemn expression.

It's starting, I thought.

I felt a touch of relief. My part in this play was over. I could leave the stage, withdraw to the wings and prepare to collect the pieces of my wife's shattered heart.

"This watch has been in our family for more than a century. Look at the casing."

Annelise read aloud. It was a date. "February 12, 1848."

Werner nodded. "It was a wedding present. Since then it's been passed from father to child. And now I'm giving it to you."

"It's beautiful, Papà, but . . . "

"You have to take good care of it, the mechanism is fragile. You have to wind it every evening, as the Mairs have always done, otherwise it might be damaged."

"Papà . . . " Annelise was pale.

Werner gave her a sad and infinitely painful smile. "I'm dying, my girl."

Annelise put the watch down on the table as if all at once she was afraid of it.

"My time is coming to an end. That's why I want you to have this watch. You know why you have to wind it every evening? Because that way you appreciate more the passing of the minutes. Those were my father's very words the day he gave it to me. God knows where he'd read a sentence like that. Maybe it was his, who knows? We've always been a bit strange, we Mairs. A bit crazy and a bit innocent. What I meant to say was that you always have to take care of time."

"Papà," Annelise murmured, her eyes swollen with tears. "You're not really dying. You're Werner Mair, you can't die. Everybody in Siebenhoch knows that. You . . . you . . . "

Werner nodded. "You remember when I fell in the attic and went to see a doctor? He did what doctors always do in these cases, he sent me to see a colleague, and so on. Except that each time, the face of the doctor I was seeing grew as long as a mule's. In the end, the last one standing had the bother of telling me the diagnosis. I have bone cancer. It's inoperable and incurable."

It was as if an invisible vampire had sucked every drop of blood from Annelise. "You can't leave me alone," she said in a low voice.

"I'm not leaving you alone, my girl. You have your husband and your daughter. You have your life." He picked up the watch and placed it in her palm, then squeezed her hand. "You still have a lot to do, mountains to climb, battles to win – or maybe to lose just enough to acquire a little bit more wisdom. And I'm sure destiny has a couple of sunny days in store for you to warm your bones when you reach the age when time is counted, not in years but in minutes. Then, at the end, you'll take this watch, you'll make a package more beautiful than mine, and you'll give it to Clara."

"But I . . . " Annelise said, shaking her head. "I don't know what to say to her. I . . . " She spoke as if she were hoping to persuade the cancer to leave Werner more time.

"When the day comes, you'll know," he replied.

Annelise threw her arms around his neck, as Clara did with me when she was scared. Except that the person crying on her father's shoulder wasn't a child, it was an adult woman, the woman I loved, the woman I'd sworn to protect from all harm.

A promise that couldn't be kept.

The devil always has the last laugh, as the *Krampusmeister* said.

I stood up, feeling like a deep-sea diver at the bottom of the ocean.

Father and daughter had words to say, secrets to reveal and tears to share. I prayed, as I left them alone, that one day, facing Clara, I'd be able to find the same serenity with which Werner was explaining the ultimate mystery to Annelise.

* * *

For the whole of the following week, Annelise wandered around the house with red eyes and a bleary expression. It was like living with a ghost. It was torture seeing her like that.

Especially for Clara, who couldn't figure out her mother's behaviour.

"Is Mamma ill?"

"A bit of flu, maybe."

"Shall we make her some fruit juice?"

"I don't think she wants fruit juice."

"Then what does she want?"

"To be alone for a while."

"Why?"

"Because sometimes grown-ups need to be alone. To think."

To cut off that cascade of questions, I tried to distract her. I invented some new games, a tongue-twister, I challenged her as to which of us could find the longest word in the world, just to shield her from all that bitterness. I knew how Annelise was feeling, but I didn't want her to withdraw into her grief and exclude the world.

There wasn't time.

One evening, after putting Clara to bed, I took Annelise aside. "You have to react, darling."

"I *am* reacting," she said irritably, as if I had distracted her from her thoughts.

"No, you're mourning your father," I said gently.

"Of course I'm mourning my father, Salinger!" she cried. "He has cancer!"

"But he isn't dead yet. You remember what he said? The drugs are doing their job right now, the pain is almost non-existent. You should be taking advantage of that."

Annelise looked at me as if I had cursed in church. "To do what?"

"To be with him," I said. "Because the most important thing we can do for our parents is make sure they leave us with happy memories."

In the Belly of the Beast

On April 20, there was a ringing at the door in the middle of the night. A furious ringing that woke me with a start. My heart seemed as if it were about to take flight.

Dazed by the sleeping pills, wondering if a fire had broken out that was razing Siebenhoch to the ground, or a war, or a disaster of apocalyptic proportions, I went downstairs and opened the door without even asking who it was who was making all that noise.

The figure that emerged from the darkness embraced me with the strength of a bear.

"Salinger!" he cried. "I always get the time difference wrong, don't I? And where's my sweetie?"

"Mike, Clara's . . ."

She wasn't sleeping.

Clara was coming down the stairs, jumping the steps two at a time. She landed in Mike's arms and he lifted her in the air, making her yell with joy.

"Uncle Mike! Uncle Mike!"

You could see the exclamation marks from a long way away.

Mike threw her so high, I was afraid she would hit the ceiling. So, to avoid a heart attack, I took the two suitcases my friend had abandoned and closed the door, leaving outside the sharp cold of the night.

"Am I allowed to know what the hell you're doing here?" I asked.

"Your Papà doesn't like Uncle Mike," he said to Clara.

"Papà does like Uncle Mike," she pontificated. "Only he says that Uncle Mike is a bit five letters."

Mike turned to me. "What the hell does five letters mean?"

"'Crazy', in this case."

Mike turned again to Clara, and threw her up in the air one more time. "Crazy! Crazy! Uncle Mike is crazy!"

Every time Clara flew upwards, I lost a year of my life.

At last he put her down, pretending to be hurting.

"Not even a beer for Uncle Mike, sweetie?"

"It's night-time, Uncle Mike," Clara said with unexpected wisdom.

"In some parts of the world, it's five in the afternoon."

To Clara, the logic of this seemed unassailable, and she disappeared into the kitchen.

I had seen grown women, worldly-wise women, succumb to Mike's absurd logic: why expect a little girl of five to be any exception?

"Since when have you had beer for breakfast?"

It was Annelise, in her dressing gown, her hair ruffled and a smile all over her face. Mike hugged her and smothered her in compliments.

He thanked Clara, who had brought him a can of Forst, and, still wearing his jacket, collapsed into the armchair in the middle of the living room.

"How are you feeling, partner?" I asked him.

"Like someone who's flown across the ocean for eight hours, spent four hours on a train, and then forked out a whole lot of money on a taxi," he replied, guzzling down the beer. "Actually, seeing as how I forgot to get a receipt, how much is 'a whole lot of money' in dollars? You owe me one, Salinger."

"Clara?" I said.

"Papà?"

"Bring me the Monopoly, please."

Clara was bewildered. It was Annelise who explained to her that it was a joke.

"Papà makes jokes," Mike said, sipping at the Forst. "Papà thinks he's funny."

"You could have called," Annelise said. "I'd have made something to eat. Would you like a sandwich?"

"How about another beer?"

"No way."

"You've lost points, baby."

"Mike?"

"Yes, partner?"

"It's three in the morning. I was sleeping with my lawful wedded wife under a warm quilt and you show up on my private property without warning."

"You could have shot me."

"I'd have happily done it. Sweetheart?"

"Yes, Papà?"

"Bring me my rifle."

This time Clara got the joke and burst out laughing.

Papà and Uncle Mike were better than cartoons, when they really got going.

"Do you want to know why I crossed the threshold of your private property without warning?"

"I think that'd be only fair, given that you've also appropriated my armchair."

"I was sitting quietly at home, after an evening in a club in Co-Op City, an incredible place with a live band doing Stooges covers and lap dancers who were the real thing. I have a couple of beers, chat a little and meet this blonde. Not bad, let me tell you. So we decide to go to my apartment and—"

"You can spare us the details."

Mike remembered Clara, who was following the monologue as if hypnotised. He cleared his throat and continued, "I take her home and tell her the story of the fox and the grapes. Sweetie, do you know the story of the fox and the grapes?"

"Is it the one about the fox who wants to eat the grapes and because they're too high he says they aren't ripe? Is it that one, Uncle Mike?"

"That's the one. Except that in my version, the fox is old and flabby and married, and so when his friend Mike starts to tell him about the latest bunch of grapes he took home with him, the flabby old married fox—"

"Go easy," I said, cutting him off.

Mike took two envelopes from his jacket pocket and threw one at me and one at Annelise.

"What's this?"

"An invitation to the premiere of the masterpiece of Mike McMellan and the now flabby Jeremiah Salinger."

The envelope contained a flyer printed on stiff card. The logo was the network's. There were too many gaudy colours. There were snow-capped mountains.

And a date.

The date was: April 28.

* * *

Seven days later, Mike was telling Clara his own version of the story of Cinderella. From what I'd gathered when I'd gone up to her bedroom for a goodnight kiss, it involved a rich Manhattan lawyer, a *Vogue* journalist and a big bull terrier. Mike didn't seem to have grasped the idea that bedtime stories were meant to get children to sleep, but it was nice to hear Clara roaring with laughter.

Annelise was finishing clearing the table, an apron tied around her waist and a tuft of hair brushing her chin and bothering her. I thought she looked delightful.

I lit myself a cigarette.

"It'll be full of assholes," I muttered.

"I know."

"Assholes who'll write bullshit."

"That's a tautology."

I cleared my throat. "We'll have to escape into the night. They'll come looking for us with pitchforks."

"Don't exaggerate."

"I'm not exaggerating. That's how it'll be."

"You're exaggerating."

"If I'd wanted to exaggerate, I'd have said: they'll set fire to the house, they'll impale me on the church steeple, and when I'm dead they'll make a barbecue out of my ass."

"Nothing of the kind will happen. You'll just have to shake a few hands and answer questions you've already answered dozens of times."

"Mike's the director," I whined. "He's the one who likes shaking hands. Remember how it went the last time I answered the questions?"

Annelise's mouth twisted at the memory of the performance that had earned me a lawsuit (dismissed by the court) and a migraine that lasted three days.

"You're the star."

"I don't want to be the star. I like keeping a low profile."

"Salinger . . ."

I raised my hands, as a sign of surrender. "O.K., O.K. . . ."

"No 'O.K., O.K.', understood? I haven't spent five hundred euros on a dress just to hear you whimpering all night."

Having said this, she turned and rubbed a grease-encrusted baking tray: Mike had made the dinner, and when Mike cooked, cholesterol levels were so high, they did somersaults.

I sat in silence for a while, listening to Clara's laughter and the clatter of the dishes in the sink, wondering for the hundredth time how come neither I nor Annelise used that modern contraption called a dishwasher. A kind of snobbery, I guess. The same kind that would allow the long list of guests at the premiere of the documentary to kick me in the ass for the next two years. My buttocks already hurt.

"Stop it right now," Annelise suddenly exclaimed.

I jumped. "Stop what?"

"Brooding. I can feel it from here."

"I'm not brooding."

Annelise let go of the baking tray, wiped her hands on her apron and sat down facing me.

"You have to do it. You have to go."

"Why?"

"Three reasons," she said.

"Just three?" I tried to joke.

"First," she said, "you owe it to Mike. He worked like a dog to finish everything. He defended you all the way, and you know perfectly well it can't have been easy."

"Right."

"Second, you have to do it for yourself. You have to write the words 'the end'. Then you'll feel better."

I tried to smile. I couldn't. My mouth was dry.

I extinguished my cigarette. Maybe it was time to quit.

"Third: you owe it to them."

"Them?"

"*Them.*"

* * *

The network had brought out the heavy artillery. Posters on street corners, banners and all the rest of the paraphernalia that Total Asshole had dreamed up for the occasion. On the internet he had launched something called a "viral bombardment" in the manual of guerrilla marketing: to me, it seemed more like a free-falling cluster bomb of bullshit, but who was I to judge?

The sleepy town of Bolzano had witnessed in astonishment the preparations for the premiere of "In the Belly of the Beast" and the in-vasion of a host of critics (those with T-shirts under their jackets were T.V. critics, those with bags under their eyes film critics), reporters (those who bragged a lot were from local papers, those who ate sushi were from the national press, and those who grumbled were Americans), starlets ("Mike?" "Yes, partner?" "Who the hell is Linda Lee?" "She made a couple of socially aware movies." "With those nuclear warheads she has instead of boobs?" "Take it easy, partner. Linda's a friend") and characters of varying degrees of weirdness who wandered amid porticos and monuments with wild eyes and bewildered expressions. The local population seemed to have taken this madness well, I thought, as we headed in a rented car with other motorists to the cinema that was hosting the event, until my eyes came to rest on a piece of graffiti, in red block capitals, which a diligent municipal employee was trying to wipe off and which said: SALINGER MURDERER.

"Is that another of Total Asshole's clever ideas?" I asked Mike.

"It may be, partner, it may be. Who was it who said: 'The important thing is to be talked about'?"

"Comrade Beria, I think. Or maybe it was Walt Disney?"

Mike was dressed with unusual sobriety that evening. A suit and tie that made him look like a stranger to me. He was pretending to be relaxed. But I knew him well. He kept cracking his knuckles. An activity he indulged in only when he was trying hard not to scream.

I knew how he felt. Oh, yes. I hadn't eaten anything that day, I'd gone though two packets of cigarettes (so much for good intentions), had complained all morning and spent much of the afternoon trying on clothes. In the end, my choice had fallen on a jacket and tie that made me look thirty years younger, rather like a schoolboy on the day of his first communion. Annelise had borne all this with patience and stoicism. She was a knockout in her new dress. But I was so nervous I almost didn't notice.

Clara, on the other hand, was simply excited. Blessed childhood.

She looked at everything with eyes like headlamps and continued bombarding me with questions, while the car with its smoked windows (another flashy idea from the twisted mind of Total Asshole) cut through the crowd in the centre of Bolzano. Half of these people had no idea who we were – I kept telling myself – and the other half considered us vultures. In any case, very few of them seemed to be paying any attention to us at all. But my paranoia had reached danger levels.

"What does T.A. mean, Mamma?"

Mike and I looked at each other.

"Terribly Astute, sweetheart," I replied.

"If he's so astute, why do you and Uncle Mike always make fun of him?"

"Sweetheart," Annelise cut in, "you remember what we said?"

"'Be a good girl,'" Clara recited. "'Papà has to work.'"

"Very good."

"But this isn't real work."

At this point, Mike and I could no longer contain our hilarity. Clara had caught us out. This wasn't real work.

The reporters were waiting for us along the sidewalk under two very cool, very minimal and very ugly blow-ups of the outline of a mountain. The red smudge that went across it was an artistic depiction of the EC135. Total Asshole had assured me of that. It was down to the genius of a Californian designer who earned thousands of dollars for his consultancy. To me it looked just like a red smear, not even very well drawn, but if a guy had really managed to get himself paid a fortune for that stuff, hats off to him. You have to appreciate talent when it shows itself.

The car came to a halt.

The driver cleared his throat.

"We have to get out," Mike said.

"They'll tear us to pieces."

"Isn't that always the case?"

"Can we turn back, partner?"

Before opening the car door, Mike gave me an encouraging wink. Annelise squeezed my hand hard. I returned the squeeze and turned to Clara.

"Give me a good luck charm, honeybun."

Clara imprinted a kiss on my forehead.

If you happen to see photographs of that evening, you'll see that yours truly has a kind of washed-out little heart between the eyebrows. It's my daughter's lipstick (yes, Annelise had put *lipstick* on her).

Waiting for us, a gangly guy whose name I didn't know. There were a few flashes. Mike showed index finger and middle finger in the gesture made famous by Winston Churchill. I limited myself to not zipping away at the speed of light. It has to be said that with Annelise by my side, I looked pretty good. I clenched my fists and my buttocks.

The inside of the building was packed. A babel of tongues into which we insinuated ourselves while everyone watched us. Slaps on the back, thousand-dollar-a-bottle perfumes mingling with one another to the point of nausea.

Total Asshole had got an artisan in the Val Gardena to put up something like an army of lanterns in the shape of a *Rosengarten* (even though a *Rosengarten* had nothing to do with the movie), the light from which was torture to me all the time Mike and I, with Annelise and Clara standing to one side, spent pretending to know the people greeting us.

"Salinger."

Mr Smith had hauled his butt out of New York and flown all the way here. I was horrified, even though I should have felt flattered.

He was wearing an impeccable dinner jacket, with a cigar in his breast pocket instead of a handkerchief. His handshake lingered long enough for a couple of flashes. He had put on weight since the last time I'd seen him.

For a moment, I was afraid I'd said that out loud.

"What do you think, son?"

"Amazing."

He smiled smugly. "Have I introduced Maddie?"

Maddie was a wrinkled little thing in a baby-pink dress, with a Martini in her left hand and her right held out as if she were expecting me to kiss it.

"Maddie?"

"Maddie Grady, *New Yorker*."

I felt a tightness in my stomach. And while Mr Smith withdrew to go and spread charm over the buffet, I spotted Mike (the girl on his arm must be Linda Lee, judging by the abundant bosom overflowing her low-cut dress) putting a hand over his mouth, trying not to seem the amused caveman he was.

"I've been looking forward to meeting you in person," I said. My sarcasm didn't escape Annelise, who pinched me. Maddie Grady was the journalist who had slaughtered and deboned the first season of "Road Crew" with all the delicacy of a squadron of nosediving Stukas.

I'd lost a lot of sleep over that article.

"Likewise, Mr Salinger, believe me."

"Let me introduce Mike, he—"

"I know McMellan." The wrinkled little thing gestured in the direction of Mike and his unbridled companion, as if swatting a fly. "But I didn't come all the way here for some matured *speck* and a movie. I came here for you, Mr Salinger," she said, leaning on my arm and forcing me to support her. "May I call you Jeremiah?"

"Call me Plissken," I muttered.

"I beg your pardon?"

"I said, of course, Mrs Grady."

"Miss. But Maddie will be fine, Jeremiah." She emptied her glass and, as if in a conjuring trick, swiped another one from the tray of a waiter (dressed in the uniform of Dolomite Mountain Rescue, a detail for which I would have cheerfully strangled T.A.). Then she looked through Annelise with her ice-cold little eyes. "Do you mind if I steal your boyfriend, darling?"

"We're married," Annelise said, without losing her poise. "But go ahead. It's his evening, after all."

"Haven't you had a drink yet, Jeremiah?"

"I only just got here. And anyway, I prefer to avoid alcohol. The suspense, you know how it is . . . "

"Oh, nonsense, my dear," she twittered, handing me a Martini. "As my third husband said, there's nothing a Martian can't chase away."

That's what she called it: a Martian.

Now I really was terrified.

With the authority of a *grande dame*, Maddie manoeuvred me into a discreet little corner, where we pretended we weren't being watched, even though we both knew (I with dismay, she gloating like a killer whale) that most of those present were already commenting on our private rendezvous.

"Are you really that nervous, Jeremiah?"

"Only as much as I need to be. But a Martian is a Martian." I clinked my glass against hers.

"I'm sure it'll be a success. That joker McMellan wouldn't even show me a small clip."

"I assume it was Mr Smith who told him not to."

"Mr Smith? Darling, Tom's my third husband, he'd bark like a dog in front of everybody if I asked him."

She was drunk, but horribly lucid.

"How does all this make you feel?" she resumed.

I prevaricated. "Is this an interview or is it strictly off the record?"

"That depends on what you say, *chéri*."

"I'm a bit dazed, but happy. It's only right that people, especially people around here, should know what really happened." I cleared my throat. "There's been a lot of rumour about September 15," I added, making an effort to maintain a neutral, professional tone. "Now it's time to tell the truth."

"I've made a note of that. But off the record?"

"I'm terrified, Maddie."

"After what you achieved with the 'Road Crew' series? One of the two most envied *enfants prodiges* on the east coast? Terrified by a premiere?"

"People have embellished this story a bit too much. Some of my wounds are still bleeding." I tried not to notice the light that had come on in Maddie's eyes. "Luckily, my wife is by my side. Her help has been fundamental, but what happened . . ." My voice broke. "Anyway, you'll see."

Maddie emptied her glass without taking her eyes off me. "I'll see, of course."

"Now, if . . ."

Maddie held me back. She didn't have hands, she had claws, which dug into my biceps. "I see your charming little wife is getting a stiff neck from trying to seem uninterested in our little *tête à tête*, but I want to steal you for another second. I don't see anyone here from Dolomite Mountain Rescue. Do you have any idea why?"

It was like a punch in the stomach.

The witch knew exactly where to hit, and she aimed well. It wasn't for nothing that her pen was the most feared on the East Coast and even on the West, to use her own words.

I was saved by the cavalry. A tiny contingent of cavalry one metre thirty tall.

Ignoring Maddie, Clara grabbed my trousers and her little face looked up at me, demanding my attention. "Uncle Mike says we have to go. It's starting."

Wer reitet so spät durch Nacht und Wind?

I don't remember what I dreamed, something terrible I suppose, because when I woke the pillow was soaked with tears and I had such a fierce migraine that it almost turned my stomach. I had to close my eyes tight and wait for the world to come back onto its axis.

I had drunk quite a lot after the screening. I remember little or nothing of what happened later.

The end credits, grim and relentless, which concluded with "In memory of the brave men of Dolomite Mountain Rescue", and the applause, timid at first, then a torrent.

Mike looking around, relieved, while to me the noise seemed like nothing so much as the laughter of the Beast. Annelise brushing me with a kiss, and then leaning over to console Clara, who was in tears, her hair dishevelled.

I don't know if it was the applause or the sight of my daughter sobbing in my wife's arms that made me go to town on the booze, the fact is that when Maddie Grady put one of her Martians in my hand, I knocked it back in one go.

The rest was all downhill.

I remember the odd fragment of the ride back to Siebenhoch. Stopping outside a hotel in which Mike and Linda Lee were to spend the rest of the night. The road shrouded in darkness, the outline of the chauffeur against the light, Clara sleeping in Annelise's lap, Annelise replying patiently to my drunken questions – I don't remember what they were, only the urgency with which I asked them.

The stairs.

The bed.

* * *

Slowly, the spasms of pain in my temples became less intense and I realised I was alone.

It was cold.

I got up, moving like a hundred-year-old. I checked the window. It was locked. There was light, though, coming from the corridor. Maybe Annelise had gone down to the kitchen for a snack, or maybe I was snoring so loudly that she had decided to spend the night on the couch in the study. I felt a pang of remorse.

I tiptoed into the bathroom, rinsed my face and took a couple of painkillers. I drank a little water. I ruffled my hair in front of the mirror, trying to assume a vaguely presentable air.

The light was on in the study, the door slightly ajar. I knocked.

"Annelise?"

No reply.

I went in. Annelise wasn't there. The computer on the desk was on, I could see the L.E.D. flashing intermittently. I shook the mouse. When the monitor came back on again, I had to hold onto the desk in order not to fall to the floor. I had spent too many hours on the file I found open in front of me not to recognise what it was. The notes I'd made during that downward spiral that had led me from a few words heard by chance at the Visitors' Centre all the way to the entrails of the Bletterbach, by way of Siebenhoch's ghosts, Brigitte's death and Max and Werner's confessions. The file on the Bletterbach killings. The one I had thrown into the recycle bin on the desktop but which, foolishly, I hadn't deleted.

Annelise had read it.

Now she knew.

She knew the truth about Kurt, Evi and Markus. About the man she had called father and the woman she had called mother. About what had happened to Oscar Grünwald. About the justice of the forefathers.

About my broken promises.

"Annelise?" I called out.

It was almost an entreaty.

No answer.

The house was shrouded in silence. I went downstairs, barefoot. My ears were plugged up, everything was muffled. The front door was wide open. The wind was blowing hard. There was water on the threshold. It was raining. In the sky, the clouds were a compact sheet of lead. My stomach contracted.

"Annelise?" I moaned.

I don't know how long I would have stayed there, paralysed, if Clara's sleepy voice hadn't shaken me.

"Papà?"

"Go to bed, sweetheart."

"What's happening, Papà?"

I expelled all the air I had in my lungs, took a deep breath, then turned. I had to be reassuring. I had to be strong. I smiled and Clara smiled back.

"Everything's fine, ten letters."

"Are you all right, Papà?"

"I have a bit of a stomachache. I'll make myself some tea and then go to bed. You should be asleep."

Clara started playing with a strand of her hair. "Papà?"

"Clara," I said, "go to bed, please."

"The door's open, Papà. The rain's coming in."

"To bed."

I probably said it too aggressively, because her eyes grew bigger. "Where's Mamma?"

"To bed, sweetheart."

Clara tugged at the strand of hair, then turned on her heels.

She obeyed. I was alone.

"Annelise?"

I was answered by the dry boom of thunder. I headed for the door. I could feel the cold water under the soles of my feet. I tried not to slip. I looked.

The car wasn't there.

I can't remember much of the next few minutes, which I spent overwhelmed by anxiety and a sense of guilt. I only know that I somehow found myself dressed, with my cell phone in my hand and Max's voice in my ears.

"Calm down, Salinger, calm down and tell me everything from the beginning."

"Annelise," I said. "The Bletterbach."

I don't know how much Max guessed, but I must have scared him quite a bit because his reply was, "I'll be there right away."

I hung up. I stood there staring at the phone. I put it down on a cabinet.

I climbed the stairs, trying to slow my breathing.

"Sweetheart?" I said, entering Clara's room.

She lay curled up under the blankets in a foetal position. She looked much younger than her five years. She had her thumb in her mouth.

"Mamma?" she asked hopefully.

I sat down on the bed, even though every fibre in my body was urging me to start running. "We're going to fetch her now."

"Where has she gone?"

"*Nonno* Werner's."

"Why?"

I had no answer for that.

"We have to get dressed, Max will be here soon and we have to be ready for him."

If Clara had questions to ask me, she didn't ask them. She was silent all the time it took me to dress her.

By the time the headlights of the Forest Rangers' Land Rover cut through the darkness outside the house, Clara and I were in the doorway, well wrapped up in heavy waterproof coats.

Max got out of the car without switching off the engine. The wreaths of smoke from the exhaust pipe, tinged red by the headlights, assumed demonic shapes. I pushed Clara towards the back door and opened it for her.

"Annelise knows everything," I said to Max.

"How did that happen?"

"She read my notes."

Max clenched his jaw. "You're a fool."

"We have to go."

"To Werner's?"

I nodded.

* * *

Annelise wasn't at Welshboden. Werner's property was shrouded in darkness.

My father-in-law's jeep wasn't there, while mine had its door wide open. The house was empty.

I felt my eyes fill with tears. I wiped them with the back of my hand.

I didn't want Clara to see me in that condition. She was already scared enough.

"I think you know where they went," I said, looking straight in front of me.

Max didn't reply. He reversed and set off in the direction of the Bletterbach.

I summoned up my courage, turned and said, "We're going on an excursion, ten letters."

"It's raining, Papà."

"It'll be a kind of adventure."

Clara shook her head slowly. "I want to go home."

I reached out my hand and brushed her cheek. "Soon."

"I want Mamma."

"Soon, sweetheart. Soon."

I felt my voice crack.

"Do you like music, Clara?" Max asked.

"Yes."

He switched on the car radio. A cheerful little tune flooded the inside of the vehicle. It was Louis Armstrong.

"This is my favourite," Max said, and sang, "When the Saints go marching in . . . "

A glimmer of a smile on Clara's face.

"Am I out of tune?"

"A little."

"That's because the volume's too low," Max replied. And he started singing again at the top of his voice.

Clara laughed, raising both her hands to her ears.

I gave Max a grateful glance and laid my head back against the seat. The painkillers had started to take effect. The migraine had been reduced to a kind of undertow of pain.

Outside the Land Rover, rain and darkness. Inside, Louis Armstrong.

It was crazy. Simply crazy.

When we got to the entrance of the Visitors' Centre, we noticed Werner's jeep parked sideways and the gate wide open.

Max switched off the engine. The music stopped abruptly.

"We have two possibilities, as far as I can see," I said.

"Three," Max said. "The third is: we stay here and wait."

It was as if I hadn't heard him. "The cave or . . . *there*."

There where everything had started. The place where Kurt, Evi and Markus had met their deaths. Where Annelise had been born a second time.

"Or else we stay here," Max repeated. "With Clara."

I shook my head. There was no time to lose. I opened the door. "Are you coming with us?"

* * *

We were soaking wet even before we'd gone the first hundred metres. The rain was coming down as if it wanted to drown the whole world, and us with it. Up until that day, rain had meant something quite different to me. It was a nuisance that an umbrella or a windscreen-wiper brushed away. That night, I saw it for what it really was. Ice-cold water that oozed darkness and brought not new life, but death. It uprooted plants and killed animals, drowning them in their lairs. It got into clothes and made people lose heat. Heat is life.

Around us, the gorge of the Bletterbach roared. It wasn't a single voice, it was a chorus in which one instrument was added to another until it produced a cacophony that was sometimes unbearable. Even the pouring of the rain sounded different depending on the surface on which it was beating. The deep tolling of the chestnut tree, the crystalline one of the red fir tree. The pounding on the rocks.

Many voices, one message. The Bletterbach was admonishing us not to defy it.

But nothing could stop me.

Annelise was there, somewhere (even though I knew perfectly well where), in the deep. She was wounded. If not physically, certainly in her soul. And that wound was my fault.

Clara was holding my hand, head bowed. She was walking quickly, although the mud had made her trousers heavy and swollen. I would have liked to hold her in my arms, but she had refused. Rather than waste time arguing, I had done as she wanted, vowing that when I noticed signs of her weakening I would persuade her to let me help her.

Every now and again I heard her singing in a low voice. It was her way of giving herself courage.

I envied her.

I had nothing but the guidance of Max, who was in front of me in the mottled darkness.

I tried to visualise Annelise's face. The freckles around her nose, the way she bent her neck as she came closer to kiss me. I couldn't do it. I saw only the pain with which she had uttered her ultimatum. Either her or the story of the killings. I had chosen the dead, and the dead had taken their revenge on me by snatching her away.

It was a stupid thought. The dead are dead. I remembered some graffiti written on the wall of a public toilet in Red Hook: "Life sucks, but death is worse."

Evi, Kurt and Markus weren't responsible for what was happening.

I was responsible.

I had forgotten (or maybe I hadn't had the courage) to delete the file with my notes. It was my fault that Annelise had found it.

But what on earth had driven Annelise to switch on my laptop in the dead of night and look through my files? Usually, I was the one who started searching for Christmas presents before I received them, not her. What had induced her to violate my privacy (and to be so determined as to check even the recycle bin)? It had to be something serious.

Something like . . .

I stopped.

Clara knocked into me and almost fell.

"Salinger?" came Max's voice.

He was less than two metres in front of me and yet his silhouette merged with the shadows.

"It's O.K. It's just . . ."

It's just that when I get drunk, when I get seriously drunk, not after three or four glasses, not even after six or seven, but when the Martians take me and put me on their spaceship and give me a rollercoaster ride, I talk.

I talk in my sleep.

"Papà?"

Clara was still staring down at the ground.

"My shoes are dirty."

"We'll clean them."

"Mamma will be angry."

"Mamma will be happy to see us."

We had been going for at least another three-quarters of an hour before Clara stumbled. I quickly caught her and cleaned her cheeks with a handkerchief that Max gave me. There was no blood and Clara didn't cry. My brave little girl.

"Now we have to go up a level," Max said, pointing to a thicket of holm oaks above which a couple of red firs jutted. "There's still quite a way to go, Salinger. According to my calculations, we have at least another two hours' walk. Even more, in this rain. And Clara's only a child," he added, giving me a harsh look.

"Carry on."

Max heaved a sigh and started clambering up the slope.

"Do we have to go up there, too?" Clara asked.

"It'll be fun."

"Is that where Mamma is?"

"Yes, it is. But to get there, I need your help, sweetheart."

"What do I have to do?"

"I'll hoist you on my back and you'll have to hold on tight. Do you think you can do that?"

* * *

Two hours later, I had to stop. I was exhausted. I laid Clara down on the felled trunk of a pine, sheltered beneath a group of exceptionally large ferns.

She was finding it hard to keep her eyes open, and the hair that had escaped from under her hood was stuck to her face. It broke my heart to see her like that.

It was six in the morning, but there wasn't even a hint of sunlight. The rain kept pouring down. And I'd become so accustomed to the thunder that I'd almost stopped hearing it.

I accepted Max's thermos. I gave it first to Clara, then took a few sips myself. Sweet tea. It was a tonic.

The muscles of my back and legs were burning.

Max checked his watch. "Two minutes' rest, no more. It's cold."

I collapsed on the ground, heedless of the mud.

"I haven't yet thanked you, Max."

"For what?"

I indicated myself and Clara, then the whole of the Bletterbach. "For this."

"It's a search and rescue operation. The stupidest of my entire career."

"Call it what you want, but I'm indebted to you."

"Make sure you don't have a heart attack, keep that child warm, and I'll consider the debt honoured."

I took Clara and hugged her to my chest. She had fallen asleep.

"How much longer?" I asked Max.

"Not much. If there was any sun, you could see the place from here."

"We should be able to hear them, then."

"With all this noise?" Max shook his head. "Not even if they used a megaphone. Now let's go. Time's up."

I made to lift Clara, who barely protested, her eyes half closed, but a terrible spasm in my back caused me to lurch forward.

"I'll take the child," Max said anxiously. "Is that O.K. with you, Clara?"

"It's O.K.," she murmured.

"Do you like my hat?" Max asked her.

"It's funny."

"And it's warm."

He put it on top of the hood of her coat. In spite of the rain, the lightning, and the crackling of the stones, I let out a laugh. "It suits you to a T, you know, ten letters? Maybe when you're grown up, you could be a forest ranger, instead of a doctor."

"I don't know if I'd like that."

"Why not?" Max asked, setting off again.

"Because where a doctor works, it doesn't rain."

* * *

I recognised the clearing even though I'd never been there before. From the forensics photographs, of course, but also from the accounts I'd heard.

The chestnut tree was more imposing than I had imagined it, and some of the fir trees must have fallen, because the edge of the precipice seemed closer compared with the photographs from '85.

Annelise and Werner were under the rocky spur, the very same one under which Kurt and the others had camped. Werner was sitting with his back to the mountain and stroking Annelise's hair. She was huddled between his legs. He raised a hand by way of greeting. Then he gently shook his daughter.

Clara slipped out of Max's arms and threw herself on Annelise, who buried her in kisses.

"Here again," Werner said, getting to his feet. His eyes were red.

He shook hands with Max.

"We've never really left it, have we, Werner?" Max replied.

"You didn't tell me anything," Annelise said, embracing me.

"I didn't want . . ."

Annelise gently detached herself. "What?"

"I didn't want you to be hurt."

Annelise wiped away a tear. "Papà has told me everything."

"What has *Nonno* told you, Mamma?"

Annelise stroked Clara's head. "Look how wet you are, sweetheart."

"What has *Nonno* told you?"

"A lovely story," Annelise replied. "The story of the hunter who saves the princess from the monster." She looked at Max. "The *four* hunters," she corrected herself. "Werner, Günther, Hannes and Max."

"What happened to the monster?"

"The monster went back where it came from." She looked me in the eyes. "I have that from a reliable source."

"I . . ."

Annelise brushed my cheek with a kiss. "You've been reckless."

The mountain was throbbing with electricity.

I was aware of what Werner had tried to explain to me in words, centuries before. The feeling of hostility in the Bletterbach. Hostility and age. Millions of years of an open-air graveyard in which monstrous creatures had breathed their last.

I thought of the blood of Kurt, Evi and Markus.

I wondered if part of them were still here, in what they called "the deep". Not on a biological level, of course. Wind, snow, water and years had wiped out even the smallest D.N.A. trace of Annelise's parents.

But something, maybe on a more subtle level, a piece of something that we call the soul, must still be here, and it struck me, thanks to my wife's kiss, that in spite of the Bletterbach, the thunder and the cold, at that moment the souls of Kurt and Evi were at peace. Thanks to Annelise.

And to the granddaughter they had never known.

"How many letters are there in the word 'end', Clara?"

"Three," she replied immediately.

"You know something, sweetheart? I need a hug. Will you give me one?"

Clara reached out to me, and as I had done an infinite number of times and as I hoped I would do an infinite number of times in the future, I lifted her and hugged her tight. Beneath the odour of the mud and the sweat, I smelled the smell of her skin and closed my eyes.

That smell was the casket in which all the happy moments of my life were kept. Cold pizza at five in the morning during the shooting of "Road Crew". The Fight Club. *Mein liebes Fraulein* . . . "Nebraska" playing softly in the background. Annelise saying yes, in Hell's Kitchen. The nine months of pregnancy. My reflection in the mirror murmuring that strange word: "Papà." Mike's opening his eyes wide, speechless for once, when I had told him that I would soon be a father and that he would be . . .

* * *

Suddenly, something went click in my mind.

* * *

Stunned, I laid Clara on the ground.

The Bletterbach no longer existed. Nor the rain. There was only that click.

And the memory of Mike's dazed expression.

"January 3, 1985," I said, in a choked voice. "January 3, Werner. Oh, God. Oh, God."

"January 3," Werner echoed, surprised. "Yes, Annelise's real date of birth, but. . ."

I didn't even listen to him.

The click was joined by another click and then another. An avalanche running quickly from *a* to *z* in a blinding explosion of horror.

Birthdays and triangles with the point at the top. And a soul that the implacable pressure of time had made as insensitive as rock, rock that, as had happened to the Bletterbach, had been damaged to such a point by hate as to bring into the light the unspeakable buried in the heart of every human being.

The substance of evil.

"What did the four of you do?" I murmured.

Werner was staring at me with eagle eyes that didn't see. That hadn't seen for thirty years, so blinded with love for Annelise that they hadn't realised the obvious. Like those of Günther, hostage to his demons, or his brother Hermann with his sense of guilt and his determination to become someone. Like the eyes of Hannes, blinded with prejudice and then destroyed by the grief of his loss.

None of them had seen.

The answer had always been there, in plain sight. For all this time.

It was like a whiplash.

Adrenalin.

I raised my head, snarling. I grabbed a big branch from the chestnut, tore it off, scraping the palms of my hands as I did so, and clutched it like a sledgehammer.

"Annelise," I ordered. "Take Clara and get out of here."

"Salinger," Annelise said, "calm down, please."

"Go back. Now!"

I heard Clara whimper.

I ground my teeth.

"Jeremiah," Werner said, "put down that branch."

"Move away, Werner. I don't want to hurt you. But if you take another step, I will."

"God in heaven, son," he said, incredulous. "What's happening to you?"

"Do you have any rope with you?"

"In my backpack, yes."

"Then use it."

Werner gave me a long, stunned look. "Use it?"

"You have to tie him up."

"Tie who up?"

"Max. The Bletterbach monster. The killer of Evi, Kurt and Markus."

With each of these names I felt my anger increase.

And the clicks added one to another.

"That's madness, Jeremiah," Werner retorted. "It was Grünwald. He was crazy. You know that, too. He—"

"Grünwald was protecting them."

"From who?"

"*Jaekelopterus Rhenaniae*," I hissed.

"That's all a load of—"

"Grünwald," I said, without taking my eyes off Max, who was motionless, "was really convinced that those monsters existed in the Bletterbach. He knew that Evi and Kurt would be coming down here on an excursion and when he heard that a storm was about to break out in this area he thought the underground lakes would overflow and release the *Jaekelopterus*. He sent the telegram and rushed here. He was crazy, but there was a logic in his madness. Isn't that so, Chief Krün?"

"I don't know what you're talking about," Max replied softly.

His calm made me furious. "January 3, Max!" I yelled. "Four months before the killings. Four!"

Was it possible that neither Annelise nor Werner understood?

It was all so damned simple.

"You know what my first thought was when Annelise told me she was pregnant? I thought I ought to tell Mike right away. Because Mike and I are friends and we always tell friends our good news. You and Markus were the only people who'd kept in touch with Evi and Kurt. And so you were the only people in Siebenhoch to know about the birth of Annelise. Evi and Kurt were your friends. You knew about the child. But why didn't you tell Hannes or Werner when you organised the rescue party? It made no sense anymore to keep the secret."

Werner turned pale. "What are you saying, Jeremiah?" he stammered.

He didn't understand.

Or maybe he didn't want to understand.

Because the consequences of my argument were catastrophic.

"You know what I'm paid for, Max? Constructing stories that start at *a* and end up at *z*. And in this case, *a* is the ringing of a telephone thirty years ago. At one end there's you, and at the other . . . Who told you? Kurt? Evi? Or maybe the beginning of the story is Markus, in seventh heaven, knocking at your door to tell you that Evi's pregnant but that nobody is to know about it. It doesn't matter, I don't think it was then that you decided to kill them. No."

It was all so clear now.

"When Annelise was born, the two of you took the train and went to Innsbruck. Was it January? Or February? The important thing is that when you saw the baby, when you took her in your arms, it was then that you realised that Evi would never be yours, never. Because you loved her, didn't you? Only, she'd chosen Kurt and had a daughter with him. That baby was the outward sign of their love. You couldn't lie to yourself anymore, couldn't hope anymore that they would part. That was the moment you decided to kill them."

From *a* to *b*.

From *b* to *c*.

And then . . .

"But not immediately. Not then. They would have found you out, arrested you in a flash. You didn't want to end up in prison. You continued to pretend. You wanted to kill them *here*. And for a very particular reason, isn't that so?"

Max was shaking his head.

Thunder rumbled through the Bletterbach.

"Triangles," I said. "Triangles with the point turned upwards. The symbol that saved my life in the caves. Three triangles with the point turned upwards. A crown, that's what that symbol was. *Krone*, in German. *Krün* in dialect. It was your grandfather who carved those crowns on the walls of the mine, wasn't it? He was responsible for safety. The mine and the caves, a single labyrinth nobody dares enter. You're the last person in Siebenhoch to know them like the back of your hand. Did your grandmother take you there? Because madness doesn't grow by itself. It settles. Layer by layer. It takes time. Years. It was her, wasn't it? How much resentment did she transmit to you? How much hate did it take, Max?"

Max didn't react.

His stupefied expression was perfect.

Worthy of an Oscar.

Or maybe he was genuinely surprised.

After thirty years, someone had discovered the truth.

"Madness settles in layers, and then hate eats into it until a hunger for blood emerges. It's a slow, cold process. You waited. They were your friends, you knew them. You knew that sooner or later Kurt and Evi would go back to the place where their love was born. The place where you would be able to create a perfect alibi: the distance from Siebenhoch. Nobody would ever think of arresting you. Of course, it might take a long time, but what did that matter? The Bletterbach has been here for millions of years and you're a patient man. But in fact, it took only four months. Then the self-regenerating storm gave you an even better cover than you could have hoped for, didn't it? But then . . . " At this point, I exploded. "What did you feel when Grünwald sprang up out of nowhere? When he screwed up your plan?"

I took a step closer.

It was time to bring this to an end, and to attack.

"How long did it take you to get here, Max?" I pressed him. "How long does it take, cutting through the caves?"

Werner's voice filtered through my anger. A trembling voice. "It isn't possible. It means that . . ."

He had got there.

The horror.

"It means," I finished for him, "that in this story there are three innocents. Kurt, Evi and Markus. And there's a hero. Oscar Grünwald. Oscar Grünwald who saved the child, ruining Max's plan. Oscar Grünwald whom you all killed."

Just like on the Ortles, I thought. The innocents and the heroes die, the guilty are saved.

"No," Werner moaned.

That was his last word. His eyes opened wide and he raised his hands to his belly.

There was no expression on Max's face as he turned the knife in the wound he had made.

Annelise screamed, clutching Clara tight to her and turning her head away.

"It takes an hour and a half, Salinger," Max replied, in a toneless voice. "Here and back. An hour and a half. But you have to swim. *Omi* had made me do it ever since I was your daughter's age. Swimming in the caves in the dark was necessary to revive the blood of the Krüns. That's what *Omi* said. When the mine collapsed in '23, the water flooded everything. The miners drowned. My grandfather got his calculations wrong. He got them wrong because he was tired, because he was paid as little as all the other beggars in Siebenhoch even though he wasn't just an ordinary miner, he was responsible for safety. He died along with the others, although he was better than any of them."

He spat on the ground and looked at me.

"Think about it, Salinger," he said. "An hour and a half. And barely thirty minutes to find them under this spur. Thirty minutes. It was destiny. Those three had to die. And the child had to die, too."

He took out the knife and Werner fell to his knees. In a single fluid movement, Max aimed the blade at Werner's throat. "Let go of the branch."

I dropped it.

"Take three steps back."

I obeyed.

Max assumed his good uncle face. "When did you start sticking your nose in this business?"

"A few months ago."

"A few months!" Max roared. "Even that drunkard Günther suspected something. Who do you think made sure he found the report?" Beside himself with anger, he yanked Werner's head. "And you? Thirty years spent thinking you were a hero. Thirty years and you didn't understand a thing."

Werner bowed his head in defeat.

Max displayed the blade of the knife. "It'll be harder with you people, but much more enjoyable. An axe is too . . . crude."

"Wouldn't a gun have been enough?" I said. "Didn't you have a rifle?"

"They wouldn't have suffered enough. All the humiliations I'd endured. They had to pay. To taste a little of my shit. The shit Siebenhoch used to flavour everything I'd eaten since I was born. The heir to the man who'd caused the mine to collapse. As if a child could be guilty of anything. Oh, how they enjoyed taking their revenge on us. Making fun of us, laughing at our poverty. Just like Evi laughed when I told her I loved her. She thought it was a joke. A joke, can you imagine? She preferred Kurt. That son of a bitch. The rescuer. The hero. But in the end they both had to eat their words."

Annelise let out a sob, which drew Chief Krün's attention to her.

I didn't want Max to look at her. Not until I was the one holding the knife. So I tried to gain time by bringing him back to his narrative.

"But then Grünwald showed up," I said, as if interviewing one of the protagonists of my stories.

"Markus tried to run away. A coward to the end. He slipped and hit his head. I reached him to finish him off, but he was already dead. He just made me waste time. I cut off Evi's head, took it in my hands and put it down in front of Kurt's eyes. He was dying, but he was still lucid and I wanted him to see it. Then I threw it away. When Grünwald suddenly appeared, screaming like a madman, I panicked and ran." He let out a cry of annoyance. "I thought it was *Omi*. I thought she'd come back to take me to the caves. Now that I'd avenged my grandfather, I had to stay down there for ever, with him."

In his eyes there was an abyss.

"When I calmed down, I saw that Grünwald had found the child. And the axe. And an idea came into my head. A wonderful idea, Salinger. Those three bastards had got their just deserts. But what about the others? The ones who made fun of me because I went to school with broken shoes? The ones who laughed at *Omi*, at Frau Krün, because she'd lost everything when the mine collapsed? Her money, her husband and even her honour. A woman who'd been married to the Saltner of the mine! All those country bumpkins who thought they were better than us Krüns, even though we'd protected the miners of Siebenhoch for two centuries! I realised it was a way to turn their pathetic forefathers' justice against them."

Max was panting like an animal.

He was an animal.

"I turned back. I went to Verena's party. Hannes arrived, then Günther, and together we went to pick up Werner. We came here and I pretended I didn't know anything. I had everything under control. *Almost* everything," he corrected himself. Then his eyes darted towards Clara. "How many letters are there in the word 'end', sweetie?"

Hidden by Annelise's body, Clara replied in a trembling voice, "Three."

"Three," Max echoed.

The blade disappeared into Werner's throat. Werner slumped to the ground, spurting a gout of blood. His eyes rolled backwards. His body jerked. Once, twice, three times.

The end.

Max didn't even deign to look at him. He wiped the knife on his jacket. I stared, hypnotised, at the brown stripes on the rain-soaked fabric.

It was our turn.

It was at this point that I heard it.

* * *

I let go of the branch and threw myself towards Annelise and Clara just as the mud overwhelmed us. The Bletterbach was transfigured into an apocalypse of water, sludge and debris. I grabbed my daughter by the elbow and lifted her into the air just in time before a piece of wood as thick as my thigh lashed the air where her head had been. She let out a cry that was also a sob. We fell. I flailed about. I managed to catch hold of a fir tree. The rock under which Kurt had pitched the tent became a cascade of mud. Werner's lifeless body was swept away.

"Annelise!" I yelled.

She didn't respond. Some debris must have struck her. I couldn't see any blood, but her eyes were clouded over.

She was clinging to a root, looking into emptiness.

What about Max?

Where was he?

For a moment, I hoped he had been swallowed by the abyss, but I was wrong. Somehow, he had managed to grab hold of the chestnut tree and hoist himself to his feet. The knife still clutched in his hand, his face twisted in an expression of rage, he pulled away from the tree and began advancing, as the water swirled between his legs. He was inexorable.

"Mamma!"

Clara's voice succeeded in waking Annelise. She turned to me, her eyes trying to get back into focus.

Max was towering over her, panting. He was holding her by the hair, her head tilted back, her neck exposed.

"The whore's daughter," Max said. "Let's have done with it, Salinger."

I threw myself towards him. My screams were the screams of the Beast.

The blade of the knife rose to the sky, ready to cut, when a flash of lightning filled the air with electricity. The crash of thunder made the walls of the Bletterbach tremble.

A fraction of a second. A moment's hesitation.

It was enough.

I struck Max with my fist, knocking him backwards. He spat, coughed, waved his arms. I struck him again. The pain in my knuckles paid me back for all the suffering endured until that moment. I grabbed him by the throat and lifted him. I struck him a third time. And a fourth.

By the fifth, I'd lost feeling in my hand.

I didn't stop.

I wanted only one thing: to kill him.

All at once, I felt a burst of heat and the sudden pain blinded me. It was the knife, going right through my knee. Max lacerating the flesh, pushing and pulling. My flesh. My cartilage.

My leg gave way. I slipped and fell. The water dragged me away, while the pain grew and grew. I knocked into Annelise and we embraced. I felt the warmth of her body. I even felt her breath on my neck. But I also felt the tiredness. Resignation followed. It was nice to die like this. I'd been given the possibility of this last contact with the woman I loved. I closed my eyes. I felt a sensation of total peace. No more pain, no more fear.

No more Bletterbach. There was only death, and it was waiting for me.

Fade to black, as Mike would have said.

It was Clara who saved me.

"Papà!"

Her broken voice tore me from my lethargy. I couldn't die. Not yet. Clara needed me.

I raised my head from the mud. I opened my eyes. The pain returned, the fear, the anguish.

The determination.

Still clinging to Annelise, I tried to move through the debris towards our daughter. I bumped into a rock. I grabbed hold of it. Annelise pressed herself against me.

"Salinger!" Max roared. "Salinger!"

He was on his feet, standing in the middle of the current.

A demon.

He opened wide his arms, yelling my name. Maybe he would have liked to add a curse or a threat, but he didn't have time.

Something scythed through his leg at the height of his thigh, describing a half-moon of blood in the air.

Max stopped yelling.

His back went rigid. His head fell back, his mouth gaping.

I saw his body rise thirty centimetres above the surface of the water, the horrible stump of his leg bleeding and kicking, the arms flailing.

Then . . .

Something emerged from his thoracic cage. *Something* that looked to me like a gigantic claw. *Something* that smashed the bones and went right through him. The monster of the Bletterbach.

The *Jaekelopterus* was there. And it was hungry.

It had had Max. It wanted me. And Annelise.

It wanted Clara.

There was only one thing to do.

I grabbed Clara. I grabbed Annelise.

I breathed in. I breathed out.

I closed my eyes and let the current carry us away.

One Letter at the End of the Rainbow

I remember the pain. The waves of mud and the cold in my bones. The world sliding into a bottomless abyss. Even now, Clara's screams echo in my head, as does her sudden silence, which was even more frightening. The descent ended, although I don't know how or when. We waited in silence in a niche in the rock for the monster to discover us and tear us to pieces.

It didn't happen.

I cradled Clara. I cradled Annelise.

The rain began to ease off. The drops grew thin, a damp dust through which the first rays of the sun were refracted, creating rainbows. No more rocks from the sky.

The mud gradually stopped its descent.

Then, a thousand years later, the chirping of insects. The call of some animal or other. A partridge appeared amid the bushes, stared at us and disappeared in a flurry of wings.

The clouds grew thinner. The sun gained strength. It looked huge and very beautiful.

The gorge of the Bletterbach was no longer roaring. It had had its fill of death.

Then I started crying. Not from the pain. Not because of Annelise's empty eyes. Not even because of Clara, who was moaning in her sleep.

I cried because I had seen it.

The *Jaekelopterus Rhenaniae.*

The monster with claws and eyes like black wells. The creature God had decided to sweep away, but which the Bletterbach had nursed in its entrails like a loving mother. I had seen it. I had seen what it was capable of . . .

But the post-mortem report says otherwise. No claws, no monster. No *Jaekelopterus Rhenaniae.* Only a big branch from a fir tree that the fury of the current had turned into a harpoon. In other words, or so it seems, it was the Bletterbach that had closed the circle.

But in those terrible moments, as the Bletterbach abated, I cursed, I wept. I went crazy. And when the madness gained the upper hand, I saw the ghosts arrive. They got out of a bright red helicopter. Moses with his severe features, Ismaele with his Lampwick expression, Manny with his quiet confidence and Christoph with his usual air of someone who can never quite take anything seriously.

Werner was with them, too.

As they gently peeled Clara from my arms and placed a blanket over Annelise's shoulders and checked her pupils, I tried to tell them that I hadn't wanted them to die, that if I could turn the clock back I wouldn't go down into the crevasse and so the avalanche wouldn't kill them.

Their reply didn't need words.

They were there.

It's Rule Zero.

* * *

I almost died three times while I was on the operating table. The knife had severed some nerve or other and a nasty infection had done the rest. My right leg will never be the same as it was.

When Mike saw me after the Bletterbach, he burst into tears and couldn't stop sobbing the whole time. But Mike makes things out to be more tragic than they are. Deep down, he's always been a big softie. I've become pretty nimble with the stick, you know.

You should see me: a dancer.

"In the Belly of the Beast" won a prize of which Mike is very proud.

He says it'll open a lot of doors for us, but he also knows there'll never be another McMellan–Salinger production. I think, though, that constantly saying it does him good, so I don't contradict him. As Bob Dylan used to sing, "the times they are a-changin'", and they don't always change for the better.

At first, the real problem was my head. And it was a big problem. Enough to make Dr Girardi, the psychiatrist to whose care I was entrusted, fear that I would never recover my equilibrium. I put all I had into it and now I'm better. Hermann helps me to keep busy. He's planning to open a centre for recovering alcoholics. And he wants me to give him a hand. Impossible to say no to someone like him. To quote Bogart: I think this is the beginning of a beautiful friendship.

Annelise, too, has had to fight.

Her arm was in pretty bad shape. Even now, when there's a risk of rain, she takes painkillers. Three times a week, she sees a physiotherapist. She has her battles to face, like me. Nightmares, bad memories, anxiety. Often her eyes cloud over and then I know she's thinking about Werner, whose body is still somewhere in the labyrinth of caves below the gorge. But every day she smiles a bit more.

Like me.

Our medicine has five letters: "Clara". It's because of her that on bad days we find the strength to get out of bed. It's because of her that our laughter is gradually becoming genuine again. It's because of her that we make love at night, as clumsy as a couple of teenagers.

Clara . . .

I like listening to her stories, I like playing with her. Running through the meadows of Siebenhoch with a stick that makes me look like a scarecrow. But above all, I like watching her sleep. Clara sometimes smiles in her sleep and when she does that, my heart fills with hope. Her smiles chase away fear and get me one step closer to salvation. I *need* Clara to smile. Because that's how fairy tales end, those that start with *a* and always fini sh with a *z* we call a happy ending.

* * *

I've written these pages for her. Because one day Annelise and I will have to tell her the truth about the Bletterbach killings. About how it was her love that saved the lives of the final protagonists in that story.

Annelise and Salinger.

* * *

"One letter, Papà?"

"The smile at the end of the rainbow, sweetheart."

Z.

Acknowledgements

If, as many will have noticed, the Alto Adige/Südtirol described in these pages departs from the real one, the reason is simple: *The Mountain* is a work of fiction, and fiction, by definition, tends more to verisimilitude than to truth. I hope this hasn't hurt anyone's feelings. In any case, I'm sure that Clara would agree with me in stating that telling stories is always, in a way, a declaration of love.

In this regard, let me thank many (certainly not all) of the people who, with their affection and encouragement, have helped to bring the writing of this novel to fruition.

Thank you to my mother and father for always holding my hand. Thank you to Luisa and Agostino for letting me carry away the most precious thing they had. Thank you to Claudia, Michi and Asja for Alex and all the rest. To Eleonora, Corrado and Gabriele for adopting me. And thank you to Giannina for the bells.

Thank you to Maurizio who never turns back and Valentina who takes him fishing. Thank you to Michele, the unique, true and inimitable. Thank you to Emanuela, Simone and Bianca. To Caterina, Maurizio and Sofia. To Ilaria and Luca. To Chiara and Damiano. No point adding why, you all know. A very special thank-you to Loredana, Andrea and the first readers of the manuscript. You know who you are and how much I owe you.

Thank you to Piergiorgio Nicolazzini who isn't just an agent, and I want him to know that. Thank you to Luca Briasco for teaching me to hold a pen (although he insists on claiming the opposite). Thank you to Francesco Colombo for turning the editing into a pleasant outing between friends. Thank you to Severino Cesari, Paolo Repetti, Raffaella Baiocchi and the whole Stile Libero family for the kindness with which they welcomed this lost mountain-dweller to the big city and for the professionalism with which they took care of the big tome he had in his backpack.

Thank you to Dr Christian Salaroli for the mountain blues. To Raffael and Gabriel Kostner, for being everyday examples of heroism. Thank you to the courageous men of Aiut Alpin Dolomites for inspiration, kerosene and strudel. The good things about mountain rescue that you find in this novel I owe to them (whereas the errors and flights of fancy are entirely down to the imagination of yours truly). Thank you to Professor Fulvio Ferrari, always true to the motto: "Once a teacher, always a teacher." And: *Vergelsgot'n oltn Alois for dr Mappe unds Wörterbuach. Zum Wohl, Herr Luis!* Thank you, obviously, to the Bletterbach and its sign: "Enter at your own peril."

Finally: a gold doubloon to Alessandra for being the first to cry "Blow! Blow!"

The lines on p. 14 are from "Hellhound on my Trail", sung by Robert Johnson.

The line on p. 15 is from Robert Frost's poem "Stopping by Woods on a Snowy Evening". From *Poetry of Robert Frost* by Robert Frost, Published by Jonathan Cape. Reprinted by permission of The Random House Group Limited.

The quotation on p. 278 is from *Ask the Dust* by John Fante.

LUCA D'ANDREA was born in 1979 in Bolzano, Italy, where he worked as a teacher for ten years. *The Mountain*, his first novel, is being translated into thirty languages.

HOWARD CURTIS is an award-winning translator of Italian and French literature, including books by Fabio Geda, Gianrico Carofiglio, Jean-Claude Izzo and Giorgio Scerbanenco.